From the Bestselling Author of *Descent*

"Johnston writes in gracefully exact language with genuine heart . . . Reminiscent of writers like Annie Proulx and Richard Bausch."
—*The New York Times Book Review*

"Past and present merge in *The Current*, Tim Johnston's atmospheric, exquisitely suspenseful novel of two murders separated by ten years . . . A first-rate thriller."
—*The Washington Post*

"Johnston dazzled with his breakout thriller, *Descent*; his follow-up is a more ambitious page-turner, unpacking how a shocking murder impacts the denizens of a small Minnesota town as they weather suspicion, guilt, and grief."
—*Entertainment Weekly* (The 50 Most Anticipated Books of 2019)

"Tim Johnston's second novel, *The Current*, is even better than his first, which is saying something. He's a terrific writer and definitely a name to watch."
—Dennis Lehane, author of *Since We Fell*

"Tim Johnston's gripping second novel is much more than a skillfully constructed, beautifully written whodunit. It's a subtle and lyrical acclamation of the heart and spirit of small-town America. *The Current* is not your conventional, frenetically paced page-turner, although it smolders with a brooding, slow-burn tension that nudges the reader forward, catching you up in the lives of the troubled solitaries at the book's core."
—*Washington Independent Review of Books*

"Gripping as it is, Johnston's masterful novel is worth lingering over—it soars above the constraints of a traditional thriller and pulls you deep into the secrets of a grief-stricken town."
—*People*

"Pick up Tim Johnston's suspenseful novel *The Current* and you risk finding yourself glued to your chair, eyes to the pages, no thought of attending to daily obligations. Johnston's elegant, cinematic style takes us into the characters' lives and history, problems and concerns. The book examines that horrifying moment when everything changes, the before and after when love, friendship, hopes and trust turn into dread, guilt, blame and grief." —*Minneapolis Star Tribune*

"Tim Johnston's new novel, *The Current*, is an exceptional tale of suspicion and secrets—and a strong follow-up to his excellent 2015 book, *Descent*." —*The Gazette* (Cedar Rapids, IA)

"The author of *Descent* returns with a tour de force about the indelible impact of a crime on the lives of innocent people." —*The Wichita Eagle*

"[An] involving and layered thriller . . . Johnston's prose is so lyrical you want to stop and read it again." —*St. Paul Pioneer Press*

"With *The Current*, Johnston presents readers with another slate of unforgettable characters." —*Columbia Missourian*

"Along with his poetic style, the author's acknowledgment of the complicated nuances inherent in friendship, family and love, especially the love of a parent for a child, elevate this tale to literary fiction." —*The Columbus Dispatch*

"With unhurried ease *The Current* carries us along, mirroring that fatal river, as clear as winter ice on the surface while beneath flowing darkly into the past." —*The Barnes and Noble Review*

"Seriously suspenseful."

—HelloGiggles

"This novel is careful layer upon careful layer, as deceptively thick yet brutally delicate as winter ice itself. Johnston's descriptions of people, places, grief, and loneliness are subtle and evocative; the minor plot about an aging dog becomes a rending portrait of the ravages of love. Indeed, for all its harsh observations about human nature, this novel has at its heart a strong belief that love, for all the pain it brings, is the one thing that truly saves us. An apt title that functions as a beautiful metaphor for all the secrets and emotions roiling beneath the surface of every human life."

—Kirkus Reviews, starred review

"[An] outstanding thriller . . . Johnston imbues each character with believable motives. The nuanced plot delves deep into how a community—and surviving relatives—deal with the aftermath of a death."

—Publishers Weekly, starred review

"Tim Johnston's Descent, a complex missing-person thriller set in the shadowy wilderness of the Rocky Mountains, was one of 2015's most pleasant surprises. His follow-up, The Current, is equally, if not more, impressive . . . As methodical as Johnston is at unwrapping his carefully plotted story, readers will churn through The Current's 400 pages—a paradox that only the most accomplished mystery writers ever achieve. The only complaint is that we might have to wait another three years for his next one."

—Amazon Book Review (Best Book of the Month)

"The Current is a rare creature: a gripping thriller and page-turner but also a masterwork of mood and language. You'll want to go fast at the same time you'll be compelled to savor each and every word."

—Ivy Pochoda, author of Wonder Valley

"Tim Johnston is the best thing to come along in crime fiction in years. With *Descent* and *The Current* he has already established himself as one of the best writers in the game, with an original voice that calls to mind the likes of Cormac McCarthy and Dennis Lehane but is entirely his own. With its beautiful prose, deeply emotional storytelling, and craftsman's eye for detail, *The Current* made me want to read slower, and write better."
—Michael Koryta, *New York Times* bestselling author of *How It Happened*

"I would have taken a break long before 2:00 a.m. last night were it not for Johnston's masterly ability to rummage inside the heads of his various characters, revealing the frayed fabric of small-town life in the process and showing us the stand-up grit of a handful of women and men . . . We need a little hyperbole if we're going to adequately describe how much we love a Tim Johnston novel."
—*Booklist*

"*The Current* is a haunting story . . . Johnston masterfully describes people, their grief, their guilt, and loneliness. He brings out both the brutal and loving sides of human nature. It is a real treat for those who love thrillers."
—*The Washington Book Review*

"Johnston plots out intricate story lines—his character development is thorough and intensive . . . What an invigorating read!"
—*Dayton Daily News*

"*The Current* is moody, layered crime fiction at its finest; you'll be tempted to tear through the pages, but, slow down. The lyrical language is worth lingering over."
—*The Augusta* (GA) *Chronicle*

THE CURRENT

ALSO BY TIM JOHNSTON

Never So Green

Irish Girl

Descent

THE CURRENT

A NOVEL BY

TIM JOHNSTON

ALGONQUIN BOOKS OF CHAPEL HILL 2019

Published by
Algonquin Books of Chapel Hill
Post Office Box 2225
Chapel Hill, North Carolina 27515-2225

a division of
Workman Publishing
225 Varick Street
New York, New York 10014

First paperback edition, Algonquin Books of Chapel Hill, November 2019.
Originally published in hardcover by Algonquin Books of Chapel Hill in January 2019.
Printed in the United States of America.
Published simultaneously in Canada by Thomas Allen & Son Limited.
Design by Steve Godwin.

This is a work of fiction. While, as in all fiction, the literary perceptions and insights are based on experience, all names, characters, places, and incidents either are products of the author's imagination or are used fictitiously.

LIBRARY OF CONGRESS CATALOGING-IN-PUBLICATION DATA
Names: Johnston, Tim, [date]–author.
Title: The current / a novel by Tim Johnston.
Description: First edition. | Chapel Hill, North Carolina :
Algonquin Books of Chapel Hill, 2019.
Identifiers: LCCN 2018020534 | ISBN 9781616206772 (hardcover : alk. paper)
Subjects: LCSH: College students—Fiction. | Traffic accidents—Fiction. |
Murder—Fiction. | Small cities—Minnesota—Fiction. | Life change events—
Fiction. | LCGFT: Psychological fiction. | Detective and mystery fiction.
Classification: LCC PS3610.O395 C87 2019 | DDC 813/.6—dc23
LC record available at https://lccn.loc.gov/2018020534

ISBN 978-1-61620-983-4 (PB)

10 9 8 7 6 5 4 3 2 1
First Paperback Edition

For Uncle Rick & Tante Kathy,
for showing a grateful Nef how it's done:
with wit, laughter & love all the way.

And for my mother, Judy Johnston,
who continues to lead our little clan with
such grace, good humor, constancy & love.

He whispered this last so low that it was inaudible
to anyone who did not love you.

—Ernest Hemingway, *Across the River and Into the Trees*

PART I

1

THE TWO GIRLS, young women, met for the first time the day they moved in together, first semester of that first year of college, third floor of Banks Hall, a north-facing room that overlooked green lawns and treetops and streams of students coming and going on the walkways below. Roommated by mysterious processes, perhaps a computer algorithm, perhaps a tired administrator plowing his way through a thousand folders, the girls tried at first to become friends, then tried simply to get along, and finally put in for reassignment, each without telling the other, and by the end of the winter holidays had both moved into new rooms with new roommates. If they saw each other on campus after that, they pretended they hadn't; they looked away, they looked at the sky, they received phone alerts of highest importance. They seemed to have made a pact of mutual invisibility, and this pact might have gone on forever, all the way through college at least, if not for a literature class in the fall of their sophomore year.

The class—The Romantics, it was called, like the band—was crammed into a too-small classroom, a space not much bigger than those dorm rooms, and yet neither girl wanted to be the one to drop, but instead kept coming to class and taking her seat. Three weeks into the semester one of the girls, arriving late, had no choice but to sit next to the other, and from then on they made a point of it: sitting shoulder to shoulder, nearly, in the crowded classroom, eyes on the professor, notebooks open . . . a game of academic chicken that neither girl felt too great about, to be honest, but felt even less great about losing, and so on it went. Until, one day, one of the girls—the one named Caroline—turned to the other girl, whose name was Audrey, and asked to borrow a pen, setting off a backpack search of such intensity that the professor herself, prowling her narrow track of floor at the head of the class, halted, one eyebrow cocked, while the girl hunted, and dug, and at last fetched up from the very last place it could have been a plain blue Bic with bite marks on the cap. The pen passed from hand to hand, and in this simple way the girls started over. Their story reset itself, and they became friends.

On February 4 of that same school year, Caroline Price turns twenty, and two days later at the Common Grounds Café her friend Audrey Sutter is telling her that her father is sick, and she needs to get home and she doesn't have a car, and the Visa her father gave her is maxed out on tuition, and so she's wondering, what she wanted to ask is, could she possibly borrow $150 for bus fare, she can pay Caroline back when . . . well, as soon as she can? And Caroline Price, sipping black coffee, shudders at some inner picture—perhaps the interior of that bus: God-knows-how-many miles up to the Arctic to see your sick—your dying?—father and nothing to keep you company but the smell of diesel and the cold, droning miles and probably some mullet-headed yahoo with halitosis just *waiting* for you to take those headphones off, like you would ever take them off!

It's not the Arctic, Audrey could remind her, it's Minnesota, but to a Georgia girl like Caroline it might as well be. Even Memphis, less than a three-hour ride north from her hometown, is too much. An *ice storm* last week, a tree limb snapping the power line behind her apartment, and all weekend in Troy's dorm room with its stink of boys, or in the library, or right here in the café, before the city got the power line repaired . . .

Audrey sitting meanwhile across the table, holding Caroline's image in her wet blue eyes—those pale, Arctic eyes—waiting, until at last Caroline says, Sure, of course, what time does your bus leave, I'll drive you to the station, and like that the storm lifts from Audrey's face, and wiping the tears from her cheeks she says, like one who has just regained her senses after a blow to the head: "Caroline, you look so nice today. What's going on?"

Because, as Caroline herself would be the first to admit, unless she's off to see Troy on a Friday night, or unless she's going out dancing with her volleyball girls, she tends to look like what she is: a sweats-and-sneakers kind of girl, a big, loose athlete, on her way to or from practice. But when she decides to look good?

When she hits the shoes and skirts and makeup? It's like she swooped down from some other world, a sudden alter-Caroline of extreme beauty and dazzle.

But it's nine o'clock on a Tuesday morning and Caroline is on her way to class, so—what gives?

A good question, a fair question, but Caroline must fly—running late again, always running late, Audrey watching through the glass as her friend fast-walks toward campus in her short jacket and short skirt and her tights, leaning into a cold headwind that seems to push at her with actual purpose, as if to discourage her, stop her even, turn her back—*Go back to your room, Caroline Price, go back to your bed, curl up under the heavy quilt the old women of home sewed just for you, no warmth like that in the world, not even a boy's . . .*

Caroline's boot heels clock-clocking on the sidewalk, her long fingers stuffed as far as they'll go into the fake pockets of her jacket, batting tears from her thickened lashes and asking herself too, perhaps, what's going on. A meeting with a professor, that's all. After class, if she has time, said the email. So, OK. Lose the Adidas and the hoodie for a change, but that's it, effortwise.

It's not anything sexual, this looking nice—she has a boyfriend, after all.

And the professor is *old*—like, forties-old.

But there are girls she knows who want that A so badly, who learned in middle school—hell, *grammar* school—how these things worked. The world. *Power*.

But that power is a false *power, girl,* says her memaw. With her dentures and her bent little body. *That power will turn on you like a stray dog.*

And the profs themselves, these older men, these wise and fatherly teachers; you could always tell who they had their eye on. And you watched it progress over the semester, the favored girl bringing it for a 9 a.m. class: the clothes, the hair, the earrings, the lashes.

But that's not what this is. Caroline would wear a damn *Snuggie* to class if she felt like it, and she would earn her grade according to her performance, just as she'd earn a win on the volleyball court where there are no grades and no flirting, only muscle and sweat and the unambiguous counting of points.

As for the perfume . . . well, a girl wanted to smell nice when she looked nice. Just a touch, a fingerprint, on the neck. That was for you and not for anyone else.

Certainly not for some forty-year-old man who wanted to see you after class, if you had time.

But it was the good stuff, Audrey knew, having caught its scent over the smell of coffee even before her friend sat down: the little French bottle Caroline bought on her trip to New York City last summer, and the scent of which Audrey now associates with Caroline almost as intensely as the potent green slime she'd rub into her legs before practice and before each game and sometimes, in those old dorm room days, before going to bed. And it's this weird remix of scents— French perfume and overpowering muscle gel—that Audrey smells as she, too, leaves the café, stepping into that same cold wind but the wind pushing at her back as she moves in the opposite direction of Caroline—a wind not to stop her but to hurry her along home, the sooner to pack, the sooner to be ready when Caroline comes to get her, the sooner (though she knows this is not logical) to get home to her father, who of course has told her not to come, to stay in school, nothing to see here, says he, just a little touch of the inoperable cancer is all, nothing that won't keep until you come home in the spring...

And with such thoughts fluttering within her it seems actually a piece of these thoughts, like an escaped fragment, when the air itself bursts into violence just above her head—a sudden flurry and a kind of shriek as a *bird* nearly crash-lands on her head, close enough to fan her with wingbeat, low enough to sweep something soft and alive along the part line of her hair; it's the plush tail of a squirrel, she just sees, a juvenile, who rides like a pilot in the bird's claws, this bird and rodent combo descending with flaps and cries to earth behind a low wall of hedges, a troubled landing that no one—she looks: students plodding head-down, locked into phones, ear-stoppered—no one but her has seen or heard.

And she steps around the hedges slowly, coming all the way around before she sees the bird—a hawk, sure enough—standing with its back to her, wings fanned out on the dirt like the wings of a broken craft, great riffling wings that become arms, crutches, here on earth, keeping the hawk upright atop the body of the squirrel; young, round-eyed squirrel, unsquirming in its cage of talons.

The hawk rotates its head halfway round, puts two black eyes on Audrey and opens its sharp beak soundlessly. Audrey standing there doing nothing. Saying nothing, just watching. A passive but rapt witness to this instance of wildness on a college campus. Predator and prey. The hawk watching her with those black eyes, that sharp beak, considering her—Audrey's—intentions here, the pros and cons of waiting it out, until at last in a single high note the hawk says, *You little bitch*, and lifts the great wings and unhooks the talons and with one windy beat is aloft again, and with another is gone.

The young squirrel remains, wide-eyed, belly to the ground; in a state of rodent shock maybe. Or maybe it's the dead-like stillness prey is said to adopt when all hope is lost, when it's time simply to die. But then, suddenly, the squirrel leaps to its feet and flies into the hedges and there's nothing where it had been, where the hawk had been, but a random patch of ground—and no one sees any of this but Audrey, and she will tell no one, not even Caroline; it's her own personal event flown down from the sky—some kind of sign, surely, some kind of message: a last-second reprieve from death.

And so enlivened—so incited—by this vision, she takes the four wooden porchsteps of the little gray rental house in two bounds, then likewise flies up the staircase that leads to the two upstairs bedrooms and begins tossing things onto her bed like one making her own escape. Like one whose own reprieve has just been assured.

AFTER CLASS, AS per his email, Caroline follows him down the hall and into his office and watches him close the door behind her but not all the way, no click of latch, just enough gap to keep it private but not too private in the cramped little room—"Have a seat, please." Two old leather chairs from somebody's yard sale. Books everywhere. Authors on the walls: old dead white men in offhand moments, as if he'd known these men himself, snapped the shots himself between cigars and whiskeys in the sepia past.

She sits, crossing her legs, and he takes the other leather chair and crosses his too, showing her a length of brown dress sock and a light-brown wingtip, the nose of the wingtip so close to her knees the decorative perforations seem olfactory, almost, like pores by which he might sniff her. The office is so small she can smell the French perfume like there's another girl in the room, and her heart thuds with embarrassment.

He doesn't look anywhere below her throat, his eyes a light clean steady blue, and so it's surprising when he says, "You look nice today," and keeps his eyes on her face. "Is it a game day?"

"No," she says, "it's Tuesday." As if everyone, including an English professor, knows the women's volleyball schedule.

"Ah," he says, and nods, and she nods too in the silence that follows.

"So," he says, turning to lift a sheet of paper from the desk, then turning back. "I just wanted to ask you about your response to last week's reading." And holding the paper before him he reads: "'Highly accomplished work of the post-9/11 epoch, incorporating multiple points of view to great effect, but to what end? Empires, entire civilizations vanish, so what matter these living few? These little human lives?'"

He holds the paper, his eyes on the sentences. As if with patience they might replicate. Spawn others. She thinks about recrossing her legs and decides against it. Audrey Sutter's flushed, wet face comes to mind. The way a tear dove through the latte foam and left its neat tunnel.

The professor floats the paper back to the desktop, turns back again, and fixes her with those eyes.

"So—what's the deal here?" he says, and Caroline glances down at her knees, brushes at the topmost one, and when she looks up again he looks up too, just an instant late.

What is *the deal here, Prof? she thinks. How do these things generally work? Who makes the first move? In the movies, in a book, how would it go? Would I click the door shut or would you?*

"What do you mean?" she says finally.

"I think you know what I mean," he says. "Why do you make so little effort with these responses? You are a smart, articulate young woman, and I . . . well, I—" He falters, and just then a group of students pass by the gapped door—boys, laughing and cussing down the hall. *Shit*, they say. *Motherfucker*, they say.

The professor clears his throat. He folds his hands together and rests them on his knee. He looks her in the eye again.

"Caroline," he says, drawing the name out like it's something sweet and melty in his mouth. "Come on, now. Am I asking too much?"

What are *you asking?* she'd like to ask. *What do you want from me?*

But in the end she's only sorry—very sorry, she says. She understands. She'll try harder next time, she says, even as she feels pretty certain that what he really wants is another excuse to call her into this little room. That what he really wants is to open up one of those folded hands and let it fall through space, through every kind of alarm going off in his heart, and place it, under the eyes of the dead authors, smack onto her knee.

And then what, girl? What happens when the ol' dog wants a bite?

After that it's back across campus for Caroline, to Troy's dorm—she is dating a boy who still lives in a dorm—and ten hard bangs on the door before it unsticks like a gummy eye and there stands Phil, the roommate, in nothing but boxers. Annoyed and bony and pale as any cadaver, giving her the up and down—the skirt, the tights—and saying finally, "He's not here." A fact she already knows by the smell coming off him, the stink of burned weed among several notes of stink. Because Troy does not abide smoking of any kind in the dorm room, most especially weed, which just a whiff of on his clothes could get him kicked off the team. Good-bye scholarship. Good-bye college. Good-bye warm Caroline in his bed.

"Where then?" she says, checking her phone again for the time. For the text reply that won't come; she knows his class schedule, his practice schedule, his feeding schedule. As he knows hers.

Bony shoulders rise and fall and Phil says, "Cannot say, man, as I am not his keeper."

She looks beyond him, and Phil opens the door wide for her to look. Beds and desks and clothes and pizza boxes and socks and Troy's gym bag and his Nikes, and she knows just by looking, just by smelling, that he did not spend the night here. And there it goes, inside her chest: her heart stepping up to a ledge and tottering, dizzied, ready to fall. It's the sensation of losing at the net, of rising up for the block and knowing she's failed even before the ball goes sizzling by her ear to boom against the floor—a sound for her heart alone. *Beaten*, it says. Outplayed, schooled.

"You're welcome to come in and wait," Phil says. "Smoke a little bud, if you like."

Weighing his chances, she thinks. Liking the look of her legs in those tights. She sees herself in the skirt and tights and understands she's come not to see Troy but to be seen by him, at this hour, looking good.

Because if you dressed up for your boyfriend, then you didn't dress up for your professor. Although either way you are a vain and stupid girl.

Phil stands watching her. Scratching his ribs.

But now the ball comes back over the net into deep court where her girls, her sisters, take it onto their wrists, take it lightly onto their fingertips and gentle it once more her way, nice and high, and she is ready, she is coiled hard and tight, a perfect rattlesnake of timing: "Gonna have to take a pass on that invite, Phil," she says, "but could you give Troy a message for me?"

"Sure thing, man. Messages are my specialty."

"Tell him I came to say good-bye."

"Good-bye?"

"Yes. I just found out I have cervical cancer. Stage four. I'm going home and I don't want him to try to contact me."

Pale, dull-eyed Phil, speechless. His face goes one way but his eyes stay on her. "I sense a certain lack of sincerity here," he says, and without taking her eyes off his she presses her hand to his boxers and cups the whole soft works in her palm, her long fingers. His body bows and he shows the pinked whites of his eyes and gasps.

"Listen, Phil. I want you to tell Troy this—right here." She holds his gaze. His balls. "You got that message?"

Thirty minutes later she's in front of the house, fifteen minutes late, and Audrey is sitting on the porchsteps in her black peacoat and black watchman's cap and sturdy winter boots, a seaman off to sea, and the girl has got some luggage.

"Damn, girl," says Caroline, and Audrey says, "I know, I'm sorry . . . I don't know when I'll be back," and Caroline takes half the load and they get it all squared away in the back of the RAV4 and they buckle up and they're off. Five minutes later, doing forty down Union, Audrey cranes around to watch the bus depot go by and, doing so, sees the large blue gym bag in the back seat. Fully loaded, Caroline's jeans, socks, her favorite sweater busting out. Audrey looking her friend over, then, taking note of the flannel pajama bottoms she wears, the old gray hoodie, the pink Adidas, and Caroline turning briefly to meet her eyes and then turning back to the road.

"What the fuck," Caroline says. "Road trip."

BECAUSE THE TRUTH is she's glad for the excuse to get away, she says. If Audrey was just homesick for her pet chicken she'd still be on board, so will she please not sit there being so darn grateful the whole way?

They've got their coffees, and the RAV4 is climbing the eastern coast of Arkansas, up the 55 North toward Missouri. A gusty but otherwise fine day for driving.

Audrey is silent awhile and then says, "Who would have a pet chicken?"

"I'm just saying."

"What would you even do with it?"

Caroline sighs. When asked by housing why she wanted a new roommate after their first semester, Caroline wrote: "Irreconcilable species." No idea what Audrey wrote.

"Is it Troy?" Audrey says.

"Is what Troy?"

"Why you're glad to get away."

Caroline looks over, looks back to the road. "It could be a lot of things, Audrey. I might be having a psychological crisis. I might've decided college is a waste of time and money. I might be sleeping with my professor. I might've decided life is too fucking short. I might—"

"Which one?"

"What?"

"Callaway?"

"What? No. Seriously?"

"Buford?"

"*Buford?* He's like, a hundred years old and smells like old bedsheets."

"Nice eyes, though."

"Nice eyes. Jesus, Audrey, I am not sleeping with my professor, I was just making a point. I was just posing *hypotheticals*—remember those? Remember when we talked about those?"

"Yes. But it just stuck out, that one."

"Well"—pushing out the flat of her palm—"stick it back in."

"All right. Sorry."

"You don't have to *apologize*," Caroline says, flicking hair out of her eyes. Sliding a glance at Audrey, who sips at her coffee.

"Is that how you see me?" she says. "Someone who would sleep with her professor?"

"No. I never thought about it until you mentioned it."

"But you went there pretty quickly."

Audrey holds her coffee in midair. Then sips, and says, "Not because I think of you like that, though. But because you always surprise me, Caroline. You always do. I count on you surprising me. That's all."

The girls face forward. The fields sweeping by, unrolling like great corduroy rugs, brown and white, the white not cotton now but lines of ice from the storm caught in the furrows. Above them bends the deep and empty sky. Audrey reaches to touch the colorful loops of beads that hang from the rearview mirror. The beads click when they get swinging, and in the thick of them, like a little thing nested there, is a white rabbit's foot, stained in shifting spots of colored light. The RAV4 was a gift from Caroline's father, the rabbit's foot a gift from her brother. *Not so lucky for the rabbit*, said Caroline's father. And: *A moving vehicle is no place for luck, daughter. May this vehicle be safeguarded by intelligence, by great care and caution, and not the amputated paw of a rodent.*

"So what is it, then?" Audrey says, and Caroline swipes at her eye—a single tear, where did that come from?

"Let's just say it *includes* but is not *strictly about* Troy," she says, and neither girl says another word for a mile, two miles. Then Audrey says, "I'm sorry, Caroline," and Caroline says, "Screw it. Screw him. Are we going to listen to these tunes or what?"

THEY ARE JUST a few miles into Missouri when the first text comes, a two-note chime, and Caroline's heart jumps to it like a trained animal.

But she defies the chime, her heart's response to it. Eyes on the road, hands at ten and two. They've been listening to an old Radiohead CD—the RAV4 is pre-Bluetooth by, like, *one year*—each in her separate thoughts, and Caroline waits for the end of the song before she fishes up the phone from her tote bag, reads the message, places the phone in her lap and takes the wheel two-handed again. Now it begins.

The phone chimes and vibrates on her upper thigh, sending its hum, its message, deep. The times when he would text at night and she would hold it there, waiting, her heartbeat beneath it, in her belly, everywhere . . .

A full minute passes without a third text and she lifts the phone, and the car drifts and she corrects with a jerk. She holds the phone at the crown of the wheel, as if she's going to text back, and Audrey, reaching, says, "Here, let me," and takes the phone from her. "What do you want to say?"

The first yellow speech balloon reads: *WTF, C? Where r u?* The second reads: *U don't know what u think u know. In class, will call u in 1 hr.*

Caroline tosses her hair and says, "Tell him, 'You don't know what I know. Don't call me, I'm driving.'"

Audrey thumbs it in and sends the message and places the phone in her own lap, and Caroline eyes the phone there, her phone, in a lap not hers, before looking away.

She turns up the music and taps at the wheel and bobs her head to the beat, but it's no use; it's as if there's a third person in the cab now, as if they've picked up a hitchhiker. They wait to see what he'll say.

The phone chimes and vibrates on Audrey's thigh. She reads aloud: "'Please please be cool, C'—C as in the letter C," Audrey says. "'Gotta talk to you.'"

"Tell him, 'Talk to Phil,'" Caroline says. "Tell him, 'Ask Phil how he liked it this a.m.'"

Audrey looks over. "Liked what?"

"Just type it."

She types and sends the message, and Caroline tells her what happened with Phil, and Audrey sits holding the phone. Silent for a long while.

"What did it feel like?" she says at last, and Caroline gives her a look.

"What do you think it felt like?"

"I mean," Audrey says, "in that context. The fact that it was Phil."

Caroline sputters her lips and turns back to the road. "The usual, Audrey. Nothing to write home about."

The sun is going down; the swaying beads catch its light and throw prisms on the girls' legs. Music pulses in the speakers.

"Phil," Audrey says after a while, as if to herself. "I hope you washed your hand."

And Caroline laughs then, deeply and truly, and the laugh releases the Georgia in her chest like walking into her memaw's house, like the drug-strong smell of hot pecan pie, and she says in the voice of home, "Oh, Audrey, sometimes I just love you."

And Audrey—who loves this voice, who has *always* loved this voice—says, "I know. It's the same with me."

THEY DRIVE OUT of day into night, out of cotton country into wheat and then into corn, all such fields indistinguishable in the dead of winter, all brown and empty, increasingly drifted in dunes of snow. Off to their right somewhere the wide Mississippi slugs along through its turnings, back the way they've come, south as the girls drive north. The girls talking and talking until, in the midst of a lull, Audrey works her head into a pillow stuffed up against the passenger window and sleeps.

Caroline drives on, alone now and aware of the car around her—the road beneath it, the four small dashes of rubber that connect car to road—in a way she hadn't been just a moment before, and soon enough she puts it together: that this awareness, this alertness, comes with the surrendering of the same thing in her passenger, and that this is an intimacy, this exchange, modern in its specifics and yet ancient to the species, old as blood: the deep, unthinking trust of children who slept in open caves, who sleep now in cars piloted by their parents flying down deadly highways; the fierce tenderness of responsibility that pounds in the chests of parents, the father or mother at the wheel . . . and following this current of thought Caroline doesn't think of Troy for miles, and then she realizes she hasn't thought of Troy for miles and it's all over—he's back. Those eyes. Those hands. The smell of that chest.

She would like to let Audrey sleep but they need gas, and ten miles later she takes the exit and pulls into the station, and Audrey raises her head, then pushes the black knit cap up from her eyes.

"Where are we?"

"We're not in Kansas anymore."

"We were never in Kansas."

"I know, Audrey."

They take turns in the ladies' and then they look over the food: the wedges of old pizza, the paper baskets of breaded chicken parts, the fat corn dogs that crack them up just to think about putting them in their mouths, finally settling on a family-size bag of Cheetos and two milky coffee drinks in glass bottles. Audrey offers the last of her cash but Caroline waves her off. The big dude behind the counter looks from one girl to the other, boldly, as if to make some kind of point. Caroline catches and holds his eye: *Is there a problem, bubba?*

Outside the air is so cold, and there's the smell of snow although they can see the deep glitter of outer space, and they stand awhile with their faces lifted, lips pursed, blowing pale breaths that rise and vanish in the stars.

Audrey drives now, and they talk, and Caroline learns that Audrey's father has lung cancer—the cancer is back, actually—and there's no hope. Her mother died when Audrey was just seven, a rare blood disease, and there are no brothers, no sisters—Caroline knows these facts from the dorm room days, from those early days when they were still trying—and she understands that in a few months, or however long it takes, Audrey will be an orphan at the age of nineteen.

The cold night rolls by, northern Iowa, flat and snowy, a few farmhouses lit up in the empty reaches. Caroline imagines Audrey out there—walking out there in her winter boots, her black knit cap, all alone. She reaches to touch the colorful beads, the white rabbit's foot within, so soft. Everything strange from this vantage. A girl who is not her sitting in her seat, hands on her steering wheel. As if she's been transformed. If she looks in the vanity mirror now what will she see? Her mind is playing tricks on her. She needs sleep.

She sips the cold coffee drink through a straw and says, "What will you do?"

"What do you mean?"

"I mean . . . after. Will you come back to school?"

Audrey doesn't answer. Then she says, "I don't know," and sinks her hand into the Cheetos bag.

Caroline slips her own hand into her tote bag and steals a glance, but no new messages. That's seven hours now.

Not that she's counting.

Not that she's thinking where is he where the fuck is he.

Not that she's picturing certain big-eyed skanks swatting their eyelashes at him.

Audrey, at the helm, sails on. Steady as she goes. Taking her time catching up with and passing a semi, giving the old boy behind the wheel a nice long look down into the car. Caroline sitting there in her pajama bottoms with the shells and starfish so faded they could be anything, *What're you looking at, truck-driver man? Why don't you watch where you're driving?*

When they are well past the semi and back in the right lane again Audrey says, "Want to hear what he told me, last time I saw him?"

"Who?"

"My dad. The sheriff. The ex-sheriff."

"Sure."

"He said there's never a good American with a gun around when you need one."

"What's that supposed to mean?"

"That's what I asked."

"What did he say?"

"He said if it were just him and the doctors and the bills, it'd be over already. Says to me, 'I'm not afraid of dying, but I got a certain reputation to uphold, don't I? Folks sure would be disappointed.'"

"What did you say to that?"

"I said, 'Daddy, if I ever hear you talk like that again I'll shoot you myself.'"

"And what did he say?"

"He said, 'Deputy, now that would really shake things up, wouldn't it.'"

The girls smile at each other, eyes shining, and face forward again.

A swarm of bright insects dive into the headlights and burst their translucent guts on the glass. Not bugs, Caroline realizes—it's some kind of weather, thick and whitish, but not snow. *Sleet.* The pavement, gray and salty-white for so many miles, begins to darken, to glisten.

Audrey eases up on the gas. "I don't like the looks of this."

"What do you mean?"

"I mean I don't feel too great driving your car in this stuff."

"Audrey, let me remind you: Caroline from Georgia, Audrey from Minnesota. Grandpa Sven probably had you driving the snowplow when you were just a wee lad."

"I don't have a Grandpa Sven."

"Plus this car has four-wheel drive."

"Is it on?"

"It's supposed to be."

"But it's your car, Caroline. You have a feel for it."

"Audrey, we're like an hour away, aren't we?"

This is true: they are an hour, in good conditions, from Audrey's father's house, where they will say hello to the man, brush their teeth and fall like dead women into Audrey's bed. But after eleven hours on the road, the last hour will be the longest and cruelest, whatever the weather, and finally it's the girls' bladders that make the call—oh man, that coffee drink went *straight* through them—and they take the next exit, only to discover that the nearest gas station is two miles from the highway, but by now the idea of a bathroom has such a grip on them that they take the two miles anyway, a hilly and curvy two-laner that feeds them down into a valley and onto a narrow trestle bridge with a rusted and bullet-pocked sign that may have once named the river they can see below, wisps of snow moving snakelike across a black face of ice, or perhaps the sign issued a warning about the narrowness of the bridge or its tendency to freeze before the road. In any case, once across the bridge they rise out of the valley again, steeply, and travel another half mile through a gray, disheartening slush before they at last reach a remote station—a dubious, sickly lit shoebox of a building, blurry after so long on the road . . . Christ, is it even open?

It is, thank God.

BABY WHEREVER U R, whatever u r doing, I will b there. Just tell me.

Caroline thumbs in a reply, stares at it, then wipes it out and drops the phone back into her bag.

The sleet ticks and ticks against the glass. She cranks up the heat and directs it onto the windshield and lets the wipers loose for two crusty swipes. Maybe ought to get out and go at the glass with that scraper she bought when the ice storm hit last week. Inside the gas station, on the other side of fogged glass, sits the big gal with her big pink Midwestern face, pencil in her fist, solving her puzzles. Giving the girls a good long look when they came in. Hardly room to turn around in there between the counter and the racks, let alone steal any of her dusty old crap, *The ladies' is around the side of the building, girls, here's the key*, thin, cheap key attached by a short hoop of what looks like dried possum gut to a wooden souvenir backscratcher from Phoenix, Arizona, of all places, and blackened from handling, black grime under weirdly realistic fingernails, and that's what you give people to take into your nasty-even-for-a-gas-station ladies' room?

Two other vehicles are parked at the station, Caroline observes, neither here for gas, or else finished with gas and moved off to the side of the building, opposite to the bathroom side. One a low-squatting wagon with a driver's door of a completely different color and the windshield blinded over in sleet; the other an old two-tone pickup like her papaw's down in Georgia . . . Papaw forever head-first into its open hood, *Hand me the five-eighths now, Sweetpea . . .*

Caroline tapping the wheel with her nails and looking for Audrey to appear in the yellow light again, give the big gal back her backscratcher and get her ass back to the car. The falling ice ticking away on one side of the windshield and hot air blowing on the other and the thin streams of water finding their way down the curve of glass and *Come* on, *Audrey, Jesus . . .* and suddenly Caroline goes cold all over, her heart jolting as if something live has bounded in front of her, and she looks again at the pickup truck. The windshield catches the yellow light of the station, the glass recently wipered and still too warm for the sleet to build its white shell as it has on the wagon.

And she looks again at the building, the large single window: the big gal sitting there as before, unquestionable owner of the sleeted-over wagon. All alone in there.

"Shit," says Caroline, and she's out of the car and moving fast through the sleet and she can hear them even before she rounds the corner,

". . . there now, that's better. See there, Bud? We're all gonna be friends here."

The one talking has got his hand on Audrey's face, and Caroline registers in that first glance how dark the fingers look against her friend's pale face, as if they've been dipped in paint, or oil—white hand but dark fingers—and how light her friend's eyes are, even in that shadowed space. Audrey's hair is a dark mess, tossed by some roughness, and the man has got a knee between her legs and has pinned one of her arms against the wall but her free hand hangs at her side, as if by some terrible gravity—has he broken her arm? The man's face is scratched and bleeding. Both men wear cheap high-crowned caps with curved bills and meaningless logos. Jeans and canvas jackets. Leather workboots, as common as old tires. The door to the ladies' hangs open, gapped, does not shut on its own, she knows, nor lock convincingly from the inside, and there's the foul stink of that room but also the stink of beer and cigarettes coming off the two men. And all of this in the instant before they see her—before Audrey sees her and they see Audrey seeing her.

The one nearest to Caroline, the one standing back and watching, just has time to lock his eyes on what she's holding up to him before the canister hisses its load into his face and he screams and flails backwards, clawing at his eyes—trips over his own boots and falls rolling on the concrete as if on fire. Misty discharge clouds the air, the intensely bitter smell and taste of pepper, and Caroline's own eyes begin to burn. The other man—he is not a man, she sees, but hardly more than a boy, twenty if that, both of them—the boy lets go of Audrey to fling up his forearms, impressive reflexes, and the spray wets his sleeves—"Don't you fucking mace me, cunt"—and he wheels and turns his back just as Caroline lets go another round. With her free hand she grabs Audrey by the coat sleeve and pulls her away from the door, away from the bitter haze, and Audrey in turn pulls at Caroline, but to no effect. Caroline isn't going anywhere.

"What did you say?" she says. She holds the canister head-high, aimed, but he keeps his face buried in his arms, his back to her. She blinks and blinks, the cold night spangling with the burn of the pepper, but she doesn't move.

"What did you say?" she says again.

The boy just standing there, hunchbacked over his own face. The other boy squirming on his back on the concrete, blubbering about being blinded, *Jesus Christ, you fucking blinded me*, the wooden backscratcher near his head, strange thing lying there, like a doll's arm torn from its doll.

"I said don't you fucking mace me, you fucking cunt bitch," says the standing boy.

"Caroline, let's go." Audrey is pulling at her. Pulling at her.

"Why don't you turn around and say that to my face, you slackjawed muppetfucker?"

"Put that shit down and I'll do more than that."

She sprays the back of his neck. He doesn't move, but she takes a step away from the mist.

"Bitch," he says, "I swear to God . . ."

"*Caroline*," Audrey says, and pulls hard enough to get her friend off balance, and suddenly they are moving, they are stumbling, they are reeling toward the light, their bodies so slow and heavy and all they want is the light—the beautiful yellow light of the station! But when Audrey goes for the glass door Caroline grabs her once again, and there's a brief struggle before Audrey looks in and sees: the woman who gave them the key, sitting at the counter as before, solving her puzzles as before, so pink and soft and alone in the cramped little store. And maybe you can get the door locked in time and maybe you can't, but if you can't, and the boys get in there . . .

The RAV4 sits where Caroline left it, still running. Its doors fly open and slam again and the boys have not grabbed them, the boys are nowhere in sight as the RAV4 drops into gear, as it lurches and fishtails out from under the lights of the station, and the girls are in it and their hearts are slamming.

"Are you all right?" Caroline yelling through her tears—the burn of the pepper. "Audrey, are you all right?"

"I'm fine. Slow down!"

"Do you even know where we are—?"

"We're two miles from the highway. Slow down."

"Who are you calling?" Audrey holds the phone in both hands—her arm is fine, why didn't she use it?

"The police."

"The *police*? What are they gonna do?"

"Those boys might follow us."

"Fuck, I should've got the license—"

"Yes, hello," Audrey says calmly. "I'm calling to report an attempted assault."

"Attempted rape," Caroline yells.

"Yes, we're all right now. What? Where are we—?"

They are on the narrow and dropping two-lane road. They are halfway down the hill before Caroline thinks of the sleet, before she remembers the iron trestle bridge at the bottom—and yet when she applies the brakes nothing happens. Or rather, something very strange happens: the car turns quarterwise to the road and continues on at the same speed.

"Caroline, don't brake—"

"What?"

"Take your foot off—"

"Audrey, shit—"

They are briefly broadside to the road, and then they are backwards to it, looking back up the hill the way they've come—there's their tiretracks carving a long black DNA helix in the sleet—one or both of them screaming as they come around again, and the steering wheel has come loose from the car, spins with meaningless ease in Caroline's hands, and the whole world spins with it, the sleet angling crazily in the beams of the headlights—the snowy shoulder, the road, the trestle bridge all slurring by—until at last the car slips from the road and plows face-forward into the deep snow of the shoulder, the passenger-side wheels sinking into the ditch, and the car plows and plows through the snow, and it slows, and at last comes abruptly to rest, just short of the outermost ironworks of the bridge and on the very crest of the high riverbank. The two girls stiff-arming wheel and dash, looking out into empty space, their hearts banging. Sleet diving through the headlights on its way to a landing they cannot see, far below.

"Caroline," Audrey says.

"What?"

"Put the car in park, please."

Caroline puts the car in park. What they want is the lack of movement. What they want is stillness. It's like that scene in the movies when the car totters on the cliff's edge. Though the car is not tottering and it's not a cliff, it's a riverbank, but still.

The cab is an aquarium, green-hued from the gauges, encased in glass. A heavy, underwater world. Even the air smells of it—tastes of it: plant life, silt, fish. Their heartbeats pulse between them on the currents, send messages one to the other on the green and conductive air. Fine hairs lift from Audrey's head and sway like black cilia. The girls find each other's eyes and find something—perhaps their screams, still ringing in their ears, perhaps the giddy rolling of their guts as the car spun round and round—to laugh about, breathlessly.

"You fucking *blinded* me!" says Caroline, laughing. "Did you see that poor peckerwood?" And then she sees the headlights in the rearview mirror—two yellow lights descending the hill, unwavering, locked in, steady. As if this driver traveled some other kind of road, where the laws of physics still held.

"Damn, that was quick," she says, and Audrey sees the headlights too in the side-view mirror.

"Caroline."

"What?"

"That's not the police."

Caroline looks again. "How do you know?"

"They're not throwing their lights."

That's right: Audrey's daddy is a sheriff. Audrey has ridden shotgun through the Arctic hinterlands, has probably thrown the lights herself. Thrown the sirens. *Let's go get 'em, Deputy.*

Where is that sheriff now? Where is that daddy?

Lying in his bed, dying of his cancer.

Audrey remembers the phone and lifts it to her ear. "Hello? *Hello—?*"

Headlights descend and pour their light into the cab, and when Audrey looks over her shoulder her face is a kind of light itself, moon-bright, and nearly all the color driven from her eyes, the pupils like black pinholes. She lowers the phone and says as quietly as anything Caroline has ever heard from another person's lips, "*Hold on, Caroline.*"

The headlights grow so near they are blocked by the RAV4's tailgate, and still they flood the cab with light, the driver pulling onto the shoulder too but not as far over, short of the deep snow. There's the sound of tires in the snow, and then there's the sound of tires failing to stop in the snow, of tires skidding in the snow. And then there's the bump.

You couldn't even call it an impact. A love tap, Caroline's papaw would say—and the Mardi Gras beads click and sway, brilliant in the light. The tiny, multicolored rabbit's foot. And it's then, at the moment of the bump, the love tap, that the hawk and the squirrel come back to Audrey, flapping into her mind like something she once dreamed, a shrieking figment having nothing to do with real life, and she briefly thinks—briefly believes: *This, too, this is not real!*

A love tap, a miscalculation—an accident, surely. And over the edge they go.

How must this have looked to the driver who watched it happen: the RAV4 squatting in the deep shoulder snow one moment, solidly at rest, lit up in his headlights, the bags and suitcases of the cargo area, the heads of the two girls in the front seats—and then the bright oval of the passenger's face as she turned to look back at him. Was it that bright sudden face that distracted him, that accounts for the failure to stop in time, the bump of machine on machine and the resulting, the unbelievable, visual of the back end of the RAV4 rising into the air as the front end dipped and the whole of it, machine and luggage and girls and all, slipped all at once out of view? Just—gone.

Did the girls scream? Was there time? Was the outcome too swift and too certain for screaming? The forward tires locked in park, did Caroline Price slam her powerful legs at the brake pedal anyway? What thoughts fired in their brains as the car dropped, gathering speed from its own weight, flying nose-first toward the black surface of the river—a darkness and coldness too incredible to imagine. The black, smooth ice full of its own burning lights, its own stars. Did the girls in that span of two, maybe three heartbeats, find each other's hands? Like girls who have done so all their lives did they reach out in the dark? Like sisters did they find and grasp?

PART II

2

THE DAILY PAPER that once landed on his porch in the morning, rolled up and slapping the porchboards in the dark as if to announce the new day, as if no new day could begin without that sound, had been stopped years ago, and still the days came, and the day's news too by and by, though the only news he took with his morning coffee these days was the national weather from the TV, and that just so he'd know what to expect out there, though it rarely changed his plans or even how he dressed, and so he didn't learn about the accident, those two young women in the river, those college girls, until much later in the day, when he made his way at last to Eileen Lindeman's house to see about the smell she said was coming from the downstairs bathroom.

The winter sun down by then, the end of a long day of small jobs, some in town, some out. Eileen Lindeman's house was in town, on the east side of the river, and once upon a time he might've taken more care, might've parked the van a block away from the house, although it wouldn't have stopped people from talking.

Another lifetime, all that business, and anyone who saw Gordon Burke's van in Eileen Lindeman's driveway these days would know that Gordon was there to fix something in the house and nothing more. His story had changed too much for any other interpretation.

The trouble was the seal—he told her that right off, showing her by rocking the toilet in his hands. The floor tiles had not been set level and so the porcelain base did not sit cleanly all the way around, and so the gasket never stood a chance. Just the slightest corruption to the wax and you had sewer gas leaking into your house.

Brad, she told him—her ex—had set the tiles himself in one of his fits of home improvement. "Looked it up online," she said. "Said anybody who could read could do it."

Twelve, thirteen years ago, that would've been. Brad Lindeman, the lawyer, had left her for a young woman lawyer up in Saint Paul, and of course Gordon's wife had pulled pretty much the same stunt at about the same time—a *banker*, in her case—leaving him to raise a teenage daughter mostly on his own. Which, truth be told, was a relief at the time. Was a godsend to that house.

He stood looking at the toilet, the tiles. Eileen standing just behind him in the small bathroom, her face framed in the vanity mirror.

"You know what I'm gonna find when I lift this toilet?" he said.

"A leprechaun?"

"No, a two-dollar gasket about this thick that's not even squashed. I'm surprised it lasted this long."

She was watching him in the mirror, the hand he raised to demonstrate thickness, and when he met her eyes he saw what was still there, if he wanted it—just a note, a reminder, just in case. She'd been the first, after Meredith moved out. Four years without a woman's touch, including the last two years of marriage, unless you counted a woman's fists as touching, a wife's crazy little blows at two in the morning—your fault, always your fault that she was drunk. That she was sleeping with another man.

He'd not been looking for it, not missing it; he had his work, his business, a sixteen-year-old daughter to raise. But Eileen had Brad's money to spend: new water heater downstairs, new kitchen sink upstairs, new fixtures in the master bath . . . until finally there was no other reason to come over but one.

You can park in the driveway, Gordon. There's nothing wrong with what we're doing. Is there?

People talk, Eileen.

So let them talk.

What he meant was: they'd talked about Meredith. They'd talked about Brad Lindeman, and now they would talk about Gordon and Eileen, the two cheated-on leftovers running into each other's arms, for Christ's sake.

He looked at the toilet again and said, "Shouldn't be more than an hour, give or take," and Eileen told him to take his time. She offered him coffee, a beer? but he thanked her no, he'd best get to it, and she smiled at him in the mirror and left him to it.

THE OLD WAX ring came up with the toilet and peeled easily from the porcelain—greasy black but otherwise not much altered from its original shape and thickness, which was one-half inch, as predicted. He replaced it with a Harvey's No-Seep #5, walked the bowl back into place, felt the wax compressing under it, tightened down the nuts, reconnected the water line and stood watching the tank fill, then watched the water flush down.

He checked his watch. One hour, soup to nuts.

He climbed the snowy risers to the driveway and got his tools stowed away. The stars were out, bright and thick. The temperature had dropped ten, fifteen degrees.

At the front door he stomped his boots and let himself in, then stood on the small rug waiting for her to appear. She'd turned on the lamps in the living room. A light in the kitchen. The house was full of furniture, as if she was expecting a big crowd any second. She and Brad had never had any kids. There'd been a miscarriage or two, people said. Anyway it was now the house of a woman in her fifties who lived alone. Everything in its place.

He took a step and poked his head into the kitchen. "Eileen?"

A TV playing somewhere. Not downstairs, and not in the living room. The only other set he knew of was in the bedroom. He said her name again, louder. He didn't want to cross the carpet in his boots but he would not take them off. He pawed the soles once more over the rug and crossed the living room and took the two steps up to the landing where the master bedroom was. The smell there was partly her perfume and partly some other scent that was in her skin, in her hair, that made you think of the back of a supermarket where boxes of fruit were stacked and waiting. Or maybe it was because she day-managed the supermarket that made you think that. Anyway the smell was there . . . stronger when she unzipped her dress, when she stepped out of the dress in the lamplight, years ago, and stepped into your arms.

He would not stay the night, he'd told her back then, because of his daughter. Because of what she'd gone through with her mother, and Eileen understood. But then one night when Holly had gone up to her mother's for the weekend—Meredith sober then, supposedly, and living with some new man who was not the banker but a contractor with a young daughter of his own—that night Gordon had drunk too much wine and was just falling asleep when Eileen said she wanted to tell him something, something she'd never told anyone, not even Brad. And then she told him about the man who'd given her a ride. Fifteen, she'd been, and the man wore a tie and his car looked like her father's silver Buick and he wore a wedding band and so when he pulled over she'd gotten in. But when they reached the turnoff for her house the man kept going, fast. *Don't*, she said. *You're a nice man.* She could tell by his face he hadn't planned it, didn't know what he was doing, or even where to take her. She knew it was his first time. *You've seen me now*, the man said, and she said, *No, I never did. I never saw this car either, I swear to God.* He looked at her and said, *Do you believe in God?* and she said, crying now, *Yes, sir, I do*, and the man slowed down. He pulled over and stopped the car. Sat there with his hands on the wheel, looking straight ahead. After a while, Eileen simply got out of the car, shut the door, and walked home.

And you never told anyone? Gordon said after a long silence, lying there in the dark. His heart drumming.

Not a soul, she said. She'd watched the news to see if some other girl would go missing, but none did, not around there.

Dumb, dumb girl, she said in the dark, dreamily, and Gordon said nothing.

Then he said, You should of told your parents. You should of told the police, what in the hell were you thinking?—his heart pounding, his voice rising, until she switched on the lamp and said to him, Gordon, *Gordon*, as if to wake him from a dream, and he was up on his elbows and she was a frightened forty-year-old woman, and then she understood—Oh, Gordon, I'm sorry, I shouldn't have told you that story . . . Because his own daughter was sixteen and would get drunk, would get high. Would get rides home in cars he'd never seen before and would never see again, and every night that she wasn't home by midnight was the longest night of his life and he was all alone in this and had no idea what he was doing, only that he was doing it all wrong.

Anyway it wasn't long after that night—the night of the story—that whatever it was between him and Eileen Lindeman ended, just ended, like a bulb burning out. And the next time she called him, a year or two later, it was a busted pipe spraying water into her basement, she didn't know who else to call, and he'd done the job and that was all. Like none of it had ever happened.

Which was how he came to be in her house again today, easing his head around her bedroom doorjamb and saying, over the TV, "Eileen—?"

She sat in the same white reading chair with her bare feet up on the footrest. Only the feet were bare; otherwise she was dressed as she'd been when she let him in, the black pants and green sweater she'd worn to work. A glass of wine on the small table there, its shadow dark red on the white tabletop. The big white bed neat and smooth. The six o'clock news was on the TV and when he looked finally at her face he saw the stains under her eyes—dark streaks on her cheekbones like big fallen eyelashes.

"You all right?" he said, and she looked at him strangely, wet-eyed, and turned back to the TV.

It was a story about an accident, the night before: two young women in a car, just across the border in Iowa. Slick roads. The Lower Black Root River. College girls. One of the girls was local. He knew who she was. He knew her father. Everyone did, of course; he was the county sheriff, or had been, and hearing his name in the news again—or his daughter's name—opened a crack of memory, of old misery, in Gordon's heart.

Eileen pushed up out of the chair and stood holding the back of it with one hand, as if she needed to. "I heard about this at work," she said, "but they hadn't said any names." With her free hand she wiped at her face and then wiped her fingers on the back side of her slacks. Then she raised this hand toward him, as if to touch him. "Gordon, I'm so sorry. It's so awful . . ."

But he'd turned back to the TV.

It was a series of clips from the scene: a shot of the river from above, from a bridge maybe, a shot of the broken ice, beams of light crossing like swords over the ragged hole. A woman's voice reporting from off camera: "As to the question of a second vehicle, as to the question of possible foul play, no comment at this time from law enforcement." A shot of the car: a small SUV being reeled up the bank as if by an off-screen fisherman, the car coming along on its back, wheels up. One girl in the hospital up in Rochester, the other still missing. He watched until the report ended and a commercial replaced it.

Around the edges of the screen the room had gone all black. The sound he heard was like water rushing through copper pipes, a pressure like small hammers beating on the eyeballs. It was the old blackness, the old rage, and in the center of the blackness was an image of himself, on his knees as he so often was but now like a man at prayer, the big Stillson wrench raised two-handed, raised high, and swung down on the offered skull. The cracking, crushing blow. No more thoughts or feelings or memories forever, just the pink wet stew of bone and brains.

Slowly, the blackness receded, his heart pounding on but less wildly. His fists at his sides opening again.

Her hand was on his arm—for how long?

He raised his hand so that hers fell away, and looked at his watch.

"One hour," he said.

Eileen Lindeman standing close, searching his face. "One hour—?"

"Downstairs. One hour."

She was trying to hold his eyes but he wouldn't. Gordon looking instead at the room beyond her, the big bed, neatly made in white with white pillows at its head. A bed like any bed. Or a staging of a bed, with matching furnishings, as in a department store.

"Of course," she said, "of course." And she led him out of the bedroom so she could find her purse and pay him what she owed him.

3

THE NOSE OF the car drops over the edge of the bank and the world pitches, and their own weight rolls forward through their bodies as at the top of a roller coaster just before the drop—the deep human fear of falling, the plunging heart, and there's no stopping it and no getting out and nothing to do but hold on. And down they go, fast and easy in the snow, toboggan-smooth, hand in hand, their grips so tight, the grips of girls much younger, girls who will not be separated, their faces forward, watching the surface of the river, the black glistening ice as it rushes up toward them, larger and larger, until there's nothing in the windshield but the ice, dark and wide as an ocean and they are going to it, they are going to strike it nose-first with the car and they can imagine that, the sudden ending of forward motion as the car meets the plane of the ice, but after that they cannot imagine, they have never been here before and there is no way to know what will happen next except to go through it, and this is the most terrifying thing: the understanding, within those few plunging seconds, that there is no time to figure it out, to prepare—it is here, and the physics that rule the world cannot be altered, and time cannot be stopped, and no one can be called upon to help them, and they are all alone in the instant of experience and the car will strike the frozen river and that is that.

But then, incredibly—it doesn't. At the last moment the bank levels out, or the snow grows more deep, or some other variable they cannot account for lifts the nose of the car, and the impact is jarring but brief, and all at once the car sits upright on its wheels and they are spinning out onto the ice as they'd spun on the sleety road, the world once again turning round and round, headlights sweeping the perimeter like a haywire lighthouse, the beams selecting out of the darkness trees and bridge and bank and trees and bridge and bank, the bank of their descent farther away with *each turn, their bodies thrown with such turning and their stomachs rolling. When the car at last comes to rest, their minds lag behind and the world keeps spinning, as in childhood games of dizziness, until finally even that illusion ends and they are still. They are dead-still in the middle of the river, and everything is silent and dark and they are OK, they are all right.*

Still holding hands. Holding their breaths. Hearts whopping in their chests. Finally they breathe—Holy shit, holy shit—*and they see the look on each other's face and they laugh then, breathily, helplessly, the laugh of fright and relief. The laugh of love for each other and for being alive!*

Now what? *one says, and the other says,* Now we get out and walk back. We go back exactly the way the car came and we—

It's a sound that stops her, a sound they feel as much as hear—a great deep pop in the floor of the world. A sound to stop the heart and freeze it all the way through. The great pop is followed by silence: nothing but the roar of silence in their ears, of listening so hard, but it doesn't last—the ice pops again and the car shudders, it lists, and the girls let go of each other's hand, Get out—now! *and the ice is shattering, it's exploding beneath them in blasts like gunshots, and the car is on the move once again, aslant to the axis of the far bank and slipping down beneath the plane of the ice as they struggle with the latches of the doors, and for just a moment, before the water comes flooding in through the driver's-side door, there is the bizarre effect across the ice of one beam of light skimming the surface above while the other beam probes the same length of ice from below, underwater, revealing ice that moments ago looked so black and solid to be, in fact, bubbled and fissured and a terrible, ghostly translucent yellow.*

And then the car begins to roll.

4

RACHEL YOUNG WAS in her chair in the living room, writing a letter to one of her two sons, when she heard about the accident. The other son, who still lived with her and who had worked all day, had gone upstairs to bed, and Rachel had the ten o'clock news on with the volume low, and she wasn't paying much attention to it anyway; she was writing the letter to the son who lived now in New Mexico, just a few words catching him up, such as she wrote every month. In the old trunk under her feet were old photo albums and sheaves of yellowed letters tied up with string and a great hoard of hardback ledgers filled front to back with figures that meant little to her but that told the story of her grandfather's life, from the neat, fluid hand of his youth to the shaky scratchings of old age. She was using one of the hardback ledgers for a writing surface, and each time she lifted it or set it down she smelled the farm—this farm—and her grandparents' bodies, and the forever-hot kitchen where her grandfather sat over his figures, slurping coffee as thick and dark as tractor oil.

In the space between the chair and the trunk, beneath the bridge of her legs, slept the old dog, so that she would have to be careful when she stood.

Something on the TV caught her eye and made her look up. It was a young woman's face, a photograph, a nice one, probably a high school graduation portrait, and Rachel's first sinking thought was, *Oh, no,* as it always was when the news showed a pretty young woman's picture so early in the broadcast. Her next thought was that she knew this girl, had definitely seen her before, and she picked up the remote and raised the volume in time to hear the girl's name— Audrey Sutter—and she must have cried out then, for the dog raised his face and stared at her with his clouded eyes.

An accident, a slick road, the Lower Black Root River—Rachel's own heart going cold even before she saw the footage of the frozen river, the jagged hole in the ice, the car already pulled out and taken away.

By the time the program went to commercial break she was out of her chair, the letter forgotten, and she was pacing before the TV, the old floorboards creaking and the old dog watching her. Her heart thudding. Her mind tumbling. What should she do? Who should she call?

Her heart flew immediately to Gordon Burke, a man she'd known so well for so many years—or had known so well until that terrible business ten years ago, that awful business with his own daughter, in this same river—the great sorrow not just of his life but of Rachel's too. She would like him not to see it on the TV, would like him to be forewarned. But not by her. Then by whom? She thought of Meredith, Gordon's ex-wife, with whom she'd once been so close, but that friendship had died long ago along with everything else, and as there was no one for her to notify, no one from that old life to talk to, not a thing she could do, she began to clean the kitchen—quietly, her son upstairs sleeping—and when she finished there she cleaned the downstairs bathroom, and when that was done she sat down on the toilet lid and wept as the old dog looked on from his place on the bath mat.

She fixed herself a mug of decaf tea, intending to take it up to bed with her and read her novel until she could sleep, but after fifteen minutes she was still standing at the sink looking out at the cold night, the black oak tree against the snow. Those poor girls! That ice . . . the water running below—the deep, cold under-river that never froze. She stared so long out the window that the snow melted away, and there was grass, and the autumn leaves were tossing in the oak and the view was not of the farm but of the yard and the driveway where she had lived before, when her boys were boys, and she stood now not in the farm kitchen but in that other kitchen, and something had woken her up in the night.

Water.

Water was running in the pipes somewhere. Not the shower, or the toilet, or the kitchen sink: this was the distinctive one-inch-pipe gush you heard when the boys were washing the truck, or the dog, or filling the plastic pool for the dog to splash in. She'd married a plumber and she knew about pipes.

Lying awake that night, in that other house, listening. One of her sons would stay out late but when he came home he was like a burglar and if she heard him at all it was because she'd gotten up to use the bathroom, pausing by his door just long enough to hear him clicking at the computer in there, or humming to his headphones, or shushing Katie Goss, his girl.

But she'd heard none of that, that night. Heard nothing at all but the water rushing in the pipes and the wind in the trees. Late October, this was. Almost Halloween. The alarm clock's red light burning in the dark: 1:59 a.m. Then 2:00 a.m. Rachel pushing back the bedding and standing into her robe, her slippers, and padding down the hall past the boys' rooms—Danny's door open, no Danny; Marky's door shut but him in there, a mound of sleep she could feel like a current in the air—and then down the stairs and into the kitchen, where the water sound was loudest, and there, in the window, was Danny's truck, lit up by the light she'd left on for him. Two yellow smiley faces staring in at her, plastic hoods for the fog lights or whatever they were he'd mounted on the cab. She saw the truck's red front fender, the tire, a thin pool of water leaching into the gravel, but no Danny. She leaned closer to the window and just then a face popped up before her so suddenly her hands flew up. Danny, out there, saw the movement and then saw her, and Rachel's heart surged, as if he were hurt, as if he were washing out some wound she couldn't see. In the next moment she heard the dog shaking its hide, rattling its tags, and she understood: he would let the dog out in the park, where it would find some other animal's filth, or carcass, to roll in, and then later would stand under the hose, stupid and happy as Danny hosed it off.

The spigot gave a squeal and the water stopped running and in they came, and the cold air with them. Wyatt shoving past Danny's legs to dive face-first into her carpet, driving his upper body along with his hind legs, first one side, then the other, grunting in some kind of dog ecstasy.

Wonderful, Rachel said, and Danny said, I'll dry him when I get back. I gotta go help Jeff. His battery is dead.

Did you get it all off at least? she said, and he flinched, as if she'd shouted. What? he said.

Rachel gestured at the dog. Did you get it all off?

I got it all off, he said, and turned and was gone again. Nineteen and free to do as he pleased, including, apparently, drinking. There were places they could get into, he and Jeff Goss, and some mornings she smelled the bar on him like he'd slept on its floor. Other mornings she smelled strawberries and knew that Katie Goss, Jeff's younger sister, had been in the house. Rachel did not approve of such things, of course . . . but then she'd remember the night she heard them laughing behind his door and she could smell the strawberries and she'd been so angry she rapped on the door and hissed that it was late and he was going to wake up his brother, and the laughing stopped and the bed squeaked and to her horror the door swung open and there he stood, with his smile, fully clothed. Beyond him, on the bed, sat Katie Goss and Marky, smiling at her too, holding their hands of playing cards. *Ma*, said Danny, *come in, we need a fourth. Yeah Momma come in we need a fourth!* cried Marky. *Plenty of room up here*, said Katie Goss. And there they'd sat on the little bed playing cards until one in the morning, when finally she'd gotten Marky to go back to his room, and Danny had driven Katie home to her parents.

He would test her in some way, Danny would, and then he'd fill her heart with love. He'd been taking classes at the college then—engineering! Bridges and dams!—and he could've moved out, he had a good job with Gordon Burke, but he was staying home to save money, he'd said, and that was fine. He could call it whatever he wanted; she knew it was for his brother. She knew he'd stayed home for Marky.

5

THERE WAS THE direct way home, across the new concrete bridge—or new fifteen years ago, when the county had finally rebuilt it—but Gordon drove past the turnoff and kept going south, to Old Highway 20, so he could get the engine heated all the way up; the cab was closed off from the back of the van and would warm up fast, but frost was climbing the inside of the windshield, and when he put his bare fingers to the vent the air was no warmer than his fingers.

He hit the Old Highway 20 bridge doing fifty and he would not think of the other bridge, the new concrete bridge, upriver. Although it wasn't the bridge, it was the river that ran beneath it, which was the same river wherever you crossed it and wherever you looked at it and wherever you went into it.

From the county road you could see the light of his front porch, the sixty-watt bulb blinking a Morse code in the passing pinewoods, and he took the winding drive through the trees and pulled up to the outbuilding and put the van in park, then sat there with the engine running, the air blowing. The cab warmer now but not warm enough by far.

He hauled up the bay door and got back in the van and pulled in behind the old tractor plow and killed the engine, then he popped the hood and got out again and stood staring at the engine in the dark. He stood there a long time, no sound but the ticking of the engine block and his own breathing, before he dropped the hood and hauled down the bay door, booted home the side latches, and crossed the clearing to the house, his bootsoles on the shoveled path so loud in the cold, in the stillness of the woods.

He got his fire going, then clattered a frozen pizza into the oven and sat down at the kitchen table to go over his receipts and his appointments for the rest of the week, and he did not look up again until he smelled something burning—forgot to set the timer, Jesus Christ . . . and he carried the blackened pizza still smoking on the cookie sheet to the front porch and shucked it into the snow, where it hissed and steamed and went down slowly like a ship.

He found a beer at the back of the fridge and spiffed it open and took it into the living room and sat in his chair with his sockfeet up, drinking the beer and watching the fire play dimly in the dark face of the TV. He held the remote with his thumb over the button but did not push it. *As to the question of a second vehicle, as to the question of possible foul play, no comment at this time.*

There was a sound, a thump, and he looked to the ceiling. Her room up there, directly overhead. At her noisiest just before she went out again, hopping around to her music, chucking shoes into her closet . . . and then down she'd come, clock-clocking down the hardwood stairs as some girlfriend or more likely some boy pulled up the drive and whooshing by in perfume and too much leg, *See you later, Dad. Don't wait up, Dad.* And there you'd sit all night watching for headlights, listening for the slam of a car door, for the sound of her heels on the porchsteps . . .

A log popped and whistled and settled onto its bed of coals. Small flames leaping for the flue and vanishing in midair, and he thought of Eileen Lindeman again and the story she'd told him—fifteen years old and getting out of that silver Buick and walking home. Just walking into the house like it was any other day. Going to school the next day. Going to college. Getting married. Getting divorced. Becoming a woman he himself would one day desire, and take to bed.

And the man—the driver of the Buick? Walking into his own house that night with terror in his heart at what he'd almost done, and were the police looking for him at that very second? Kiss the wife hello. Kiss the kids. Sit down to dinner thinking of the fifteen-year-old girl who believed in God. Thinking of what he'd almost done. Almost become. Did that man go back to work the next day, make his money, pay his bills, raise his kids, live his life? An old man now, or dead, and what became of his desire? Did it fade with time, with age? Or did the thing you fought inside yourself just grow bigger, hungrier, until it took you over?

He got up, intending to throw another log on the fire, but instead returned to the kitchen, and from there stepped into the utility room, flicking on the light, and squeezed himself between the washing machine and water heater, reaching back into the webby dark until his fingers touched what they felt for, until he could lift it free of the webs and lay it out before him on the washer. Canvas and leather, padded and heavy. The sound of a good zipper, then the smell of oiled lamb's wool and metal and walnut rising from the opened case, and, more faintly, the cordite of the rounds that had been fired in the rifle's chamber. Built into the case was a compartment with a Velcro flap. *Just the one box?* said the dealer. As if a single box of lethal bullets was not the norm, was strange even. *Just the one*, said Gordon.

He hit the light switch on his way out and he hit the kitchen switch and he hit the switch that killed the sixty-watt bulb on the porch and he opened the door and put the gun to his shoulder and steadied himself against the jamb. He put his eye to the scope and turned the focus ring until the trunks of the pines at the edge of the clearing stepped forward, weirdly lit by nothing but the light from the snow, and so close it seemed you could reach out and touch them. And with such power of vision he scoped, he searched, panning left, then right in great sweeps, though he moved the rifle itself barely at all. He scoped, expecting any second to see something in the lens other than trees—a shape, a face in the dark, staring back at him with eyes that had no idea what they were seeing, what the man held in his hands in the darkness of the house. That sudden flash of light.

The sound of the shot and the punch to his shoulder and the burst of white in the face of the tree and the great thrill in his heart were all instantaneous, and right away he lowered the rifle and looked for the casing where it had rung like a coin on the porch, picked it up still hot and put it his pocket and closed the door again.

He returned to the utility room and zipped the rifle back into the case and set the case far back in the corner again, and all this he did in the dark. And still in the dark he got into his boots, his jacket, and he stepped onto the porch and turned the deadbolt with his key and went down the porchsteps and crossed the clearing to the outbuilding, and five minutes later he was on the 52 North, and fifteen minutes after that he pulled over to scrape the frost from the inside of the windshield, and "Just what in the hell," he said, but not to the frost or to the van. "Why don't you just mind your own business?" And after he'd scraped off enough frost, the frost falling like snow inside the cab, he put the van in gear again and drove on.

6

SHE STOOD AT the kitchen window staring out at the night, and it was still that night ten years ago, the night her son came home with the wet dog, so that when the dog now shook itself at her feet, clapping its ears and rattling its tags, she looked down absently, unthinkingly, and was shocked by the sight of him—the hunched and wasted body, the whitened muzzle, the filmy eyes turned up to her, searching for her in the fog of his world—and it was the shock that returned her to her place in time, to this kitchen, this farmhouse where she lived now with the old dog and her other son.

She took the dog's face in her hands and felt his trembling and tried to soothe it from him with her touch and her voice but it was not enough, it never was anymore, and finally she stood again and picked up his vial of pills, shook one into a cereal bowl and began crushing it with a spoon. She folded the grit into a soft dog treat, and when she turned again his snout was already raised, his nose tracking the treat's descent, his yellow teeth taking it gently from her fingertips.

She watched him chew, swallow, lick his lips.

"Go drink your water," she said, and he limped over to his bowl and lapped sloppily, then turned to her once again, dripping water onto the floor she'd just mopped. Staring at her with those milky eyes, waiting to see what she would do next, where she would go. Rachel staring back at him, going nowhere, saying nothing. She was back in time again, at the old house, ten years ago. Danny had gone to help Jeff and she'd gone back to bed, she remembered. But half an hour later she heard him knocking about in his room and she'd gotten up again. The door to his room open, Danny hunched over and stuffing clothes into his duffel. Stink of wet dog in the room, and the dog lying on the bed, watching Danny's every move.

Now what are you doing? she'd said from the doorway.

Gonna go see Cousin Jer, he said without turning. Shoot some birds.

On a Wednesday night?

Why not?

T-shirts, a pair of jeans, purple Vikings sweatshirt.

Danny, she said. It's two thirty in the morning. Does he even know you're coming?

Of course he does, he said—it was all set up: he'd be at Jer's in an hour, he'd sleep a couple of hours and then they'd head up to Uncle Rudy's cabin. Back by Friday, maybe Saturday . . .

Rachel stood watching him, confused and strangely heated. As if she'd done something stupid. Something embarrassing.

And all this is fine with—your boss? she said, and her son paused then, they both did, as the idea of Gordon Burke came into the room: His smell of earth and copper, a certain kind of deodorant. His big good face. His hands. There'd been a few men over the years, after Roger, but there hadn't been any for several years, and at forty-three, with two grown sons, she'd been ready to believe that that part was over for her. But it wasn't, not quite. Gordon Burke's daughter was still at home, Holly, a moody girl all her life and now a troubled girl who did not make things easy, and so the going was slow. But it was going. When the phone rang these days Rachel's heart jumped. New bras and panties waited in her bureau. She'd gone down two sizes.

The only reason Danny was out late tonight, with work in the morning, was because she and Gordon had made plans for the following night—Thursday night, a date—and Danny had agreed to stay home with his brother.

I'll call Gordon in the morning, he now said. Jeff will cover for me.

And me? Rachel said, swatting at him lightly. Danny, we had a deal!

He shrank from her and said nothing. Then he said, You can still go out, Ma. I'll take Big Man with me.

Oh, you will, will you? Hunting? She stared at him, waiting for one of Marky's howls to fill his head. Most recently it had been the torn heap of rabbit at Wyatt's feet, but a mouse in a mousetrap could do the job.

The bedroom window shook with the wind. The dog watching Danny and Danny standing there staring into space, frozen, his plans crashing. She couldn't bear it.

She shook her head, she sighed, and that was that: he was free. She'd see Gordon Burke in the morning, at the Plumbing & Supply. A change of plans, she'd say. Home-cooked dinner instead. She'd get Marky to turn in early . . .

But Gordon Burke wasn't at the Plumbing & Supply the next morning, his van wasn't in the lot, and Rachel had followed Marky into the store with something childish, something silly and persistent jabbing at her heart.

Big Man! Jeff Goss calling as they came in, and Marky raising his hand for a listless high five before disappearing into the back, stranding Rachel with no good-bye . . . because he felt what he felt, this boy, and what he felt this morning was that it was her fault Danny and Wyatt had gone off to the cabin without him, and nothing to do but let him feel it until he didn't.

She'd stood among the pipes and fittings. The smell of the place was a smell she loved: pipe dope and PVC glue and sweated copper and cigarettes and men. She remembered the summer when Gordon and Roger had bought the building and begun fixing it up. Sawdust in the nostrils, freckles of paint on all their faces. Rachel and Meredith had fallen for each other like schoolgirls, the kind of gushy, overnight friendship men don't even try to understand. They'd both gotten pregnant the same month, and then, five months later, when Rachel and Roger learned there was trouble with the twins—one healthy, one not; they could terminate one to save one, or risk losing both—it was Meredith and Gordon who loaned them money for more tests, a second opinion, the monitoring that saved Danny's life. He had his heart murmur, but he'd grown strong as a lion. And Marky . . . well, Marky was Marky. No one had seen that coming.

Twelve years later, Roger was dead. The cancer they'd been fighting in one lung had jumped to the other like a clever rat. Rachel had to give up their share of the business to keep the house. Her and Meredith's friendship began to falter, and she realized that, after all, it was the men, not the women, who kept the two families close.

Then, a year after Meredith had moved out—had run off, actually, with a banker—here came Gordon Burke again, with jobs: custodial duties for Marky and the secrets of the trade for Danny. Gordon had never gotten around to changing the BURKE-YOUNG sign on the side of the building, and a hyphen that had once said *family* to Rachel, then *loss* (a minus sign), suddenly said *family* again. Gordon was involved with another woman by that time, Eileen Lindeman, but that was his business; it didn't affect their own friendship, hers and Gordon's, their history, one bit . . . and anyway it didn't last, whatever that was with Eileen Lindeman.

Now, standing among pipes and fittings, Rachel asked Jeff Goss if he knew when Gordon would be back, and the boy replied cheerfully, Can't say, Mrs. Young. He hasn't been in yet.

Oh, she said, puzzled—actually bothered by this answer.

Anything I can help you with, Mrs. Young?

And there it was: Jeff Goss had opened up the store. Gordon had given him keys.

She'd thought Danny was the only one.

7

At the front desk they told him she was in the ICU but when he got there they told him she'd been moved to the third floor, and when he got up there the girl at the desk said visiting hours were over and she was sorry but there was nothing she could do, he'd have to come back in the morning.

Gordon stood looking down at the young woman in her chair. Her large brown eyes. A hundred small tight braids drawn back from her temples and collected in a thick snakeball on top of her head. MONIQUE ROSE, said her ID.

"What about the father?" Gordon said, and the young woman's brows bunched up.

"Sir?"

"Can the father go in there?"

"Into her room? Yes, of course he can. But you are not the father."

"How do you know?"

"Pardon me?"

"How do you know I'm not him."

The young woman turned her face a little to one side and spoke carefully. "Because I've seen him? Because I know him by sight?"

"You know him by sight."

"Yes, sir."

"When was the last time you saw him?"

"Sir, I'm not sure I understand—"

"Did you see him tonight?"

"Yes, sir, but . . ."

She looked Gordon up and down. She was looking for some evidence of his authority, of his right to ask her such questions. He could see that she found none.

"Look," he said more gently. "I drove all the way up here and all I'm asking now is can you go tell him that I'm here, and that I'd like to talk to him?"

"Tell who?"

"The father. Her father."

The young woman said nothing. Her mind was working.

"He might be sleeping," she said, and Gordon looked at her. He tried to give her a smile.

"Trust me," he said. "He's not sleeping."

He took a seat in one of the plastic chairs and sat staring at nothing, the opposite wall, the TV up in the corner, and he stared at the dark screen of the TV for a long while before he realized that the man sitting back in its gloom, as if in another room altogether, or another world, must be himself; when he got out of his jacket in the overheated room, the man in the TV got out of his too. Some minutes later another man came into the image of the room, and into the room itself, and except that he was waiting for this man, expecting to see this man and no other come around the corner, Gordon would not have recognized him, and not because the man wasn't in uniform. He saw what he'd already known but would have known anyway in that first glance, which was that this man coming toward him was not well. Considerably down in weight, his flannel shirt hanging on him as it would on a hanger, and when Gordon stood he saw that the man had grown shorter too, as old men do, though this man was a good five years younger than Gordon himself. And yet when the man put out his hand, Gordon was surprised by the strength of the grip. Surprised by the blueness of the eyes too, down in the wells of their sockets, blue and sharp as ever.

"Gordon," said the man in that same rough smoker's voice.

"Sheriff," said Gordon. "How is she?"

"She's OK. She's busted-up some, but she's gonna be all right."

The man, Tom Sutter, passed his jacket from one hand to the other and stood looking at Gordon, Gordon looking at him. Sutter's face so thin now. His hair, gone purely white, looked as if it would blow from his skull in a strong wind, like milkweed seeds. The man was sick and there was nothing to say about that. It was too big a thing to ever say aloud.

The young woman behind the desk sat watching them. Light tubes hummed in the ceiling. Machines beeped behind doors.

Sutter raised the jacket and said, "Well, you're here, Gordon. Do you care to join a man for a smoke?"

THEY HAD THE shelter to themselves and they stood in its weak light, Sutter smoking and Gordon blowing into his hands. He put his hands back into his jacket pockets. Sutter was watching him.

"I saw it on the news, is why I drove up here," Gordon said.

Sutter flicked the ash from his cigarette, raining tiny embers that flared out before they hit the ground. "She's hardly been awake two minutes," he said. "I'm not even sure what in the hell happened down there, except that she's alive, and her friend isn't."

Gordon looked down and toed his boot in the thin remains of ice. "I figured it was too soon to see her," he said. "But I came anyway."

Sutter blew smoke and was silent.

"I remember when she was just a little girl," Gordon said. "I remember seeing her sitting there in the cruiser that day. She couldn't have been more than six years old." He looked up again. Sutter was looking at the building.

"No, she's nineteen now," Sutter said, "so she must've been nine back then. She'd been sick at school that day and I had to take her with me." He turned back to Gordon. "I was always sorry about that."

"I knew you had your reasons. But, hell, seeing her there, just sitting there, waiting for you to come back to the car. I never did forget that."

Sutter took a pull on his cigarette and blew the smoke.

"I won't stand here and tell you I understand, now, Gordon, what you went through. Because I don't. These situations, our situations, they aren't the same, not even close. I know how God damn lucky I am—how lucky she is." He shook his head. "I never could imagine what you were going through. And I can't imagine what those folks down in Georgia are going through right now. A young woman like that. A daughter . . ." He coughed, then turned his face and coughed again, from the lungs, wet and ragged. He took a step away and spat, and stepped back and dropped his cigarette down the plastic throat of the receptacle.

"Well," he said. "I best be getting back."

"On the news they said there might of been a second vehicle," Gordon said, and Sutter's right hand, raised for shaking, lowered again.

"I don't know what bigmouth said that," he said, "but if he was one of mine we'd have us some kind of talk."

Gordon watched the ex-sheriff's face. His eyes. As he'd always watched them. *What does this man know that he isn't telling me? What right does any man have to know something about my daughter's death that I don't know?*

"I know it's none of my goddam business, Sheriff," Gordon said.

Sutter shook his head again. "There's just nothing I can tell you, Gordon. Like I said, she's hardly been awake two minutes. I'm not sure she even knows where she's at yet. I don't think she knows about her friend. I called in some favors just to keep the cops off her a while longer, until she's out of the woods. And I tell myself it doesn't really matter right now anyway. Tell myself that all that matters is that she's going to be OK." He looked to the sky. "And I tell myself that all that matters to those folks down in Georgia right now is that they get their daughter home so they can begin to do what they have to do. But I don't know. I don't know what they need from me. I don't know what they need from my daughter."

"Hell, Sheriff," said Gordon, "you're not even close to knowing."

Sutter watched him. "Meaning?"

Gordon shook his head. His heart was thumping in his neck vein. He thought he could put his fist through something.

"Meaning," he said, "grief is just about the smallest part of it, Sheriff. Meaning if it turns out there's some person out there who had something to do with this, and that son of a bitch just goes on living his life—?" Gordon swallowed. He was choking. Sutter standing there watching him.

"That man down in Georgia," Gordon said, "that girl's father? Hell, he ain't even the same man anymore, Sheriff. He's already some other man."

Sutter had not looked away as Gordon spoke, and Gordon saw a light come on in those eyes, bluer than before. Brighter. But whatever was behind the light, whatever he was thinking about saying, Sutter said nothing.

You don't have to say it, went Gordon's own mind. *You can just turn around now and go back home. Saying it won't change a God damn thing for anyone and you know it.*

"Tell you one more thing, Sheriff," he said, "and then I'll let you get back up to your girl."

Sutter waited.

"The things I called you when you let that boy go, when you just let him walk away? Those words weren't nothin compared to what I wanted to happen to you. I knew you'd lost your wife. I knew you knew something about loss. But this thing that happened to you here, with your daughter—I wished it on you. I wanted you to know what that was like. I'm sorry I wished it, and I'm glad your girl's OK—but I did wish it, back then."

Sutter was silent. Then he said, "I have to say you picked one hell of a time to tell me that, Gordon. With my daughter lying in that hospital room and that other girl in a box on her way to Georgia."

"When would be a good time?"

"How about never? Did you think about that?"

"I did," Gordon said. "I thought about it hard." He looked down at the concrete, the crystals of salt. He ground at them with his bootsole, and the gritty crushing sound was the only sound. "But I just kept asking myself: What would Sheriff Sutter do differently now, if it was his girl instead of that other one who didn't make it? What would he do for himself that he didn't do for me?"

He looked up again and the two men stood watching each other, their breaths smoking between them.

"If you're waiting for an answer to that," Sutter said, "you're gonna wait a long time, Gordon. All I know right now is my daughter's OK. She's alive. Jesus Christ—" he said, but then looked away. He took a breath and blew a long white cloud into the stars, as if to rid himself once and for all of whatever it was inside him—his cancer, maybe. The poisonous little cloud drifting through space with all the other gases and junk up there.

"I'm just as sorry today as I was back then, Gordon," he said finally, like a man done talking. "I never stopped being sorry and I never will. There just wasn't a God damn thing I could do."

"I know," said Gordon. "That's what you told me ten years ago."

Gordon offered his hand then, and Sutter stood looking at it.

"I just came up here to tell you I'm glad she's OK, Sheriff. I'm sorry as hell about that other girl, but I'm glad your girl's OK. I mean that."

Sutter said nothing. Finally he shook Gordon's hand. Then he stood watching as the man walked off toward the parking lot, as he climbed into his van and turned over the engine and backed out of his spot. He watched until the red taillights had disappeared into the darkness, and when he was alone again he got another cigarette to his lips, and he fished up his Zippo and he stood turning it in his fingers, the old familiar weight of it, before at last flicking it open and flicking the flintwheel once and raising the flame to his face.

8

IT DOESN'T TAKE long for the drug to find the dog's bloodstream, his heart, his brain, and she carried her tea to the living room and sat in her chair so he would find his spot under her legs, turn an unsteady circle on the rug, and sleep. Usually she would get him upstairs and into the bedroom before the drug took effect, but she was not ready to go up there herself, not ready to be alone in that bed with nothing but her thoughts of those two girls, and anyway it was easier for both of them, her and the dog, to carry him up when he could not feel all the pain of being carried.

She aimed the remote and turned on the TV, looking for something, anything, but it was all that late-night noise—jokes and bands and studio audiences and famous people talking to famous people and all the happy beauty of a wealth you couldn't even imagine, and she turned it off again and picked up her novel and found her place and began to read. But the page never turned, and in time she understood she wasn't reading, she was listening for signs of Marky upstairs, his heavy tread on the hardwood floor as he passed from his room to the bathroom, the sound of him at the toilet, the heavy stream of a grown man and not her little boy, a sound she'd never gotten used to. What did he do with that body when she wasn't around? What did he think about? What did he think when he saw a good-looking girl—or woman? What did he feel? The boys had both stopped talking to her about such stuff when they turned twelve. Like some switch had been thrown. Danny would never tell you what was between him and Marky, but they must've talked about it; there must have been much that Danny, who even then never lacked for the attention of girls, could've told Marky about how the world worked. Men and women. Sex.

What could she herself have told him? Not much. A virgin when she married, she'd carried that innocence well into adulthood. Surprised, shocked, by the things other women knew. The things they said.

Oh, honey, Meredith Burke said one night, *I could tell you stories.*

And Rachel, surprising herself, had answered, *I dare you to.*

Meredith had refilled Rachel's glass, then her own, and looked toward the house and listened. Gordon had taken Roger to the basement to talk about turning it into a playroom for the kids, and she and Meredith sat alone on the deck with the wine. The babies all sleeping in the playpen just inside the screen door, the twins and little Holly. The bellies of insects pulsing green in the pinewoods. It was Rachel's second glass and Meredith's third, not that Rachel was counting... although if Meredith didn't slow down she'd begin to get that look in her eye, that edge in her voice that said the night was over, that it was time to go home.

When I was a junior in high school I slept with one of my teachers, Meredith said, and Rachel felt as if a notorious man had just grinned at her.

What kind? she said. Of teacher.

Art, said Meredith. Mr. Beckman. Mr. B. He'd thought Meredith had talent. She thought he was a fairy. Everyone did. He passed her one day in his car, an Oldsmobile. She was wearing her best skirt.

Meredith was quite a bit smaller than Rachel—had snapped back to her original size after pregnancy—and she had the most beautiful skin. At sixteen— Lord, Rachel could not even imagine.

They talked about Dalí, Meredith said. They parked. He had a mustache that tickled. He wanted to see her again. He stood behind her in class, as she drew. He began slipping her these little drawings—very good, very dirty. An artistic fever, he said into her ear. She showed the drawings to just one person, her best friend, but that was enough. Two days later a substitute teacher came to Mr. B.'s art room and stayed. The halls hummed with low voices, with stories. Meredith's father heard it at the plant from some other kid's father, came home and slapped the living crap out of her.

My God, Meredith. Rachel put her fingers on her friend's bare forearm.

Her dad had all these brothers, Meredith went on. One of them, Uncle Terry, was a piece of work. In and out of jail, drunk at Christmas, fuck this and fuck that. One day, about a month after the Mr. B. scandal, in the middle of a snow-storm, Uncle Terry came by the house. He was there just a minute, barely said hello, and the next day they found Mr. B. walking down the middle of the high-way. His head was cracked. His teeth were busted. All his fingers were broken.

Laughter came to them from the house, from the basement, making them both turn to stare. Meredith lifted her glass again and Rachel heard it clink against her teeth.

She waited for the cops to come, Meredith said, resuming. She stopped eat-ing. She couldn't sleep. She typed a letter at school and sent it anonymously, but no one ever came. Mr. B. was in the hospital a long time but he couldn't recog-nize you, they said, so what was the point of going up there? His parents came and took him away, finally, like a child.

My God, Meredith, Rachel said. She could barely see her friend in the dark. Her heart was beating with pity and love. After a while she said, What do you do with that?

Meredith was silent. A long, unnatural silence. Fireflies like little bombs going off in the pines and spruces. Men coming up the stairs, loud and huge, forgetting about the babies. Finally Meredith lifted her wine and said, gazing at Rachel over the rim of the glass, Not a God damn thing, honey. That's what you do with that.

Such thoughts, such memories, as Rachel gathered up the drugged old dog in her arms and carried him up the stairs.

THE NEXT MORNING, driving back to the farmhouse after dropping Marky off at work, she searched the radio but there was nothing but music and DJ jabber and ads, nothing about the accident, nothing about those two girls. The drive was ten miles coming and going—south and then north along the Upper Black Root, crossing it twice on the old trestle bridges, and why not just drive up there? Why not drive up to Rochester, leave some flowers with the nurses at least? But the thought of running into Tom Sutter, those eyes of his, those lawman's eyes, made her shudder, and she drove on toward the farm.

Ten years. Like yesterday. A cold, clear day like today. She would've been going in the opposite direction then, five miles almost exactly from the Plumbing

& Supply to the Edendale Mall, where she worked. Looking forward to seeing Gordon Burke later that night. Thinking about Danny, the way he'd taken off in the middle of the night. Hunting with Cousin Jer? What the heck was that all about? Mysterious boy! The morning at the store passing like any other: Rachel in the back room tagging sweaters to the muted bursts of ringtone from the jackets and purses of the salesgirls. At ten o'clock she'd walked to the far end of the mall, to the building's—maybe the world's—last pay phone (the cell phone Danny and Marky had given her for her birthday—*Look, it takes pictures!*—sitting dead in a kitchen drawer, next to the dead camera). She intended to call Gordon, tell him the new plan, but at the last moment she dialed Danny's cell phone instead, got his voicemail. She asked him to leave her a message at home, just to say he'd arrived at Cousin Jer's OK, then she hung up and began the long walk back to the store. She would call Gordon later, on her lunch break. It was Thursday, and they had a date.

But back at the store something had happened. Leslie stood alone on the sales floor, her thin arms folded over her thin stomach. Fifteen years younger than Rachel, she would talk about things like chakras and third eyes and orgasms. Now she came toward her as if Rachel were some teenager with a hundred-dollar blouse stuffed up her shirt. In the door of the back room Rachel saw two salesgirls, heads down and thumbing feverishly at their phones.

There's been an accident, said Leslie, and the store rolled and Rachel pitched backwards, sickly, into a scene on the highway, Danny's truck upside down on the shoulder, wheels to the sky . . .

No, no, Leslie said quickly. Not that, not one of yours. It's Holly Burke, she said. Gordon Burke's girl. They found her this morning in the river.

9

SHE WENT UNDER. *She went under and she swam those cold yellow waters for days and days, tumbling in the river's underworld, its constant current, constant deep pull, the lights of the car spinning through the yellow water and lighting up the hair of the other girls who were down there with her, so many girls, or maybe just one girl passing again and again through the lights, the way this girl's hair moved in the lit-up currents like the hair of a mermaid, like seagrass, the way the light caught the whites of her eyes, and her teeth when she smiled. How smooth her face when she reached out and brushed the girl's cheek with the back of her hand, how soft her lips when she kissed them, how warm and thrilling the breath this girl blew into her own empty lungs . . .*

And when she surfaced at last and drew her first breath in the new world, the new life, she was not cold, and she was not wet, and she was not in the river at all, and a man was sitting next to her, and after a few spinning, blurry moments she saw that it was a man who looked like her father, only older, thinner-faced, his hair gone white and wispy on his head, but those same blue eyes that she'd looked into all her former life.

Holding her hand, this man, and she lay in a bed in a room she didn't know and there was a window and it was early morning, or late in the day, and something hard and annoying was up inside her nose but she could not lift her right arm and there was pain all up and down her body as if she'd been pounded on by fists as she slept.

That you, Sheriff? she thought—only she must have said it aloud, because he smiled and gripped her hand more tightly and said, "It's me, Deputy. I'm right here, sweetheart."

"Where are we?"

"We're in Rochester. The hospital in Rochester. You're OK. You're going to be just fine."

She ran her tongue over her lips and swallowed thickly. "Thirsty," she said.

With his free hand he brought the plastic cup and the straw to her lips and she drank. She drank and drank. All that time in the river, drowning, and now all she wanted was water—there would never be enough of it for her thirst! She emptied the cup and kept sucking noisily at the air of the cup.

"Easy, easy," he said. "I'll get you more in a second. I'm gonna go get the doctor now so he can look at you."

"Don't go. Please." Gripping his hand, or trying to. She was so weak.

He smiled. How thin his face was! She felt the tears on her cheeks and watched as he wiped them with his thumb, his good big old thumb.

"I drowned, Sheriff."

"No, you didn't, sweetheart. You're right here with me. You're just fine. The doctor—"

She squeezed at his hand. "I did, though. We both did. Caroline and me, both together. But it was all right, because we were together. And also—"

He waited. "Also what, sweetheart?"

She rolled her head and looked up at the ceiling, and the tears ran from the corners of her eyes. She shook her head.

She turned back to him, to his eyes. Nothing but love and worry in those eyes.

"Did they find her?" she said.

"You rest, sweetheart."

"Daddy."

He swept the hair from her forehead.

"I saw her go under, Daddy. I saw her go. The current got her and carried her off under the ice."

"OK, but not now. You just—"

"Did they find her? Did they find Caroline? That's all I'm asking."

He nodded. "Yes, sweetheart. They found her at the dam. At the power plant in Riverside. The water never freezes there. That's where she was."

Audrey watched his face, his eyes. "How far?"

"How far what?"

"How far from where we went in."

He frowned. He shook his head.

"Daddy."

"Two miles. Maybe three."

All that way in the dark, under the ice. Beautiful, strong Caroline.

She turned and looked at the ceiling again. Her body was so sore. She could not lift her free hand, her right arm. As if it were frozen to the ice. The bed. She felt profoundly and forever drugged. Her eyes would not stay open—*But stay awake*, she told herself. He is sick and he needs you with him. How much time? How much did you waste by sleeping? Stay awake!

"You used to take me fishing there, Sheriff. Remember?"

"That was another dam," he said. Then he said, "Of course I do. In the summertime."

"The trout like it behind the dam." Her heavy lids lowered. Her hand relaxed in his.

"Hush now, Deputy," he said from far away . . . *don't spook the fish.*

"The water's so cool and deep there, behind the dam. We'd . . . we'd stand on the bank and cast and . . . the bait just . . . down to them in the current."

10

HE WAS AWAKE and out of bed while the house, and the woods all around the house, were still in darkness, with only a lesser shade of darkness in the east-facing windows, and that shade a good ways farther along than he cared to see in his windows before he was shaved and dressed and downstairs for coffee, but he'd slept poorly, passing in and out of a nagging dream in which he walked and walked, like the last man, over a burned land, and when at last he got up from his bed and walked to the bathroom his legs were all rubber and ache, and there was a thickness in his head and a drainage at the back of his throat that he kept swallowing like a sour rope, and by the time his coffee was brewing he knew he'd taken sick, as his mother used to say, and only then did he remember his trip to the hospital the night before: Tom Sutter coming out to meet him, standing outside in the cold so Sutter could have himself another cancer stick, then the long drive home with no heat in the van and his entire body shivering, until at last he was under his covers and shivering there too until he slept and then shivering in his strange dream of walking. He'd gone out into the world and taken sick and brought it home.

In the kitchen he washed down a handful of aspirin with orange juice, then fried up two eggs, and carried eggs and coffee to the living room. He hauled his chair closer to the fire and took up the old blanket from the sofa and shawled it about his shoulders. His face was hot to the touch, and yet he was so cold—the mug trembling when he lifted it.

He cocked his ear to a noise above him. What day was this? School day? He thought to look at the paper but he would have to go out to the porch to get it. And he did not remember hearing it hit the porchboards, so was it Sunday?

That would explain why that girl was still in bed. How late did she come home? Or did you fall asleep again waiting for her? A great clomping, thudding, music-playing, phone-yammering creature except when she chose not to be—quiet as a ghost in slippers then, able to pass soundlessly through doors, to float by you and up the creaky stairs without a creak and into the bathroom to brush the beer and smoke from her mouth, into her PJs and into her bed, late as hell again but safe, thank God, not out with some drunk boy driving, not in some accident but home, safe . . .

Until one morning it's a sheriff's deputy who brings her home, drunk, high, something. Her license long gone. Her face puffy, her eyes red, wobbling in her shoes. You should just let her go to bed but you can't. You can't. It's all out of control. A goddam sheriff's deputy!

Grounded? she says, and laughs. *You can't ground me, I'm nineteen.*

Hell I can't. My house, my rules.

Oh, really? Whatever happened to our house? Our home?

If you spent more time here. If this wasn't just a place for you to sleep it off.

You want me to find somewhere else to do that? Is that it?

You know I don't. I want you safe.

You want to control me. You're ashamed of me, just like you were of Mom.

Don't say that. I'm not ashamed of you.

Yes you are! And you—jabbing her finger at him—*you think I don't know about that grocery store woman, that Irene or whatever her name is? The whole town knows, Dad. The whole freaking town. So who's ashamed of who, here—huh?*

By the time she comes downstairs in the morning, stretching and stumbling half-asleep, wild-haired and smelling of bed, all the anger will be gone from you like a bad night's dreaming, forgotten in the light of day—home again—forgotten in the smell of her as she passes by—safe again—and you will get up, however sick you are, and make her those thick, half-burnt pancakes she loves.

But then again, on such a morning, with the new sun spilling into the living room, with the flames rising and dropping in the woodburner, a man might hear, instead of his daughter's footsteps overhead, instead of the clap of the bathroom door and the moments of silence and then the toilet flushing . . . he might hear instead the sound of car tires in the drive—at this hour?—and setting aside his breakfast he might get up from his chair and go to the window in time to see a man stepping out of a white sedan in the dawn and putting a hat to his head—stiff, wide-brimmed hat such as a sheriff or state trooper would wear, and then he'd recognize that the car is in fact a sheriff's cruiser, and that the man putting the hat on his head is in fact the sheriff.

The heart spins, the mind falls backwards as you understand that she is not upstairs in her bedroom at all—has not been there all night—and you look again at the cruiser, waiting for her to emerge: blond head of hair followed by a small frame followed by a too-short skirt and bare legs and shoes that say to you nothing but trouble, her head hung low in shame, you'd like to think, although more likely it's the heaviness of whatever kind of high got her a ride home in the sheriff's cruiser, in bad trouble maybe but safe, thank God, with the sheriff...

And then, when no second figure appears, when you understand that the girl in the passenger seat is far too young, far too dark-haired—that the sheriff's cruiser has brought only the sheriff and this little girl who is not yours—that is the moment your heart truly falls and somehow you are already on the porch when the sheriff, coming up the walking path, sees you, and does not pause but in some way flinches, as if you've drawn down on him with a weapon, and on he comes, and reaching the bottom step raises one of his hands to his sheriff's hat and actually, what in the hell, *takes the hat off—Don't take your hat off, Sheriff, you son of a bitch, what is wrong with you?*

Gordon, says the sheriff.

And some time after that, unremembered time, the sheriff's cruiser is on the 52 South and the bright world is sweeping by and yet there is the sense of not moving at all, of the cruiser standing still while it's the land, the trees, the wire fences that rush by. Like a fish holding its place in a stream.

Just the two of them now, the sheriff having stopped at the station to drop off the little girl, and the sheriff driving ten miles over the posted limit not out of official urgency but out of decency maybe, or maybe the sooner to get his errand over with, and only when he comes up on drivers who slow him down on the rural two-laner does he throw his lights and give a short whoop of siren. Passing these drivers without a glance while his passenger looks hard at every face, every car, each one of them worth pulling over, questioning, searching. She'd been struck by a vehicle, the sheriff believed, her body pushed afterward into the river. A drunk in a panic. A kid or kids high and believing, in that moment, that the river would carry the evidence away like a bad dream and their lives could go on—college, marriage, kids of their own.

Do you want a smoke, Gordon?

The sheriff, Sutter, pushing his pack at him. Gordon can smell it, taste the smoke in his lungs, feel the nicotine speeding to his brain. He hasn't smoked in years, not since Roger Young's cancer. The cigarette would be good but who wants good. Who wants relief of any kind if it isn't the relief that will last forever. He raises his hand no thanks and Sutter withdraws the pack, and it's a long while before Gordon thinks to say, You go ahead, and Sutter goes ahead—lights up and draws the smoke deep and cracks the window and exhales into the rush of wind.

Next he's moving slow and heavy down a hospital corridor, the air reeking of sickness and ammonia and old burned coffee, Gordon a step behind Sutter, who pushes through a gray metal door saying AUTHORIZED PERSONNEL ONLY, and on the other side of the door the linoleum turns to concrete and the walls are cinderblock and the air is almost too cold for smell but not quite, smell of chemical fumes and the faint putrid stink of meat. A third man emerging now from somewhere, thin man dressed like a surgeon down to his surgical gloves, and this man leading them to the large stainless-steel what, refrigerator? A bank of three square doors side by side at waist level and each with a large latch handle. Rubber-gloved hand on latch, the unlatching echoing on concrete and cinderblock, the suck and gasp of rubber seal pulled from metal, the greased clicking of the large industrial glides as the bed—what else do you call it? slab? gurney?—floats from the dark square like a magician's trick all the way into the room, into the light.

Morgue man standing on one side of the floating bed, Gordon and the sheriff on the other. A body in the white bag, under the zipper. Shape of a female chest. Shape of a face. A nose. Sheriff standing back and Gordon stepping forward for the unzipping, the most terrible sound, and the breath of the river it releases.

And there she is. Her hair tangled and damp. Her face blue. Lips a darker blue and slightly open, the white of her front teeth bright in the blue. Eyelids down over the curve of her eyeballs, tender thin lashes on her cheeks, washed of all makeup. Over these blue, unmoving features play living expressions, like projections, faces of her youth surfacing, rippling, sinking away again into the blue mask. *Wake up, daughter. Wake up. Breathe.* Placing his large hand over her forehead as if to take her temperature. So cold. Smooth, cold skin over a hard curve of bone, nothing more. Her bare blue neck, enough of her blue chest to see that she is naked in the bag—yes, Gordon nodding yes, it's her, and the zipper makes its sound again.

The morgue man wants a moment alone with Sutter but Gordon isn't going anywhere. Hears his own voice in that place: Whatever you're gonna say to him you can say to me. And the morgue man fusses with the fit of his gloves, pinching latex over his knuckles and letting go with sharp little snaps until Gordon wants to slap him, until Sutter says, Go ahead, Doug, and the morgue man, Doug, looks up and says, Well, Tom, there was water in the lungs. A good deal of water.

Sutter standing there taking this in. Nodding. Gordon looking from one man to the other, his sight crossing over the body and back. Neither man speaks. Neither man will look at him—and then he understands.

He stands staring dumbly at the white bag. The white shape of her. This body once tiny enough to hold in one hand. To lift over your head two-handed, a squirming, soft giggling little girl. To hold by her hands and spin her around until her skinny legs lifted from the earth and flew.

A hand rests on his shoulder and the sheriff says, Gordon—and he shrugs the hand off.

I know what he's saying, he says, and turns and walks away before he has to watch the morgue man slide her back into the dark.

11

THE STORY WAS going around, pushed along by the thumbs of girls: Holly Burke had been walking home from her boyfriend's. No, she was walking home from the bar. She was alone. She was not alone. She'd been drinking. She was high. The girl had problems, no question about that—she'd lost her license to a DUI the year before; Rachel knew this from Gordon. The girl had been cutting through the park, along the river, and had fallen in. Jumped in. Been pushed in. She'd been in the water all night. Someone crossing the bridge on foot—the new concrete bridge, a good mile away from the park—had seen her, pinned up against the concrete piling below like driftwood.

Rachel had left the mall and was in her car again, driving across town. A brilliant, cold blue day. The sun, the blazing trees, the silvered bend of river, all exactly as it should be on a day in October, a pristine day. She was trying to picture it: Holly Burke, this girl she'd known since birth, bobbing in the water with the branches. But all she saw clearly was the blouse, the one she'd given the girl on her nineteenth birthday, Gordon looking on uneasily: a smart silk blouse she'd spent too much on, even with her discount, all night in the river under the black sky, the fabric wetted to the girl's skin except where air slipped in, raising white, trembling swells on the water . . .

Gordon opened the door and stood blinking in the brightness. Startled, confused to see her. His gray face, the bruised, unfocusing eyes sweeping away anything she might've been ready to say. Not asking her in. Not even letting go of the stormdoor so she could put her arms around him. She wasn't surprised— certainly not hurt. It had nothing to do with her; he had to handle things his own way, in his own time, like Roger, like every man she'd ever known.

I'm so sorry, Gordon, she said.

They took me to her, he said. The sheriff.

Oh, Gordon. By yourself?

He didn't answer. He seemed to be listening, and she listened too: someone else in the house, on the phone. A man's voice. A voice of calm male authority. She glanced at the extra car in the drive, a black, spotless Volkswagen sedan.

Someone's with you?

Edgar, he said, and she said, That's good. That's good, Gordon.

His brother Edgar, she remembered, was some kind of lawyer for the state. She'd met him once and had been struck by the cleanliness of his fingernails, a thing she was not used to in men.

Can I do anything, Gordon, is there anything I can do?

His roving eyes found hers briefly and moved on. He said, Meredith's on her way. Her sister's driving her down. I thought it was them when you knocked.

Rachel nodded but couldn't speak. She hadn't seen Meredith in years, not since before the split-up. She remembered that night on the deck, with the wine—Mr. B., the art teacher—when her heart had filled with pity and love. They were going to be friends forever, old ladies, arm in arm in Mexico, Europe, after the kids were grown, after the husbands were gone.

They think now someone did this, Gordon said.

They—? said Rachel.

The sheriff and them. He dug at the whiskers on his face. They think someone hit her with a car, or a truck.

My God, Rachel said.

They think this . . . person didn't see her maybe, Gordon said. Then tried to cover it up by pushing her in the river.

He looked off toward the woods as if he'd seen something, and she looked too, and for just a moment she thought she heard them—the kids, running through the woods, laughing. Holly in her purple Easter dress, searching for the poorly hidden eggs.

She turned back to Gordon, but he was still looking into the woods and it was like watching the eyes of a sleepwalker; they did not register what he saw of the world or even what he was seeing in his mind. What could you say? What could you possibly say? A child. A daughter.

If there's anything I can do, Gordon, just anything, she said, and Gordon, looking beyond her with those shut-down eyes, said, Still breathing.

What?

When they pushed her in, he said. She was still breathing.

Oh, Gordon. Oh no— Rachel reaching for him then, but before she could touch him the brother, Edgar, called to him from inside the house and Gordon turned and let go the stormdoor, and she stood watching her own reflection swing into view as the door bounced once on its cylinder, gave a long hiss, and clicked shut.

12

SHE AWOKE TO the painful brightness of the room, and there were men in the room, looming over her like trees, and she immediately looked down at herself in the bed—but she was covered up, the thin sheet pulled neatly to her armpits, and beneath the sheet she wore a thin blue gown.

Her right arm lay below the sheet and her left lay above, a clear plastic tube fixed to the crook of the elbow by strips of white tape, a plastic clip attached to the tip of her forefinger. The tug of the tape on that tender skin and the bite of the clip made her feel as though this arm had been left out so that other things might feed on it while she slept.

One of the men was her father, and one was the doctor, and one was a man wearing a sheriff's uniform like her father used to wear and she knew this man too; he'd been one of her father's deputies. Deputy Moran. Ed Moran. He stood tapping his hat against his leg and trying to look confident that he belonged at the bedside of a young woman lying in her thin gown under a thin sheet. She herself was too foggy-headed to question his presence; he'd once been a regular feature of her life, joking and teasing her when she was little, growing quiet and awkward as she got older, and now here he was again.

The doctor bent to look into her eyes and she smelled mint and the alcohol of hand sanitizer. The other smells, the outdoor smells of snow and smoke and car exhaust, came from her father and Deputy Moran. She seemed able to smell everything in the world, the way you would if you'd been underwater, truly, all this time. The doctor watched her eyes, then moved away to lower the blinds, and the room dimmed and she could see the men without squinting.

The doctor returned to the bed and picked something up and the bed hummed, hinging her slowly at the waist until she was nearly sitting up. "Is that all right?" he said, and she nodded, and he said, "Good. How many fingers?"

"Fourteen."

"Try again."

"Four."

"Excellent." He had a young face but his buzzed head showed the dark map of hair loss. He was looking in her eyes again. "How do you feel, Audrey? Are you in pain?"

"No. But I'm thirsty," she said, and her father was already lifting the cup and the straw to her lips. She raised her hands to take it from him—did he think she would let him hold it for her in front of the doctor and the deputy?—but only her left arm, with its tube and finger clip, rose from the bed. This was puzzling, but she was so thirsty she took the cup one-handed and sucked at the straw, water running coldly down her throat and coldly into her stomach, and only after she'd handed the empty cup back to her father did she say, looking at the shape of her arm under the sheet, "I can't lift my right arm."

"No," said the doctor, "that arm is broken and we strapped it down to the bed." He raised the sheet so she could see the cast—purple—and the white strap holding it down. "Can you wiggle your fingers for me—just the fingers? Good. Now the thumb."

"Why's it strapped down?"

"So you didn't whack it against something in your sleep, like your head." He pulled at the strap and there was the rip of Velcro, and her arm was free. She raised the cast and looked at it, turning it this way and that. It encased her forearm from the elbow to the middle of her palm, with a neat thick eyelet for the thumb. Now that she could see it she felt its weight and its pressure and its prickly heat, as if her eyes were all at once undoing the work her body had done to get used to it while she slept. She felt an itch she knew she would never get to and she remembered a blackened wooden backscratcher—PHOENIX, ARIZONA— and she remembered the filthy old piss smell of a bathroom and the greasy stink of a hand over her face.

"Do you remember breaking your arm, Audrey?"

It was the deputy who spoke.

"Ed," said her father, and put his hand on her good forearm. "Audrey, you remember Ed Moran."

Audrey lowered the cast and looked from her father to the deputy.

"Sure I do," she said. "How are you, Deputy Moran?"

Moran was about to speak again but her father was quicker: "It's Sheriff Moran now, Audrey. Remember?"

"Right. I remember. And there's the badge and everything. I'm sorry," she said. She was not ready to call the man Sheriff. Her father was Sheriff.

Moran shifted his weight and smiled at her. When she was young she'd thought him handsome in some manly, gum-chewing way. Now she wondered why. His lips were thin and his eyes were too far apart and a little bulgy, like a frog's. Her head was clearing and she remembered that he was not the new sheriff here, he was not her father's replacement, but had gone down to Iowa, just over the border, and after a few years down there had been elected sheriff. And now he'd come back up to his old turf to stand in his sheriff's uniform next to her father, who was now a common civilian, and conduct his interview.

As if confirming these thoughts her father said, "Your accident was down in Iowa, sweetheart. Pawnee County. That's Sheriff Moran's county, and I asked him to come up here just by himself for now. Dr. Breece said he thought you could handle a few questions—just a few," he said pointedly. "But if you don't want to right now, if you don't feel up to it, you just say the word and the sheriff will come back another day."

She could see by Moran's thin-lipped smile that he'd have liked to tell her father to stand down and let him handle this. And she could tell by her father's voice, and the way he kept close to her, and the pressure of his hand on her forearm, that he'd rather not have his old deputy in the room at all; that it was too soon. Or maybe it was that he'd rather be asking the questions himself. In any case, she knew she could send the deputy away with one sentence, chomping his gum all the way back to Iowa, but he would only be more thin-lipped and more determined when he returned. And so she told him everything she remembered, from the boy who grabbed her at the gas station to the spinout on the road to the car behind them that failed to stop, that bumped the RAV4, to the fast ride down the riverbank and the spinning out onto the ice and the first sounds of the ice cracking.

And then she told him what she didn't know she remembered until she heard herself saying it, and even then she couldn't be certain it wasn't some dream from the time that she was underwater, from the days and nights of swimming underwater—she told him that the ice had cracked and the car had tilted and she'd let go of Caroline's hand so they could open their doors, but the driver's side went under first and Caroline couldn't get out that way, and she herself was climbing out of her door right up onto the ice, but the ice was breaking under her hands, under her knees, and she knew how cold the water was but she didn't feel it at all, and she turned back and saw Caroline climbing up through the car toward her and she reached for her hand again and grabbed it, but then the car began to roll over and the door closed on her own arm like a shark and twisted and she had to let go of Caroline, she had to let go, and the car rolled and it took her under with it, and it held her. It held her underwater and it began to wheel slowly around, upside down, in the current, and the tires or something must have been caught on the ice because it didn't go under the ice, and there was nothing to see under there but the beams of light in the yellow water, nothing in the water but water and bubbles until, all at once, there was Caroline—she'd gotten out of the car on the driver's side, or had been swept out of it by the water, and she was in the lights and she was in the current and she was trying to swim back, she was trying to swim back to the car, her sweatshirt rippling in the current, the hood gaping behind her head like the mouth of a fish, like the bell of a jellyfish, and the current had her and she was growing smaller, smaller, and then she passed out of the reach of the headlights—and she was gone, Daddy, she was gone.

HER FATHER HELD her good hand in both of his. Squeezing so hard it hurt. Something private, secret, burning behind his eyes.

"Daddy—?"

"What hand?"

"What?"

"What hand did that—boy put over your mouth."

"Tom," said the deputy. The sheriff.

She did not look away from her father's eyes. "He was holding my right arm with his . . . his left, so it must've been his right hand over my mouth."

"His right hand," he said.

Moran standing there looking hard at her father, and her father finally relaxing his grip.

He took a breath and sat back. "Go on, Sheriff," he said.

Moran shifted his weight. He adjusted his black, gadgety belt. "So you were underwater, Audrey, but then you got out."

The water so powerful and so deep and yellow in the lights. She saw hair, golden hair, sweeping in the current, or was it grasses from the floor of the river? The current pulled at her, wanted her too, but the car would not let her go.

"How did you do it, Audrey? How did you get out of the water?"

"I don't know," she said. "The car was stuck on the ice and I was stuck on the car. I guess I must have climbed up. I must have gotten the door open far enough to get my arm out and I must've used the door to climb up on top of the car—on top of the underside of the car—and I must've climbed from the car to the ice. But I don't remember that. All I remember is lying on the ice, on my stomach, and looking at the lights through the ice, the headlights, the way they were shining on the underside of the ice just as steady and clear as anything. Like I was underwater looking up at them from below. Like everything was upside down. The sky, the water. Everything."

13

HOLLY BURKE IS dead, her mind kept repeating. *Gordon's daughter is dead.* Rachel saw his face again . . . his shut-down eyes. *Still breathing!*

She wanted to see her boys. Craved the weight of them in her arms as she had when they were babies. The smell of them. Her breasts aching for them once again.

Momma guess what, Marky said when she returned to the Plumbing & Supply that afternoon. He was at the glass door, spritzing away smears and fingerprints.

What, sweetie, she said, fitting her hand to the back of his neck.

He shrugged off the hand and said, The sheriff was here Momma the sheriff and the deputies and they were all asking questions and all wanting to find Danny.

Jeff Goss sat behind the counter, unsmiling, listening.

Did the men talk to you, Marky? she said. Did they ask you questions?

Yes Momma they asked me where is Danny and I told them he didn't take me with him he went up to Uncle Rudy's cabin him and Wyatt but he never woke me up he never told me anything he just went.

She turned to Jeff Goss and he said, his eyes on Marky, or perhaps on the half-cleaned glass beyond him, They're going around talking to people. Anyone who might've seen her last night.

He scooped up some pink receipts and studied the topmost one. They talked to Big Man, Jeff said, but I don't think they understood much.

Did *you*? she thought to ask. But didn't. Jeff had been around Marky long enough, had heard enough of Danny's translations, that he'd acquired, without much caring one way or another, she believed, a passing comprehension of Marky's meaning in any number of routine situations. But did he understand what Marky told the sheriff and his men? And understanding it, did he then translate? *Uncle Rudy's cabin, he's saying*, Jeff might've said. *Do I know where it is? Sure I do, Sheriff . . .*

Jeff raised the receipt to study the one beneath it. Rachel standing there. Thinking. Trying to think. She'd come into the store intending to ask Jeff about last night—Danny had gone back out to give him a jump. But now she didn't want to look at him again. She couldn't seem to breathe.

Holly Burke is dead. All night in the river.

Marky, she said, get your jacket, please. We have to go now.

Gotta clean the glass Momma.

Tomorrow, Marky. Today's a short day.

At home she was barely in the door, had barely glanced at the answering machine—no blinking red light, no call from her son—before she saw the car outside, in the street: the sheriff's white cruiser, parked as if it had been there all day, when she knew it hadn't been there just seconds ago. Tom Sutter and one of his deputies coming up the walk in their tan jackets, their stiff hats.

In the living room the TV went mute. They're here Momma.

I know, sweetie. He could not see the drive or the walk from where he sat, but he'd heard the car doors shutting and it was not the sound of Danny's truck, or he'd seen some reaction in her at the window, or felt it—she'd stopped concerning herself with how he knew the things he knew a long time ago; it was just who he was. If you were sad, if you were missing your husband, for instance, he would find you and put his arms around you. If you stayed up waiting for his brother to come home, and Marky yawned and went to bed, then you knew you could go to bed too.

Marky getting up from the couch now and coming to stand beside her. Her little man, so big now! Too big to send to his room, but she didn't want the sheriff staring at him, asking him questions, upsetting him, and she said, Sweetie, go on up to your room, OK? Just for a little while. And he stood looking into her eyes like he understood perfectly—all her fear and all her love for him, and for Danny too—before he said, OK Momma I'll go upstairs, and she put her hand on his face, and he turned and went up the stairs.

The sheriff introduced himself and his deputy, then told her they'd like to speak to her son, they'd like to speak to Danny, watching her face as she explained that she didn't know where he was, hadn't seen him since last night, and the sheriff making sure she was aware of the unfortunate news regarding . . . while the other man, Deputy Something, brushed past her with his eyes, ransacking with his eyes all he saw beyond her in the house, working his wad of chewing gum. They were trying to learn as much as they could about the night before, Sheriff Sutter was explaining. They understood that her son Danny had been at the bar, at Smithy's, where Holly Burke was last seen alive.

Rachel wasn't sure if this was a question, but she said she couldn't say about that, she didn't know where he'd been.

The deputy stopped chewing, watching her with his buggy eyes, and resumed chewing again.

After a moment—after Sutter asked—she let them in.

14

SHE'D SHUT HER eyes for just a few seconds, she thought, but when she opened them again the room had changed: the bright, hard sunlight gone from behind the blinds, doctor gone, the smell of cigarette smoke stronger.

"How long was I asleep?"

Her father handed her the water cup. "Not long. An hour."

She sucked at the straw and swallowed the cold water. "I'm sorry."

"No, I am. We made you talk too much."

"It's the drugs. Can you tell them to stop giving me the drugs?"

"It's for the pain, sweetheart. For your arm."

"I don't care about that. Please, Dad."

"I'll ask the doctor."

She turned to look at Moran then, who'd been standing back and staring at the floor, or his boots. Her father looked too, but when she said "Sheriff" both men turned to her.

"Can I ask you something, Sheriff?" she said, and Moran stood straighter.

"Of course, Audrey," he said.

"Where is Caroline now?"

He glanced at her father, and her father said, "She knows. She's asking about the body," and Moran turned back to her.

"She's gone back home, Audrey. Her folks flew up to get her yesterday and they took her back with them. Mr. Price, her father, drove up here to see you but you were still . . . sleeping. He and Caroline's mother wanted to get her back home and put her to rest."

Audrey looked away and the tears ran to her jaw and from there fell to her collarbone. She wiped her face with the palm of her good hand and turned back to Moran. He wasn't finished with his questions, and she waited for the next one. He'd removed his jacket—they both had—and when he stepped up to the side of the bed she saw the sheen of sweat on his forehead.

"I was hoping you could tell me more about those two boys, Audrey. From the gas station."

"What do you want to know?"

"Did you get a good look at them?"

"It was dark back there, and they were both wearing caps with, you know, bills, so their faces were dark."

"Were they black?"

"Their faces?"

"Were they African American."

"No, they were white boys. They smelled like car engines and beer. And cigarettes."

"How old were they?"

"I don't know. Twentysomething."

"Names?"

Audrey shook her head. Then, as she remembered it, she said, "Bud."

"Bud?"

"The one Caroline sprayed, the one on the ground—the other one called him Bud."

"As in the *name* Bud?" said Moran. "Or 'bud' as in 'buddy'?"

She thought about that. "I thought it was his name. But now I'm not sure."

Moran flipped open his notebook and wrote it down. The notebook was small and black and just like the one her father had used. "And the other boy?"

"I never heard his name."

"Did you get their license plate?"

"No, sir."

"Did you see what they were driving?"

"No, sir."

"You didn't see them follow you?"

"No, sir."

"Did you see who came up behind you at the top of the bank—who gave your car a bump?"

"It wasn't my car."

"Caroline's car then. Was it those boys?"

"I couldn't see who was driving. The headlights were in our eyes."

Moran nodded. "You said, earlier, that Caroline pepper-sprayed those boys pretty good. They must've been mad as heck."

"So was Caroline."

"Do you think they were in any shape to drive?"

"I don't know, Sheriff. We didn't stick around to find out."

Moran looked at her father, as if out of some old habit, but quickly turned back to her. "Did you see the vehicle that came up behind you, what kind of vehicle it was?"

"The lights were real high, and I thought maybe it was some kind of truck." Then she remembered something she'd forgotten, something she'd seen as Caroline's car spun around and around on the ice.

"It was a truck, Sheriff. I saw it from the river, when we were spinning around, before the ice broke. It was just sitting up there. And the next time I looked up, when I was lying on the ice, it was gone."

"Did you see what kind of truck it was?"

"What kind of truck?"

"Yes."

"Like a Chevy or a Ford or whatever?"

"Yes."

"I have no idea. Plus I was, like, spinning around on a frozen river."

"Could you see the color?"

"No, sir."

"Was it new-looking or old?"

"I don't know. It was just a truck, Sheriff."

"Audrey," said her father gently. "The sheriff is only trying to help us here."

"I know he is. What did I say?"

Moran stood looking at her.

"I'm sorry," she said.

"I'm sorry to badger you, Audrey. I know you must be upset about the accident. And about your friend. But I have to tell those folks down in Georgia what happened up here. I have to tell them what happened to their daughter. That truck that bumped you, that sent you and Caroline down the bank—do you have any reason to think it was intentional? That whoever was driving it meant to do you harm?"

"No, sir. Only he didn't do anything to help us either, did he. Or she."

She drank more water. Moran waiting, watching her. Her arm under the cast was throbbing like a heart.

"I just have to ask you one more question and then I'll get out of your hair," he said, and she nodded. "If you saw those boys again, either one, together or separate, do you think you'd recognize them?"

She thought about that. She tried to piece them together from her memory but it was like trying to climb onto the broken ice, and all she found of the two boys were hands and shadows and caps and clouds of breath that stank of beer. She found the feel of his hand over her mouth and the oily smell of the hand and she found the muscles of his leg as he wedged it between hers.

But then she saw the scene from another vantage too: she saw the boy pressing her against the wall with his hand over her mouth and she saw his leg forced between hers and she saw him holding her by her right wrist and she saw the scratches that ran under his eye from ear to nose, weirdly small lines like a bar of sheet music and the dark little drops of blood that were the notes. And she saw the second boy's face clearly when he turned, the look in his eyes as he tried to understand what she was pointing at him, and she saw the first boy's face again as he raised his arms to block the burst of pepper spray. She saw all this as clearly as anything she'd seen with her own eyes and she knew she was seeing the scene through her friend's eyes, through Caroline's eyes, and she knew how crazy that was and yet she knew it was true just the same and she knew she could never say it out loud to Moran, or even to her father. Not because they could never use it against the boys—they couldn't—and not because they would never believe it—they wouldn't—but because to say it out loud would be to lose it, the realness of it, forever.

"I think I'd know them, Sheriff," she said. "I'm pretty sure I would."

Moran nodded. "That's good, Audrey. That's real good. You rest now and take care of that arm, you hear?" He seemed about to pat her on the knee but thought better of it. Turned instead to her father and said, "Care for one last smoke, Tom?" and her father looked at her and she said without saying it, *Go,* and he gave her hand a squeeze and both men collected their jackets from the chair and left her alone in the room with her crazy thoughts and the beating of her arm under the cast.

When he returned some minutes later her father smelled of smoke and the outdoors, but an outdoors that was much later in the day and colder, although when she thought about it she did not think a person could know the time and temperature of the day by its smells on a man's clothes, and the moment she thought that, the smells lost their meaning and her certainty was gone.

He stood at her bedside but seemed far away. His eyes a faint blue down in their shadows.

"What did he want to talk to you about?" she said.

"I think he just wanted to let me know he had it under control. So I could rest easy, and stay with you."

"So you wouldn't get any ideas about going down there yourself and getting all sheriffy."

He smiled. "Maybe."

She watched him. "You weren't very nice to him."

"I wasn't?"

She just looked at him, and he shrugged.

"I guess I didn't care to see him in my daughter's hospital room."

"Him—?"

"Any lawman." He placed a hand on her wrist and she flinched, and he removed his hand again. "I'm sorry—"

"It's OK. It's just—your hand is so cold."

He cupped his hands and blew into them. "I can't ever seem to get them warm anymore. It's like they're dunked in ice water all day long. Although I guess you'd know more about that than I would." His smile was uncertain and she reached for his hand.

"I barely felt it, Sheriff."

"I don't know how long you were underwater, but you were on that ice a long time. The EMTs had to chip you free with ice scrapers."

"They did not."

"Honest to God." He smiled at her smile, but it didn't last. "If that old man hadn't driven by and seen the lights, the headlights, under the ice—"

"What old man?"

"The old man who called in the accident."

"Who is he?"

"I wish I knew. He declined to give his name. Said he was just driving by and was too old to go down there and help. Felt real bad he couldn't help, Ed says. But didn't give his name and didn't stick around."

She looked off and said quietly, "Poor old feller. Didn't they get his number from the call?"

"He called from a pay phone."

"At the gas station?"

He narrowed his eyes. "Now who's getting all sheriffy?"

She held his eyes. Outlasted him.

"The old feller is a dead end, Deputy," he said. "Called and vanished. But thank God he called."

They were silent. Then he looked at her and said, "What is it, sweetheart?"

She shook her head. She wouldn't cry again. If you tell him you wish you'd never asked Caroline Price to loan you bus fare you are just telling him that the only reason Caroline Price is dead is because you were coming home to see him, because he's so sick. Because he is dying. All of which he already knows.

She gripped his hand tighter. "I just wish I'd never left, Daddy. That's all. I wish I'd never gone back down there after Christmas."

"Sweetheart, I never could've let you do that. I needed you to be in school. You should be there now."

"But we don't have time, Daddy. There's not enough time." Now came the tears. She couldn't stop them.

"Sweetheart. We've had lots of time. Your whole life. And they have been the best damn years of my life. Hell, I wouldn't trade another hundred years of living if it cost me one day of knowing you. Do you believe that?"

"No. You're exaggerating."

"The hell I am."

He watched her. Then he smiled, and patted her hand again. "Can I get you anything? Aren't you hungry?"

"No, thank you."

She looked at the cast, looking closely at the purple surface of the plaster, the edges of the individual strips where they'd been layered and shaped by another person's hands before they dried into this hard shell. She wiggled fingers that did not look like her fingers so much as the pink legs of a creature that lived inside the shell. She said, watching the wiggling legs, "I thought of something when I was under the water, Daddy. Something I hadn't thought of in a long time. Someone, I mean." She didn't look up. She could feel him waiting. Could feel his tightening heart between the dying lungs. "She was blond, wasn't she," she said. And now she looked at him.

"Yes," he said.

"Long blond hair."

"Yes."

"I remembered that when I was in the water."

"You were just a little girl then. You shouldn't have known about such things." He turned his head to cough. "I never should've had you in the car with me."

"That didn't make any difference, Daddy. We all knew. We'd stand around on the playground and say her name: *Holly Burke*."

She saw the effect of this name in his eyes, darkening the blue like a cloud over water. He'd not found the girl's killer—or had not found the evidence the law required. Had never given her that, given her family that, and now he never would.

"She seemed so old to us then," Audrey said, "so grown-up and mysterious. But she doesn't seem old now. She seems young. Even younger than she was." The beautiful hair, that long fine girl's hair, lit up and swaying in the current, in the lights.

He squeezed her good forearm. "I wish you wouldn't think about that." He patted her—kept patting until she looked at him and he stopped.

"There's something I didn't tell the deputy—the sheriff," she said, and the moment she said it she felt him grow tenser yet. She felt his heart begin to slide.

"That's all right," he said. "It takes time, sometimes, to remember things. The brain just kind of . . ." His mind was running to the worst, she knew: What hadn't she told him about those two boys, what they'd done to her?

She shook her head. "It's nothing like that, Daddy. I just didn't want to tell the sheriff something I wasn't sure about. And I'm not sure I didn't just imagine this."

He waited. Watching her run her fingers up and down the purple cast.

"What is it, sweetheart? Tell me, and I'll tell the sheriff if I think he ought to know. I'll tell him you're not sure—how's that?"

She nodded. Then she told him about the scratches on the one boy's face, the one who grabbed her. The scratches were fresh, but she knew they didn't come from her own fingers; they ran small and neat across his face, ear to nose, like the scratches from a cat.

"Did Caroline do it?" her father said, and she said, "No. I did it. I must have done it with the backscratcher."

He looked at her. "The backscratcher?"

"The backscratcher," she said. "From Phoenix, Arizona. The lady at the gas station will show you. Can I have that, please?"

He handed her the cup and she sucked at the straw and handed the cup back.

"I must've hit him with it," she said. "But then he took it away from me and I stopped. I stopped fighting, Daddy."

He squeezed her hand hard. "Sweetheart, don't—"

"Caroline fought, Daddy. She fought them so good. She fought them so beautifully."

15

THERE WASN'T MUCH she could tell them, as there wasn't much she knew, and just a few minutes after they left she had trouble remembering what they'd said, what they'd asked, trouble believing they were ever there at all.

She tried to call Danny again. Kept trying until, in the space between dialings, the phone rang and she answered, —*Danny?* But it was Rudy, her brother, telling her that everything was all right, Dan was all right, they'd found him up at the cabin, and there was no trouble and he was in custody.

In custody? Rachel said.

Not arrested, her brother said quickly. Not charged.

But in custody, Rachel said.

There's a gray area, he told her, and he went on reassuring her, but Rachel's mind was reeling. She was at the kitchen window, as she'd been the night before. Two yellow eyes looking in, the twin smiley-faces. *Water*, she remembered. The dog had rolled in something. She saw her son's face, the look on his face when he saw her in the window.

There was nothing out there now. No truck. No son.

In custody.

It was dark when tires crunched in the drive, and she quickly turned off the TV. A car door slammed, tires crunched the gravel again, and in walked Danny. Rachel was up from the sofa but everything about him said *Stop, don't touch me.* Marky lifted him in a bear hug until Danny said, Put me down, idiot.

Danny, Rachel said.

As if he hadn't heard her, as if she weren't there, he headed for the stairs.

Hey Danny where's Wyatt? Marky said.

I had to leave him up there, with Jer.

Marky put his hands to his head, but he said nothing. He stood like that watching his brother.

Danny, Rachel said, talk to me—and he stopped on the stairs. Then turned back to her.

Why are you even here, Ma?

She stared at him.

Why aren't you on your *date*?

Danny, she said again, but then faltered. His eyes so hard, so cold. What had she done?

They stood that way for a while, he on the steps above and she below, before he turned again and continued up the stairs. Marky watching him go, turning back to Rachel, and finally going up the stairs too.

She moved woodenly from room to room then, locking the doors, drawing the curtains. It crossed her mind to pull the phone line from the wall, and at that second the phone rang. Rudy again. There was nothing for her to worry about, he told her, he'd been talking to the lawyer . . . telling her other things she hardly heard, something about physical evidence, the phrase *erratic, troubled girl*, and Rachel mechanically took down the number of the lawyer.

There was a silence, and then she said, Do you think he knows?

Who? said Rudy.

Gordon Burke. Do you think he knows, about Danny?

You haven't talked to him?

Yes, earlier. Briefly. He wasn't— He . . . She didn't finish.

He's a good man, Rach, Rudy said. And he's been good to those boys. But what he's going through right now . . . Hell, I don't even want to imagine.

SHE WAITED FOR the sheriff to return, but he didn't—not that night, not all day Friday.

She waited for Gordon to call, although she knew that wouldn't happen either. And then it was Friday night, Halloween—Danny emerging from his room at last, on his way to Jeff Goss's waiting car, and off they went. Rachel sitting at home with Marky, who sat in his Vikings helmet and jersey ready to dish out candy for kids if any came, and then announcing after a while that none were coming. And none did; not one. It was a bad night for it, a bitter wind blowing, so no wonder.

Later, after Marky had gone to bed, something sailed through the living room window, puffing out the curtains and dropping with a light thud to the carpet. A small stone out of the sky. Surprising, what a clean, small hole it made in the glass, with only a few slender shards to pick up. The pieces were still in her hand when the phone rang.

Hello? she said. *Hello—?*

Hello? Mrs. Young?

Mrs. Young! The blood went out of her. She steadied herself on the counter. It wasn't him, it wasn't Gordon. It was his brother, Edgar.

Rachel managed to give her sympathies, then listened while Edgar explained that Gordon wasn't going to open the store tomorrow, so the boys should plan on staying home.

She saw the scene over there, at Gordon's house: Edgar at the phone and Gordon beyond him, heaped in a chair, staring into his coffee. Meredith on the sofa, and their daughter, their only child, laid out somewhere in some cold, awful place, dead.

—under the circumstances, Edgar was saying, they should plan on staying home until further notice.

After he hung up, Rachel kept the phone to her ear, listening to the strange silence there, a sound from outer space, an eerie wind. She stood frozen in it, her chest hollow. There'd been a day, years ago, when something happened, or nearly happened, between her and Gordon Burke. A gray afternoon, the windowpanes ticking with bits of ice. She'd come out of a bath and felt weak and had sat down on the bed. Before her was the cheval glass that had belonged to her grandmother, then her mother, now her. Who would she give the mirror to, this girly keepsake?

Rachel—?

A man had come into the house, downstairs. There was the sound of his footfall across the living room, and then her name again, lobbed up the stairs. A stair tread creaked and she reached for her robe but stopped.

Two days ago they'd buried Roger. This afternoon, Gordon had picked up the boys and taken them to a movie so Rachel could sleep. Now they were back.

Rachel—? he said from around the corner.

Yes, she answered. That was all. He came anyway, into the frame of the door.

Oh— he said. His big face filling with the sight of her there, on the bed. I'm sorry, he said.

She heard the kids in the yard, already into some kind of contest. Holly could be mean but Danny would keep things fair and good for Marky.

Brought the boys back, Gordon said, not looking away, looking her in the eye. He reached up and worked the flesh under his jaw with a coarse, sandpaper sound. He was a man who was sure before he acted, who didn't operate by guesswork or even intuition, but who held in his head all the hard facts of mechanical things. Over the years there had been moments, yes, when she'd wondered what it would be like to be with him instead of Roger, to simply switch. Innocent, helpless thoughts such as every wife must have.

He took a step, then came certainly toward her. In the wash of movement she smelled the outdoors, the steely clouds and the wet, moldering leaves. Her heart was beating in her breast. She turned to the mirror and the picture there was incredible: this naked, wet-haired woman, this man beside her dressed for cold.

Rachel . . . , he began, and in the next instant Holly's voice, cold as a queen's, penetrated the room.

Hands off, retard.

Out there in the cold, Danny said something low, and there was silence.

Gordon's face had gone red. His jaw muscle jumped.

She knows better, by God, he said.

It's all right, Rachel said.

The day was going dark. In the mirror she saw Gordon's arm drift toward her shoulder, then beyond it. She saw the robe rise up like a phantom, felt it brush her skin. In the mirror, as in the flesh, he got the robe over her shoulders and over her breasts without quite touching her.

THERE WAS GLASS in her hand, Rachel had noticed standing at the sink. Slender fragments pressed into her palm, and after a moment she remembered the broken window, the strange little stone. She dumped the glass in the trash and rinsed her hand under the faucet. She had wanted to tell him something, that day—something true and unafraid, such as how she'd often felt, her secret thoughts. Holly's voice had stopped her.

And if it hadn't? If everything had gone just a little bit differently? Meteors, they said, were on their way, right now, crossing billions of years of chance. The smallest bump changed everything. If Holly had not spoken and Rachel had—would things be different? Would Holly be alive?

It was late, almost midnight. Wind was moaning in a gap somewhere. She began locking doors, switching off lights. She was halfway up the stairs before she remembered that Danny was still out, but she didn't go back down to turn on the light. In a few weeks, he'd be gone. Taking off one day while she was at work, leaving just a note saying he'd gone down to Saint Louis, to work construction with a friend of his. Leaving the dog behind. His classes. His girlfriend. When Rachel would try to call, a message would tell her the number was no longer in service. There'd be a postcard, the Gateway Arch—they'd gone once when Roger was alive, Marky terrified to go up until Danny explained the mechanics of the thing, the strength of arches!—and a few sentences on the back saying he was fine, he was working, he'd be back in a month . . .

But he wasn't. Two months and he wasn't back. Six months. One day she'd see that Gordon Burke had finally changed the sign on the side of the Plumbing & Supply building, whitewashing out the hyphen and everything after—and that's when she'd decide to go too. Her father still had the farm and there was room for her and Marky and the dog. It was a place, a life, she'd left behind. But you never do, and the first time she cooked for him, at the old stove, her father wept. Two months later he too was gone, laid to rest next to her mother and her father's parents, Grammy and Granddad Olsen, those dusty souls, those ghosts.

16

TOM SUTTER STOOD just outside the shelter, alone and listening to the sounds of his own smoking, the faint cracklings of tobacco and paper when he inhaled, the sighs of his breath when he exhaled. He smoked the cigarette down and dropped it to the concrete and crushed it under his boot toe before he remembered the receptacle with its long plastic neck. He thought of Gordon Burke—the pain, the anger in those eyes all these years later. Of course still there, of course—where would it go? And he thought of Danny Young, nineteen back then, Gordon's daughter's age. Audrey's age now. What had become of him? Would you even recognize him if you passed him on the street?

Of course you would.

Sutter looked up at stars, the billion stars—far more than that, sending light from distances you could never imagine. Coldness and silence and total indifference as to himself or anyone else alive now or ever alive. He looked into these so-called heavens and said: "Well, what have you got to say about it?" And stood listening.

"That's about what I thought," he said. Then he walked to the parking lot and got into his car and began the long drive home. He'd not slept in his own bed for two nights and they wanted to keep her for one more night at least; she was out of danger but they didn't like her temperature, and they would know more tomorrow.

On the highway, the sedan up to speed, he lit another cigarette and left it to burn between his knuckles. After a while he said, "Why don't you just say it?" But she stayed quiet. Sometimes he would smell her lipstick. Her skin. The whole complex scent of her. Would see her hands in the corner of his eye. The flash of the diamond he'd put on her finger, years ago.

You don't need to hear it from me, she said finally. *You already know it.*

He drove. The cigarette burning down.

"Shoot," he said. "That never kept you from saying it before."

TWO HOURS LATER he stood near the trestle bridge, in the rutted and trampled snow there, looking down the beam of his MagLite at the river. The rupture had frozen over but was still visible by its outline of jagged ice. From where he stood it had the mouthy look of a great fish, a prehistoric monster, frozen at the moment of striking. He saw the iced-over hole and he saw the story it told but he could not see his daughter there, struggling to get out, pawing at the busted ice, pulled under into that coldness, that darkness, by the car as it rolled. Could not see that.

Of the car's tiretracks going down there was nothing left; they'd been plowed under by the car's body coming up. Nothing left of the tiretracks up top either, where the car had first come to rest; too many vehicles had come and gone and you couldn't expect first responders to concern themselves overly about evidence—and he wouldn't have it any other way in this case—but God damn.

He doused his light and stood at the top of the bank with his arms at his sides. The breath smoking from his nostrils. Winter smell of woodfire in the air. Listening, but not a sound. Then, from downriver, traveling some distance along the ice, the baying of a hound dog. Baying. Pausing. Baying again, but answered by nothing Sutter himself could hear in all that hushed valley. He crossed the road and got back in his sedan and shut the door and sat in a darker, closer silence.

Don't even say it, she said after a moment, and he didn't. But then he did: "Just one more stop," he said, and turned the key in the ignition.

THERE WAS A pay phone at the corner of the station but when he went to pick up the receiver there was no receiver, no cable, and he moved on, passing the window—the woman sitting there, at work on her puzzles, much as he'd pictured her—and stepped inside.

"Oh," she said, looking up from her work. "I didn't see you pull up."

Sutter turned and looked out the pane of glass and said, "No, I guess I parked out of view, didn't I?"

"That's all right. I guess you can park anywhere you like, Officer."

She sat on her stool behind the counter, soft-faced and blond. The pin tag on her chest said PAMELA. He took in the cluttered countertop, the disposable lighters and ChapStick and other plastic junk for sale.

"Is it about the accident again?" the woman said. "Those two girls? Just so awful."

Sutter shook his head—somber, dumbfounded. "It doesn't get much more awful, does it?"

"No, sir. It just chills me to the bone to think about it."

"It had to be mighty cold in that water."

"Well, yeah, that—but I mean seeing those two girls just a few minutes before, right here? Right where you are standing now? I still can't hardly believe it."

"I guess you remember that night pretty clearly, ma'am."

"I guess I'll never forget it."

He stood a moment, giving the comment room. Then he said, "I know they've already asked you questions up and down, ma'am, but I just want to ask one or two more, if you don't mind." He watched to see if she would look more carefully at his sheriff's jacket, but she did not. Good warm jacket for a cold night, if anyone cared. Beneath it he wore a plain khaki shirt, no tie, and he wore jeans and a plain leather belt and his old leather workboots. His sheriff's hat and belt and holster, his badge, were all back home in his bedroom closet. The county-issue .45 was back with the department, turned in one year ago on his last day, as per regulation.

The woman said, "I'll answer whatever you want to ask me, Officer. If it'll help, I'll answer."

"Thank you, ma'am—Pamela, is it?"

"Yes, sir."

"You can call me Tom, Pamela."

She placed her hands in her lap and waited. He glanced about the cramped little store. In a dark recess at the back an exit sign glowed above a metal firedoor. Adjacent to that door was a narrow wooden door leading, he guessed, to some kind of storage room or back office.

"You tend to be here by yourself, Pamela?"

"Yes, sir. Six to midnight on weeknights."

He'd already looked for security cameras and seen none. "It doesn't seem like the safest of shifts for a woman alone, if you don't mind me saying."

She laughed. "You'd have to be crazy to come here looking for money, or any other kind of nonsense. For one thing, Ron—that's my boss—he takes all the day cash away at five p.m., and most folks use cards for the gas anymore. Heck, I asked for this shift. It's nice and quiet, mostly."

"And the other thing?"

"Sir?"

"You said for one thing," he said. "Sounded like there was another thing."

"Oh." She glanced toward the back, the shadowed recess, and he saw the color come to her face like a sunburn. She flung a hand and said, "I was just gonna say that Ron, my boss, comes in kind of regular. At nights. He stops by to check on things." She fussed with the ChapStick dispenser.

"But he wasn't here that night?" Sutter said. "He didn't stop by?"

"No, sir. Not that night."

Sutter nodded. "You get a lot of regulars, then?" he said, and she looked up at him big-eyed and hot-faced and he added, "Customers, folks filling up."

She gave a breathy laugh. "Oh, sure. Plenty. I mean, we're the only station out this way you know, so."

"How about a boy—a young man named Bud?"

She shook her head. "It's like I told the sheriff before, I don't know anyone named Bud around here. I mean he might've been in here, but I didn't know him by name."

"Did you know him by sight—him or the other boy?"

"When?"

"The night of the accident."

Her face crimped in confusion. "Well, I mean, I already told the sheriff, Officer. I never saw those boys."

Sutter watched her face, her eyes.

"Yes, I know. I know that's what you told them." He gave her a smile. "But just to be clear, Pamela: You saw nothing of those two boys whatsoever?"

"No, sir."

"They never came into the station while you were here?"

"No, sir. I've seen plenty of boys come in here at night. I've seen some pretty sketchy characters. But no real trouble, ever, and I've been here, oh gosh, two years come March."

He watched her. "What about their truck?"

"What about it?"

"Well, ma'am, what kind of truck was it?"

"I couldn't tell you, Officer. I couldn't even say it was a truck."

Sutter looked out the window. "I guess it'd be hard to miss a truck pulling into the station, if you were sitting right here the whole time."

"I was sitting here, all right. The whole time. I went to use the ladies' once, but that was a good hour before those girls ever got here."

"And you saw the girls' car—the RAV4?"

"Yes, sir. They pulled up for gas right there at pump number one."

"Mm-hmm," said Sutter. "And how do you figure you never saw that truck?"

The woman sat up a little straighter. Somehow, the softness had left her face.

"Well, Officer, either that truck was never here, or else it was parked off to the side, same as you did."

Sutter coughed into his fist.

"That's sensible, Pamela. That helps a great deal. Thank you very much."

"I'm only trying to help, Officer. I feel awful bad for those girls. But the first I ever heard of those two boys was when the sheriff came asking about them earlier, and I'll tell you what I told him: if those boys were here, they'd of had to park where you parked, off to the side, and then they'd of had to walk around the back of the station to get to the restrooms on the other side. Otherwise I'd of seen 'em go by the window there."

Sutter looked to the firedoor at the rear of the building. "You reckon they went tramping through the snow back there?"

"No, sir. There's no snow back there. We're required by law to keep that sidewalk clear of snow and ice. It goes clear around the building. But I don't know why anybody would go back there, unless they just plain didn't want to be seen."

Sutter stood looking at the back door. Then he looked out the window again.

"Did you see the girls leave?"

"I sure did."

"How did they look?"

"Sir?"

"Did they seem frightened, upset?"

"They just seemed in a hurry. I figured they were trying to get out of the weather. It was sleeting pretty good. As you know." She shook her head. "I sat here a good half hour before I realized they never brought the key back, and by then every sheriff's car and ambulance and fire engine in the county was going by, and I just sat here wondering what in the world—"

"I'm sorry, Pamela—the key?"

"The key to the ladies," she said. "They took off without ever giving it back. Ron had to put in a whole new lock, cost him forty-five dollars." She lifted the new key from below the counter to prove it.

"May I?" he said, and she handed it over. The new key was attached by a loop of shoelace to what looked like the sawed-off stick-handle of a plumber's helper drilled through with a quarter-inch bit. LADIES inked along the shaft in a blocky, near-angry hand.

"Can I ask, what was the old key attached to?"

"A backscratcher."

"A backscratcher?"

She rolled her eyes. "I know. Ron asked the sheriff and them did they find his backscratcher in the girls' car and they looked at him like he was crazy."

"They didn't find it," Sutter said simply.

"No, sir."

"Can I borrow this a minute?"

"Oh, sure. But they've been all in and out of there already, the sheriff and them."

"I know. I just want to see for myself. If you don't mind."

"I don't mind. It's just around the side of the building."

"Thank you." He began to lift his hand to the brim of his hat but stopped himself, as he was wearing no hat. At the door he turned back.

"Where was it from?"

"Sir?"

"Where'd the backscratcher come from?"

Her face clouded—and then brightened: "Phoenix, Arizona," she said. "That was printed on it. Don't ask me how it ended up here."

He went around the side of the building and unlocked the ladies' and flicked the switch and stood in the humming light. The dirty tile floor and the reek of old urine. A dinged sheet of aluminum where a mirror would normally hang, engraved forever with obscenities. Did the ugliness of places bring out the ugliness in people, or was it the other way around? He shut the door and stood where she'd stood. He sniffed the air and he could smell it: the hand over her mouth, the greasy right hand. His heart was pounding and he patted down his pockets before he remembered he'd left them in the other jacket, in the car, his smokes, and what a way to go, his heart banging itself to pieces because he couldn't get his hands on his smokes—and on the very spot where his daughter had been cornered by those boys, those reeking punks, and would these be his last thoughts, these angry and hateful images, these smells?

That other time, when he'd woken up in the hospital, he'd had no warning, and no memory of any of it—no visions, no lights. Just nothing. Helping his deputies move desks around one second, in the hospital the next. The deputies, Halsey and Moser, had worked on him until the EMTs arrived.

You were just all the way gone, Sheriff, Wayne Halsey said later, and the doctor confirmed it. Full cardiac arrest. Full stop. Lights-out.

And it was those tests that led to finding the cancer. Double-whammy day.

But no connection between the two? he'd asked the doctor.

Other than the smoking? No. I'd say you mostly inherited the heart. It's an old heart.

An old heart?

Older than you.

Will it last?

How do you mean?

I mean will it do the job before the cancer.

It darn near did.

What about those stents?

A temporary fix, said the doctor. What he needed was bypass. Double, maybe triple—he couldn't really say until he got in there. And that was that.

Sutter had watched his own father go through all that, a year of recovery only to die six months later sitting in his chair watching baseball.

He never told her about the heart. The cancer was enough. Audrey still in high school then. Nineteen when the cancer came back, a college girl, and he only told her because the money was running out and you didn't want your daughter getting some kind of notice that her daddy had failed to pay her tuition. Or that her daddy was in the hospital taking his last breaths.

He did not want her to come home—had made her promise not to, but she'd broken that promise, and otherwise would never have come to this stinking place, would never have stopped here for gas with Caroline Price.

And if Caroline Price had not been with her, with her pepper spray and her toughness?

Caroline fought, Daddy. She fought them so beautifully.

He swept his beam all around the cleared pavement in front of the bathrooms and over the heaped up snow at the pavement's edge and over the snowy, undisturbed reaches beyond—did he throw it? And how far could he throw it? Sutter ran his beam up the boughs of a solitary pine tree, then followed the beam down the length of sidewalk behind the building and around to the other side and trained it on the spaces where he'd parked next to the old Ford wagon. Then he took the key back to Pamela and thanked her again.

"Officer," she said as he turned to go.

"Yes, ma'am?"

"Are you all right?"

"Ma'am?"

"I mean, you just don't look like you're doing so hot there. I thought maybe you had the flu or something."

"No, ma'am. It's not the flu. Good night, now."

17

IT WAS JUST gray dawn when his crying woke her, and whatever she'd been dreaming fled from her like the warmth of the bed as she drew back the covers, as she sat up and pulled the robe around her—"It's all right, boy, I'm up, I'm here"—and in the dark there was the weak thump of tail as she bent to collect him from his nest of blankets and old stuffed toys at the foot of the bed, the dog like an old stuffed thing himself with all the stuffing dragged out, all the living heaviness gone from him now, hardly more to this creature in her arms than the sack of skin and the brittle bones it held, the riddled bones, and her dream, whatever it was, was gone.

Downstairs she set him on his feet by the door and waggled her own feet into the soft boots there and fed her arms into her father's old canvas jacket and unlocked and swung in the wooden door, "Watch your toes, boy," and pushed open the stormdoor and followed him out onto the small wooden deck that overlooked the long slope of the yard and the wire fence and the fifty acres beyond that she rented to old Jimmy McVeigh, or, rather, to his sons now. The dog making his way over the top crust of snow to the iron clothesline bar, and no sound at that cold hour but the soft press of the snow under his paws. Stopping and lowering his haunches at the foot of the iron bar, no longer able to lift his leg, the snow hissing and steaming beneath him.

There he squatted, the dark outline of a dog in the glistening white. A thin and homely shadow of a dog, much as he'd looked when the boys had first brought him home, what—thirteen years ago? Brought him to her as if there would be no question, no resistance, this starved and dirty animal. Danny and Marky coming up the walk with the animal wobbling along behind them and nearly through the front door before she pushed them back outside, then reached to pull the boys toward her, to separate them from the animal, the shocking thing, a creature that surely would've died given another day.

Get inside, she'd told them. She would call the pound, the Board of Health, the county sheriff.

But Danny had looked at her, and then at Marky, who with his strange agility had twisted free of her and stood petting the animal's skull.

You know what they'll do to him, Danny said quietly.

He was sly, her Daniel, so sly. And Marky knew at once what he meant, and the fight was over; she could never do that to her son.

Danny kneeled next to his brother and began stroking the dog's ragged spine. What will we call him? he asked, and Marky said Snickers, but then rethought; the boys had been watching westerns on TV. Wyatt Earp! he said, and Danny nodded. The outlaw sheriff, he said.

Fifty feet of hose lay sun-heated in the grass and as they washed the filth from his coat Wyatt Earp stood docile, soaked, the more wasted and pathetic for his soaking, a living skeleton. Rachel at the kitchen window shaking her head. Her good fabric shears flashing in the sun as the boys snipped the burrs from the dog's coat, the boys quiet and serious as surgeons. Danny emptying one of Roger's old jelly jars of screws and pouring in lawnmower gas and dropping into this—he alone, not Marky, who could not be the cause of any creature's death—tick after tick, some as fat as blueberries. They cleverly made a collar out of an old leather belt, and lastly they pooled their savings for the vet's shots and for dogfood. The county would do the neutering for free.

Well. He'd been a good dog, after all. Smart, obedient, happy—devoted to Danny as if he'd never forgotten that day, that sudden change of fortune. When Danny went away, years later, leaving him behind with Rachel and Marky, he was not the same animal. His heart was broken. Sickness saw an opening.

Now in the dawn, in the cold, the dog returned to her. "Good boy," she said and held open the stormdoor. So much life, so much love, and memory, and grief in such a short-lived life. Does he have any idea what a life is? What his might have meant?

In the kitchen she filled the kettle and lit the burners and took out the half can of dogfood from the fridge and spooned the remainder into the saucepan. She crushed up one of his pills and added that to the dogfood, and with the spoon began to break it all down over a low flame while he sat on his kitchen blankets, watching her, shivering with cold and pain. Rachel at the stove stirring his breakfast, her eyes on the window where the new day was coming, the sky growing pale in the east and you should put him down, Rachel. The only kind thing to do. The vet's advice.

But Danny is far away and Marky knows only his love of the dog, his terror of death, and Roger is gone. There's no one but you to make that choice, to say whether this animal, this member of the family, after all, goes on living or has come now, so quickly, to his end.

It was the water, she remembered—the sound of water in the pipes. If he had not used the outdoor spigot she would not have come downstairs. She would never have seen him standing out there with the hose in his hand. Would never have seen the look on his face the moment he knew she was there, the moment he knew he'd been seen.

Of course, if she had not had a date with Gordon Burke—if she'd never had feelings for Gordon Burke—Danny would not have been out at all that night.

This was her final thought on the matter, again and again, all these years later. Standing at her grandmother's stove, the winter sun rising, stirring dogfood and drugs in a saucepan for the outlaw sheriff.

18

SUTTER WOKE UP coughing as if he would drown and he coughed his way into the bathroom and put his hands to his knees and stood bow-backed until at last he hocked the thing up and into the bowl, thick ball of Jesus knows what that bobbed in the water in a spreading cloud of pink. He spat again and wiped his mouth with the back of his hand and stood over the bowl dizzy and sweating.

He got into his jeans and his shirt and stepped barefoot onto the cold concrete of the motel's second-story walkway and lit the day's first cigarette and stood looking down on the gray lot below. Birds somewhere, calling and whistling. Iowa birds. Semis somewhere, brakes gasping, the big diesel engines rumbling. He looked down from the height of the balcony and he remembered falling through space and then he remembered his dream: he'd been on the river with his father, the two of them in his father's old johnboat way up north above the falls, his father heavy in the stern and himself just a small boy riding high in the bow. But in the dream they had no outboard and when he searched the floor for the paddle he found nothing but dead fish, the boat rocking in the current and moving fast as the falls roared louder and his father yelling, *Just hold to the gunwales, Tommy, and don't* . . . but he could not hear for the roar of the water, and then the bow was out in open space and he with it, way out over the drop with the weight of his father in the stern, nothing under the bow but the plunging water and the open air and the far small rocks below. He hung there and he hung there, the world below him, before the boat fulcrumed over the edge and began its dive and he'd woken up with his fists gripping the gunwales and his lungs full of water.

THE GARAGE DIDN'T open until eight a.m., the sign said, so he drove back two blocks to a café and then drove another block and parked, and killed the engine, and sat with the keys in his fist.

"What?" he said. She hadn't said a thing.

He half expected to see Ed Moran's cruiser on the street, or parked before the café, and when he went inside and sat at the counter he half expected to see Moran himself walk in with his deputies, and he half hoped he would. Save everyone a lot of trouble, probably.

But no sheriff walked in, no deputies, and at eight a.m. he let the waitress refill his mug. She was forty or so and on the big side and she had a bright patch of pink on her neck he took to be a birthmark. Her tag said RHONDA.

"You sure you don't want some real breakfast, hon?" she said, regarding with an unhappy look the untouched half of his buttered toast. The other half he'd swallowed just so he could take his heart pills and not vomit them right back up.

"Thank you, but I gotta watch my figure," he said, and there was a half beat of nothing before she cocked her head back and laughed.

"Hon, you call that a figure?"

When she'd gone away again he sat drinking his coffee until he'd emptied the mug—no sheriff, no deputies—and then he left a few bills on the counter and walked out a free man, a free citizen of his own country, and he walked to his car and got behind the wheel and drove back past the café and pulled into the lot of the mechanic's garage and parked off to the side, out of the way of the closed bay door.

An electronic chime sounded when he entered, and there was no one at the desk and he waited to see if someone would respond to the chime. Stink of grease and tire rubber and sweat, decades of it in the crammed little office and no one coming, so he stepped into the garage through the open door and stood watching the only man in there heft a tire from off its bolts and bounce it away on the blackened floor. Finally Sutter said Hey and the man looked up from his work and said Hey yourself. Stood and came over, working a red rag in his hands. He was a squat and strong-looking man with enlarged gray eyes behind thick lenses. Midforties. His face was not marked, scratched, in any way.

"Can I help you?" the man said.

Sutter looked for a name on the blue mechanic's shirt but saw none. "Maybe so," he said. "Are you the owner?"

"I am, and my old man before me and his old man before that." He stuffed the rag in his back pocket and set his hands to his hips.

"Any chance you've got a young man name of Bud works for you?"

"Bud," said the man, merely repeating the name. He took Sutter in anew. Sutter wearing his regular canvas jacket, now. His jeans, his khaki shirt. "You mind if I ask who's asking—not to be rude or nothin."

"Not at all. Tom Sutter," he said and put out his hand.

"Pete Yoder."

"Glad to meet you, Pete. I'm just asking because this guy Bud gave me a jump up in Decorah awhile back, said if I was ever down this way I should stop by the shop and say hey."

"Which shop did he say?"

"Said best shop in town."

"Well, you found it. But I only got one man working for me and his name ain't Bud."

"Well, shoot," said Sutter. "What's his name?"

"I just told you. Pete Yoder."

Sutter smiled. "That's how I liked it myself, back in the day. My name on the door, my name on the work. Well," he said, turning to go.

"What kind of work was that? If you don't mind me asking."

Sutter turned back. "I was a sheriff for fifteen years."

"That so. Whereabouts?"

"Up north. Just over the state line."

"That so." Yoder adjusted his smudged lenses. "Then you probably know Sheriff Moran."

"He used to be a deputy of mine," said Sutter.

Yoder nodded and studied his own fingers, front and back. He pulled the rag from his pocket and began working it in his hands again. "Well, Sheriff. I reckon this brake job ain't gonna do itself."

"Sorry to keep you from it."

"Sorry I couldn't help you. There's two other garages in town, but I'm guessing you already know that."

Yoder walked him back into the office, and there he paused, and Sutter paused too.

"How do you like that rig there, Sheriff?" He was looking at a grid of black bars over the office window. Raw steel frame bolted to cinderblock. Welds of dull pewter, unpainted. New-looking.

"I'd say you had you a break-in," Sutter said.

"You'd say right. Twelve hundred dollars' worth of hand tools, according to the insurance, walking right out that door. But you can't buy those kind of tools no more. Those were my granddad's tools." He looked away. Then he looked back and said, "Not sayin nothin against your old deputy, Sheriff. But ever time I think of some son of a bitch walking around in here, taking his sweet time, and then walking right out that door with my tools . . ." He looked like he might spit, but spit where, on his own floor? "I know it's just tools," he said. "But I think I could kill a son of a bitch if I got the chance."

19

By the time he pulled into the parking lot of the garage the cab of the van was no warmer than when he pulled out of his drive—or if it was warmer it was his own body heat that had warmed it—and Gordon left the engine running so there'd be no doubt, so no one could sit there running the engine for an hour before they could tell him what he already knew, which was that his goddam heater was shot.

He felt a little better for the day off, for the night's rest without fever dreams, but still his eyes ached in the winter light and his body felt like he'd fallen down a flight of stairs.

Just a few other cars and trucks in the lot and none he recognized other than Wabash's Ford pickup and the black Crown Vic he kept as a loaner. Anyway the garage opened for business at seven thirty so she would have already come and gone by now and would not return again until five o'clock to pick the boy up again, just as she'd done when the boy worked for him. That other lifetime. And he would go to another garage if he could find one within twenty miles that did not take twice as long and charge twice as much and do half as good a job and was somehow also run by Dave Wabash, a man he'd known since high school and who sent customers his way just as he sent them Wabash's way.

He stepped into the office and stood there a full minute, waiting, tasting more than smelling, thanks to his jammed-up sinuses, the gasoline and tire rubber, before finally he pushed through the glass door, stained with many black handprints, into the garage and made his way toward the only sound, which was the ratcheting of a socket wrench—steady, rhythmic, like the call of a great bug. He tracked the sound to the far bay, where a man stood under a gray sedan, or did not stand exactly, as the lift only went so high, and there was no pit and a man had to stoop under the chassis or else scoot around in a chair on casters—Wabash too cheap to buy new lifts, which was fine by Gordon if it kept his prices down.

All he could see of this man was his dark-blue mechanic's pants and his leather workboots, and Gordon said, "That you under there, Dave?" and there was a final turn of the wrench before the boots shifted and took a step and a face appeared. Not Wabash's face or the face of any other mechanic he knew, but the face of the boy he'd not seen in ten years, and seeing it appear now from beneath the car did something to Gordon's legs so that he had to take a step to get his balance. His heart rolling like a boat. Time rolling back.

But of course it was not that boy—he knew it before his heart or his legs knew it. It was the brother, Marky, who he'd seen maybe half a dozen times since those days, usually right here in this garage, the boy blurting out, *Heya Mister Burke!* as if he had no sense of time, no sense of history. And maybe he didn't. Maybe he was the only one.

You could tell him from his brother by the eyes, always the eyes, if that's all you had to go on: the lights on in there but a different kind of lights. You didn't say *retard* anymore; there were other words, though Gordon hadn't learned them. The boy had not been expected to live, once upon a time, and now here he was—twenty-nine, thirty?—big as a horse and working on a car. That was the thing, that was what threw him, and Gordon said without thinking, "What the hell you doing under there?" As if it was his place and not Wabash's. As if he'd caught the kid trying to sweat copper in the back room of the Plumbing & Supply, trying to blow himself up and the whole building with him.

The boy grinned and said, "Heya Mister Burke!" and showed him the socket wrench and told him in a burst of Marky-talk, within which Gordon caught just enough English, that he was pulling the pan because the gasket was bad and Jeff had told him to do it . . . Gordon pinching his eyes shut against the pain the boy's yammer put into his brain and saying, "Where's Wabash, Marky? Where's your boss?" to which the boy gave a big shrug and went on yammering.

"All right, all right," said Gordon, "where's Jeff, then?" and as he said it a door squawked open at the far end of the garage and Jeff Goss stepped out, tucking his blue shirt back in, behind him the sound of the refilling toilet tank Gordon himself had installed maybe twenty years ago, Goss looking down as he walked and then looking up and stopping—or almost stopping at the sight of Gordon standing beside the crouched and yammering Marky, and then continuing on toward them. No taller now than he'd been at sixteen, still looking up to look you in the eye. Not the worker Marky's brother had been—or that Marky had been, for that matter—not even close. But he'd hired the three of them as a set, figuring three boys who were almost like three brothers would be stronger than three who weren't. That the best of them would shape the other two and bring out something better in all three—or at least something better than had been there otherwise.

And then you wake up one day wishing you'd never set eyes on any one of them. Wishing they'd never been born. That they'd died all together in a car accident at sixteen.

"Hey there, Mr. Burke," Goss said. Then, to Marky: "Big Man, give it a rest," and the stream of Marky-talk abruptly stopped, as if by some valve.

"Wabash has got him working on cars now?" Gordon said.

"That ain't work, Mr. Burke, he's just draining the oil pan."

Gordon turned to Marky again, the boy standing hunchbacked under the chassis still, looking from Gordon to Goss and cranking the wrench handle slowly with one hand as he held the socket in the other, as if to raise some tricky bolt from his own fist.

Gordon grunted and said, "Maybe you better tell him that. He thinks he's pulling the whole goddam pan and changing out the gasket."

Goss gave a small jerk of the head and put on a smirk. "He tell you that?"

"That's what I heard."

"Heck. He don't know himself what he's saying, Mr. Burke, you know that. He gets going sometimes he just can't stop—can you, Big Man." Goss grinning at the boy under the car until Gordon wanted to cuff him one to the back of his head and Marky standing under the old lift like he was just waiting for it to give out and squash him, the dope, and finally Gordon couldn't stand it and, gesturing at the boy, he said, "Get out from under there already, you dope, you're making me nervous," and Marky came out from under the car and stood to his full height, somehow still looking like someone who was worried about cracking his head on something.

Gordon turned once more to Goss and said, "Where's your boss?" and Goss told him Wabash was out on call with the wrecker, wouldn't be back until after lunch, and was it something he could help him with? Gordon standing between these two boys, daylight burning, his head pounding . . . Jeff and Marky waiting, watching as their old boss took his forehead in his hand and shook his head and said, "Son of a bitch." Then said to Jeff, "It's the goddam heater," and turned and walked back toward the office.

Jeff followed, and Marky stood alone by the raised car, still turning the socket in his fist and saying nothing to his old boss, no *Good-bye Mister Burke!* Because Jeff had given him a look, a face that said *you just be quiet Marky, you don't need to say good-bye to Mister Burke*, and he watched them go into the office and then watched them through the bay windows as they crossed the lot toward the van, good old Mr. Burke, who looked mean and talked mean but wasn't really mean because he let you work for him in the Plumbing Supply when you were just kids, you and Danny and Jeff, and Danny still lived at home, at the old house in town, not the farmhouse, and Poppa had died and *this is how you dry-mop a floor Marky, and this is how you wet-mop a floor*, Mr. Burke pushing the mops awhile and then handing them to you and patting you two times on the back to get you going, always two times, *one two off you go, and here's how you clean a window and here's how you keep the supplies neat on the shelves and here's what you say if a customer asks you something, you say just one second ma'am or just one second sir while I go get Mister Burke or Danny or Jeff*, and all the nice people coming into the Plumbing Supply and saying *Heya Marky* and Danny always there to show you stuff Mr. Burke wouldn't show you like how to clean the copper fittings and paint them with the little flux brush, *stand back now while I light this torch and don't ever do this without me Marky, I'm serious, this is just for show*, and the hissing gas and the scritch-scritch of the sparky thing and then the WOOSH of the flame *and see here how you heat up the joint until the copper turns that bright new penny color and the flux starts to bubble in the seam and then you touch the solder to the seam, see how it just kinda sucks into the joint and when you see the solder all the way around the seam you know the joint is filled and you can stop then and that's how you sweat copper Marky and don't ever EVER tell Mister Burke I showed you that, you promise, you swear on a monkey's uncle?*

And you never told Mr. Burke anything Danny said not to, not even the time Holly showed you the jewelry she had in a shoebox in her closet and made you swear you wouldn't tell a soul and Danny said where'd you get all this and Holly said the mall and Danny said you better be careful and she said I am careful dummy, that's why it's here and not in the mall, and later after you went home Danny made you promise all over again not to tell anyone about the jewelry and you said but stealing's bad Danny, and he said I know it is Marky but telling on people is worse, especially your friends, especially after you promised not to, and after that you didn't want to go upstairs into Holly's room anymore . . .

You never told Mr. Burke anything you promised not to, not about sweating copper in the back room or about Holly's jewelry, but Mr. Burke got mad anyway, Mr. Burke got so mad and so sad and so quiet after Holly went into the river, and then one day after the sheriff came and asked questions you couldn't go to the Plumbing Supply any more, you or Danny or Jeff, and Holly was dead, and Danny coming home from the cabin without Wyatt, and Danny so mad too and so quiet, and then going away to Saint Louis and to Houston and to Albuquerque and only coming home at Christmas and some years not even that, poor old Wyatt so sad, he doesn't understand anything you tell him he just looks at you and he looks at the door and he sniffs all around the house looking for Danny and he lies in his bed, Danny's bed, and he doesn't want to play anymore and just let him be, Marky, Momma says, he's old, and he just lies around old and sad and waiting waiting waiting . . .

20

THE GARAGES WERE just something to do—one thing he knew he could wrap up by midmorning, be back up to Rochester before noon to check on her and see if he could take her home. It was something to do other than sitting around going crazy.

Like driving down here with your sheriff's jacket isn't crazy. Questioning that poor girl at the station.

"I know what I'm doing."

I know you know what you're doing. That's what scares me.

"Hey, I'm her father—all right?" he said, but she said no more.

At the third and last garage, three miles from the second, he pulled in and parked and walked slowly past the three bay doors, one of them just raising and four or five men at work in there, a face here, a face there, but mostly their backs, their blue mechanic's shirts. Lug-nut removers shrilling. A radio tuned to country. In the office a redheaded woman sat tapping at her keyboard, squinting at her screen. Thirtyish. On the wall behind her a round clockface set in a small-scale Goodyear tire said ten minutes to ten.

"Hi there how can I help you," said the woman, and Sutter waited for her to look up.

"Yes, ma'am. I'm here to see the young fella who worked on my car."

"All right, what's his name?"

"Well, that's a good question." Sutter scratched his head. "I wanna say . . . Bud?"

"Bud?" She frowned. "There's no Bud here. How long ago was this?"

"Coupla weeks back."

"No Bud then, either. There's never been a Bud worked here since I've been here."

"How long is that?"

"Sir?"

"How long have you worked here."

"Too long. You sure it was here you had the work done?"

Sutter glanced again at the tire clock. "Well, I'll just talk to someone else then."

"All right, who do you want to talk to?"

"A mechanic."

"Any mechanic?"

"Your best one."

"Best one? I couldn't say, sir. It depends on the problem."

Sutter placed his fingertips lightly on the countertop. He nodded toward the glass door that led to the garage. "How about I just go on in there and talk to one?"

"I'm sorry, sir, customers aren't allowed, for safety reasons."

Sutter smiled. "All right." He lifted his fingertips from the counter. *How about just fuck it then, how about that?*

Then aloud he said: "How about that young one then, what's his name."

"Which young one?"

"I forget his name. The tough one."

She made the face of guesswork: "Ryan . . . ?"

"That's him," Sutter said. "I'll talk to him."

She smiled thinly and said, "He might be on break, but I'll try," and she picked up her handset and pushed a button and said into the receiver, "Ryan to the front desk, please, Ryan to the front desk," and through the glass door at the same instant came the same request in electronic echo.

She hung up and regarded him. "There's coffee there, and chairs."

"Thanks," Sutter said and stood where he was. He looked at the tire clock again and checked it against his watch. The woman resumed tapping on her keyboard. *Just go back out and walk in there and look each of them in the face and walk out and get in your car, what are they gonna do, call the cops?*

He'd already turned toward the glass door he'd come in through when the other door opened and a young man walked in wiping his hands in a rag and looking around. No one to see but the woman behind the counter and Sutter, and Sutter's heart slapping once on his breastbone when he saw the lines on the young man's face—four neat scab lines running from cheekbone to jaw, like he'd been swiped by a large housecat. The markings gave him a strange, primitive look, like some Indian brave in the making, dressed weirdly in blue shirt and blue Dickies and grease-darkened workboots, and Sutter's first impulse was to grab the young man by the throat.

"Help you?" the young man said, stepping toward Sutter. RYAN stitched in red in the white oval on his shirt.

"Hey, Ryan."

"Hey," said the young man, taking a closer look.

"Tom Wilson."

"Sure. Hey, Tom." Brown eyes half-hooded and underslung with blue shadows. Brown hair too, buzzed on the sides and thick on top, tossed and peaked. Sutter gave the young man's right hand a shake and let go. He described his problem and the young man was happy to follow him out to have a look and a listen. Sutter pulling the hood release and turning over the engine, then stepping out and standing beside the young man, who was aiming his ear toward the whirring pulleys, the snaky blur of the belt.

"I don't hear it," he said, and Sutter said, "That figures. Doing it all week long and now it stops."

"Probably the tensioner rod. They do that on these old Fords. Sounds like somebody dumped a jar of bait crickets under your hood."

"Yep," Sutter said. "What do you drive?"

The mechanic's eyes swung up from the engine. He looked at Sutter, then gave a slight toss of his chin toward a half dozen parked cars and trucks. "That Chevy there."

"The two-tone?"

"Yep."

"'Eighty-seven?" said Sutter.

"'Eighty-five."

"They don't make 'em like that anymore, do they."

"No, sir."

They stood listening to Sutter's motor.

"Well," said Sutter. "Looks like I wasted your time, Ryan."

The young man looked at him again. Trying to place him. He put fingertips lightly to the scab lines on his face, one to each line, as if to make a chord on them. Then he said, "Hell," and swung down the hood. "It's the boss's time, not mine."

"I hear that."

They stood there, Sutter holding the young man in place with his eyes.

"That's some scratch."

"What?" He raised his hand again but stopped short of touching his face. "That ain't nothin."

"Cat?"

"What?"

"Looks like a cat scratch."

The young man looked at him and looked away. "It ain't nothin." And turned to go.

"Well," said Sutter, his heart thudding. "Thanks anyway."

"No problem."

"Say hey to Bud for me."

The young man paused.

"Bud?"

"Bud. He said go see Ryan at Anderson Auto."

The young man nodded, sucked at something in his teeth, and when he said nothing more, asked no more questions—*How do you know old Bud?*—Sutter knew he'd made a mistake, although he wasn't sure where, which was the worst kind. He saw the young man glance at his Minnesota plate before he moved on. But then after a few steps he turned back to toss Sutter a kind of two-fingered salute and an empty smile. "If those crickets come back," he said, "you bring her on back and we'll get her fixed up."

21

THE WOMAN PUT him on hold and in those minutes Sutter ordered a coffee from the waitress and received it, stirred milk into it, and drank half of it down. From the booth window he could just see the garage a half block away, the two-tone Chevy in the lot.

At last the doctor came on the line to tell him that Audrey was doing much better today, stronger, her temperature considerably down, and he was taking her off the drugs.

"When can I take her home?"

"Let me have another look at her after lunch, and we'll see about sending her home this afternoon. But no promises."

Sutter hung up, then sat staring at the phone's home screen, at the image of his daughter and himself smiling out at him, that time she got him to go skating with her, both of them red-faced and wearing black knit caps like a father-daughter burglar team. Then he dialed the same number and asked the nurse on duty to let Audrey know he'd called and that he'd be coming in after lunch to see her.

The waitress returned and he found the simplest thing on the menu and she wrote that down on her pad and collected the menu and went away again— unsmiling, no-nonsense; another breed entirely from the one at the café, with the birthmark.

He drank his coffee and watched the garage. He pulled out his wallet and his notebook with the names and numbers of the garages and set them before him, and after a while he opened his wallet and slid the white business card free and held it at its four points between his thumbs and forefingers.

She might remember more when she's feeling better, Tom. I know you know that.

Keep it, Ed. I've got your number in the phone.

Well, take the card anyway. And Tom . . . I've got this. I promise you.

SHERIFF EDWARD MORAN, the card said, in raised black. Little sheriff's star up in the corner that caught the light like gold, that looked damn near like the real deal. One good-looking card, Sheriff.

He looked out the window for a long while. His phone was under his hand and he kept turning it round and round on the tabletop.

You could just take the bastard's picture and show it to her.

That still wouldn't prove it.

Be enough to bust him, though.

It'd still be his word against hers. Only one thing can prove he was there. Hard evidence, pal. I know it.

He took another sip of coffee, then picked up the phone and punched in the number and held the phone to his ear. The woman who answered was the same one he'd spoken to thirty minutes ago, in person, and he said, "Yes, is Ryan working today?"

"Ryan Radner?"

Sutter hesitated. "Is there another Ryan?"

"Not today there's not."

"Well, Radner's the one I want."

"Did you need to speak to him?"

"No, ma'am. I was just wondering how late he'll be there today so I don't miss him."

"He'll be here till five today, sir. That's when we close."

"Thank you very much," Sutter said.

"You're very welcome, sir."

HE WAS AT the hospital at half past noon and when he looked around the doorjamb she was sitting up with a spoon halfway to her mouth and she looked so much like her mother in that bed, in that place, that his heart went out from under him, and she looked at him, the spoon halted in midair, and said, "—What?"

He corrected his face, his heart, and stepped into the room.

"Nothing," he said. He held up the white paper bag, and her eyes widened.

"Is that a Portman's bag?"

"Kept it in the trunk all the way up here."

"Strawberry?"

"What else?"

She set aside the pudding and pulled the large paper cup with its coat of frost from the bag and fastened her lips on the straw and caved her cheeks and shut her eyes.

The doctor floated in, the wings of his open labcoat riding his currents, greeted Sutter and stepped up to Audrey. "Don't mind me," he said, and she went on sucking at the straw while he shone his penlight into her eyes, put his stethoscope on her back and on her chest, held her cast out of view from her and pressed his ballpoint pen to the tips of her fingers, asking her to wiggle each finger when she felt it. He seemed to like all he saw and heard, but at the end of it he said he wanted to keep her one more night just to be on the safe side, and Audrey shook her head at Sutter and Sutter said, "Whatever you say, Doc," and the doctor floated away again.

She released the straw and pushed her head into the pillow as if for a better view of him, standing there.

"Did you sleep at all last night, Sheriff?"

"I got my share."

"I think we need to go home."

"You heard the doctor."

"I don't think he sees the big picture."

"What's the big picture?"

"That staying here isn't making me any better and it's making you worse."

"It's not making me worse."

"It isn't making you any better."

He rubbed his open hand on his thigh to warm it and then placed it on her forearm. "It never has and it never will, sweetheart."

"Oh, Daddy, don't be morbid."

"It's just the truth."

"That's not what you said when Mom was sick."

"That was different."

"How was it different?"

"You were just a little girl then."

"Maybe I needed to hear the truth."

He kept his hand on her arm. "Maybe. But I couldn't say it. Not then."

She stared at the ceiling. "I missed her funeral."

It took him a moment. Caroline Price. "Yes, sweetheart. I'm sorry."

"I want to go down there. I want to see them. Her family."

He nodded. "All right. When you're stronger."

"I don't want to wait."

"Well." He squeezed her arm.

"Well what."

"Well, they may want you to. Wait, I mean."

She turned to look at him. To see his eyes.

"They don't want to see me, you're saying," she said.

"I don't know what they want, sweetheart. I can't even imagine. But I think maybe those folks need a little time just to themselves."

She stared at the ceiling again. She wiped at her eyes.

"They don't think they want to see me," she said, "but they do. I'm the one person they want to see."

He stayed until she slept again, then stayed a while longer just watching her face, the faint tremblings of her eyelids, seeing her face from long ago, a little girl in her bed, night after night when he'd read her to sleep. And then he saw that hand, Radner's greasy right hand pressed over her mouth, and his heart began to bang again. Finally he got up and crossed the room and drew four purple rubber gloves from the size L dispenser and tucked them into his jacket pocket and walked out of the room.

Sutter, she said once he was in the car again, on the road again. When she wanted to be sure she had his attention she called him Sutter.

"Please, woman," he said aloud. "Just . . . for a little while here."

22

WABASH HAD THE one loaner and Gordon could take that or he could wait for Wabash to get back with the wrecker, Goss advised him, and then Goss himself could drive him home—he couldn't leave Marky alone at the garage—but if it was a bad heater core, as Goss would bet dollars to donuts it was, then Gordon would have to leave the van for a day at least, because to get to the heater core you had to remove the AC housing and to get that out you had to remove the blower and the filters and to take those out you had to pull the dashboard and to pull the dashboard you had to—*Jesus Christ, gimme the loaner*, Gordon had said, and he'd taken the key from Goss and left the van and all his tools and his supplies behind and he would have to cancel his appointments for the day and that was just as well anyway, way he felt.

The loaner was solid, clean, fast. A ten-year-old Crown Vic Interceptor that Wabash had picked up at the Minneapolis PD auction and painted all black, but even so when you were behind the wheel you had the feeling that everyone who saw you coming saw the black-and-white and they slowed way, way down or they hit the turn signal and turned off the road you were on, because a certain kind of man knew the shape of the Crown Vic whatever the paint job and did not like having that shape in his rearview one bit.

Gordon drove the car slowly through town, but when he hit Old Highway 20 he opened her up and let her run. Clear, cold winter day with no snow or ice on the road, the car soaking up the sun, heat pouring from its vents, and he did not ease off the gas until he hit the narrow bridges that crossed over the Upper Black Root as it snaked its way south toward the state line and its new name, the Lower Black Root . . . upper, lower, all the same river as far as the Indians were concerned, back in the way-back days before highways and bridges and Crown Vics.

Not Indians, Daddy: Native Americans.

Twelve years old and her eyes bright with knowledge. With education—with wonder at his lack of it.

Do you think the Sioux, or the Crow, or the Cheyenne changed the name of the river at the Iowa border? she wanted to know.

Sure, he said, teasing—such seriousness, such big eyes! *Why not?*

*Daddy—do you think they had borders at all? A line that said 'America' on one side and 'Canada' on the other? No, they didn't. It was all one land, all one river, all part of the big open everything. Until we came along. Lying to them, cheating them, killing them but keeping their names, Minnesota, Iowa, Dakota—*ticking these off on pink, serious fingers—*Mississippi, Miami . . .*

We, she'd said. The bloody old work of her own granddad's granddads: kill off the people, kill off their buffalo, kill off their songs and their stories but keep their names.

That young girl gone now too, lost to the river that was the same river whatever you called it and that emptied into a greater river that once had no name and that emptied into an ocean that once had no name, and that ocean evaporating into the sky and coming back down in water that ran over the land whatever you called it and found the creeks, and the creeks found the rivers once again . . . and so ran his thoughts, winding north through Sioux country in a machine that spewed from its backside the smoke of creatures that lived and died a million years before any man, Sioux or otherwise, took his first breath, until he reached the sign that warned him of a reduced speed limit and he slowed the Crown Vic and drove lawfully into the little town, and stopped at the one light and then sat there after it had gone green, no one behind him, no one anywhere that he could see, and after the light turned red he drove through it and no alarms sounded, no sirens wailed, and he drove on.

Fields buried in snow, windbreaks of black winter cottonwoods and then the old farmhouse rising out of the land just as he remembered it—twelve, thirteen years ago that would've been. Anyway it was before she moved out here and before her father passed, because she'd asked him to come out and talk to the old man, who seemed to think there was something wrong with the septic—he was smelling it all the time now, and no wonder because he hadn't had the thing pumped in three years, and there was a broken pipe, and it was high summer and by the end of the day Gordon was so covered in filth and flies she'd turned the hose on him like a dog, the two of them laughing like they hadn't laughed in a long time. Since before Roger died. Since before Meredith left.

Thin line of smoke rising now from the chimney and that could mean she was home or not home, but then he saw her green wagon in the drive and the sight of it did something funny to his guts, to his heart, and he almost drove on; she might recognize the Crown Vic as Wabash's loaner but she would not put it together with him.

Unless the boy told her so, when she picked him up later in the day; unless the boy told her Mr. Burke had been at the garage that morning and had driven off with the Crown Vic, and then she'd know it was him who'd driven by, who'd slowed down but hadn't turned in, and he said, "Just to hell with everything," and braked and made the turn in time, fishtailing a little in the packed snow of the drive.

He parked behind the wagon and stepped from the Crown Vic and shut the door and looked for her to come to one of the windows so he wouldn't have to stand on that porch waiting for her to answer the door. But she didn't come to any window and he was making his way to the porch when he heard something off to his right, toward the back of the property, out of view, and he stopped where he was, ear-cocked, until he heard it again: a muted, earthy thunk. Like something pounding at slow intervals on the stony ground.

He turned back and trudged through the snow alongside the house, making his way to the backyard, where the sound was louder—hard metal and hard earth and also the breaths, the grunts, of human exertion—and as he came around the corner he saw the figure in the middle of the yard, standing beside the T of the iron clothesline bar. A man's canvas workcoat, his watchman's cap, his rawhide gloves. The man standing knee-deep in the snow and not moving, taking a moment, gathering his strength and his breath before he raised the pickax shoulder-high and swung once more at the frozen earth, dull ring of iron, sharp grunt of effort in a high register. Not a man, of course. A woman. Rachel Young, dudded up in her dad's old workgear.

Somehow—maybe her exertions, maybe the noise of the pickax—she didn't hear him until he was nearly at her shoulder, and then she turned abruptly and faced him, the pickax held crossways to her body, smoke huffing from her mouth and nose, her eyes pink-veined and wet, and there she stood, trying to make sense of him. Gordon trying to make sense of her, the pickax, the rough box of space she'd cleared in the snow down to the turf, big enough for her to stand in and to swing at with the tool. And only then, after he'd taken all this in, did he understand that the darkness in the snow to her left, that dark bundle, was the old dog, Wyatt, wrapped in an old blanket.

She held the pickax as if to stop him, as if to meet him in battle—seeing him, not seeing him, seeing God knows what in those raw eyes, but when he said her name, "Rachel. Rachel . . ." and reached for the pickax, she lowered it. Or the pickax lowered itself, by its own weight. Like something she never could have lifted in the first place.

He took one step forward into the space she'd cleared and took the pickax from her and held it one-handed at his side as she fell sobbing to his chest.

23

It was just dark when they began coming out of the garage. A light snow falling through the headlights of their cars and trucks as they started them up and pulled out of the lot one by one and onto the street, some going left, some right.

Sutter tailed the two-tone pickup as it crossed through town, as it passed under an old railroad overpass, as it drove another half mile down industrial streets before turning, finally, into the lot of a small bar with the name JACK'S in failing red neon over the door. He watched Radner park and get out of the truck, wearing a billed cap now, and cross the lot toward the gray metal door and pull the door open and step inside. Then he parked his own car and gapped the window and killed the engine. He lit a cigarette and sat watching the gray door, the few other cars and trucks in the lot. It was Friday, a quarter past five, and as he sat there another truck, a black Ford, pulled into the lot and two men got out and slammed the doors and walked toward the gray door and opened it and went inside.

A red dust of snow fell before the neon sign and vanished. He smoked, and when the cigarette was gone he stubbed it out and turned the key and put the sedan in gear and drove out of the lot.

When he returned to the lot ten minutes later he was on foot, and he walked up to Radner's Chevy and tried the driver's door, then walked around and tried the passenger's. He glanced around the lot; he watched the door to the bar, the red-stained flecks of snow in the neon, then pulled the thin metal tool from his hip and fed it down the glass into the guts of the door and felt with it for perhaps a second before he gave one quick yank and slipped the tool back under his belt.

The dome light came on with the opened door and he got into the truck and pulled the door shut and removed the plastic light cover and took out the little bulb and put it in the ashtray, replaced the cover and got out of the truck again and stood in the open door. He adjusted his mini MagLite for its tightest spot and roved it over the benchseat and the junk that lay there: plastic Mountain Dew bottles, mechanic's rags, a rumpled back issue of *Field & Stream*, a black watchman's cap, a flattened box of tissues. He probed the light under the benchseat on both sides of the tranny hump and saw nothing but garbage and dust and a long metallic ice scraper. In the glovebox he found a handgun, a Colt .45, with much of the factory bluing worn from the slide. The safety was on and a round was chambered. He slipped the gun into his jacket pocket, then slid the benchseat all the way forward and ran the spot over the garbage behind it, stirring it with his free hand. He saw a skinny wooden length and his heart jumped, but when he pulled the stick free it was another ice scraper, this one about as old as the truck.

He stood in the open door for a long while, darting the beam here and there, over and over again. Finally he slid the benchseat back and shut the door and peeled the rubber gloves from his hands and stuffed them in his pocket and wiped his slick hands on the sleeves of his jacket. He found his cigarettes and got one lit and, leaning his weight against the front fender, watched the gray door of the bar and the snow that fell red and silent in the light above it.

24

WHEN SHE TURNED from the stove he'd taken the chair at the table where her grandfather would sit in the evenings bent over his ledgers, sipping mug after mug of boiled black coffee, Gordon taking the chair with no thought of her memories, of course, but only because it gave him a direct line of sight, through the window, to the fire in the yard—the fire burning strong now, sending white smoke into the sky and filling the deep snow before it with a strange trembling blush. Good old hardwood this was, he said, oak and walnut, and after it had burned down to cinders they could dig the grave and it would all be done by the time she had to go pick up Marky from the garage and tell him . . . what? That their old Wyatt, their old friend, was gone forever.

Rachel turned from the stove with the two mugs and glanced at her feet so as not to step on him, not to trip over him—hot tea everywhere, shattered mugs, shattered bones!—and her heart broke again because he was not there, was nowhere in sight and never would be again, and she fought back her tears because it was only a dog after all and what was that next to the loss of a child, a daughter, your only child?

She set one of the mugs before Gordon and he looked away from the window to thank her. He hooked his big finger through the handle but did not lift the mug, instead sat looking into the steam, and how strange he should choose today of all days to show up, so that she would not have to be alone, not yet. Even if he just sat there, even if he never said another word.

He did not look up until she'd sat down and then he looked slowly around the kitchen, and when his gaze came around to her she wanted to hold it, to read his thoughts, but he moved on again, back to the window and the fire beyond. The pale tips of flame rising above the snow, the thick and twisting smoke.

"It's a good old house out here," he said. "It's good you held on to it."

She could just see his reflection in the glass. She lifted her mug and sipped and set it down again with care. The furnace had come on and the dusty heat blew on the dog's empty blankets where they lay before the vent and blew the smell of him into the room.

"It gets noisy here, sometimes," she said.

"Noisy?"

"Yes. Walking sounds where no one's walking. Smells too. Cooking smells where no one's cooking. Bathroom smells where no one's been for hours."

"You might have that toilet gasket checked."

"I might have my gasket checked, you mean."

"Didn't say that. The mind gets . . . active when you're on your own, that's all. It can get to be a tricky son of a gun."

His big hand lay on the table beside his mug, palm-down. Her own hand might cover half of it. She remembered standing on his porch that day in October as he held the stormdoor open but would not ask her in, nothing in his eyes to say he needed her or even knew her name, a gray-faced man whose heart had been torn out. The very worst thing, the unspeakable thing. He didn't know then that the sheriff was looking for Danny. And neither did she.

Gordon turned the mug, and watching the turning said, "I guess you know all about those girls by now. Those two girls that went into the river."

"Yes. You were the first person I thought of. I wondered if you'd seen it on the news, or if anyone would tell you. I . . ." She didn't finish. Didn't know how to finish.

"I drove on up to Rochester, night before last, to the hospital," he said.

She watched him.

"I thought I wanted to see her," he said, "but when I got there I realized what I really wanted to see was her father. Sutter. Wanted to see his face, what it looked like now."

"And did you?"

"I did." He nodded slowly. "He's a sick man. He doesn't hardly look like the same man." He stared into the mug. "I guess I wanted to know did he have any better understanding now. Did he understand any better why I said the things I said to him. Back then."

She waited. "And did he?"

He tilted his mug and frowned. "It just isn't the same situation. What happened to his daughter, he'll get over that. He'll just pay more attention to every part of her life from here on out. Or as much of it as he gets to see. He won't carry this thing that I carry around with me every day and every hour, these"—his hand circled in a buffing motion to the right of his temple—"thoughts that go through my head, these . . . ideas."

He lowered the hand and looked at her from under his eyebrows, and a coldness poured into her.

He turned back to the window. The fire was burning down, the smoke thinner now and calmer.

"Is that why you—" she began, and faltered. "Is that why you came out here? Because of those two girls?"

"I don't know. Maybe." He turned back to her. "I saw your boy this morning. Marky."

"You did?"

"At the garage. I had to take the van in. I hadn't seen him in a while, I guess. For a second there I thought it was the other one. And then I remembered that that boy was long gone, and—"

He stopped. She was blotting up her tears with the handkerchief he'd given her earlier, outside, when she'd first turned and seen him standing there. The thin cloth damp now and no longer smelling so strongly of him as it did that first time.

"Ah, damn it," he said. "Don't listen to me." Shifting his weight in the old chair. Patting the tabletop with his fingers. "I never should of come out here like this, out of the blue like this. I must be crazy."

"Don't say that. Please don't say that. I don't know why you came but you came. You came, Gordon, and I'm so . . . I'm so grateful."

He turned once more to the window, and so did she. The fire had burned down out of view. A weaker cloud of smoke rising into the dusk. The light had dimmed in the kitchen too; soon she'd have to go pick up Marky.

"I sure didn't come out here to talk about any of this," he said. His shoulders raised with a deep breath and lowered again. He did not look at her. "I drove up to Rochester two nights ago and I saw your boy this morning and I guess that's what put it in my head to see did you need any help out here." She was nodding, yes, wiping at her eyes. "And now it looks like that fire is near about spent," he said, "so why don't we go on out there and see about giving that old boy a proper place to rest."

25

AN HOUR LATER Radner pushed through the gray door and began to make his way to the truck, loose-legged and head-down, his face shielded by the bill of his cap.

Sutter got out of the truck and shut the passenger door behind him, wondering at the strangeness of his own legs, calling it the time he'd spent sitting in the cold truck waiting and not his nerves, or his sickness. He saw Radner look up at the slam of the truck door. Saw his eyes under the bill when he saw him, and saw his gait change hardly at all as he kept on, hands in his jacket pockets. He stopped a few feet short of the truck, of Sutter, and stood taking him in, jacket first, then the face. Then the rest, down to his boots.

"I know you," Radner said. "You're the man had me looking under his hood today."

In his breath cloud Sutter smelled the Seagram's and 7. A smell and a taste from the old days, before she got him to give it up for good.

"But you weren't wearing that jacket earlier," Radner said, raising one forefinger in the air and wagging it at him. Playacting a man who would not be duped.

"Is this your truck?" Sutter said.

Radner lowered the finger. "What's the trouble, Sheriff?" At the movement of Sutter's arm he glanced down, then showed his hands. "I'm an unarmed man here, Sheriff."

Sutter studied him. The hooded eyes. The smirking and wet, almost girlish lips. Sutter raised the gun. It was his father's old .38 revolver. Now his. He stepped aside and gestured with it.

"I want you to shut up and place your hands on the fender of the truck."

"What's this about, Sheriff?"

"What did I just say?"

Radner regarded him blankly, drunkenly. Then he stepped forward and put his hands on the fender of the truck.

"Spread your feet."

Radner spread his feet and Sutter patted him down. He collected the young man's keys and phone from his jacket pockets and slid them into his own. He glanced at the door of the bar. If anyone else came out it changed everything.

"Put your hands behind your head and lace your fingers."

Radner did so and Sutter gripped the fingers in his free hand and pocketed the .38. He pulled the bracelets from the hip pocket of his jeans and drew down Radner's left wrist and cuffed it, then drew down the right and cuffed it to its fellow.

Radner was glancing around the lot. "Where's that Ford of yours, Sheriff? With the Minnesota plates and no whattayacallit. Official insignia."

"I won't tell you again to shut up."

Sutter opened the truck door and gave Radner a push and Radner got himself in and Sutter shut the door, then walked around to the driver's side and got in. The smell of the young mechanic had already filled the cab: booze and grease and gasoline.

"Whatever this is—" Radner began, and Sutter struck him with the back of his hand.

Radner sat looking at his lap, tasting his lower lip with his tongue.

"You want to say anything else?" Sutter said. He saw Radner's eyes go to the door of the glovebox. "It's a short drive," Sutter said. "It won't kill you to keep that mouth shut till we get there."

The truck started up, the wipers swept snow from the glass, but under the snow was a film of ice and Sutter sat staring at it, his heart pounding—all that waiting and you never thought to scrape the windshield? He tried to crank down the window but it was either frozen or didn't work, and finally he reached under Radner's legs for the metallic scraper, got out of the truck again and went quickly and foolishly at the ice, and with each scrape he saw more of the cab, more of Radner, and it was like the reveal on one of those lotto games, one of those scratch-and-play cards, only this one told you not what you'd won but what you'd lost.

He turned left out of the lot and drove down the road two blocks and turned right, and then right again, down a lampless road where the buildings were all dark and window-boarded and the lots had not been plowed, and he pulled into a lot where the only tracks in the snow were his own tiretracks going in and the tracks of his boots coming out and he followed these to the back of the building, a one-time machine shop, according to the faded signage, and pulled up along-side his sedan and parked the truck and killed the engine.

He turned to Radner, but Radner was looking out the ragged hole Sutter had scraped, and Sutter looked too: the flat, undisturbed snow of the lot, the dark old building. The snow that fell on everything with no prejudice and no sound whatsoever.

Sutter got out of the truck and walked around with his eyes on Radner and opened the passenger door. "Get out."

Radner stared at him. The smirk gone from his lips. His face shining. Then he looked away. As if not seeing Sutter was the same as Sutter not being there.

Sutter took him by the arm and pulled him stumbling from the cab. He walked him a few steps and turned him around again.

"Get on your knees."

Radner did not. He said, "Sheriff, I'm not putting up any kind of resistance here."

Sutter stepped behind him and put his boot to the backs of Radner's knees, and down he went. He swatted the billcap from Radner's head and took the cuffs in his hands and jerked up on them and leaned over until his face was near Radner's right ear.

"Do you remember where you were three nights ago?"

"What?"

"You heard me."

"Three nights ago—?"

"Tuesday night."

Radner shook his head. "I got no idea. I swear. I coulda been anywhere."

"You weren't anywhere, you were at the Shell station on County Road F24 and you were assaulting two young women with your buddy."

"Hell I was."

"How'd you get those scratches on your face?"

"At work. A tire blew up in my face."

"You are full of shit."

Radner shook his head again. "Swear to God, Sheriff. Ask any of them at work. Ask Toby, he was standing right there."

Sutter's heart was banging. He saw his own ragged breaths bursting white into the air. The empty lot, the old machine shop, the falling snow, all seemed to be turning in some sickly way. You can still drop this. Right now. You can get into that sedan and just drive away. Go talk to Toby . . .

"You watch the news?" he said.

"What?"

"Do you watch the news."

"Yeah, sometimes." Radner groaned. "Please, Sheriff, you are breakin my arms."

"Do you know what happened to those two girls, after you ran them off the road down the riverbank?"

"I never did. I never ran nobody down no riverbank."

"One died, Ryan, and the other one almost did. So guess where that leaves you and your buddy."

"You got the wrong man, Sheriff. You got the wrong man."

"Assault, attempted rape, attempted murder on two counts, murder on one count."

"All right," Radner said, "so take me in. Haul me in, man. Let me talk to a real sheriff. Let me talk to a—" He howled. Sutter had raised the cuffs.

"Where is it?"

"Where's what?"

"You know what."

He shook his head. "I swear I don't."

"The backscratcher, Radner. Where is it?"

Radner craned his neck to look at him. Fear and pain in those dark eyes.

"You're crazy," Radner said. "You're just plain crazy. You better let me go before this gets any worse. I won't say nothin. People make mistakes, I get that. I won't go to the sheriff or nothin. You just go your way and I'll go mine, how about that, huh? What've you got to lose?"

Sutter was silent. His breaths smoking. His heart slamming. He looked up at the sky. Slow tumble of flakes, landing cold on his face and melting. Faintly there was the fishy, muddy smell of a river . . . but any river would be frozen and you wouldn't smell it, and then he understood that the smell came from Holly Burke—from her wet hair, from the air trapped in the white bag and escaping like breath when they unzipped it, and—

Tom, she said. *Sutter* . . .

Something buzzed at his side, and he heard the muted tune, and with his free hand he reached into his jacket pocket and fetched up the phone and along with it a louder rendition of the same tune that sounded in the emptiness of the lot like some tiny and maniacal bugler.

"Let me answer it," Radner said. "Let me talk to someone."

Sutter read the name on the screen, MARY ANNE, and with his thumb ended the tune, and with another press of his thumb shut the phone down. He returned it to his pocket, then raised his watch and looked at it. Like a man of appointments and schedules. Like a man who needed to be somewhere else and had been here too long. He stared at the watchface and he saw the three hands and he saw the time markers, but however he moved the watch it seemed to float in a blind spot in his vision and he couldn't read it, and this was somehow the most frightening thing, the thing that made him sick at heart.

He felt out the key in the clutter of his pocket and fitted it into the cuffs and pulled them away, and Radner pitched forward onto his palms in the snow and there he remained, like a man heaved up ashore.

Sutter stepped around him and stood where Radner could see his boots.

"Look up here."

Radner looked up. Sutter standing against the flecks of snow, the gray sky. Radner got up on his knees, rubbing at his wrists. He'd not been told to stay on his knees but he stayed on them just the same.

"Do you believe in God?" Sutter said.

"What?"

"You heard me."

Radner looked at him as if he'd never really seen him before.

"You ain't no sheriff. What are you?"

"Answer my question."

Radner hung his head and shook it. "God," he said. "What's he got to do with this?"

"That's a good question, but it's no answer."

Radner looked up again. Sutter watched his eyes. He could see that the boy was seeing last things, wondering at the coldness, the meaninglessness of it all. The unfairness—in a parking lot, in the snow? As a young girl might've looked up at pine trees, at the cold moon, as she was carried, or dragged, toward the river.

"Yes, sir," Radner said. "Yes sir I do believe in God. And Jesus too."

"Is that the truth?"

"I swear to God it is, Sheriff."

"Good," said Sutter. "In about thirty seconds I'm driving away from here and this never happened and you never saw me."

Sutter saw hope enter the young man's eyes like some drug.

"I never saw you," Radner said. "This never happened."

"But on one condition."

"Name it, Sheriff."

"I want you to raise your right hand and swear to God you had nothing to do with what happened to those two girls that night. At the gas station and at the river."

Radner raised his right hand, the palm clean and pink but the fingers stained with oil and grease—this stinking hand on his little girl's face—and he said gravely, "I swear it, Sheriff. I swear it to God and Jesus. I swear it on my mother's soul." And as the young man said these words Sutter pulled the other gun, Radner's .45, from his pocket and thumbed off the safety and took one step forward—

"Don't," said Radner.

—and put the barrel to the center of the raised hand and pulled the trigger and saw the hand whip away. Saw the pink cloud and thought he saw small bones from the center of the hand fly off into the snow and he knew that that hand would never again hold a wrench, or any other thing.

The gunshot rang off the back of the machine shop and flew from building to building until it became a volley of gunfire, a sudden shoot-out in the night. Radner's howls and curses followed but Sutter didn't hear them. He'd pulled a mechanic's rag from the benchseat and he was wiping down the steering wheel, the gear lever, the handles inside and out and he even wiped down the keys. Lastly he wiped the empty .45 and set it on the benchseat and shut the door.

Radner remained on his knees in the snow, folded over his hand and still cursing but quieter now, like a man in argument with himself.

"Here," said Sutter, and Radner looked up, white-faced, grimacing. He looked Sutter in the eye, then snatched the red rag from him and wrapped it around his hand. "I'm throwing your keys in the bed of the truck," Sutter said. "You find them and you drive yourself to the urgent care clinic on Highland. You know where that is?"

"Gimme my phone so I can call an ambulance."

"You don't need an ambulance."

Radner hung his head. A string of drool swinging from his lip. "Crazy moth-erfucker. Think they won't find you and lock your ass up?"

"They might," he said. "But I got a feeling after you think on it awhile you'll come to remember that you shot yourself in the hand. Happens every day to people even smarter than you." Then he walked to the sedan and got behind the wheel and turned over the engine and drove out the way he'd come, and the last thing he saw in the mirror before his view was blocked by the building was the dark figure rising from the snow and staggering toward the tailgate of the truck, and he did not hear the figure's curses but only saw them, bursting from its mouth and following its head in clouds of rage.

ON HIS WAY back through town he pulled over and sat thumbing through the contacts on Radner's phone. His heart was still pounding and would not let up. There was no Bud that he saw. He checked the texts but they only went back two days and no Bud there either. He checked the phone log— nothing. Bud as in "buddy." Jesus Christ. He saw that hand again, that filthy hand, the bits of pink and bone flying.

He wiped down the phone and got out of the car and stepped up to the blue public mailbox at the corner; there was the dull bong of the phone on the floor of the box, and he returned to the car and drove on. Past the last stoplight. Past the Shell station out there on the county road—same blond head in the window as before, bent over its puzzles as ever, steady as a monk, or a lifer in her cell. Over the trestle bridge, over the river. North.

Silence in the car. Sutter waiting for her to say something, anything—*A crazy man, I married a crazy man*—but she would not. Saying everything with her silence.

The snow was falling heavier, shaping out the beams of his headlights before him like two great cones. He was five miles out of town, heading north again on the 52, before he took up his own phone and thumbed at the lighted menu. He'd not charged the phone, and the battery was in the red. A deputy answered and transferred the call and Sutter drummed the wheel as he waited. He looked at his hand, the pale, intact palm, and drummed the wheel again.

"What's the word, Tom?" said his former deputy.

"I've got a couple of pieces of information for you, Ed, but I gotta be quick before my phone dies."

"Hold on a second." Sutter heard the TV in the background before it went mute and he heard Moran tell his complaining boys to go watch it downstairs.

"I'm listening, Tom."

Sutter told him he might have his deputies check the urgent care clinic for a young man name of Radner with a gunshot wound to the hand, self-inflicted, and that he might get the postmaster to let him into the mailbox on the corner of Main and Park Street before morning.

There was silence on the line. Then Moran said, "Tom, what have you done?"

"Just calling you with some fresh intel, Ed." He heard Moran draw a deep breath through his nose and release it the same way.

"You couldn't just let me do my job. You couldn't just be patient."

"Patience has kind of lost its meaning for me, Ed."

"I know that, Tom. I know all about that."

"I doubt you do."

"All right. But I know one thing. I know it doesn't give you the right to fuck with my investigation."

Something in Sutter darkened. This man, this former deputy of his . . . the total lack of respect in his voice. Of memory. Of gratitude.

Into the silence, into Sutter's rising blood, Moran said, "I mean, Christ, Tom—what if the tables were turned? What if it was your case and I'd done the same?"

Sutter thought about that. Watching the road, the diving snow.

"Tom—?"

"I'm here."

Moran said nothing. Breathing through his nose again. Finally he said, "Is that it?" and Sutter said no, it wasn't, and told him about the backscratcher, the scratches on the boy's face. The hard evidence that would place the boy at the scene.

Silence again—not even the breathing, and Sutter glanced at the phone.

"Funny she never mentioned a backscratcher when I interviewed her, Tom."

"She didn't remember till later."

"Ah."

"I know he took it with him, Ed, this son of a bitch."

"Yeah? You reckon we'll find it under his pillow?"

Now Sutter was silent. He could see his deputy's hardened jaw, the thin lips pressed to a single hard line in his face. But when Moran spoke again he did not sound so angry. He sounded tired, sounded discouraged.

"Tom," he said, "it won't change a thing, going after this boy down here like this."

"The hell it won't."

"I mean it won't change what happened before, up there. That boy up there—well, he's no boy anymore. He, or some other man, is walking free today and he'll be walking free tomorrow."

The mention of the boy dropped Sutter back in time—ten years. Holly Burke in the river. The boy himself, Danny Young, sitting across from him in the interview room, scared but not stupid. Careful. Not under arrest but knowing his life was on the line, right there, right then . . . And you let him go.

"We were the law, Tom," Moran was saying. "We followed the book. And we'd have thrown his ass in jail if we could have. But there was one problem— remember?"

Sutter said he did but Moran reminded him anyway: No witness, no evidence, no case.

There was another silence. Sutter realized he was nodding and stopped it. He said, "How're your boys, Ed? Little Ed and the other one—Eli?"

"What? They're fine. Jesus, Tom—are you gonna tell me you're just doing what any father would do?"

"Not any father, Ed. I wouldn't say that. Just the father of a daughter."

Moran said nothing. Sutter watching the snow in his beams, thick and constant.

"A man doesn't really ever know himself, Ed," he said. "He thinks he does, but he doesn't. There's something in him that goes deeper than anything in his raising or his beliefs or his badge or whatever the hell he lives by. And once he reaches that place, well. Right and wrong are just words."

Moran did not respond, and Sutter moved the phone from his ear to look at it again and nearly drifted off the road—corrected, and shook his head at his stupidity. How many times had he warned his own daughter? The dead kids he'd seen, their mothers or girlfriends or boyfriends still on the line saying, *Hello, hello—?*

"Shit, Tom," his deputy said. "This is all just words."

"I know it, Ed. But listen, my phone is dying here and I gotta let you go. I'll call you tomorrow."

He hung up and set the phone on the seat and drove awhile with both hands on the wheel. The snow diving into the headlights. The click and squeak of the wipers. His heart was going and he got a cigarette into his lips and cracked the window and lit the cigarette and blew the smoke into the draft.

She was silent. Then she said, *He's right, you know.*

"About what."

You know what.

Sutter smoked. He drove. He crossed the state line into Minnesota and continued north into the town of Charlotte, and he could not drive through that town without thinking of the morgue there, of the bodies that had waited in those cabinets to be seen by parents, by wives or husbands, by grown children. Gordon Burke looking down on his daughter and putting his hand to her forehead, a father taking his child's temperature. And he saw his own daughter looking up at him from her bed, red-faced, and he saw his own hand pushing her hair from her forehead—and his heart abruptly plunged, and then began to pound, and "Jesus Christ," he said, and reached for the phone once again, thumbed it on and stared at the screen: the two smiling faces in those black caps.

Tom—the road!

He corrected again, and thumbed at the phone again, but the screen went dark.

"You son of a bitch," he said. "You dumb son of a bitch."

He sped up, and when he flew by the turn for home she said, *What are you doing?*

"I'm going up there. To the hospital."

Why?

"I need to see her. I need to talk to her."

It's late, Tom. She's sleeping.

He drove on. He felt a great panic in his heart. Like the car would not make it. Like it would blow a tire or throw a rod before he got there, before he could see her again.

Tom . . . she said. *Sutter,* she said, and he glanced over. *You can't do this now. You need to come home.*

"I have to do this, Annie. Just—please . . ."

He gripped the wheel and drove on, into the diving snow, and she did not speak to him again until he'd pulled over and put the car in park. The motor running. The lights on, the wipers sweeping.

It's all right, she said. *Just get your breath.*

He thumbed at the phone—no light, no nothing—and he popped open the glovebox and pawed everything out of there but there was no cord, no charger—what kind of an idiot, Jesus Christ—and it was then she caught up his hand in hers, held it in both of hers until it was still, until it was quiet.

She rested her head on his shoulder and after a while he put his head to her head and like that they rested. They breathed, looking out the windshield at the endless snow, how it dove into the lights and dashed itself soundlessly on the glass, how the wipers in their quiet rhythm swept it away and yet the snow kept coming . . . a million flakes, a billion, just diving and diving into the lights and no end to it that they could see.

26

HE WASN'T SUPPOSED to come before eight a.m. but she'd been sitting in the wheelchair since seven, face washed, teeth brushed, dressed and ready to go, glancing back at the clock—the plain round clockface strategically placed so that you could know exactly how slowly time moved when you were stuck in a mechanical bed with your broken arm that itched and itched under its cast—glancing at the clock every minute, until at last eight o'clock came. And went. And he was late. Ten minutes. Fifteen minutes. Well, wasn't he always? People called, they needed him—car accidents, fights. Law and order. Weekends included. That was his job, or had been, and so she'd waited: after band practice after school, after the movies with Jenny White, who was her best friend for one year of middle school, after her shift at Portman's Dairy the summer before she left for college and she had her license but no car because he couldn't afford even a used one, he said, but really it was because of all the teenagers and pieces of teenagers he'd seen strewn all over the roads. She waited for him on street corners and in the shade of trees and on Mrs. Aberdeen's porchsteps as the old woman's next student pounded out her scales inside the house; she waited for him as he went into her mother's hospital room alone, and now she waited for him in her own hospital room, in the wheelchair, facing the open door, watching the open door, watching the clock behind her, waiting.

The hospital had cleaned and dried the clothes she'd been wearing when she came in—which now that she thought about it, should they have done that? Shouldn't the clothes have been preserved? Or did the river already ruin them as evidence? In any case, she was dressed as she'd been dressed when Caroline had come to pick her up four days ago, minus the peacoat and the black knit cap, both still in the RAV4, or in the river, or else hung out to dry with the rest of her clothes on the bars of some jail cell down in Iowa, and she would ask him to find out and they could stop and pick them up on their way down to Georgia . . . but he had to get here first and get her out of here, and when she looked back into the room it was only the clock she saw and not the terrible mechanical bed or the dying flowers or all the little stuffed animals she was leaving behind, a childish menagerie sent or dropped off one by one by old childhood friends or the mothers of old childhood friends she hadn't seen in years, none of whom stayed long or said anything she could remember now.

Audrey rolling the wheelchair forward and back, listening to the squeak of the rubber tires on the floor, and she didn't need a wheelchair obviously but who knows—you might slip on the squeaky floor and crack your head before you got out of here and you could sue because you were still technically under their care, and she had waited for him one time in the nurse's office at school and not outside because that was school policy, the nurse said, and at last he'd come for her in full uniform and all business and impatient with the nurse, hearing just enough to learn it wasn't anything serious, something she ate maybe, and then he'd done something he never did in his full uniform and in front of people; he bent down and took her into his arms and held her close and kissed her near her ear with his sandpaper jaw that smelled of smoke and he squeezed her, hard.

Then it was just his hand on your shoulder as he led you down the school hall and outside to the cruiser, where he'd parked in the fire lane, waiting for you to buckle in before pulling away from the curb and right away talking into his cell phone as he drove, and something was happening, something was going on, and you still felt a little sick to your stomach but you couldn't ask him to slow down on the turns, because he was talking . . . and then after a long moment of saying nothing, the phone resting on his thigh, he said they'd have to take a detour, he needed to make a stop and he didn't have time to take you back to the office to sit with one of the deputies and you wanted to know were they going to arrest someone but he didn't seem to hear, but then he did and turned to you and almost-smiled and said no, it wasn't that kind of stop, but he needed you to sit in the car and mind yourself for a bit while he talked to a man and did you think you could do that, did you feel well enough for that? and of course you said Yes, Sheriff, I can do that.

And it was another two, maybe three days back at school—the huddled, whispering girls, the passed notes and the big eyes and the open mouths—before Audrey finally put it together, that the man they'd gone to see that day at his house in the woods and then driven into town was the father of the girl in the river, Holly Burke, a high schooler who'd been walking home through the park and had been beaten up or hit by a car or messed with by some man or men, or boy or boys, who had then tossed her into the river as you would toss an old piece of wood to see it splash and float away.

It was her boyfriend, my dad said, said one girl. *He says it's always the boyfriend. How would he know?*

My sister said it was a college boy, said another girl. *He got her drunk and took her to the park and gang-raped her.*

Oh, was your sister there, Christine? Do you even know what gang-rape means? Do you?

Yes, do you?

Ten years ago that was and no one talked about Holly Burke anymore, the whispering girls grown into teenagers themselves, into young women gone off to college or some of them staying put and having daughters of their own, and whoever had done that to Holly Burke was still alive in the world, somewhere, still walking around, and whenever Audrey had seen the man she'd first seen on that porch in the woods—saw him getting into his van outside the hardware store, or pushing a cart down the cereal aisle, or walking toward her on a sidewalk—her heart would race and she'd try to meet his eyes, to see if he would recognize her, say hello or even nod at her, but he never did, he never did, and it was exactly as if she'd become invisible to him.

Or maybe it had nothing to do with her, and everyone had become invisible to him. He was a ghost who everyone could see but who could see no one else.

And her father had not found the man or men, or boy or boys, who'd done it and no one talked about that anymore either, or at least not in front of Audrey they didn't. Nor did they talk about it themselves, she and her father, although she knew he thought about it always, that it was in him every day like his cancer and maybe it was even part of his cancer. Or his cancer was part of it, had grown out of it, feeding on it . . . And just then the particular sounds and smells of hospitals, of human sickness, returned to her in the moment and she remembered she was in a hospital once again, and she turned her head just enough to see the clock and not the bed itself, not the wilted flowers and the stuffed animals.

Forty-five minutes late now.

An hour late now but she wasn't angry, she wasn't mad, she could never be mad at him again, there wasn't time for that. But finally she couldn't sit there any longer, and she rolled to the open door to see was the coast clear, and she'd no sooner crossed the threshold than she saw a doctor coming toward her, and it was her own Dr. Breece—less breezy than usual, the wings of his white coat weighted down by his hands like stones in the pockets, a man deep in thought, and she thought she could roll back into the room without him seeing her but she couldn't—he looked up and saw her there and she saw him catch himself up, saw the recognition in his eyes and she knew at once he wasn't passing by but had come to see her especially, walking all the way from some far wing of the hospital, some altogether unrelated place where people weren't waiting to leave their quiet little rooms but were arriving in bursts of noise and urgency, nurses converging, doctors commanding, a place of blood and pain and emergency.

And next she knew, she was walking in a dream to that far other place in the hospital, one hushed and squeaking long hallway after another, a long humming elevator ride down, just she and the doctor alone, and following him toward a gray metal door that hissed open for them like it knew them, was expecting them—ICU PERSONNEL ONLY—and lastly there was the silvery cold whisking sound of metallic rings along a metallic bar as the doctor drew the curtain aside and there he lay on the bed—partly raised and neatly tucked in as if for a night's sleep and not for the long cold forever sleep that she saw everywhere she looked, starting with his hands so white and still on top of the sheet. The bony pale chest neither rising or falling as she watched. The eyes that would not open and the mouth that would not smile and say to her in its old torn-up voice, *There you are, Deputy . . . was just coming to get you.*

PART III

27

WHEN SHE NEXT awoke, rising once again through depths of water and color, she was not in the hospital but in her father's house. As if they'd made it there after all: Caroline upstairs in her bed, sleeping off the drive, she downstairs on the sofa, a corduroy throw pillow that smelled of smoke pressing its design into her cheek. The dampness on the pillow was from drool, she thought, but then she remembered the tears and then she remembered everything else. Caroline gone. Her father gone. The house so empty and quiet you could hear his watch ticking on the coffee table.

But something had woken her—a ringing, or chiming—and she reached out with her good hand and picked up his phone and pressed the button, pressed it again, but the screen remained dark. The room itself was dark, or almost dark; the sun going down. She sat up and put her feet to the floor and as she did so the doorbell rang again. Her boots were still on her feet—so heavy as she crossed the floor, as if still soaked from their time in the river. The plaster cast a strange weight on her arm.

She drew aside the little curtain on the door just as he raised his fist and rapped his knuckles on the wood, and he stopped at once, opening his hand in hello, in apology, and by the time she turned the bolt and opened the door his hat was off and in his hand. Standing there in full uniform on the porch, winter sheriff's jacket, sheriff's badge shining. His cruiser was parked in the driveway behind her father's car, and her first thought was of her stuff—her suitcases, her backpack with her school books, all of it dried out and repacked and hand-delivered. But there was nothing else on the porch other than him. Then she looked into his bulgy eyes and knew what he would say, and he said it: "Audrey, I'm so sorry. I am just so sorry."

"Thank you. Sheriff," she said. Her mouth strange and thick. She'd taken one of the pills, the pain pills, after she'd gotten home from the hospital, she remembered. Remembered crying on the sofa—and nothing after that.

Moran stood holding the stormdoor in his free hand. Audrey holding the wooden door in a mirror image. She noticed snowflakes in the brown nap of his jacket collar, and then she noticed the snow falling beyond him. The snow on the windshield of her father's car did not look thick and she didn't think she'd slept very long. And he'd had to drive up here from Iowa—so how had he known?

She asked him this, "How did you know so fast?" and he looked down, and looking up again said, "I've been calling his phone since noon and finally I decided to just drive on up here, and on the way I called the hospital and they told me."

There was movement and she looked beyond him to see Mr. Larkin standing in his driveway. All geared up in boots and parka and both his gloved hands resting on the handle of his shovel. The snow still falling and him out there shoveling. Or not shoveling. Moran turned too, and Mr. Larkin coughed a pale cloud and began pushing the shovel over the concrete, raising a grinding scrape that was terrible to hear in the snowfall, in the quiet of the cul-de-sac.

Moran turned back and said, "Audrey, I sure don't want to bother you right now—" He looked past her. "Are you alone?"

"Yes."

"No one's here with you?"

"No." Grandma Sutter and her husband were on their way from Illinois, and Uncle John was flying in from Houston, but it was too much to say.

Moran stood looking at her. "Well. Do you mind if I step inside for just a minute or two?"

His tone, his face, woke her somewhat from her stupor, and she stood aside so he could enter. He kicked the snow from his boots before stepping in, and Mr. Larkin in his driveway pitched a white cloud of powder with his face turned to watch the sheriff go into the house, before the front door shut off his view altogether.

She turned on the light and they both stood looking around. It was weird and she knew what the weirdness was: she'd never been alone with him in the house before.

She saw him see her father's things—the watch, the phone, the Zippo lighter, the cigarettes, the little black notebook, the ring of keys and the old .38 revolver—all in a row on the coffee table.

"Can I get you anything?" she said, remembering her manners. "There's probably coffee."

"Thank you, no," said Moran. He was looking at her face now. He put a finger to his own. "You've got these . . . lines."

She reached and felt the small ridges on her cheek. Tried to smooth them out. "It's that," she said, gesturing, trying to think of the word. "Pillow."

He looked. "You were sleeping," he said. "Shoot, I'm sorry. What a time to have some guy in a uniform banging on your door."

"It's all right."

He stood there. Then he fanned his face with his hat and said, "Warm in here. I'll just get out of this jacket if you don't mind."

"Glass of water?" she said.

"Water, OK, sure."

"Sit down, if you want."

In the kitchen she ran the tap into two clean-looking tumblers and carried them back to the living room and handed him one where he sat on the sofa. He was sitting forward, forearms on his knees. She knew he'd picked up the revolver and checked it. If there'd been bullets, someone had kept them.

She sat in the armchair opposite him and crossed her legs.

"How's that arm doing?" he said.

She lifted the cast from her lap. "Itches like crazy."

"Bet it does. My dad fell off a ladder once and broke his shinbone. He had one of those backscratcher things he'd wiggle on down there."

She raised the tumbler and drank, lowered it again. Outside in the dusk Mr. Larkin scraped the powder from his drive. He'd scrape one way across the drive, pause, scrape back the other way.

Moran looked around the room again, and she looked too: the hodgepodge of wooden chairs and little tables. The small walnut dining table where he sat to pay his bills, do his taxes. Stacks of unopened envelopes there. An electric print-out calculator. An ashtray. A coffee mug. Vials of prescription pills. She followed his gaze to the fireplace mantel, where paperbacks stood racked between two leaping bass that were the cast-iron bookends she'd gotten him one Christmas. Antiques, supposedly. The framed photographs to either side of the books: her father and her mother, both young, on their wedding day. Herself as a newborn in her mother's arms, still at the hospital. She and her father in Granddad's johnboat on the river, her first fish, a perch, swinging from her pole. Her high school graduation picture, which she hated.

Moran's eyes came back around to the coffee table and the items lined up there. He sat staring at them. Then he drank from his water and looked for something to set the tumbler on and finally set it on the table, matching it to one of the rings already there. He cleared his throat and looked up at her.

"Audrey, I just want you to know I thought the world of your dad. He was a good lawman and a good man. When I lit out of here he didn't hold any kind of grudge about it like some other man might have, and he didn't say anything against me to Sheriff Gaines down in Iowa either, and I'll never forget that."

She said nothing, and Moran went on talking, but she was thinking about a time years ago when she'd run from her father in tears, because he'd snapped at her . . . and he'd snapped at her because she'd asked why Deputy Moran was leaving the department and he'd said it was none of her concern, which only made her more curious, of course, pestering him until finally he turned on her and said, *What did I just say?* and she'd run from him in tears. Because she was his deputy too, and she understood then that that was just for play and there were things she would never know about—grown-up things. Real sheriff and real deputy things.

". . . so I just want you to know," Moran was saying, "you need anything, and I mean anything, you give me a call." He unsnapped a breast pocket flap and plucked out his card and set it on the table and snapped the button again. She saw the bright gold star of the card.

"Thank you, Sheriff. I will."

He laced his fingers in the space between his knees and seemed to study them. Then he said, "Shoot, there's just no good way to get into this, especially so soon after . . ."

"I'm all right, Sheriff," she said. "You drove all the way up here so you might as well just say it. Is it about those boys?"

"It is. It surely is. It's about one of them anyway."

She waited. He looked up.

"Did you know your dad headed down there, two nights ago?"

"Down where?"

"Iowa."

She shook her head.

"Well, he did. He went looking around, asking questions at that gas station, and then he spent the night in a motel and in the morning he went looking around some more."

She watched him. Waiting.

"And so now I gotta ask you, Audrey: Did you tell your dad anything about that night, about those boys, that you didn't tell me? Anything you might've remembered after I left the hospital?"

She knew what he was after and she didn't pretend she didn't. She told him about the backscratcher, and how she thought she'd scratched the one boy's face with it.

"You said at the hospital you never got a good look at their faces," he said. "That it was too dark."

"It was. But I felt it when I got him. And he yelled, and yanked it out of my hand. So I knew I got him."

He was watching her face, her eyes, her hands. As he would anyone he was questioning.

"Did he find it?" she said. "When he went down there?"

"No. It would seem not. If he had, he might not have shot that boy through the hand."

Audrey said nothing. She knew at once that it was true.

Moran raised his own right hand and pointed at the palm with his opposite forefinger. "Right there. Close range. Then left him bleeding in a parking lot."

She looked at the old .38 on the coffee table.

"He didn't use that," Moran said. "It was the boy's own .45."

Audrey was silent, staring at the .38. "Was it him?" she said at last.

"Was it who?"

"That boy. From the gas station."

Moran watched her with those eyes of his. "How am I supposed to know that?"

She stared at him. She couldn't think. "I mean—didn't you talk to him?"

"I did. Talked to him this morning, but all he said was he wasn't talking to any more cops without his lawyer. Said he knew who shot him and wanted him arrested. That's why I was on my way up here."

"To arrest him?"

"No, I couldn't do that up here—I'd have to go through the whole extradition process and . . ." He waved his hand. "I was coming just to talk to him, to see how he wanted to go about it."

Audrey began to get up but then sat down again. Her legs wouldn't do it.

Moran stood and collected the tumbler from her and walked into the kitchen. The tap ran, and he returned and handed her the glass and took his seat again on the sofa.

"Do you mind if I hold on to this?" He'd just finished thumbing through the little black notebook and he was holding it up.

"Will I get it back?"

"Of course. I'll make copies of anything of relevance." He slipped the notebook into the same breast pocket from which he'd taken his card.

Audrey took another long drink and when she was finished he said, "I know he was sick, Audrey. I mean, I know the cancer had come back and that it was . . . that there was nothing . . ." He looked at the coffee table and shook his head. "I think between that and what happened to you, and to Caroline Price . . . Well, heck. I think it pushed him over some kind of edge."

He stopped. He seemed to study the remaining items on the table one by one: The watch. The Zippo lighter. The gun. She would like to have it in her hand, she realized—the good familiar weight of it. The silver finish rubbed off the forward edge of the cap by his thumb, and by hers too, flicking the cap in play for as long as he'd let her: the sound and the feel and the sparky smell of the flintwheel, the burning fuel.

"You remember that girl ten years back who was pulled out of the river up here?" Moran said. "Holly Burke?"

"Yes."

"I guess it's the same river, isn't it?"

She waited.

"Well. We had a boy we knew did it sure as shit smells like shit—excuse my language. We had him in the same bar as her on the same night, and we had him drunk-driving in the same park later, Henry Sibley Park, where she went into the river. We had everything but hard evidence and a living witness, so what did we do?"

"You let him go."

"We let him go. Made a whole lot of folks just mad as hell too. Her father most of all. As you can imagine. Gordon Burke. Who has not said one decent word about your dad or any of us ever since, I can promise you that."

Audrey looked down into the water of her glass. When she looked up again Moran was watching her. He said, "I don't believe your dad ever got over that, Audrey. Letting that boy go. Never making an arrest. No trial. That boy walking free today, doing God knows what. I think your dad had that on his mind too, when he drove down to Iowa. I mean he was thinking about you, of course, and Caroline Price. But he was thinking about that other girl too, and it all just . . ." He shook his head again. Looking at her as if she might explain it to him. She said nothing.

"I don't even know what to say about it," he said. "It just beats everything. On top of kidnapping and shooting that boy, he has gone and screwed the pooch on any kind of case we might have made against him for your assault, and maybe even Caroline's death. The whole thing's just a great big cluster-mess, that's all. I don't even know how I'm going to explain it to that girl's family down in Georgia."

He fell silent. Mr. Larkin had finished with his driveway, or else stood as before, watching, listening. Her father's watch lay ticking on the table. Then, like an old memory, she remembered the hospital—was it just that morning? Waiting for him in the wheelchair. The long walk through the halls. His body under the sheet. So thin. So gray . . .

"How did he find him?" she said, and her voice seemed to snap the sheriff out of his own thoughts, whatever they were. He drew a sharp breath through his nostrils and shook his head again.

"Looks like he just went driving around to the local garages, looking for some young grease monkey with scratches on his face. Found one. Waited to get him alone. Interrogated him. Shot him through the hand."

"But he had the scratches on his face?"

"He had *scratches* on his face," said Moran. "And a story for how he got them."

He watched her and she could see the anger in his eyes at all her father had done to his investigation. To his authority. To even more than that. Leaving him nothing but this daughter, this girl, to answer for it.

He sat on the edge of the sofa, fingers laced again and mashing his palms together as if to crack a nut.

"What's his name?" she said. "The boy with the scratches." She wanted the notebook back, suddenly. She could see its shape in the breast pocket of his shirt. She knew he would not give it back now.

"I think I'd better not give you a name just yet," he said.

She thought a moment. "Because I might look him up online."

"Yes, ma'am. And that could bias you one way or another."

She tried to see him again: his face under the shadow of his cap. She could smell—taste—his hand over her mouth, the grease. His hot beer breath. The burning taste of pepper spray. But she could not see his face. She saw the other one rolling around on the concrete, hands to his face.

"Can you say if he has a friend named Bud?" she said.

"No, I can't."

She watched him. "Can't or won't?"

"Can't. I have not found one person so far who admits to knowing any young man by the name of Bud." He opened up his hands, palms to the ceiling, brought them together again. "Bud as in 'buddy,' it looks like." He watched her. She saw him take her in as if he'd not looked closely before. He said, "Did they say anything else before then—before that moment outside the ladies' room?"

Something fluttered in her chest. She held his gaze. "I'm not sure I understand the question."

"I'm asking did you talk to them before—in the parking lot? Something like that?" Moran the sheriff, sitting there. Watching her with those eyes.

"I'd have told you if I had," she said.

"Maybe you forgot. Like the backscratcher." He gave a kind of smile, but it came too late.

"I didn't talk to those boys at all, Sheriff."

"It's no crime if you did. Girls talk to boys, boys talk to girls."

She stared at him.

"I'm just saying," he said, "it would make more sense if there'd been some kind of . . . interaction, before they just showed up outside that ladies' room."

She blinked at the sting in her eyes but she would not cry.

"There was no interaction, Sheriff. They just showed up."

He raised one hand and said, "All right. I'm just making sure, that's all."

She watched him. Then she looked away, toward the window. Night had fallen, and the room was repeated in the glass like a painting in its frame, their two seated figures the painting's subject: Moran sitting there looking at her, she looking out at the viewer, who was herself.

She turned back to him. "Is there anything else, or . . . ?"

He said nothing. Then he sat up straighter and said, "Matter of fact there is," and popped the snap on the other breast pocket of his shirt and wiggled something free—a short stack of white rectangles—and sat squaring them up in his hands as if about to deal them out. And so he was. "By the book I should bring you back to the station for this," he said, "with witnesses other than myself. But under the circumstances . . ." He dealt out the rectangles; they were pictures, printed on photo stock, and he placed them one at a time on the coffee table all in a row, parallel to her father's things and oriented so that she didn't have to do anything but lean forward and look.

"I just need you to look at these real careful, real slow, and tell me if you think any one of them is that boy who grabbed you."

Five pictures, and they made a poor hand: five young men of about the same age, all poorly shaven, blond to brown hair, eyes of all colors and all staring into the camera with the same dumb criminal emptiness.

"What's the tape on them for?" It was a little square of masking tape stuck to each of the pictures in the same place.

"One of these boys has scratches on his face. Or what's left of them. So I had to put tape on all of their pictures. Just try to ignore that. Look at their features. Their eyes."

She studied them one at a time, right to left. She wanted so badly to peel off the pieces of tape, to see the face that bore the scratches.

"Anything?" he said.

"It was dark," she said.

"Take your time."

She looked again, left to right, while her heart slid. She'd seen him so clearly, or believed she had, when she was in the hospital bed—when she'd seen him through Caroline's eyes. Now she waited for one of the faces, one of the sets of eyes, to bring that vision back, to put the boy's face together with the feel and the taste of his hand over her mouth. Instead, the more she stared at the faces in the pictures the more that vision, that clarity, slipped away from her, and when she closed her eyes it was not to give up but to hold on, to keep that feeling of Caroline—of being Caroline—alive in her heart.

Moran said her name. And said it again before she opened her eyes.

"Nothing?" he said.

She shook her head.

"You're sure?"

She would not look at the pictures again. "Yes."

He sat watching her. Then he leaned forward and swept the pictures into a stack again and fit them back into his pocket and snapped the button to. He tapped his forefinger on his business card where it lay on the table. "You call me, Audrey. I mean it. Anything you need."

He stood then from the sofa and picked up his jacket and hat, and she stood to see him out and it was all a dream: the two of them in that living room, her father's gun on the coffee table, even her voice when she heard it ask him what would happen next.

"With what?"

"With the case."

"Well, we'll finish our investigation, our interviews, and then we'll take everything to the county attorney and see what she says."

"What might she say?"

"She might say let's prosecute this SOB, for the assault at least. Or she might say we haven't got enough even for that."

"I might know him if I saw him in person," Audrey said.

"Might," said Moran.

She opened the wooden door, and he pushed open the stormdoor and put on his hat. The snow had stopped. Mr. Larkin was gone, the light of his television playing now on the living room curtains and Larkin himself standing in the dark of some other room watching to see would that Iowa sheriff ever leave that house. What did he imagine was going on in there? Did he even know her father had died?

"And what about my father?" she said, and Moran paused with one boot down on the first step.

"What about him?"

"I mean what he did down there."

Moran adjusted his hat. He squinted up at something in the night sky. "Well," he said, his breath smoking. "They might pursue monetary compensation, I suppose. But as for criminal charges, under the circumstances . . ." He didn't finish, and didn't have to.

"Thank you, Sheriff," she said, and Moran nodded.

"You have my card," he said.

"Yes, sir. I have your card."

28

AND THEN IT was Sunday—a long day of sobbing and sleeping. Of dreaming and waking and remembering and sobbing again. Of finding him in everything she touched and smelled, from the paperbacks on the mantel to the stained coffee mug in the sink to the rounded cake of soap in the shower.

Grandma Sutter and her husband, Kent, spent most of the day trying to take care of her, but then Kent told her they couldn't stay, he had to get his wife away from this house for a while, just too many reminders of her son . . . and they were not gone fifteen minutes before the other son, Uncle John, arrived—but he was so restless and talky, so determined to keep her distracted, that finally she pretended to fall asleep on the sofa, then fell asleep for real, and when she woke up he was gone.

Others came too: the same mothers of childhood friends who'd visited her in the hospital, bringing this time casseroles, bringing lasagna, *Just put it in the oven at three-fifty, sweetie, or do you have a microwave . . . ?*

Lastly came another lawman, the man who'd replaced her father when he retired: Sheriff Wayne Halsey. The sheriff looking so awkward on the porch that she didn't even bother inviting him in; she thanked him for checking on her, promised to call if she needed anything, watched him walk back to his cruiser, waved when he waved, then shut the wooden door again and locked it.

The sofa was still warm, and she lay staring at her father's things on the coffee table, listening to the ticking of his watch, and when she woke again it was morning—Monday morning. The weekend was over.

SHE'D REMEMBERED TO charge his phone, at least, and the first thing she saw when she lifted it was his face, next to hers—the two of them red-faced and smiling in their black knit caps.

Audrey, this is a bad idea . . . Her father, the sheriff, mincing out onto the ice in the rented skates. He was from Illinois and had not played hockey as a kid, and had not been on any kind of skates since he was ten years old, he said.

It's like riding a bike, she said.

Have you ever, in your life, seen me on a bike?

She wiped her eyes, her face. Then she found the number she was looking for, and a woman answered the phone and put her on hold—no music, just fizzy silence. The phone smelled like smoke. The woman came back and told her yes, he could see her at ten thirty this morning, would that be all right?

She was in the shower a long time, lathering and scrubbing and shaving all one-handed, a plastic bag rubber-banded over the cast, and afterwards she found socks and underclothes in her dresser and she stepped into a pair of old jeans once too tight and now too loose and she took an old flannel shirt from the hanger it had hung on untouched for maybe three years, and lastly she brushed out her hair and bound it tightly in a damp ponytail at the back of her head.

The canvas jacket was too big and too heavy and it reeked of smoke, but her cast slipped right into it, and she loved it. She stood outside on the porch, squinting in the sunlight and rooting up the sunglasses from the breast pocket and putting them on, the glasses loose at her temples and heavy on her nose. Dark- green tint. The aviators he'd worn for years.

The Ford sat where it always sat. A male nurse from the hospital had driven it while another nurse, a woman, had driven Audrey in a little car that stank of the nurse's gym bag, both nurses making sure she got inside all right, that she would be all right—could they get her anything, was she sure they couldn't call someone?—before leaving her alone in the house at last.

Now, climbing into the Ford, she thought she'd cry again from the smell of it—the smokiness, yes, but also something beneath that, or within it, some old sheriffy scent or combination of scents that was the very smell of—what? Of safety.

She didn't cry. She scooted the seat forward, buckled up, made an adjustment to the rearview mirror, and put the Ford in gear, and with each of these movements her father's watch slipped and swung on her wrist like a heavy bracelet.

It had snowed but not enough to bring out the plows, and the river when she crossed it was snowy at its bends but clean at its center—glassy black ice maybe a foot thick, maybe more depending on the currents underneath, how fast or slow, and was there an equation for that, such as the rate of descent for a projectile depending on its weight and its speed? For ice thickness you'd have to figure temperature too. And the temperature over how many days. The ice on her river—their river, the Lower Black Root—had been thick but not thick enough. The current too fast there, rushing toward the dam where the water never froze.

Oh, Audrey, sometimes I just love you.

I know. It's the same with me.

She fed the meter with quarters from his console and crossed the sidewalk toward an image in the glass she took to be someone else altogether, someone on the other side of the glass coming out, before she realized it was her, and she removed the sunglasses and stowed them in the breast pocket of the canvas jacket and opened the glass door and stepped inside. Ten minutes later by her father's watch the lawyer came up to her in his shirt and tie and took her good hand in both of his as she stood from the chair. "Audrey, I am so sorry. I am so sorry." Holding on to her hand, looking into her eyes. "I came to see you at the hospital but you were absolutely conked out. How's your arm?"

"It's fine, Mr. Trevor, thanks."

"Please, call me Tuck. What can I get you?" Letting go her hand and turning to the counter. "Debbie, is there yet some coffee back there?"

She'd known him since she was young, tagging along with her father to the courthouse, or he'd show up at a campaign rally when her father had to campaign, or she'd see him at school, where his girls were in the class ahead of hers, the Trevor twins, a double dose of pretty and mean. *Call me Tuck*, he always said but she couldn't do it.

He walked her back to his office and told her to please sit, and before he'd even settled into his own chair behind his desk he said, "I don't know where to begin, Audrey. All you've been through. Your friend Caroline. And now your father. I have to say I'm surprised to see you up and about at all."

On the wall behind him was a framed photograph of the Trevor twins in their high school graduation caps and gowns, their white smiles. They'd gone to a school out east, some big-deal college where they could go on being pretty and mean together.

"He told me to come see you, if this happened," she said.

"Yes, he told me the same thing—to make sure you came to see me, that is. He wasn't a man who liked to leave things to chance, was he."

She watched him—did he know? Maybe he did and maybe he didn't. What did it matter now anyway?

She said, "I guess you know about what he did then."

"I know what they say he did. News travels fast along certain channels. And if there's a bigger group of gossips you'd have to prove it to me."

She looked down at the water bottle the woman had given her. She twisted the cap to break the plastic seal but did not remove it.

"As a father," the lawyer said, and when he didn't go on she looked up. Trevor sitting there, not quite looking at her. "As a father, under the same circumstances, I can't say I wouldn't have done the same thing. Not that I expect that to console you."

She didn't know what to say to that.

Trevor adjusted his glasses. He cleared his throat. "It may be a poor time to ask," he said, "but have you heard anything more about the investigation?"

She told him about the sheriff coming to see her at the house and showing her the pictures.

"He brought you a photo array?"

"Yes."

"To your house?"

"Yes."

Trevor frowned, watching her. "And was he there?"

"Sorry?"

"The boy who attacked you. Was he in the photo array."

"I don't know. I couldn't say. They all looked like the same boy to me."

"Well, don't you worry about that. It doesn't do anybody any good if you're not one hundred percent certain."

She looked at him, her heart suddenly thudding. "Like Dad was?" she said.

Trevor sat watching her. "How do you know he wasn't certain?"

"Because he didn't find evidence. Hard evidence. He found some boy with scratches on his face."

"Yes," said the lawyer. "But how do you know that boy didn't say something to your father? Didn't admit to it?"

"At gunpoint?"

Trevor almost smiled. Then he looked off toward a bookshelf that ran floor to ceiling, each shelf jammed tight with law books.

"A professor of mine used to say Justice is blind," he said, "but she also can't see worth a shit." He turned back to her. Adjusted his glasses again.

"I guess I'm not sure what that means," she said.

"It means," he began, and stopped. Looking at her more keenly. "It means your dad loved nothing more in this world than you, Audrey. And he knew as well as anyone how the system works, and how it doesn't work. And the clock was ticking, as you know. The clock was ticking." He shook his head. "I believe he believed he was doing the best thing he could do as a man. As a father. And in my opinion that's the only thing you need to remember about that. All right?"

She watched him. Then she nodded. "All right."

"Good," he said. "Now let's get to what you came here for."

He read it aloud, glancing up to meet her eye from time to time, and when he was finished he folded his hands on top of it and sat looking at her.

She didn't know what she was supposed to say, or do.

"I don't think he had any savings," she said. "I think he used everything to pay the hospital bills."

"Yes, I suspect you're right about that."

"And there's about ten unopened letters from the bank at home. I think about the mortgage."

Trevor looked down at his desk and nodded. "There's just nothing like illness to take everything a man's got right out from under him. Illness and injury. No one is as ready for it as they think they are, and most aren't even close to ready." He looked up again. "Be that as it may, and however things shake out financially, Audrey, clearly nothing was more important to him than you finishing college and getting your degree."

She nodded.

"And what about that boy," she said.

"What boy?"

"The one he went down there and shot."

"What about him?"

"Do you think he could go after the house, or anything like that?"

"You mean as compensation for damages?"

"Yes."

"Possibly. I'm no expert in Iowa law, but I suppose he could get a judgment down there which could result in a lien against the property."

"A lien?"

"Yes. Meaning, the amount of the damages would be due at the sale of the house."

Audrey was silent.

"But I don't think you need to worry about that, Audrey. He'd have to be one dumb buckaroo to go anywhere near a court of law, under the circumstances."

"Or innocent."

The lawyer smiled but said nothing.

She turned her father's watch on her wrist until the crystal was faceup—its tick-tick sound now synced with the movements of its second hand—but when she let go it all slipped away again in a silvery, top-heavy slump. She'd already taken up too much of the lawyer's time.

"Can I ask you one more thing?" she said.

"Of course."

"I was just wondering—" she began. Then began again: "I was just wondering if you were involved with a case of his, from ten years ago."

Trevor adjusted his glasses. "The Holly Burke case?"

"Yes, sir."

"Do you mean professionally, as a lawyer?"

"Yes, sir."

"No, I wasn't."

"And he didn't talk to you about it—my dad?"

"Not that I remember. A lot of people talked about it—everybody talked about it. But not your dad." Trevor waited. "Why do you ask?"

That yellow hair, that long fine girl's hair streaming in the fast water, just hanging in the light as Caroline swam against the current, as she fought to get back to the car, back to Audrey . . .

"Audrey?" said the lawyer, and she looked at him. She shook her head.

Through the door, or the walls, a phone began to chirp and then it stopped chirping and she could hear the woman, the secretary, speaking.

Audrey looked again at the photograph on the wall.

"How are the twins doing?" she said, and he turned to look at the photograph too.

"Costing me a fortune but doing great." Smiling when he turned back to her, the smile of a father. He got to his feet. "I'll walk you out," he said.

29

HE'D DAMN NEAR missed it—not only the funeral but the news itself, all of it. He hadn't watched the evening news in years, but for some reason, that Saturday—maybe it was those two girls, the Sutter girl and her friend; maybe there'd been some new development—he'd turned it on, and boom, there it was, the top story: Local ex-sheriff Tom Sutter dead at the age of fifty-one.

Son of a bitch.

He'd thought to call out to someone to come look at this but there was no one to call out to.

Three days later—just six days since he'd talked to Sutter outside the hospital in Rochester—Gordon got out his suit and he worked his tie into a knot at his throat and he wiped the dust from his shoes and he drove the van with its new heater core out to the funeral home and slipped in a few minutes late and took a seat at the back.

Old dusty church smell in the overheated room. Smell of bodies giving off heat, perfume, sweat. Thick smell of flowers. He saw profiles he recognized, backs of heads. Ladies sniffling into tissues. He did not expect to see Rachel Young in the crowd, or her son, and he didn't.

The coffin was white oak with brass handles, flowers on the curve of the lid. The blown-up photo on the easel was his campaign picture from eight years back, when he'd had to run to keep his job. Before he lost all that weight.

Deputies and cops and sheriffs sat in their uniforms, Ed Moran among them, a sheriff down in Iowa now, and Wayne Halsey, Sutter's replacement up here. Halsey taking the podium now to tell a quick story, with the mic pushed aside because he didn't need a mic, and though the story had some laughs built into it, by the end Halsey had to wrap up and step away from the podium before his voice let him down. He was followed by Sutter's older brother, John, a talky guy with a tanned face, telling about when they were boys, then young men, then men . . . and when he finally went back to his seat in the front row Gordon saw what he guessed was the back of the girl's head. Dark, glossy hair combed down straight. More family seated to either side of her. Grandparents, maybe. He expected the girl to get up and talk but she didn't. Finally the director walked to the podium and asked for the pallbearers to meet him at the side of the building.

Gordon sat in the van until the last of the cars and trucks and cruisers had filed out behind the hearse and then he pulled out of the lot and brought up the rear at a good distance, and when they reached the grounds he parked on the shoulder with a few other cars. The mourners ahead of him all took the path to the right but he turned left, following a path that had not been cleared, and when he reached the intersection of a third path he swept the snow from the iron bench there and sat and watched from that distance as the mourners gathered under the blue canopy, some taking chairs, the rest standing.

Old brown leaves chattering in the oak trees. The far-off call of a crow somewhere.

The coffin had already been placed on the straps over the vault and there was no dirt in sight but only the apron of AstroTurf around the grave, bright green and fake in the snow, in the cold. The skirt of the canopy rippling like the side fins of a fish, the roof filling with wind and whopping as though it would pull free of its ropes and fly, but it didn't, it held. The preacher or whatever he was stood before them in a black overcoat, and Gordon could hear the man's voice if not his words, and anyway he didn't speak long before all said amen and then came the ratcheting sound of the lowering mechanism carrying loud and clear across the snow, and he stood up from the bench and walked on.

The stand of oaks that once marked the far border of the cemetery now marked the border between the old grounds and the new grounds, and a white marble stone that had once been the only one out here, ten years ago, had since been joined by twenty-three other stones, all shapes and colors. None of them as old as hers and none of the souls they named as young.

He got down on his haunches and ran his bare fingertips over the engraved words.

Holly Catherine Burke
Beloved Daughter

Two dates and a dash between them. A whole life in that dash. From first breath with blood on her little face to her last. From water to water. Nineteen when she died and almost a stranger by then, but here she is no age at all. She is a smile, she is big green eyes looking up at you. She is giggles. She is the limp little body fitted to your chest, the head that falls into place on your neck as you carry her up the stairs. She is the smell of her face when you kiss her good night.

You could curse God if there was anything left of him to curse. If he were not already dead and gone. In the end it's you. Just you. You had one thing to do with your life and that was to protect her. To keep her safe.

And you did not. You did not.

30

WHEN THE KNOCK came at the aluminum door, a quick rap on the square of glass, the man at the desk looked up from his work and did not wave the other man in until he'd bent once again to his calculator and his receipts. The room was in fact the interior of an old worksite trailer that had been converted into an office, and whenever a body was added or subtracted from it, or crossed from one end to the other, it teetered on its tires like a balance scale. The trailer made its corrections now and grew steady again, and still the man, whose name was Ben Holden, did not look up but instead finished entering a last sequence of numbers into the old calculator, set its works into motion, held the length of paper as it rose from the printhead, ripped it free and said, fussing with the coil of paper, "Yeah."

Danny Young, having removed his cap, ran his hand through his hair front to back and pressed his fingertips into the cords at the back of his neck. Behind him at a small workbench sat old Billy Ramos, working on an old Hitachi nail gun. Billy had worked for Holden's father since he was fourteen, and some of the men said he was Holden's half brother by a Mexican señorita, covering their mouths when they said it because the old deaf bugger could read lips at a hundred yards.

Holden looked up at last and Danny said, "I just came in to tell you I gotta take off, Ben."

"You gotta take off."

"Yes, sir."

Holden looked at the punch clock on the wall, and Danny turned to look too. The clock said 3:45.

Holden said, "You're telling me you can't wait fifteen minutes and finish out the day?"

"No, sir. I'm telling you I gotta take off as in I can't keep this job. I wrapped up early so I could come in here and let you know."

Holden leaned back in his chair and began a slow rocking, raising the same birdy chirp from the chair's spring with each backward tilt. Danny watched him, then looked up, as if to inspect at close range the rivets in the metallic ceiling. Outside, in the hollows of the building, men were gathering tools, shutting down compressors, coiling cords and air hoses—all men, this crew, no women. You could hear in their voices that it was Friday. Payday.

Holden said, "I don't even consider a raise till a man's been with me six months, but I might make an exception if I knew you were gonna stick around. And I wouldn't say that to just anyone, so."

"I appreciate that," Danny said. "But it's not the money. This has been a good job. I wouldn't leave if I didn't have to."

Holden's eyes narrowed. "You in some kind of jam?"

"Jam?"

"Jam. Like the kind where some man comes knocking on that door tomorrow flashing me his badge."

Danny looked back at Billy Ramos. Working on the nail gun, not watching, feeling the vibrations of the trailer, of Holden's voice.

"Don't mind him," Holden said. "He's just in here for ballast."

"No, sir," Danny said, turning back. "Nothing like that. I just have to go, that's all."

"Just go."

"Yes, sir."

"You gonna tell me where you're just going to?"

"Just heading home."

"Home, as in Minnesota home?"

"Yes, sir. My dog died."

Holden's chair stopped chirping. Billy, behind him, paused too in his tinkering.

"Did you say your *dog*?" Holden said.

"Yes."

"Thought so. Well." He resumed rocking. "A man can get close to his dog, sure enough. Can be a real loss. I remember a dog I had as a boy, just an old dumb mutt from God knows where, but the day he died, oh boy . . ."

The letter was folded back into its envelope, and the envelope was folded into the back pocket of his jeans. It had come the day before but he'd opened it today on his lunch break, sitting alone on the far side of the building. Familiar paper, familiar handwriting—even the smell of the air that escaped the opened envelope. Writing first of the weather as she always did and then of the farm, any repairs that had needed doing and how they'd gotten done or if they would have to wait—not mentioning money, never mentioning money, in case he thought she was asking him to send more, had told him over and over not to send any, to take care of himself and not worry—and then writing a little about Marky, one funny thing or other he'd said, before moving on to tell him some news she wasn't sure she should include but just wanted him to hear it from her first, and this was the two college girls who'd gone into the river in their car, just a few miles south, into the ice, and one of them, the one who lived, was Audrey Sutter, Sheriff Tom Sutter's daughter, and not a week later Tom Sutter himself, who was in stage four cancer, was dead from a heart attack. The funeral two days ago, the man buried in the same cemetery where so many had been buried: her father and mother, her grandparents, Danny's father.

Tom Sutter. Sheriff Sutter. The name conjured blue eyes and a small room and the taste of cigarette smoke and the feeling of choking on your own voice.

Lastly, and abruptly, as if she'd been putting off the true point of the letter and must write it quickly to get through it, she wrote, *Danny, I'm sorry to tell you we buried old Wyatt too. It was his time, and his pain is over.*

Old Wyatt, that old outlaw. Gone.

Whatever Holden was saying about his own childhood dog, he finished and fixed his eyes on Danny.

"I won't ask you again to stay," said Holden. "But I will say one thing since you're going anyway, and just so you get the whole picture here."

Danny waited. Billy snapped something hard into place.

"I did a check on you, Daniel Young from Minnesota. Not an all-out background check like I do on some guys. Hell, most guys. But you . . . you were kind of the opposite of most guys."

Danny said nothing.

"I one time hired this guy, crackerjack framer, and six months later I find out he used to teach poetry at Princeton."

Danny waited.

"So," Holden said. "Before I hired you I got on the internet, and lo and behold."

There was a rap on the door then and the door opened and the trailer rocked on its wheels and a man's head appeared, but he did not enter. It was Jones, the foreman.

"Give us one more minute here, Vernon."

"Sure thing, Ben." Jones stepped back out and the door shut and the trailer rocked once more and settled.

"I was never charged," Danny said.

"I know you weren't. I can read." Holden shrugged. "I just wanted you to know I knew, that's all." He sat forward and shifted his calculator to some better angle. "You go ahead and punch out and I'll cut you a check."

Danny stood where he was. He studied the inside of his cap. "I guess I just have one question," he said.

"Why'd I hire you?"

He looked up. "Yes, sir."

Holden sat staring at the old calculator. "My dad used to say a man can only prove himself once in this business, good or bad, and that's while he's *your* man. I've always tried to keep that in mind."

Danny punched his time card and stood by as Holden entered the figures into the calculator and ripped the receipt from the machine, as he wrote out the check and ripped that from the book and handed it over.

"Stay outta trouble, Danny."

"Yes, sir," he said, and he turned then and found Billy Ramos watching him, and he said, "See you around, Billy," and Billy said in his rubbery voice, "See you around, Danny," and Danny stepped from the office and nodded to Jones—who nodded back and stepped into the trailer while it was still rocking and shut the door behind him.

31

THE OLD DEAD tamarack had been there long enough, stopped in its fall by the lower boughs of a balsam fir and doing the balsam no good either, so he gathered his gear and walked to the site just a few paces into the woods and broomed the snow from a crook in the branches of the tamarack and wedged the chainsaw there and broomed off the rest of the tree. Then he took up the snow shovel and cleared a path along the fall line, and when that was finished he fetched down the chainsaw again and stood studying the tree. Like a man saying last words, though saying nothing. No other sound but his own smoky breaths. Finally he looked up into the branches overhead for widow-makers and seeing none he pulled the choke and jerked the cord. The engine came to life and he worked the throttle trigger to keep it running. Cold gray Sunday morning and these woods his church. The revving saw the only sermon he cared to hear.

He lopped off the limbs, then dropped the tree into the path, and he'd begun bucking it into lengths when there was a flash of light in the corner of his vision and he stood to watch the white sedan pull into his drive and come to a stop. His heart pitching strangely because he knew the car—had seen it dozens of times around town, on the roads, in the time since Sutter had retired and gone civilian. The driver's door opening now and a figure stepping out wearing Sutter's sunglasses and Sutter's canvas jacket, and where was this, where was he, was he dreaming? He removed the fogged safety glasses and looked again and as he did so Sutter turned his head and Gordon saw the dark ponytail and his heart swung back to its place and he shook his head at himself—old fool, what did you think?

He held still, watching her through the trees. She looked at the house and she looked at the outbuilding, and then she turned toward the woods and looked right at him and he realized the saw was still running, puttering low but puttering all the same in that silence. She raised a hand to him, then began making her way toward him through the snow. When she reached the woods where the snow was not so deep she paused to kick her boots one against the other as you would at someone's doorstep, then she took off the sunglasses and continued on to the small clearing where he stood beside the fallen tamarack.

Her mouth moved and he cut the engine and set the saw down on the tree.

"Say again?"

"I said, Mr. Burke?" She was winded from her walk through the deep snow and trying not to be. Bright pink blotches on her pale face.

"I am."

"I'm Audrey Sutter. Tom Sutter's daughter?"

"I know who you are."

The girl nodded. Looking right at him, her face so smooth and young but with Sutter's blue eyes.

He said, "I'm sorry about your father."

"Thank you. Thank you for coming to the service."

"Well. Wanted to pay my respects. He was a good man."

"Thank you." The girl standing there with both hands in the big pockets of that jacket that made her look so small. Young, pretty girl. Look you in the eye. Looking to see did you mean what you said, so don't look away, give the man's daughter that much, at least.

She stepped up for a closer look at the tamarack. As if to inspect his work.

"Will you burn all this yourself?"

"Yes, I will."

"You won't sell it."

"No, I won't."

She looked up into the branches overhead. A male cardinal landed on an upper bough, sending a small avalanche of powder falling without a sound. The bird whistling for its mate.

"You should have something on your head," he said.

"I know." The girl nodding, looking all around. She wanted to say something, had driven out here to say something, but he couldn't help her say it and he didn't know that he cared to hear it anyway.

"You like trees?" he said finally, and the girl looked at him.

"Do I like them?"

"Yes, ma'am."

"I like them," she said.

"All right then, follow me," he said. And he turned and began down a path through the trees, holding the boughs so they wouldn't whip back on her, she following close behind in his tracks.

HE POINTED TO the trees as they walked and seemed to give them their names: Jack pine. Black spruce. Balsam fir. Hemlock. White pine. He told her his old granddad was a logger from the old days and knew everything there was to know about trees. Signed up when he was fourteen and worked every job there was, you name it: Chokerman, chaser, high climber. Faller. Bucker.

"He'd show you his scars," he went on. "Just everywhere. His face. Showed me one time where a one-inch jagger—that's a sliver of cable wire—went into his hand one summer and where it come out the next on his thigh." He held a wing of black spruce for her until he was sure she had it.

"Funny thing is, I do believe a tree was the most beautiful thing in the world to that old man. When he looked at one he saw a hundred things all at once. Logging put clothes on his kids' backs, food on their plates. That's all there was to it."

He stopped and she came up beside him in a place that looked like every other place in the woods: the boughs of the trees with their burdens of snow, the shapes of fallen limbs under the snow and sometimes the branches reaching up like hands. Tracks of creatures everywhere.

"There it is there," he said, and she looked where he was looking. Trees and more trees. He pointed. "That one there."

She looked again. "Is that a white pine?"

"Yes, it is."

The tree rose straight and bare until about her height, then opened like an umbrella in gray-green boughs, soft-looking boughs, then came to a point high overhead.

She looked at him, but his eyes were up in the tree's branches. He said, "She asked me one time how fast did a tree grow and I said I don't know and she said was it faster than a little girl and I said I don't know but there's one way to find out. So out we come and she walked around and around till she found this one. Just her height back then."

Audrey looked at the tree again. At its highest it just caught the sun, and the whole tree seemed an elaborate structure for lifting that highest, palest point into the light.

"How old was she?" she said. "When she found the tree."

"Seven. That tree was just four foot tall back then and it's grown twelve inches a year ever since, give or take, so I put it at right around twenty-six foot tall."

"Was she disappointed?"

"About what?"

"About how much faster it grew."

He shrugged. "Tell you the truth she didn't have much interest after that first year. It was me who kept coming out to measure. Until it got too tall and I got too old to be climbing trees anyway."

Audrey swept at her cheeks with her fingertips, both sides with both hands, and Gordon Burke, watching her, said, "I didn't see that cast till just now."

She held out the purple cast as if she'd not noticed it herself.

"That other girl," he said, "who was with you . . ."

"Caroline."

"Was she a good friend of yours?"

"Yes, she was."

He nodded, then shook his head and was silent. The silence of the woods all around them. Dead silence. Not even a bird.

"I missed her funeral because of this," Audrey said, raising the cast again.

"I expect she won't begrudge you that," he said, and when she said nothing he added, "No disrespect. Just saying, under the circumstances."

"I still need to go down there, though," she said. "I need to see those people. Her family."

He looked at her, then looked up into the trees again. "Looks to me like you've got your hands full where you're at. And it's none of my business, but it's my guess those folks could use some time on their own."

"That's what Dad said."

He stood looking up into the trees. Then he said, "Well," and turned as if to head back.

"I guess you've heard about what he did," she said, "down there in Iowa," and Gordon Burke stopped.

"No, I can't say that I have," he said.

And so she told him. About the boys at the gas station. About the back-scratcher and about the mechanic with the scratches on his face and the new bullet hole in his right hand, Gordon Burke all the while listening, watching her, and when she was finished he looked away and shook his head.

"Be damned," he said. "Just be God damned." He turned back to her. "Did he get the right man at least?"

"I don't know. I looked at a photo line-up but I couldn't say."

"A photo line-up?"

She told him about Ed Moran and his deck of mug shots. "He's the sheriff down there now, where it happened."

"I know he is." Gordon Burke shook his head again. He looked up into the branches of the white pine. "And you still alive even," he said. "It just beats all."

"It wasn't all about me."

"What wasn't?"

"What he did down there. Or about Caroline either."

He raised a hand to stop her. Something flashing in his eyes. "We're not gonna talk about that."

"I'm sorry—"

"Don't say you're sorry, just—" He dropped his hand. Turning away from her. "I've talked my limit for one day, that's all," he said. "More than my limit." And he turned to go then, and she turned too and they went back the way they'd come, following their tracks to the fallen tamarack, and there they said good-bye, and before she'd opened the car door the chainsaw chugged back to life and she turned for a last look at him, a man in his woods, bent over in the smoke and the noise and the woodchips flying all around him.

32

It was Saturday afternoon before he got on the road—before he got his room and the little bathroom cleaned, before he got the truck packed up, and before he got his deposit from the old widow who owned the house and who believed only in cash—and he'd planned to drive all night, but after nearly drifting into the median just outside Kansas City, he pulled into a rest stop and spent the next four hours shivering under a packing blanket while the big diesels geared down and hissed and rumbled all through his broken dreams. Around dawn he gave up and drove on, and he didn't stop again except for gas and coffee.

When he turned at last into the drive and there was no car and no sign of anyone around, he thought in his exhaustion that she'd moved somewhere and hadn't told him. Or that she'd told him and he'd forgotten. But then he saw the time on the dash, 5:15, and it was what, Sunday now, and she and Marky would've gone into town for groceries, and so he parked the truck and got out and stretched, and stood looking over the farmhouse and its outbuildings. The shapes of abandoned machinery under the snow; Great-Granddad's old Massey-Harris, flat-tired and snow-heaped and the red paint all gone to rust—a miracle that that old Swede didn't come back from the dead to raise holy hell. The coop yard where he told Marky to go make the chickens fly and Great-Grammy Olsen coming out with her broom and Marky flapping his wings away from her as she cussed him in a foreign blue streak.

They had liked playing around the farm but they did not like that kitchen. Did not like sitting around that table.

Why on earth not? she'd wanted to know, staring them down.

Just don't, Ma.

Why?

It smells Momma. Marky spitting it out.

What do you mean it smells?

Shrugging his shoulders. *It just smells Momma.*

He means it smells like them. It's hot in there and it smells like them.

Smells like them?

Yeah, Ma. Don't you smell it?

Putting her hands to her hips, looking from him to Marky and back. *You know what that smell is? Do you? That's the smell of working people. Of hard work all your life. Of never having money for yourself but making sure your kids are fed and have shoes on their feet. The kitchen smells!* Shaking her head. *Next time we'll just have Grammy throw your food out to you in the yard like a couple of dogs. How will that be?* Raising her finger and pointing it at Danny's face. *Don't even think it, wise guy. Just keep that smart tongue of yours still for once, OK?*

The side door was not locked, was never locked, and when he stepped into the kitchen he thought the old smell was still there, faintly. Then he thought it might be the smell of old Wyatt who'd had his nest of blankets near the stove. Who did not raise his head now at Danny's entrance, or come hobbling in from the living room, wagging his old tail. No sound of his dog tags rattling, his ears clapping as he shook off sleep. No sound at all in the house, not even the refrigerator running its compressor, though when he opened the door the light came on and the jug of juice he picked up was cold.

He went back out the way he'd come in and stood looking at the Minnesota sundown. Bright bands of red and pink in the west, but dark winter clouds overhead. Near the middle of the yard the snow had been disturbed—excavated, and darkened with what looked like soot, and he knew what it was before he reached the edge of the site.

The fire had melted back the snow and left sharp fins like rock formations, and down in the pit lay the upturned earth, the dirt patted down with the back side of a shovel. At the head of the grave, or the foot of it, stood the rusted iron T-post, rising from the snow at its tilt like a ship mast—just the right height for boys to swing from, one to each side, making the bedsheets shimmy on the lines . . . until one day the post shifted down in the turf and they felt it going and *Oh shit oh shit*, they dropped and ran for their lives.

No idea then that they swung their sneakers over the future grave of their dog. No idea they'd ever have a dog. How many times had they asked her? Begged her. Promised to take care of it, to feed it, she wouldn't have to do a thing. *No, no, and no*, she said, *I know how that story ends.* But then one day you take off to the tracks, the forbidden tracks, and *The train is coming Danny*, Marky says, *hurry!* and you center the penny on the rail and jump back down the bank and into the trees so the conductor won't see you, and it's then, the train growing big and your hearts beating, that Marky says, *Danny there's a dog.*

And you look and look before you finally see it in the weeds and shadows. Hardly recognizable as a dog at first with its shabby, mud-brown coat, every kind of burr and thistle in its low-slung tail. Big animal in any case, though starved almost to death: ladder of ribs and caved-in stomach and hunched, bony spine. Dark lips drawing back to show its teeth, and the train keeps coming, shoving air and sunlight before it.

The engine roars by and the boxcars follow, clack-clacking over the seams of the rails while no one moves, boys or dog, and over that steady clatter you say loudly but calmly: *Marky, don't even think about petting that dog*, and Marky says, *It's all right Danny he's just hungry that's all* . . . and then you know you have to go first, before he goes to the dog himself, and the dog looks spring-loaded, so you go—one hand out, knuckles up for sniffing, and you know Marky has fallen in step behind you by the sound of his excited, open-mouthed breathing.

The dog's eyes are a golden color and they watch you and you only, your every movement: Your hand going slowly into a pocket. The hand coming out again. The thing you hold in your hand now, a Snickers bar, your lunch.

And you were halfway home, the dog wobbling along behind you, before you remembered the penny, and by the time you and Marky were in the driveway you'd sworn off the penny altogether—it had already done its work, hadn't it? You'd always wanted a dog, always, and now here he was! And if she said no, if she tried to say no, you knew already what you'd say to make her say yes . . .

And it wasn't Wyatt down there in the hard ground now; it was just his body, just the organic remains of what he'd lived in while he was on the earth and the rest of him, the most of him, had gone back into the world. Because life was organic and that was one kind of energy, ashes to ashes, but there was also energy between living beings, currents that traveled between them outside of biology, and that energy could not be buried, and neither could it fade into nothing, because energy never just ended, it transformed and recycled and you felt it even if you didn't believe in it. Souls. Spirits. Whatever you called it there was a current and you were in it always and you couldn't bury it.

He heard the sound of tires on packed snow and gravel—then slamming doors, then boots stomping up the front porchsteps before he could call out, "Back here, I'm back here," and the boots stomping back down again and then stomping through the snow, and it was no boy coming around the corner of the house but a full-grown man in blue jeans and his blue mechanic's jacket with the Wabash Auto patch on one side of his chest and his name stitched in red on the other. Marky hustling up the path in the snow, grinning and his arms out, and Danny opening his own arms and bracing for it, but the two of them nearly falling backwards anyway onto the little grave. Righting themselves and holding each other at arm's length to look at faces grown a little older—two years gone by since his last visit—but still at twenty-nine more alike than unalike.

"How you doing, buddy?"

"We saw your truck Danny and Momma said whose truck is that and I said that's Danny's truck and she said how do you know and I said I just know and I was right."

"You were right. How do you like that truck?"

Their mother was making her way up the path, smiling at the sight before her: two boys, not one. Wiping her cheek with gloved fingers.

"That's a Ford F-150 XLT four-by-four two thousand and one," said Marky. "V-8 or V-6 Danny?"

"V-6."

"Four-point-two-liter engine. Wyatt died Danny. Momma buried him right here so you could find him when you came home."

"I know, buddy. I'm sorry I wasn't here."

"It's OK Danny I wasn't either I was at work."

"He was a good dog, wasn't he, buddy."

"He was good dog Danny. He was our dog."

"Yes, he was. But you took care of him."

"Yeah but he missed you Danny. He was always missing you."

"I know. I was missing him too. Now make room for your old mom here."

"Oh, Danny." Her arms tight around him, Danny stooping so she could press her wet cheek to his unshaved jaw. The familiar good mom smell of her out here in the cold. Smell of the farm and the smell of Minnesota in the cold winter dusk.

33

HE'D HAD NOTHING but coffee for the last twenty-four hours and he didn't like tea so she made him hot chocolate, and Danny sat at the table and watched as Marky helped her put the groceries away, then they all sat around the old table as in the old days when the boys were boys, and he answered their questions about Texas and New Mexico and the jobs he'd held since he'd seen them last. He told them about some of the men he'd worked with, like deaf Billy Ramos who could fix any broken thing you put before him. Told them about New Mexico and the old adobe ruins and he told them about the coyotes you heard at night right outside your windows.

"Wild coyotes?" said Marky.

"Is there another kind?"

Marky sat thinking about that.

Danny sipped his hot chocolate.

"Is that the only jacket you own?" he said, and his brother looked down at his mechanic's jacket. He brushed at the oval where his name was stitched.

"What's wrong with it Danny?"

"It's Sunday."

"So?"

"Nothing's wrong with it," said their mother. "Your brother is cranky from his long drive, that's all." She put her hand on Marky's jacket sleeve. "Do you want to take your shower before dinner, sweetie, or after?"

Marky chewed on his lower lip and began to jiggle his right leg. He didn't want to leave, but his habit was to take his shower before dinner and he did not like to break his habits.

"Go," Danny said finally. "You won't miss anything."

"Don't go anywhere Danny," he said, and Danny said, "I just got here, knucklehead," and Marky said, "You're the knucklehead Danny," and he scooted back his chair, and rose from the table, and took his leave—all very impressive until he reached the stairs, and Danny's mug began to chatter on the table with the speed and force of his brother's climb.

Their mother stood and went to the stove, shaking her head. "He's just so excited to see you."

He watched her adjust the flame under the pot. She looked smaller than he remembered her. Grayer. Older.

"He's the same old Marky, isn't he," he said. "Just bigger." He turned the heavy mug on its base. "What does Doc Keogh say?"

She was stirring a wooden spoon in the saucepan and she went on stirring, as if she hadn't heard him. Then she shrugged and said, "What can she say? He's healthy, he's happy." She rapped the wooden spoon on the rim of the pot and turned back to the refrigerator and said from behind its door, "What do you prefer, broccoli or cauliflower?"

"French fries."

"Broccoli it is."

Overhead there was the squeak of the shower faucet and then the sound of water running in the pipes in the wall. When they were growing up there'd been the hospitals. The specialists. The surgeries. These things came with being Marky, and the two of them, he and Marky, had never known any other kind of life. Then, when they were thirteen, she'd sat Danny down alone and told him about statistics. Genetic anomalies. Life expectancy. Their father had been dead for a year by then and Danny knew that a long life was not assured, but as for Marky, it was not even a safe bet.

Twenty-nine now, and there'd been advances, and no one was making predictions anymore, least of all their mother.

"How did he take it?" Danny said to her back. "With Wyatt, I mean."

"He was heartbroken, of course. We both were. Are. You keep expecting to see him lying there, or under your feet." She shook her head.

"I'm sorry I wasn't here, Ma. I'm sorry I wasn't here to help with that. And with Marky."

"Marky was so brave, Danny. He was much braver than me. Even before I could tell him he had his arms around me. 'It's OK, Momma,' he said. 'It was time for him to go.'"

She looked at Danny with wet eyes, smiled, and turned back to the stove, and he turned to the window again. Nothing to see there now but his own reflection, and beyond that the snow—big white flakes tumbling in the shallow light from the kitchen.

"It must have been a job, thawing out that ground," he said.

"Yes, well, that was one of the strangest things," she said, and she told him about the pickax, the ground under the snow like concrete, and Gordon Burke showing up, just—out of nowhere.

Danny had raised the mug halfway to his lips and stopped. Then he sipped and set the mug down again.

It was Gordon's idea to build the fire, she said, to thaw the ground. She didn't know what she'd have done otherwise.

He watched her at the stove, stirring a column of steam at its base so that it rose circling like a twister before her.

"But why was he here?" he said.

"Why was he here?"

"Why did he come out here in the first place?"

She shrugged. "He said he'd seen Marky at the garage that morning. At Wabash's. He said it made him think of us. If we might need any help out here."

Danny watched her. "And when was the last time he did something like that?"

She frowned. She shook her head. "Never. Not since your grandfather was alive and needed some work done on the septic."

Danny stared into the last of the chocolate in the mug, the sludgy remains. Suddenly he could smell the Plumbing & Supply, the cab of Gordon Burke's van. He remembered sweating copper in someone's musty basement. Hauling an old sloshy toilet out to the van and hauling the new one in.

"Well, that's just curious as hell if you ask me. After all this time."

She looked at him, then turned back to the stove. "I suppose so," she said. And said something more, but he wasn't listening, he was staring at the floor. At the blankets there where the dog would lie. As if the dog were still there.

Then he got up and walked over and scooped up the blankets and said, "Do you mind if I get these out of here, Ma? I mean, why are they still lying here like this?"

She looked at him. "Oh, Danny. I just didn't . . . I just didn't want to clear everything out like he was never here."

"It's been over a week, Ma."

"I know."

"Is it OK now? Can I throw them out?"

"Don't throw them out, I'll wash them. Just toss them down the stairs for now."

"You're gonna wash them."

"Yes."

He went to the door and opened it and stood at the head of the stairs looking down. Smell of earth and damp concrete and musty old things passing over him like air from a tomb. Like stale ghosts escaping. The blankets stank of the old dog, but nothing like that stink from that night in the park—dumb-ass dog jerking free and taking off into the park and nothing to do but go after him on foot with the flashlight. The jingling of the tags. The eerie moons of his eyes in the beam of the flashlight. The stink of him when you finally got hold of his leash, some kind of animal shit all over him, *Dumb-ass dog, I oughta just throw you in the river, you know that?*

Danny standing there holding the dog's blankets in his arms, his mother watching him, until finally he pitched them down the stairs like she'd asked him to, shut the door again, and went back to the table.

WHEN THEY PULLED into the lot the next morning the cars all lay under fresh coats of snow—all but one, and he knew this car right off. *Once a Camaro man, always a Camaro man*, Jeff Goss liked to say, and apparently it was true.

"That's Jeff's car Danny," Marky said as they walked by the car. "That's a nineteen ninety-four Chevy Camaro Z28 with a three-fifty pushrod V-8 engine and oh boy is it fast."

They walked up to the glass door in the morning cold as they'd done when they were young, but the smell that hit them when they stepped inside was not the smell of the Plumbing & Supply at all but a trapped smell of grease and rubber and gasoline. No one around in the outer office and no lights showing in the glass door that opened onto the mechanic's bays, but then they heard his whistling and the lights stuttered to life in there and the glass door swung open and Jeff Goss stepped through and saw them and stopped whistling. Stopped walking. Like he'd stepped into a room that was not the one he'd expected.

"Hey Jeff look who's here," Marky said, pumping his thumb over his shoulder. "It's Danny."

Goss's eyes pinged back and forth between their two faces, then he shook his head in a cartoonish way and said, "Thank Christ. I thought I was seeing double." And he stepped forward and Danny stepped forward and they clapped their hands together soul-shake style and half embraced and stepped away again, grinning, shaking their heads. Danny at the sight of a boy he'd known since they were both six, standing now in his mechanic's blues, blond whiskers on his chin, and his blond hair, once so thick and shaggy, cut back and thinning on top, and his face the face of any nearly thirty-year-old man you'd see anywhere, including a mechanic's garage.

Did anything bring home the meaning of time like the human face? And did Jeff see the same, looking at you? Or was he used to your older face because he saw it every day on your brother?

"You've upgraded the Camaro," Danny said, and Jeff said, "Yeah, one piece of shit for a more expensive one. If I wasn't a mechanic I'd be broke. You still got that Chevy?"

"He's got a two thousand and one Ford F-150 XLT with a V-6 engine Jeff."

"He does, does he?" said Jeff. "Well, that'll get you here and there."

"It has so far," said Danny.

They all three stood looking at each other. Then Jeff said, "And so what the hell, Dan? You just visiting, or what?"

"Danny came home because Wyatt died Jeff and he came to see where Momma buried him in the backyard and say good-bye."

Jeff watched Marky's lips as he spoke, then looked to Danny.

"Old Wyatt died," Danny said.

"I got that part. He already told me and I was sorry to hear it. He was a good old dog."

"Yes, he was."

"A good old dog," said Marky.

"I thought I'd come home and see how things were going with Ma and the knucklehead here."

"You're the knucklehead Danny."

"Yeah, I know it. I stayed away too long."

"Well, God damn," said Jeff. He glanced at the clock on the wall behind the counter, old yellowed Pennzoil clock with its light gone out. "I wish we could stand here shooting the shit all day, but Wabash is gonna walk through that door any second now and for some goddam reason he likes to see us working when he walks in, doesn't he, Big Man."

"Mister Wabash could give you a job too Danny and we can all be working together again like we did at the Plumbing Supply."

"I doubt it, buddy. I better let you get to work here. Good to see you, Jeff."

"You too," said Jeff, and Danny stepped out into the cold morning again, but the glass door did not shut behind him, and he turned back to see Jeff holding it open, squinting against the glare of snow and sunlight.

"Shit, Dan," Jeff said. "Are we gonna grab a beer or something, or what?"

Danny nodded. "Yeah, sure. Let's do that."

"What about tonight?"

"Tonight?"

"Why not? The Gophers are playing."

They agreed to meet at the Hilltop Tavern at eight o'clock, and Danny was just climbing back into the truck when a black sedan pulled into the lot. It was an old Ford cop car repainted all black and it turned off to the side of the office and parked next to Jeff's Camaro. Danny started up the truck and put it into reverse, but Wabash had seen him and was walking over. Short and round and wearing a black winter jacket with a woolly collar like a cop's jacket. And cop-like Wabash rolled two fingers in the air for Danny to lower the window, and Danny lowered the window. He left the truck in reverse, his foot on the brake.

"Morning, Mr. Wabash."

Wabash returned his hand to his jacket pocket and there it stayed. No handshake. He said, "I pulled up I thought I saw Marky getting ready to drive this truck."

"No, sir. It's just me."

"I see that now. Up close and all." He roamed his eyes around the inside of the truck and then leaned back to look from hood to tailgate. "Two thousand one?"

"Yes, sir."

"How do you like her?"

"She gets me from here to there."

"That's more than some or I'd be outta business."

Danny nodded. "Well," he said.

"So which is it then?"

"Sir?"

"Which is it then? Here or there?"

Danny looked into the eyes behind the lenses. Pale, watered-down eyes looking back.

"I'm here now," he said. "That's all I know."

Wabash sniffled. "I guess there ain't no law against it," he said. "Is there."

"Not that I know of."

Wabash turned and leaned and spat with care, straightened again and drew a knuckle along the underside of his mustache.

"I guess you heard about Tom Sutter then," he said. "Sheriff Sutter."

"I heard he passed away, yes, sir."

"Heard about his daughter going into the river down there in Iowa."

"Yes, sir."

"That other girl too, from down south."

"Yes."

Wabash staring at him. Shaking his head. "Folks around here," he began, but didn't finish. As if he could not put such thoughts into words.

Danny sat with both hands on the wheel. The truck idling. No other sound in the lot, in the new cold day, until from within the garage there came the shrilling of the pneumatic lug wrench, a short burst followed by the clunk of a lug nut dropped in a tin pan, or an old hubcap. Another burst of the wrench and another dropped lug.

"Well," said Wabash. As if he were finished. But he wasn't. "I ain't one to stick my nose in other folks' business," he said, "but I run a small garage in a small town and your brother in there's an employee of mine and so it ain't exactly not my business either."

Danny looked toward the garage, then back to Wabash. "I guess I'm not following you, Mr. Wabash. I don't see how he has anything to do with it."

"With what?"

"With whatever it is you're saying."

"Not saying nothin here. Just standing here talking with a feller."

Danny nodded. "Well," he said. "I ought to get going."

"Will say this one thing though," said Wabash. "Maybe you already know it, maybe you don't." He nodded in the direction of the garage. "But when I hired them two in there I was pretty hard up for help. I'd lost one man to retirement and another just run off heck knows where and the cars were stacking up. Didn't need no geniuses, just needed hands on deck. Even so I wasn't too keen on hiring them two after all that happened, and one of them being the way he is. But a man asked me to do him a favor, and I'd known that man a long time so I done it. And I ain't been sorry. They've been good workers and they've stayed on where others have come and gone. But even so. Even now I guess I could still be sorry I done it."

He squared himself in his black jacket and waited for Danny's response.

Danny said, "Yes, sir. I know how much my brother loves this job. And how much it means to my mother. To our family."

Wabash sniffed and looked away down the road. He shook his head and said, "It's a small town, mister, that's all I'm saying here. A real small town. I'd think a man would want to keep that in mind, that's all."

He looked back at Danny and when he did Danny said, "Yes, sir, I've kept that in mind. I've kept that in mind quite a lot."

34

THE DAY AFTER she'd come out to his house, Gordon drove to hers, or the house that had become hers, but when he saw the unshoveled snow on the drive he stopped short of it and sat there, his hands on the wheel. Snow on the Ford sedan too, bumper to bumper, and no fresh tiretracks or even foot tracks in the snow on the drive and none on the porchsteps either. It was already three o'clock in the afternoon. A snow shovel stood on the porch, propped against the house like something no one seemed to know the use of. All the curtains were drawn. No smoke from the chimney, no steam even from the exhaust tubes in the roof. He didn't want to go packing down the snow with his own tires before she got a chance to shovel, and then he remembered the purple cast and shook his head and cut the engine and got out.

He went up the porchsteps and stood before the door, listening. No sound inside. No one around on the cul-de-sac that he could see, no one to wonder at an unmarked white van parked in front of the sheriff's house. Ex-sheriff's house. No dogs barking at him from the neighbors' windows.

He cleared off the steps first, then he shoveled the walkway and then he shoveled the drive, working around the sedan, and in the fifteen minutes this took she did not come out, did not come to a window, not that he saw anyway.

He got back in the van and backed into the drive alongside the sedan, cut the engine again and got out and opened up the rear double doors. It was a quarter-face cord, give or take, and it took him twenty minutes to get it all stacked on the porch, turning each piece for fit, and when he was finished he set the bundle of kindling in its belt of twine on top of the stack, then stood brushing the bark chips from his jacket sleeves. Then just stood there, looking out over the houses of the cul-de-sac, as the man must've stood a thousand times, smoking his cigarettes, a full day of law enforcement before him or behind him. Of the half dozen driveways, hers was the only one that had not been shoveled, and when he looked at the house two doors to the right a curtain fell shut. Yeah, you should hide your face, buddy. Can't shovel the drive for a girl with a busted arm. With a dead father.

He turned back to Sutter's stormdoor. In the inside door was a small square of window, head-high, thin white curtain drawn over it on the other side.

He coughed. He scratched at the back of his head. He looked at the stack of firewood. Finally he went down the steps once more and closed up the van's double doors with more bang than necessary and took one more look at the house—nothing—then climbed into the cab and turned over the engine and pulled out into the street. Three, four blocks away he stopped at the yellow light and sat there through the red.

Hell, you don't even know that girl. Scare her to death showing up like that.

A car honked and he said, "All right, all right," and drove through the green and then without signaling or braking he pulled a sudden left into the Phillips 66 and navigated the van around the pumps and back toward the road—pulling out onto the road again and accelerating back the way he'd come and just making the yellow, and there were no more lights after that and when he reached the house he pulled nose-first into the drive and left the van running. He went up the porchsteps and pushed his finger into the button and listened to the two-note chime sounding inside the house. Waited. Pushed the button again. Then he opened up the stormdoor and rapped on the square of glass.

"Audrey—?" He'd never said her name aloud that he remembered and it felt strange in his throat and strange in his ears.

He waited. Rapped again.

"Son of a bitch," he said, and the door was not locked.

The room was dark, and so cold he saw his breath. But cold as it was the smell was strong and no mistaking it. Daylight spilled in around him and in this light something moved and he stepped aside to let in more light, and a white face rose up from the sofa, up from a dark mound of coverings. Bleary, unfocusing eyes blinking in pain at the light. In confusion.

"Daddy . . . ?" she said. Her voice so thin and hoarse. And then he realized she couldn't see anything but his shape and he stepped in and shut the door behind him and said, "No, it's Gordon here. Gordon Burke."

". . . Who?"

"Gordon Burke. Why's it so cold in here?"

"Oh," she said, and her head dropped from view again. As if she could not hold it up a second longer.

He came closer. She'd piled every kind of covering over herself—blankets, jackets, sleeping bags. Like a great cocoon. Mail was strewn across the coffee table, and even in that gloom he recognized the Water & Gas envelope. FINAL NOTICE printed slantwise in red, as if hand-stamped by some angry little lackey.

"How long have you been lying here in the cold like this?"

From down in her cocoon she said, "I'm sorry." Or seemed to say.

"Audrey," he said.

She didn't answer. He stepped between the coffee table and the sofa and nearly kicked over the small plastic wastebasket there on the floor. Slosh of liquid and a sharper stink of vomit. He moved it so he could get closer.

"I'm going to feel your forehead now."

No answer, and he moved aside the clinging hair and shaped his hand to her forehead. *Holy God.*

"OK," he said, "that's it. I'm taking you to the hospital." He began peeling back the layers one by one.

"No," she said, weakly reaching for the peeled-away layers.

"No argument here. You are burning up." He peeled her down to the last thin damp blanket and stopped. Then peeled that slowly until he saw that she was wearing a shirt—red flannel shirt many sizes too big. She was folded up inside the shirt, and from the knees down she wore thick dark socks. She lay curled up and shivering. Heat and sweat and sickness rising from her in a rank steam.

"Please," she said, "don't."

"Can you stand up? Come on, I'll help you."

Slowly she rose to sitting and the moment she did so she reached for the wastebasket. He held it for her, held her hair as she heaved and coughed and spat. Almost nothing came up.

"Come on." Helping her to her feet. Her father's jacket was among the layers and he found it and got her to put her arms through the sleeves, cast and all, and as she stood swaying he reached down and fed the zipper and drew the metal tab up to her chin. "Here, let's get these boots on you."

"Mr. Burke," she said.

"Yep." He was trying to help with the boot and at the same time keep his grip on her arm so she wouldn't fall over. He was doing it all wrong.

"I can't go back there."

He looked up at her. He had to think a moment.

"We're not going up there," he said. "We're going to Charlotte."

She shook her head. "Not there either. Can't go to a hospital."

"You have a fever and you're dehydrated."

"Please, Mr. Burke."

"Audrey . . ."

"Please, Mr. Burke."

35

He was five minutes late and Jeff was already sitting at the bar with his arms crossed before him and a half-gone glass of beer at his elbow, his face lifted toward the TV above the back bar. Two other men sat at the bar in much the same posture, and all three glanced over their shoulders to see who had come through the door and all three turned back to the TV once they'd seen. No other sound in the bar but the sounds of the game, the announcers and the crowd and the squeaking sneakers.

He took the stool to Jeff's left and the man behind the bar flipped him a cardboard coaster and asked what he could get him and Jeff said, "Mike, this is a old, old buddy of mine, Danny Young. Danny, this is Mike. He's good people." Danny shook the man's hand and watched his face to see if the name meant anything to him, but he saw no such sign. He ordered a beer and Mike stepped away to draw it.

"You still follow the Gophers?" Jeff said. He was watching the game again and Danny watched too.

"Not much."

"Smart man. Nothing but aggravation and heartbreak."

Mike returned with the beer, and after he'd stepped away again they raised their glasses and clinked them together and Jeff said, "Old friends," and they drank and set the glasses down again. On the TV a young man stood at the free-throw line and they all watched to see if he would make his shots and when he did the man to Danny's left slapped the bar and said, "Praise the Lord."

Danny looked over his shoulder at the half dozen empty tables, their surfaces stained red and blue with the neon in the front window. Four booths along the back wall, all unoccupied. A dark and timeless place. A place their own grandfathers might have gone to in a time before there were televisions.

They watched the game. They drank their beers. Jeff asked Danny about his jobs, the places he'd lived, and Danny told him about his travels as he remembered them, unable to make them sound more interesting than they were. After a silence he asked Jeff how his mother was and Jeff shrugged.

"Still alive," he said. "Still up there in Rochester at the home."

"You get up there to see her?"

"Holidays. Mother's Day. She don't even know who I am anymore. Sometimes she thinks I'm my dad. Sometimes she thinks I'm this guy George Munroe, who I guess was some kid she knew in high school."

Danny shook his head, no idea what to say.

"Katie works up there now," Jeff said.

"In Rochester?"

"In the home. As a nurse. Mom doesn't know her from any of the other nurses."

Jeff watched the game, and Danny watched too but he was seeing Katie Goss. Her thick blond hair and her dark eyes. Her smell of strawberries and her laugh—she was a good laugher and you had to shush her at night when you snuck her in, and even put your hand over her mouth, because she'd laugh when you touched her, when you kissed her anywhere below the neck, *Shh, shh*, your hearts beating because you must be quiet, you must be quiet and secret. Summer nights with the windows open and the bugs so loud in their rhythm, their one great pulsing song and *Oh Danny*, she'd say, *Oh Danny*. Both of you too young to know how sweet, how fine. To know what could be lost.

Jeff said, "Aw, Jesus Christ" to something in the game, and Danny took a drink of his beer.

"I heard she got married," he said. "Had a kid. A little girl."

"That what you heard?"

"Ma wrote something, a few years back."

Jeff took a drink and set his beer down again. "Had the kid but never got married. Guy was a total douche. Left her high and dry."

Danny shook his head, in real sadness. "I'm sorry to hear it," he said, and Jeff shrugged again and said, "It is what it is, man." And saying this he looked at Danny, as if to give greater weight to the words, and Danny held his eyes—eyes of childhood, eyes of boyhood in the face of this man sitting at the bar drinking his beer, a man still in his mechanic's jacket and smelling of the garage.

Jeff turned back to the game. Then he gave Danny a backhanded swat to the arm. "You wanna sit at a table? This game is killing me, man." And they took a table far enough from the bar that they would not be overheard by the men at the bar but not so far that the men would wonder what it was they had to move so far away to discuss, and when they sat they arranged themselves so both had a view of the game, as if that were still their top priority. The man who'd sat to Danny's left watched the move dull-eyed over his shoulder, and Danny and Jeff returned his look until at last he swung his head back around and lifted his glass and drank, the back side of his skull gleaming under a few dark strings of hair.

"SAW YOU OUT there talking to Wabash this morning," Jeff said. He'd put his boots up on one of the empty chair seats and crossed them at the ankles and likewise crossed his arms, and his eyes were still on the game.

"He felt like a chat, I guess," Danny said.

"What'd he have to say?"

"He seemed mainly to want to tell me what a small town it is."

"Meaning?"

"Meaning I guess I might just want to think about that."

Jeff picked up his glass and before taking his drink said, "Well, maybe you might."

Danny looked over but Jeff kept his eyes on the game.

"You got something on your mind, Jeff?"

"Just saying," Jeff said. "A man might wonder what you're doing back here, Dan."

"I don't know why a man would. I've been back plenty of times."

"I know it. Big Man always tells me. Christmastime, usually. But then you go back to wherever. You don't go driving him to work. You don't go parking your truck in the lot and walking right in. Standing around jawing with Wabash all day."

Danny looked at him, then looked away.

"I guess I shouldn't have bothered you, Jeff."

"Aw, shit." Jeff brought his boots to the floor, and the man at the bar with the stringy hair glanced back at the sound, his brows bunched up over the dark mound of his shoulder. Jeff waited for him to turn away again.

"It ain't about that, Dan, and you know it."

"What it's about?"

"You know what it's about." Jeff leaned forward, and Danny turned, the better to face him, and they looked into each other's eyes—and finally with a smirk Jeff said in a lowered voice, "It's about what everybody has always said every time they've seen you back here and what they're gonna say now—especially now."

"Why especially now?"

Jeff looked at him. "Seriously?"

Danny waited.

"Not two weeks since those two girls went into the river down in Iowa? One of them dead and the other the sheriff's daughter. What sheriff? The sheriff who let that son of a bitch Danny Young go scot-free and who is now dead himself in the ground."

Danny stared at Jeff, Jeff staring back.

"I gotta say, Jeff. I thought you of all people would cut me a little slack."

"Why me of all people, Dan?"

Danny looked at him. Sitting there waiting. All tensed up like some kind of animal. Spring-loaded. It made him so tired, suddenly. Then in a voice only Jeff could hear he said, "We drove right by her, Jeff. We both of us drove right by where it happened. Where they say she went into the river."

Jeff shook his head and laughed but there was no humor in it. "That ain't what you mean."

There was a disturbance at the bar and they both turned to watch as the man with the stringy hair righted himself and stood blinking glassily at the room. At the two of them sitting there. He let go of the bar and made his way step by step to the dim hallway, then pushed his way into the men's room and forced the wonky door shut behind him.

"I was the one they wanted," Danny said. "That's all that's ever mattered to anyone."

Jeff said nothing to that. They sat staring at each other. So many years to their friendship. All the years up to that night ten years ago—years of play, of school, of hockey on the frozen lake, summer camp. Of secret hideouts and talk of girls and then the girls themselves. And then all the years after when they said nothing more about it and did not see each other or even talk on the phone but just got on with their strange, separate, suddenly adult lives.

"What," said Danny. "You think I'd come back here to say something now I never said back then? That I'd just suddenly start telling some other story?"

"Maybe you figured enough time has passed nobody'd do nothin about it now anyhow. Statue of limitations or some such shit."

"There ain't no statute of limitations for that, Jeff."

"Well, that's a fuckin relief." He drank his beer and looked at the TV, and Danny looked too but the game had ended and the news was on. The bartender had gone somewhere out of view. The remaining man at the bar appeared to be asleep on his forearms. In all the time they'd been in the tavern no one else had come in or left. As if the world outside had stopped for that time. As if the last of the world were right here in this dark and random place.

"What I told them was the truth, Jeff. I was out there chasing down that goddam dog and I didn't see anything else. Not a God damn thing. End of story."

Jeff took a breath and let it out and all the fight seemed to go out of him with the breath.

"Shit, Dan. It coulda been either one of us. They had us at the bar and they had me as the old boyfriend but they had you in the park. But it coulda just as easily been me."

"You weren't the old boyfriend. You didn't even date her, technically."

"She didn't date anyone technically."

"That's what I'm saying."

Jeff ran his thumb down the curve of his beer glass. "I had a thing for her, though. You know I did."

"A lot of guys had a thing for her."

"You knew I did, though. And you knew how drunk I was. Shit. I'd be sitting in jail right now. And my Ma would be in the state hospital in a paper gown with all the crazies. Or dead. Which would be preferable, actually."

"They had no case, Jeff."

Jeff shook his head. "That sheriff, Sutter, and that deputy, what was his name?"

"Moran."

"Moran. With those bug eyes of his. They sure didn't like nothing about either one of us, did they."

"No, they did not."

Danny looked into his beer. Jeff sat pulling at the whiskers on his chin. Then he said, "Tell you one thing I never could figure."

"What's that."

"Why old Gordo stuck up for me with Wabash, after all that. I never would of got that job otherwise."

"He knew about your ma. He knew you needed the work."

"Maybe. But I think it was about Big Man, mostly. I think he had a soft spot there."

"Maybe," said Danny. "But I'll tell you something."

Jeff waited.

"Marky never would've got that job without you there with him. You've watched out for him, Jeff, and I won't ever forget that. None of us will."

Jeff rolled his eyes. "Don't be thanking me, for Christ's sake." He shook his head dismally. "All these years. All that time away from your family."

Danny looked down at the floor, at his boots. "How about this," he said. "How about we just give the whole subject a rest. That work for you?"

"That works for me. You just watch your ass, Danny-boy, all right? There's no telling what some folks might do."

"I'll watch my ass."

Danny raised his glass and after a moment Jeff raised his too and as they did so the men's room door rattled open and the drunk man emerged and came toward them on a wandering course. He reached their table and stood balancing himself. Wet pink eyes disappearing in long, slow blinks.

"A word of caution, boys, if you will allow it," he said, and swung his face from one of them to the other. Danny looked to Jeff, and Jeff looked to Danny but before either could speak the man said, "He is everywhere, boys. Everywhere. Even here, in this reportedly godforsaken place," and he raised both hands and looked to the ceiling like a man preparing to catch something, and holding this pose he began to pitch forward, slowly, like a great statue falling, and he would have crashed face-first into their table except that both of them rose at once to take an arm and stop his fall and set him back on his feet again.

He nodded at them in turn. Patted their hands. Their shoulders.

"You see?" he said. "Even here, boys. Even here."

36

HE'D COME OUT of the men's room wiping his hands on his jeans to dry them, and Jeff was not at the table and he thought he'd gone ahead but then he saw him at the bar. Jeff, he'd said, reaching him before he could order, taking hold of his arm. Come on, Jeff, we said we were going.

Just one more.

That's what you said last time.

What's your hurry?

I gotta get home.

No you don't.

Yeah, I do, Danny said. I gotta open the store in the morning.

Jeff sputtered his lips and flung his hand.

Fine, Danny said. Stay if you wanna stay, but I'm going. And he'd made his way through the bodies and was pushing through the door before Jeff caught up with him, You hard-ass, Young, you killjoy, the two of them stepping out into a strong October wind, Aw be quiet you old drunk, their voices carrying across the lot and the dog's head popping up in the rear window well before they reached the back of the lot where they'd parked their vehicles, the car and the truck, side by side. Jeff wrestling his keys from his jeans pocket and dropping them in the gravel and stooping to pick them up and nearly toppling in the wind.

Let me drive you, Jeff.

I'm all right.

Danny leaned against the fender of the old Camaro and after a moment Jeff did too. They stared back at the building. The faint beat of music from within. Bodies moving dimly behind the glass. The cold night wind felt good after the heat of Smithy's on a Wednesday night—Wednesday nights being a night of low enforcement, so far as carding went, and therefore one of the bar's busiest.

Where do you think she is now? Jeff said.

Who?

You know who.

Why do you care?

I don't care. I know where she is. Blowing some dumb-fuck for her ride home.

I thought you were over her.

I am over her. He snorted and shook his head. He said, You could see right through that goddam shirt or whatever it was she was wearing.

I know it, said Danny. She knew it.

Jeff looked up at the sky, the moon. His blond hair tossed by the wind. And it's fuckin October. You think he knows she goes out dressed like that?

Who?

Who do you think? The old man. Old Gordo.

Yeah, I think he knows.

Abruptly Jeff leaned forward and put his hands on his knees.

You gonna puke?

No I ain't gonna puke.

Why don't we walk around awhile? We can walk the dog.

I'm all right. He straightened and combed his fingers through his hair. Just then a car pulled into the lot, a family wagon, and three girls they knew spilled out, all legs and high heels. Clutching at each other as they crossed the pitted lot, holding down their skirts in the wind. When they saw the two boys leaning on the Camaro one of them, Loretta Woods, called out, Get a room, you two, and Jeff called back, Only if you join us, and the girls went into hysterics, Dream on, Goss! and even Jessica Fisher, who was a shy girl, stuck out her hip and gave herself a spank and on they went laughing into the bar.

Now you see there, said Jeff. Let's get back in there and get some a that.

We're not getting any of that, Jeff.

Are you kidding me?

Shit, said Danny. Those girls will get you buying them drinks all night and when you go to take a piss they'll go right out the door, laughing their asses off.

Jeff looked at him and shook his head. Pussy-whipped.

What?

Heard me.

That's a fine way to talk about your sister.

Not talking about her, talking about you.

Danny looked at the big window in the front of the bar. The moving shapes within, the muted pulse of music.

He wasn't going to say it. Then he did.

What's up with her, anyway? he said.

Who?

Your sister, dumb-ass.

Whattaya mean what's up with her? She's Katie.

Danny watched the bar. Something's up, he said.

Well, said Jeff. I didn't know if I should say anything, he said, all at once sober. I mean—shit.

Danny turned to look at him. Jeff looking down. Shaking his head.

I think she might be cheating on you, buddy, he said, and looked up. He held his expression, then lost it. Sputtering into his hand.

Fuck you, said Danny.

Relax, man. She's cramming. Entrance exams and shit. You should know all about that, college boy.

Yeah, Danny said. Cramming. That's what she keeps telling me.

Jeff shook his head. Pussy. Whipped.

Danny pushed off from the fender. You coming with me or not?

No, I am not. Jeff rolled to his right and opened the driver's door and lowered himself into the bucket seat. Got his legs in and shut the door. He put the key in the ignition and powered down the window but did not start the car. Gonna just sit here awhile, he said, and then I'll drive on home. He tilted the seat back and closed his eyes.

I can wait and follow you home, Danny said.

I ain't no drunker'n you.

Hell you're not.

Whatever. Go home. I'm fine.

You won't go back in there?

No, I won't.

You promise?

Yes, sir.

And you'll drive straight home?

Yes, sir, Officer Dan.

All right. I gotta let that dog out before he explodes.

Oh, Danny-boy, Jeff sang.

I'm gonna call you later.

The pipes, the pipes are clo-ogg-ing.

The dog rode with his nose pointed into the wind and he knew where they were going and he began to whine: he could smell the park, the river. At the last light on the business drag they turned right and took the winding blacktop into the park. The limbs of the big oaks bending in the wind, the points of the spruces stirring the stars like spearheads. Midway through the park the river swung into view through a single-file row of pines, and on it sat a bright gob of moon swimming against the current, keeping pace with the truck, and when Danny pulled off onto the dirt shoulder and came to a stop the moon stopped too and sat shuddering on the windy face of the water.

He cut the engine and the lights, then snapped the leash to the dog's collar and opened the door—Wait, stupid, let me get out first—and when he was out of the way the dog jumped down and at that same moment something went skittering by them in the dirt, some night creature small and fast, and the dog leapt after it and the leash sang through Danny's grip and sailed free and the dog was gone, his paws pounding over the turf and there was the frantic jangling of his tags and then no sound but the wind as he ran deeper into the park, into the darkness under the trees.

No point even calling his name, you couldn't bring him back from that chase until he'd given it up on his own.

Danny pitched the truck seat forward and found the MagLite and tested it—the beam not at its strongest but strong enough—then he took the keys from the ignition and set off into the park. Following that beam into the woods, listening for the tags, for any sound that wasn't the autumn leaves in the wind, the high limbs creaking. Calling casually to the dog, Wyatt, come on. Whistling. Cold wind, now. First bite of winter in it. The moon following him through the treetops like an interested party. Like a fellow searcher.

Dumb-ass too drunk to hold on to a dog leash. He thought about going home with no dog. Or a dog that had been hit by a car. Thought of his brother's face when he saw the body. Not good.

He heard the tags and swept the light, but nothing there. The tossing branches, the blowing grass. He called to the dog and told him he had treats— did he want a treat? He knows you don't have no treats, dummy. Pressing on under the swaying branches and boughs, the moon keeping pace. Good ol' moon, there's ten bucks in it for you if you find him first.

It was called a park but where were the lamps, the friendly walkways—the swing sets and the shelters and the grassy spaces where parents could set their kids loose to kick a ball while the wieners roasted? It was like the city planners had dreamed of a park but then, having engineered a single road through the little wilderness end-to-end, had forgotten their dreams and moved on. As kids you'd come here with your crew to drink PBRs and smoke and shove each other around, but which of you would ever come here alone? In the dark, in the moving shadows of the trees?

For all the distance and the wind he heard the motor clearly and when he turned he saw the headlights skimming along the road and he knew the sound of the motor and he even knew the cast of the headlights and he thought Jeff would stop when he saw the truck or honk at least, but he did neither and instead drove on at a good clip and at least he was going home, at least he had the good sense to go through the park and stay off the streets where the cops were parked and waiting for the kids as they got out of the bars with their fake IDs. Later, Danny would remember the headlights, and think, and try to remember more. But there was nothing more to it than that: the Camaro passing by and not stopping, not honking.

His cell phone buzzed and he fished it up from his pocket and flipped it open, thinking Jeff, but it was Jeff's sister.

Hey you, he said.

Danny—?

Katie—?

—hear me?

I hear you!

Where are you, it sounds like a—

What? I'm in the park. The wind is insane. Wyatt got loose.

You're where? I can't—

The park! I'll call you back, I think I see him.

Danny—

But he'd flipped the phone shut and returned it to his pocket. Tags jingled and he swept the dying beam in the direction of the sound and just caught two eyes in the dark, lighting them for an instant like weird marbles floating in the night, green and see-through and blinking out again. Stay right there, God damn it, he said. Tags jingling. Sound of paws rooting in the turf. A desperate snorting and snuffling. When he reached him the dog had just been on his back, paws to the sky, and now he was on his feet again and shaking the debris from his coat. Danny put the light on his own face and said the dog's name quietly, calmly. The dog stood watching his face, waiting, and Danny reached and took up the leash and wrapped it twice around his fist and pulled the dog to him. The smell was just awful.

Jesus, what is that? Is that bear shit? You dumb dog. Christ—it's all over you.

He began making his way back to the river, the dog panting happily alongside him, the chase forgotten, at peace and much pleased with his adventures.

Dumb-ass dog, I oughta just throw you in the river, you know that?

The dog panting and padding alongside him and no remorse in him whatsoever.

The dog was a good jumper and he leapt onto the tailgate and Danny fastened the leash to a tie-down cleat. He drove through the remainder of the park, then out onto the county road on the other side, and he'd not gone a quarter mile before he saw the headlights in the rearview mirror and then above those he saw the blue-and-red barlights flashing and *Shit, shit*, he said and pulled off onto the shoulder and threw the truck into park again.

He got out his wallet and he thought to get the registration from the glovebox and then he thought again—the cop back there running the plate, watching him—and he put his hands high on the wheel and waited. He tried to remember if you were supposed to agree to the test or say no and ask for a lawyer—but now the cop was out of his cruiser and walking up with the beam of his flashlight slashing before him, his free hand holding down his hat in the wind. Wyatt began barking and the cop stopped and swept his light over the dog and he swept it around the truckbed and then he stepped up to the driver's-side window and Danny powered down the glass. He was with the sheriff's department— Danny just had time to see that before the light was in his eyes.

You want to cut that engine, sir?

Yes, sir, Danny said, and did so. And turned off the headlights.

The deputy or whatever he was swept his light over the seat and then he put it on the passenger-side floor and he put it on Danny again. The deputy was chewing gum; the wind blew the minty smell of it into the cab.

Think you can get your dog to shut up a minute, sir?

Danny leaned out the window and yelled the dog's name and told him to hush and he did. In the cab you could hear his nails ticking on the truckbed. The truck rocking slightly as he paced the length of his leash.

Can I see your license, sir?

Yes, sir. He handed over the card.

And your registration.

It's in the glovebox.

Is there a firearm in there too?

No, sir.

All right then, go ahead and get it.

Danny reached over and opened the glovebox and found the registration and handed that over too, and the deputy put his light on the document and on his license and handed both back, then stood there not quite square to the window, his beam aimed at the ground now and looking at Danny.

You been drinking tonight, Daniel?

I had one a while ago.

Just one?

Yes, sir.

And where was that at?

Smithy's, sir.

You got a fake ID?

No, sir. They didn't ask for my ID.

The deputy leaned in and sniffed at the cab. What is that smell? Did you shit your pants, Daniel?

Danny stared at him. The deputy staring back.

No, sir. That dog back there rolled in something in the park.

What was she doing in the park?

I took him there so he could do his business but he got away from me.

Did you see the sign when you entered the park?

Which sign?

The one that says the park is closed after dark.

No, sir. I'd have to say I didn't notice it. I was just driving through on my way home.

Just driving through.

Yes, sir.

You just told me you took your dog there and let her out. Did she jump out of the moving vehicle?

No, sir. I stopped and put the leash on him but then he got away.

The deputy looked at Danny.

Sit here, he said. And then he walked back to the truckbed and raked his beam inside it again. He walked behind the truck and he walked to the passenger side and he walked all the way around to the front, and when he got there he put his beam on the windshield and into Danny's eyes as if playing some kind of game. As if to see how his face would look in the bright instant before a head-on crash. Then he came back full circle and looked once more into the cab.

I've got half a mind to make you walk a line, Daniel. But I don't think I'll do that tonight. Tonight I think I'll let you get on home. Straight home. No more stops for nothing. That work for you?

The deputy's flashlight was off and Danny could see his eyes under the brim of the hat. Wide-set eyes that bulged slightly and didn't seem to center on him exactly. As if they were not quite designed for forward vision, like the eyes of a fish, or a frog. He stared at Danny with these eyes and Danny said, Yes, sir, that works for me. One hundred percent.

37

AFTER HE LEFT the Hilltop Tavern he drove through town, and at the end of the business drag he pulled into the park once again, and once again it was after dark—but no dog with him this time, no Wyatt with his nose out the window and his entire body quivering with his need to get out of the truck, to sniff and to lift his leg and to know the whole world by its smells.

The road had been plowed but not plowed well and there were three distinct tracks in the snow, the center track shared by cars coming and going, and if anyone came along you'd have to inch by each other to pass or else drive into the deep snowbanks, and he could see where some of them had done just that. His lights in the turns swept over the naked trunks of the oaks and the snowy boughs of the pines, and no other cars coming or following as far as he could see.

When he reached the stretch of road that ran along the river, with just the row of pines between the road and the riverbank, he shifted the truck into four-wheel drive and plowed into the snowbank and let the truck come to rest on its own, one headlight glancing off the deep snow and one yet on the road. He killed the engine and stepped down into the road and shut the door behind him. No sound but the ticking of the engine and no light but the light of the snow itself and a faint glow of moon drifting behind the dark clouds above the treetops.

He crossed the road and stepped up into the snowbank on the opposite side and trod through the drifts between the pines and came to the edge of the river and stopped, winded, his bare hands in his jacket pockets. Before him the river lay flat and still from bank to bank and buried in white except where the wind had scoured away the snow and left black, glassy ponds of ice, like portals for looking into the water that flowed below. It was two bodies of water really, one holding in place for the long winter while the other flowed on beneath it. One staying, one going. When they were kids they played hockey on the pond behind Shep Porter's house first and then, later in the winter, out on the lake, but they were not allowed to play on the river because of the current. And there was that time on the lake when Shep's little brother Royce went out for a runaway puck and everyone saw him drop, just drop, like he'd hit a trapdoor, and the whole gang of boys taking off yelling *Human chain, human chain!* and you were the first one out there and you went down on your belly and Jeff Goss had you by the ankles and someone had Jeff, and you reached first with your hockey stick but that wasn't enough, and you had to crawl right up to him, the whole chain crawling too, and Royce waiting with his arms spread on the ice before him and his face already blue and when you saw his eyes up close you knew you'd never really seen fear before, not even on your brother's face, and you told him *Royce, you're all right, I got you,* and you had to shuck off your gloves to get a good grip on his jacket, and the kid pawing at your arms, your neck, and when you reached into the water for his legs it was just amazing the coldness, like putting your hands into fire, and only then did you think about the deepness under you and how you would go in face-first and upside down . . . but then somehow you were moving away from the hole, Jeff and the boys behind him pulling you back and you pulling Royce and when you were clear, you all half carried him on his skates back to the warming shack that was not warm but it was out of the wind at least and the kid was too cold and too shocked even to cry, and it was another month easy before any of you were allowed back on the ice and only then after Shep and Royce's father had gone out there with his augur and tested the thickness.

And he thought of those two girls down in Iowa, Sutter's daughter and her friend, the moment when they knew they were going through the ice but had no idea what that meant, no idea really that there was a second river under the river and how the water was so cold it would feel like fire, so cold all the blood would rush to their chests to keep their hearts from stopping.

They said Holly Burke was still alive when she went into the river. Said she'd been breathing but unable to swim. Unconscious or too broken from the impact of the vehicle. That was in October, when the river was just one river. Vehicle, they said—not car, not truck. If she'd died from the impact it might have been just manslaughter. An accident. Might have been. Unless you were drinking. Then you were looking at vehicular homicide. But if you moved her and put her in the river, well, that was a whole other deal, they said. That was murder.

Murder.

That word, spoken to you by men in uniform, real cops in the real world, was unbelievable. It couldn't be happening. It was a word to take the life you knew and turn it instantly into something else. Which, all right, was nothing compared to what had been taken from Holly Burke. From her parents. But it was a kind of death. It was the death of how the world thought of you and even how you thought of yourself. You didn't know that you had been happy, that you had been free and happy and that you had loved life until you heard that word. Only then did you know, but too late.

It was two steps down the bank to the ice and he put one boot down on the ice to test it, feeling for give, listening for pops, and after a moment he brought the other boot down and stood with his weight centered over his feet and his back to the bank. And then he walked. The snow bright and undisturbed except where small animals had passed, and if there were pops from the ice they'd be muted by the snow and obscured by the sound of it compressing under his boots, and he walked all the way to what he judged to be the middle of the river and there he walked onto a clearing of black ice and stood listening. No popping. No cracking. Just the sound of his own breathing. The strange vantage of the wide river before him, the banks far away to his left and right. Like walking on water. When he looked overhead for the moon behind the clouds he had to put his arms out for balance.

He got down on his hands and knees and smoothed a glassy place with the palms of his hands and shaped his hands into a diving mask and put his face to his hands and he made his heart cold with the thought of something bobbing into view out of the darkness, sudden and horrible, as it would in the movies—a face, blue and frozen in its last moments of terror. But there was nothing to see in the ice but darkness.

You want to kiss me, don't you, Danny, she said to him once, in the woods behind her father's house, in the winter, when they were kids. They were following the tracks of a fox, Marky up ahead of them ducking under the snowy branches. When she said it Danny had felt the heat go through him like stepping into a hot bath. A sudden weakness in his legs.

No, I don't, he'd said.

Yes, you do.

How do you know?

I see you looking at me, Danny Young.

And though his face burned he looked at her then—her soft lips and her pretty eyes and the pink blotches on her cheeks from the cold. It's OK, she said, I don't mind, and she stopped, and he stopped. But then Marky yelled, C'mon Danny c'mon Holly, and Danny walked on. She followed, caught up with him. She swept snow from a pine bough and said, Maybe I'll let Marky kiss me. He's better-looking anyway, and Danny's heart was suddenly pounding. He stopped again and she stopped too.

What? she said.

You leave Marky alone.

He saw the change in her eyes—the moment when play, teasing, fell away.

I was just kidding, she said.

I'm not.

She stared at him, and he saw the meanness coming. But ahead of it came the tears.

Like I'd let either of you retards kiss me, she said, and turned and ran—flat-out ran from him through the woods, and he'd stood watching her go, her red girl's coat, her red knit cap, her winter boots kicking up snow, until she was nothing but small bursts of red in all that thickness of green and white.

THE TRUCK SHRUGGED itself from the snow and rocked back onto the road and it was flinging snow to its undercarriage when he heard what sounded like a good-size rock striking the inside of the wheelwell, and he thought nothing about that, or even about the flash of light he thought he'd seen from deep in the trees, just a small splash of light in the darkness, until an instant later when his heart, his whole body jolted with fear and he ducked down low and floored the truck—all four tires shuddering in the tracks, and there was no one coming on the road ahead and he barreled down it cutting the turns so close to the snowbanks he sheared them off with the side of the truck, and when he reached the end of the park he didn't slow down, he blew through the stop sign and the truck skated almost broadside to the road before the wheels caught and the truck heaved into line with the road, and he sped away down the county road with an oncoming car pulling over to give him room, this maniac, and his heart was pounding and all his blood was ice but there was no one coming, no one following, and after a mile or maybe two he eased off the gas and he remembered to shift back to two-wheel drive and he was all right, he wasn't shot, he was all right.

38

He DID NOT stop, did not pull over to look at the truck.

He thought of calling 911 or even driving to the police station but he had a vision of getting out of the truck and finding nothing there, no bullet hole, and the cops wanting to see his ID and looking him up, *Daniel Young—that Daniel Young?* and as he thought through these scenarios, and others, he arrived, as if suddenly, at the farmhouse and he slowed down well before he reached the drive, because parked just before it on the side of the road was a car—his own headlights picking up the rear lenses first, then the barlights on the roof, and lastly shaping out the man who sat behind the wheel—and his first thought was that there had been some report, that already they knew about the shot in the park and the officer had been dispatched to meet him.

But that made no sense—and anyway why wouldn't the officer pull into the drive and knock on the door?

Then he understood, and he knew that he should not pass the officer and pull into the drive himself, but should instead pull over behind the cruiser and put the truck in park, turn off his lights, and wait, just sit there and wait, and he did each of these things in turn and only then, after perhaps another full minute, did the door of the cruiser open and the man step out putting on his hat and begin his walk to the truck, and Danny knew him before he put on the hat and before he stepped out of the cruiser even.

The deputy carried no flashlight this time and he walked up to the truck with no caution at all, his hands loose at his sides, and when he reached the window he stood square to it and put his hands in his jacket pockets and he was already shaking his head before the window was down.

"I was hoping I had the wrong information," he said. "I was hoping you wouldn't pull in here tonight but had gone back to wherever you came from."

"I'm just here to see my family, Deputy."

"That's Sheriff, buddy," he said, tapping his badge.

It was an Iowa badge, Danny saw. "Have I done something wrong?"

"You mean other than coming back here? I don't know. Have you?"

"No, sir. In fact I think someone just took a potshot at me."

"A potshot? What do you mean a potshot?"

"It sounded like my truck got hit by a bullet."

"Sounded like."

"Yes, sir."

"You didn't get out and see?"

"No, sir. I didn't want to get shot."

"Where was it?"

"I think in the back there," he said and thumbed toward the truckbed.

"I mean where did it happen."

"In the park."

"Henry Sibley Park?"

"Yes, sir."

The deputy—sheriff—stared at him. Danny could see the smug look in his eye and he thought, Go ahead and say it, smart guy: *What were you doing in there this time?*

But Moran didn't say it. He stopped himself, and said instead: "Did you have your cell phone on you?"

"Yes, sir."

"Why didn't you call the police?"

"I wasn't sure. I wanted to be sure about it first."

Moran shook his head again. "Well, come on out of there and let's get sure about it." He stepped back and Danny got out and walked to the back of the truck looking, running his bare hand over the fender, over the tailgate, while Moran followed along with his Mini MagLite, roving the little spot here and there. When Danny got to the opposite side of the truckbed he found it right away—a neat quarter-size indentation in the rear fender just above the wheelwell, a hole at its center not quite big enough for the tip of his index finger.

Moran leaned in with his light. The paint had chipped away, leaving a clean ring of bare metal around the hole. He put his finger to it and felt around as if this would tell him something.

"That's a potshot all right," he said. "Looks like a .30-30, wouldn't you say?"

Danny couldn't say. The only gun he knew was Cousin Jer's Remington 20-gauge, and the only load they used was birdshot.

"Deer rifle, I expect," said Moran. He stood and put his thin beam into the truckbed. "Didn't come through here." He got down on one knee on the pavement and put the beam up under the truck. "No telling what it hit under there or where it went but it's for sure gone now."

He stood again slapping the grit from his knee. He doused the MagLite and restored it to its place on his belt and then stood looking at the bullet hole.

"I guess the deer don't have much to worry about from this feller, do they," he said.

Danny said nothing.

"Else he's a crack shot and was just trying to tell you something. That's a possibility too. Pretty good one, maybe, right about now."

"Right about now?" said Danny.

Moran turned to him. "You think I'm up here on a social visit?"

"I wouldn't know."

"You wouldn't, huh."

"No, sir."

"You wouldn't know about Sheriff Sutter's daughter going into the river with that other girl?"

"I heard about it."

"You and everyone else. That's my investigation, buddy. My witness. I got no other reason to be up here."

Danny was silent. Moran staring at him.

"But then a man told me you were in town and I thought, now there's a curious piece of timing, all things considered."

He stared at Danny. Danny said, "I'm just here to see my family."

"Yeah, you said that." Moran turned to look at the house and Danny did too. Light in the downstairs windows and in one upstairs window. Marky's room. Getting ready for bed. Moran sucked at something in his teeth and said, "Question is, are you doing them any favors."

Danny stared at his profile. "Not sure I follow you, Officer."

Moran looked at him. Then he turned back to the truck and he seemed to study the bullet hole once more. "No, sir," he said. "I expect this was just some gomer out in the park with one too many beers under the belt, thinking he could poach him a deer maybe, and instead decided to put one in your fender just for shits and giggles."

He turned then and walked back to the road, back toward his cruiser, and Danny followed, watching Moran's back, the smooth patch of neck above the collar and *Just keep your mouth shut, Danny-boy, don't say another word, just get in the truck and get your ass into the house.*

But Moran stopped in front of the truck door and Danny stopped too. Stood looking down at his own boots. The fraying laces. The scuffed and scarred-up toes.

"Folks talk," Moran said. "They love to talk. But I'll tell you one thing."

When Moran didn't go on, Danny looked up. The other man was looking up at the sky, the night clouds. No other cars were out, no headlights as far as you could see. Somewhere in the night a dog was barking but not at them.

"I hope," Moran said, "I truly hope the next thing I hear about you is nothing, buddy. Just nothing at all."

LATER THAT NIGHT a wind came up to rattle the window in his room, and the rattling was the sound of the sheriff's Zippo lighter rapping the metal table, and he could smell the smoke and he sat up suddenly in the dark room looking all around him, his heart pounding and a drop of sweat running down his chest. He'd just been here—the sheriff. The Zippo lighter rapping lightly on the tabletop. The cigarette smoke. The two of them caught in the mirrored glass . . . And with his heart still drumming he switched on the lamp and swung his legs out and sat on the edge of the bed, his bare feet flat on the old thin rug. It was not his old room but his new room in the farmhouse; she'd brought his things and arranged them as they'd been: his desk, his desk lamp, his chair, his bookcase. Going so far as to put the books back out because the empty shelves were just too much, she'd said, just too much.

He sat staring at his reflection in the rattling window. Awake now but that Zippo still rapping on the tabletop, the sheriff's voice continuing on as it had in the dream, a voice he'd spent so many years pushing from his mind: *And Holly Burke was at the bar too, at Smithy's, when you were there with Jeff Goss?*

Yes, sir.

Did you see her leave?

No, sir.

You didn't see her leave.

No, sir.

You didn't give her a ride?

No, sir. I had my dog with me.

So? The sheriff waiting, turning the Zippo slowly on the tabletop now, like he was trying to tune in a station. Up in the corner above the door a red dot of light glowed on the little camera.

You're recording this?

We record all our interviews.

Something tells me I should ask for a lawyer.

The sheriff, whose name was Sutter, smiled, friendly. I already told you you're not under arrest, Danny. Like I said, we're interviewing everyone who was at Smithy's. Who saw her there.

Did they have lawyers?

Who?

Everyone.

They weren't under arrest either. Do you mind if I light one of these? It's not allowed, strictly speaking, but I don't want to keep you here any longer than necessary just so I can go outside and smoke.

Danny shook his head and the sheriff lit his cigarette with the Zippo and blew a cloud toward the ceiling. There was no fan, no vent, and the smoke hung in the air. The smell reminded him of his father, before they got him to quit.

Sutter gave him a nod: Go on, now. Continue.

Danny sitting on the edge of the bed, in the cold room, staring at the spines of the books. Titles going back to middle school, the Hardy Boys, Ellery Queen, on up to Raymond Chandler and the assigned books of high school: Hemingway,

Salinger. Flannery O'Connor, who wrote the story about the killer, The Misfit, that he'd read more than once. Above these on the top shelf stood the textbooks from his one semester in college. As if he might come back and pick up where he'd left off. Classes. Equations. Exams.

He stood from the bed in nothing but the boxers he slept in and crossed the room, floorboards creaking, and he took down the largest book on the top shelf—*Applied Structural Dynamics* by Field and Leery, the hardback edition he'd bought used and already marked-up with highlighter pens—and standing there in the draft from the window he held the book faceup in his hands. The familiar dense weight of it and the familiar cover with the little doodle man still dangling from the underside of the bridge by his noose, hung there in permanent marker by a previous owner. When he opened the cover the spine crackled and the sound made his heart kick. The pages parted with the stickiness of old glossy pages that have sat too long with no parting, no airing, some of them sticking to each other as if by glue, and maybe it was trapped in one of these pairings, the pages reacting to the foreign material in some chemical way as if to consume it, as if to digest it slowly over the years until there was no trace left, not even the shape of it. But then the book opened in another place and there it lay. Flat and square and white. Strange thin bookmark, or rare leaf pressed flat and delicate and so sheer you could read the text beneath it. The window rattling behind him. His skin goose-bumping from his neck all the way down.

All right, Danny. Where did you go when you left Smithy's?

I went home.

You went straight home.

Sutter smoking, watching him with those blue eyes of his. Danny picking up the Coke and taking a drink and setting the can down again. He looked at the mirrored glass, as they always did in the TV shows. Who was behind there? More cops? The deputy who pulled him over? Drinking coffee and watching. Cop banter as they watched.

No, sir. I went into the park.

Sutter had been about to take a drag on his cigarette and stopped. Then took the drag and blew the smoke.

Henry Sibley Park? he said.

Yes, sir. The smoke was thick and Danny coughed.

Sutter tapped his ash on the floor.

Just to be clear, Danny, he said. After you left Smithy's, you drove into Henry Sibley Park.

Danny wanted to cough again but fought it down. The sheriff was fucking with him now. Wasn't he?

Yes, sir.

And why did you do that, Danny?

To walk my dog for a minute.

You didn't follow Holly Burke into the park?

No, sir. I didn't even know she was in there.

The sheriff watched him. Then he moved his notepad closer and wrote something down, studied what he'd written, then put his pen down and took up the Zippo again.

Was there anyone else in there—in the park?

Anyone else?

Yes.

Danny gave the Coke can a quarter turn on the tabletop. I couldn't say, he said.

You couldn't say what?

If there was anyone else in the park. It's a big park. And it was dark.

Sutter was silent.

You didn't see anyone else in the park, Danny?

Danny resisted looking at the mirrored glass—the cops, the deputy, watching him. He'd seen the deputy, but that was outside the park, on the county road.

No, sir, he said truthfully. I didn't see anyone else in the park.

Did any vehicles drive through?

Danny wiped his hands on his jeans. Sutter watching him. There was a loud ticking but he saw no clock in the room and he realized it was Sutter's watch. He could see the second hand moving with the ticks.

I was pretty deep in the woods, chasing my dog.

That's not what I asked you, Danny. Did you see any other vehicles in the park while you were there?

No, sir. I didn't see any other cars. Not while I was there. And that was true too: he'd seen the headlights and he'd heard the motor but he'd never seen the car itself. And it might not have been Jeff's car at all.

Although he knew that wasn't true.

He pinched the square of cloth at its corner and it came away clean and he closed the textbook one-handed and set it flat on the shelf, and then he laid the bit of cloth on his open hand. Weight of a feather. Weight of a butterfly. Great square wing of a strange nightmoth. They'd searched his room and they'd searched the books, or at least had pulled them all from the shelves, but the cloth had hung on.

And if it had fallen out when she moved the books, boxing them up and then unboxing them, years ago? Would she have put it back, not recognizing it? Or would she have sat there with it in the palm of her hand, knowing exactly what it was and what it meant. And then put it back anyway?

He stared at the cloth where it lay on his own palm, of such thin stuff it stirred with his breath. Exactly the thing they'd been looking for when they came to the house. The thing that no one else knew was missing but them—and you, and no way for you to have it unless you'd taken it yourself. A memento. A keepsake to press in a book and find again one day, or to be found by someone else and wondered about. Sheer stupid luck that you'd seen it at all that night. Seen it before they did. Stupid luck that the dog got away from you and rolled himself in shit or else you wouldn't have taken him to the front of the truck where the hose was and would not have been there hosing him down in the light your mother left on for you and would not have glanced at the license plate, you didn't even know why, and then looked again because there was something there, a bit of white paper or something stuck between the plate frame and the bumper, fluttering in the wind.

Then what happened, Danny?

What do you mean?

What happened next, after you got your dog and got back in your truck?

Danny held the sheriff's eyes. He knew what was coming next. What the sheriff already knew: the flashing lights in his rearview. The deputy with the bug eyes.

I drove out of the park.

You didn't see Holly Burke then, on your way out?

No, sir.

You didn't hit her with your truck—by accident? You were at Smithy's and you were drinking, Danny. Cruising through the park, feeling that buzz . . . You didn't come around a bend and there she was but you couldn't stop in time? An accident, Danny? Sutter opening his hands like a man offering something. Or ready to receive it.

No, sir. I never saw her.

You never saw her—that's why you hit her?

No, sir, I never saw her and I never hit her either.

And still holding the dog by the collar you set down the hose and tugged this bit of whiteness loose and stood there hunched over and looking at it in the light—a square of thin material, maybe silk, with tiniest threads like spiderwebs where it had been sewed on and it was the pocket of a girl's top and you knew it, you recognized it immediately, because you had looked. You had looked at it when you'd seen it earlier that night and you could see right through it and you couldn't help looking—even if it was just the quickest of glances, you'd looked, you'd wanted to see. And now here it was in your hand and you knew what it was and you knew in your gut, in your heart, that it could not be here except that something terrible had happened and maybe you'd been too drunk to know it. Was that even possible? Not see her? Not feel the impact?

Or not remember it?

Look more closely at the bumper. Look for the break in the plate frame, the bent plate, the dented bumper. The bit of blood and hair. Wrap the dog leash around the hosebib and get the flashlight out again and go over the tires, the treads, all the way around with the dying beam. The underside of the bumper. All the jagged parts of the undercarriage that might catch and snag and rip and hold on to—and was she out there still, lying there, alive? Go back, find her, call 911?

But what if they were there already? What if someone else had found her and called the cops and here you come driving back to the scene, having already driven away?

But what if she's alive and lying there? Holly Burke, Gordon's daughter, lying there cold and broken and trying to stay alive?

It could've happened to anyone, Danny. Who would expect a girl to be walking through that park, that time of night? Maybe you thought it was a deer. You'd had a few beers and you were cruising along and then suddenly—wham. You hit something and you think, Holy crap, I hit a deer. So you stop and get out and walk back and there she is—holy shit, there's a girl lying on the side of the road and she's no deer and you know you hit her . . .

Danny shaking his head, No, sir . . .

. . . you didn't mean to, she just came out of nowhere, and you tried to stop but you couldn't. And now there she is and you can't believe it. No life in that body, you think, and this is no dream, this is real and you've done it and you can't go back five minutes, not even one minute, and not do it. It's done. The girl is dead . . . and so are you—everything you've ever known or wanted. Your plans. Your degree. Your family. Your girlfriend, Katie Goss . . . You have hit this girl and she's dead and you can't take it back.

No, sir . . .

And so what do you do, Danny? Standing there in the cold and the wind, looking at her—what do you do? You're not a bad guy, you've never been in trouble before, but you've been drinking and you're not thinking straight, and all you know is that you want to live, you don't want your life to end this way—because of an accident? Because of nothing but chance and bad luck?

What if you were never here? you think.

What if you'd not gone through the park at all?

What if she just vanished and no one ever knew?

No, sir, it didn't happen like that.

How did it happen, Danny?

It didn't happen.

Why did you drive up to your cousin's cabin, Danny, after you got home?

To go duck hunting.

At two thirty in the morning.

Yes, sir. So we could get an early start.

Could you get rid of the truck, a whole truck, just make it disappear—into the river, or into the lake far away?

Don't be stupid. Don't be crazy. Take the hose and spray it all down, plate and bumper, tires and undercarriage. Uncle Rudy has a cabin up in the woods and Cousin Jer has the key and by the time you get up there, going over the dirt trails and across the stream and through the mud there won't be anything left of anything you might've missed . . .

But to not see her? Not feel the impact?

And what if she's still alive . . . ?

Tell me about Holly Burke, Danny.

What about her?

What did you like about her?

What do you mean?

Sutter taking a last drag on his cigarette and mashing it on the heel of his boot and dropping the butt to the floor. You know what I mean.

I've known her a long time. Our fathers were business partners.

Did you ever date her?

No, sir.

Did you ever want to?

And he thought then not of Holly Burke but of Katie Goss, and felt again that bang in his heart when the sheriff had asked to see his cell phone, hours ago, up at the cabin, because Danny had remembered then—only then—that Katie had called him when he was in the park, and he'd thought somehow that the phone would tell the sheriff where he'd been when she called, like some kind of tracking device, and he had not understood that what the sheriff really wanted to see was had he called Holly Burke, or had she called him. And now he could use that same phone to show the sheriff that not only had they not called each other—at least not on any cell phone—but that she was not even in his contacts!

But there'd been plenty of time for him to delete every trace of her from the phone, the sheriff would point out, and anyway Danny had already told him he didn't think he had to show his cell phone to anyone if he wasn't under arrest, and the sheriff had said that was true, and at last he answered Sutter's question, No, Sir, I never wanted to date her.

Never?

No, sir.

An attractive young woman like that? Never thought about it—ever?

And with the flashlight in one hand and the hose in the other you stood up then and you saw her, your mother—standing at the window and looking right at you, and how long had she been standing there, how much did she see? Where is the square of cloth?

It's in one of your pockets.

Put the flashlight down and finish rinsing the dog. Rinse your hands. Take a good long drink of the cold water and shut the water off and take the dog inside and tell her you gotta go back out and help Jeff, he needs a jump and you gotta go and you'll be right back. Just go back there and look, that's all—the truck is clean, or as clean as you can get it, so drive back now, your heart pounding, and see from the edge of the park that there are no cops, no flashing lights, and drive all the way through the park and all the way back and no sign of her anywhere, and was it some kind of joke, that piece of cloth? A gag executed by drunk girls just to mess with you?

Other scenarios, other possibilities, won't even enter your mind until later, when you are driving north toward Cousin Jer's, strung-out and seeing things—figures, young women, running out of the darkness into your headlights—and thinking you will never make it, that the lights will come up fast in the rearview and the colored lights will go off like bombs in the early morning darkness and that will be that.

But that's later. First—get back home and get your stuff and go, because you need to get away from here and you need time. You need time right now like you need the air to breathe.

You can say it, Danny. She was a good-looking young woman and you desired her. You wanted Holly Burke.

No, sir.

You wanted her, and so you offered her a ride, cold night like that, her dressed like that, and she gets in. But then you try something in the park, you get grabby and there's a fight, and she gets out and starts walking, and that's when you hit her with the truck—maybe not on purpose, but you hit her. And you panic. You see her lying there and you think you killed her and you're drunk and you panic. You need to get rid of the body—but how . . . ?

No air in that little room, as if Sutter's voice were using it up with each word, and that voice so thick in Danny's head like smoke—expanding like smoke until his brain was swimming in it, spinning in it—

. . . and next thing you know you're lifting the girl in your arms, and you're walking her to the riverbank and she weighs nothing, and all you can think is how cold she must've been, out here with no jacket, nothing but that blouse . . . and you

lay her down again, and with a push you send her over, and down she goes, her face rolling once, twice to the sky before there's the splash and the waves go rippling out and the body in its white, flimsy blouse lingers, the blond hair spreading, the body pulled slowly out into deeper water, stronger current . . . and the last you'd see is a pale shape of fabric on the surface of the water, air-filled, trembling in the wind like some living creature, before even that went under, sinking into darkness and you could not take it back you could never take it back and it was no nightmare, it was real, and you'd done it . . .

No, sir, Danny heard himself say. Shaking his head, shaking off this vision.

But you hadn't killed her, Danny, Sutter said. She was still breathing when you pushed her into the water. And that right there—that's not manslaughter. That's not even vehicular homicide, Danny. That's murder.

Sutter watching him, no expression whatsoever on his face, in those blue eyes. The camera watching. The men behind the glass watching.

The room spun. His stomach pitched. He thought he might be sick.

Sutter picked up his pen again and tapped it twice on the notepad.

Talk to me, Danny. Tell me about that night. Tell me what happened.

The room came to rest. Danny took a breath and let it out slowly.

I'm ready for that lawyer, he said. Either that, or I walk out of here right now.

And in the few seconds you had before she stepped into your room—*Danny, we had a deal!*—you pinched the cloth up from your jeans pocket and opened up the textbook and laid the cloth flat between the pages and put the book up on the shelf and you can't even say why. Just down the hall sat the perfect solution: a contraption that filled itself with water and emptied itself with gravity into a four-inch waste pipe as dark and forever as the bottom of the sea.

Instead you put the thing in your textbook. Knowing full well it was the one thing that could end your life. That could flush you down some dark and forever hole yourself.

Because, at the same time, in some new part of you that did not exist an hour ago, not even fifteen minutes ago, you knew that the same piece of cloth that might end you might also save you. If only you had the time to figure out how.

39

SHE SLEPT AND woke, slept and woke, through day and night, or many days and many nights. She might've been in the river again, but now there was heat—hours of heat that set her skin on fire, and then hours of cold so deep her jaw chattered, and she slept and woke and did not know one from the other because everything she saw in either state was equally vivid and equally unbelievable and equally ordinary. She saw glass beads swaying in a river of color and lights, and the colors smelled of fruits no one had ever tasted before and the lights played on the bare shoulders of three young women who stood on the bottom of a lake with their toes in warm sand and their hair rising and falling in cool passing currents of light. She saw a corona of light around dark curtains, the light pulsing and blooming like a living thing, and she saw the bedroom where she lay and it was not her bedroom and it was, and she knew everything she would find in the closet down to a pair of high black boots that zipped up the back and she knew if she got up and looked in the mirror she would see her new face, her new hair, and there was a silver brush on the desk and she knew how the brush would feel in her hand and how it would feel in her hair, and she felt a new heart beating in her chest and this heart broke just to feel all that it felt all at once, all its love and pain and want and fear all at once.

She saw the curtains open on their own and a figure appear in the dark of the glass and she saw this figure put its hands to its face and peer in through the air bubbles and the tiny cracks and when it stood she saw the soles of its boots as it walked off into the night. Pale hair moved in the water like silky smoke, and she smelled smoke, and her father was sitting with her, *Here, Deputy, drink this*, and he raised her head with his hand and tilted the cool water to her lips, then he cleared the hair from her forehead and said, *You have to help him now, sweetheart*, and she said, *Help who, Daddy?* but he was gone.

She saw the faces of boys she did not know all lined up in picture frames and they were all the same boy, and the images darkened and sank away until all she saw was their teeth like the grins of skulls. She watched a large bird like a hawk or an owl glide soundlessly across the ceiling. She saw a man and a woman dressed in black climb stone steps, their heads high but heavy, so heavy, and they walked into a great hall that was washed in every color, because the river of light flowed through the great hall too and they walked hand in hand down the aisle and they looked down on the girl who lay there and the girl's hair shifted colors in the light, dark to light and back to dark again, as if the shadows of great fish or boats were passing over her.

She saw herself rise from the bed and walk through a wall of heat to the window and draw the curtains, the light so bright, and unlatch the window and raise it with pain shooting all through her and the air so cold flooding in and she saw the dark shapes of two men standing next to a truck and they were faced off and talking and she could hear every word they spoke as if the two men floated there outside the window, and as she listened she saw a man in a sheriff's hat driving down a dark road and there was a girl sitting next to him but she could not see their faces and she was frightened, and then the car vanished and next she saw dogs, or wolves, running down the middle of the river chasing something she couldn't see and the thing they chased howled and cried but the dogs themselves were silent as they ran, white smoke jetting from their snouts as from furnaces and no sound to them at all.

40

HE CARRIED THE tray back downstairs and set it on the kitchen table and stood looking at the glass of orange juice, the bowl of soup, the soda crackers. Then he sat down and crumbled the crackers into the bowl and ate the soup. It was just past noon. The house seemed strangely quiet and after a moment he realized it was because there was no fire in the woodburner, because he'd not built the fire, because the heat from the fire would keep the furnace from kicking in and blowing heat into the upstairs rooms, exactly as it was supposed to do.

A man could put a space heater up there and have his fire and his heated bedroom, both. Could, if he cared to burn the house down. That time the alarm went off in the middle of the night and it was the alarm in her room and he'd thrown open the door with his heart slamming and there she sat cross-legged on the floor with a candle on a cookie sheet, her eyes so wide, and she was blowing at the blackened feet of a Barbie doll like it was a birthday cake and you had to carry the doll dripping hot, pink plastic into the bathroom and put it under the tap, and when you got back she was facedown on her bed and the alarm still going until you stood on the chair and took it down and got the battery out, and only then did you hear her crying. And she would not turn over, she would not look at you and she was so small and she trembled and cried until her mother moved you away and scooped her up and held her sobbing against her chest as you stood there, as you did all you could think to do, which was to open the window and fan the air with the cookie sheet.

You frightened her, Gordon, Meredith telling him later. And Gordon saying, *I frightened her? I frightened* her?

There was the sound of car tires on the packed snow and the sound returned him to his kitchen—smoke gone, girl gone, wife gone—and he sat listening, frowning, thinking Doc Van Allen was back, had forgotten something. But when he went to the window it was not the light-blue Olds he saw coming to a stop in the drive but a dark-blue pickup. The sun was on the windshield and the driver sat with the truck idling, white clouds chugging from the tailpipe—rechecking his directions or his information, whatever it was, this dumb cluck, and Gordon standing at the window looking for the guy to turn the truck around and drive away again. Instead the exhaust clouds stopped and the driver's door swung open and a young man stepped out in a billcap and shut the door again and faced the house, and although the young man's face was half in shadow under the bill, Gordon knew him at once. Knew him by shape and by stance and by movement and by other signs he couldn't name but that were as old as the young man was himself.

I will be God damned. I will be God damned. His heart pounding and all the blood going out of him.

The boy took a few steps toward the porch and stopped and came no farther. He'd seen Gordon in the window. He stood with his hands in his jacket pockets, looking at Gordon and waiting.

Gordon stepped from the window and sat on the bench by the door and pulled on his boots, and every movement was strange, like déjà vu, and the side of his neck was beating and he fumbled with the laces as if his fingers were half-frozen and when he got them tied he held his hands before him to see if they were shaking but they were not, they were steady. He got into his jacket and opened the door and stepped into the winter brightness and the boy was still there—he was no trick of the eyes, no dream—and Gordon closed the door and went down the porchsteps, never once looking away from the boy and the boy never once looking away from him and all of it no trick, no dream. He walked up to the boy and stopped short of him and stood looking into his shadowed eyes, and the boy lifted a hand and tilted back the bill of the cap and returned his hand to his jacket pocket.

"If you're gonna slug me go ahead and slug me, Gordon," he said.

Gordon felt the skin under his left eye twitch. "What makes you think I'm gonna slug you?"

"Those two fists at the ends of your arms."

Gordon held the boy's eyes. Then he brought his hands together and ran one through the grip of the other as if they were cold. As if that was the only way to straighten them out.

He said, "I'd say you got some nerve showing up here but I know you haven't got any nerve. So now I'm thinking maybe you're just plain crazy."

"I might be."

"You might be shot for trespassing."

"It wouldn't surprise me, after last night."

"Am I supposed to know what that means?"

"I thought you might."

"I got no idea what that means."

"It means this," the boy said, and he turned and stepped back to the truck, moving around it to the far rear fender. And looking back at Gordon he tapped his fingers on the metal.

Gordon didn't move. Then he came around and, taking his eyes off the boy for the first time, leaned down to see. And stood again.

"You think I did that?"

"It crossed my mind."

"You think I'm the only one in this town who'd take a shot at you?"

The boy didn't answer.

"Where did that even happen?" Gordon said.

"In the park."

Gordon stared at him. "Henry Sibley?"

"Yes, sir."

A black insect swam across Gordon's vision. "You were driving through that park at night?"

The boy was about to answer, but just then there was a sound from the house and they both turned to see an upstairs window raised and a face framed briefly in the dark square, a girl's face, pale and half-covered in dark strings of hair, before the curtains fell and the face was gone again.

When he turned back to him the boy was still watching the window. The knuckle of his throat rose and fell. Finally he turned back to Gordon and stared at him. As if Gordon might bother to explain what he'd just seen.

Gordon said, "I won't even try to tell you all the ways you are crazy if you think I shot your truck but I will say this. If I was gonna go to all the trouble to lay down on you with a rifle I damn sure wouldn't put my bullet in the side of your truck."

The boy had no response.

"And one more thing," Gordon said. "If I was gonna shoot you, why wouldn't I of done it ten years ago? Why would I do it now?"

"Maybe you'd figure nobody'd suspect you, all these years later."

"Just like nobody'd still suspect you, all these years later."

The boy stood looking at him. Then he looked down at his boots.

"I'm just a dumbfounded son of a bitch," Gordon said. "Whatever gave you the idea to come back here anyhow?"

"My old dog died." The boy looked up.

"I know it. I helped your mother bury him."

"I know you did."

Gordon did not believe the boy would go so far as to thank him for that and he was right.

"That was for your mother and your brother, period."

"I know it, Gordon."

"And God damn it, whatever happened to respect?"

"Respect?"

"Respect. Like calling a man by his proper name."

The boy seemed to think on that. Then he said, "I guess that stopped when you stopped having any respect for me."

"Respect for you. Are you standing there shitting me?"

"No, sir. You never even tried to ask me directly about any of it. You never gave me a chance."

Gordon stared at him. Jesus God what was happening here. *Just go inside*, his mind told him. Begged him. *Just turn and go on inside before you kill this boy.*

"Is that what this is?" he said. "You come out here to tell me all about it?"

"No, sir. I came out here to see if you'd let me say one thing. If you'd give me the chance to do that."

"Why would I do that?"

"I don't know. I just wanted to try. I didn't want to—" He hesitated. "I didn't want to go away again without trying."

Gordon stared into the boy's eyes. Somewhere in there was the young boy he'd known, before he grew up and turned into this other thing.

"You didn't do it, I suppose," said Gordon. "That's what you wanted to say."

The boy held his eyes. "Sometimes—" he began, and swallowed. "There were times when I thought maybe I had, Mr. Burke. That I'd hit her with my truck but just didn't know it. That I'd blacked out or something."

Gordon's heart was banging. He watched the boy.

"I'd been drinking, Mr. Burke. I'd had a few beers—"

"I already know that. That's in the record."

"Yes, sir. And it was dark, and windy, and trees everywhere . . . and I thought it was possible. It could have happened that way. It could have. But even if it did—even if I hit her, by accident, how did she end up in the river?"

"Because you put her there. You panicked and you put her there. And she was still breathing."

The boy shook his head. "No, Mr. Burke. That's what the sheriff said. That was his version."

"The sheriff had you in the park—right time, right place. And afterwards you drove off to that cabin." Gordon's heart pounding with rage like it had all happened yesterday. He looked at the truck again. It was not the same truck but it might as well have been. "Sheriff had you," he said. "Dead to rights. And he let you go."

The boy was staring at him, nodding slowly. "I know how it looked, Mr. Burke. I'd been at the bar, I'd been in the park. The deputy had pulled me over. I drove up to my uncle's cabin. I know how it looked. But—"

"Hold on," Gordon said, and the boy stopped. "Pulled you over?"

"Sir?"

"You said the deputy pulled you over."

"Yes, sir."

"Pulled you over when?"

"As I was coming out of the park."

"That night?"

"Yes, sir."

Gordon shook his head, his mind already reversing, searching itself. "Pulled you over for what?"

"For being in the park after dark."

And his mind went all the way back then, ten years in time . . . Sutter showing up at his house the first time, and then the other times. The officers going through her room, her dresser drawers. The questions: *What time did she go out? Did she call? How was she getting around without her license, without a car? Who was she seeing?* He had not been in his right mind but he would remember this—he would know if they'd told him the boy had been pulled over coming out of the park. It would be in the record. There would be no question he'd been there.

"That makes no sense," he now said. "Why wouldn't I know about that? Why wouldn't everybody?"

The boy was silent. Shut down. Staring blankly at him. Then he said, "They never told you I got pulled over?"

"No, they didn't. And I know that report backwards and forwards and there is no mention of any deputy pulling you over. Says you *admitted* to being in the park."

The boy staring at him, taking this in.

"Why wouldn't that be in the report?" Gordon said.

"I don't know, Mr. Burke."

"You don't know? Is this some kind of game?"

"No, sir. I'm trying to understand it too."

"You better by God hurry up."

The boy shook his head. He said, "If you didn't know about it, Mr. Burke, it means nobody knew about it. They'd have told you everything they knew. It means the sheriff . . ." He didn't finish.

"It means the sheriff what?"

"Didn't know," said the boy. "He didn't know the deputy pulled me over."

"How would he not know that?"

The boy was silent.

"What are you saying," said Gordon, "—the deputy never told the sheriff? That it just slipped his goddam mind?"

The boy said nothing.

"Speak up," Gordon said.

"That night," the boy said, "when he pulled me over, the deputy, he walked all around my truck with his flashlight and then he let me go. No DUI. Not even a ticket for being in the park at night."

"So?"

"So he would have seen it, Mr. Burke. He would've seen it then—wouldn't he have?" The boy's eyes had a glassy, faraway look to them. Like his mind had wandered off somewhere.

"Seen what?" Gordon said. "Seen what," he snapped, and the boy came back, blinking. Then he pulled his hand from his pocket and held the hand palm-up to him. As if offering him something to eat.

It was a square of white cloth, so thin and light it would've blown from his hand but for the thumb holding it there.

Gordon's heart began to slip. "What is that?" he said thickly.

The boy said nothing, and Gordon's heart slipped all the way into coldness, into blackness. He knew what it was. He knew what it was and he knew there was no other like it in the world and he knew that only a handful of people even knew about it—ripped from her blouse, they said, ripped clean off and never recovered—and only one person in the world could have it and here he was. And then with no other thought or even movement he was aware of, he had the boy by the jacket and had thrown him up against the truck. No idea what he was saying, just the sensation of speech in his throat, as if he'd gone deaf. The boy holding his wrists, his cap fallen away, and though his head shook with the violence of Gordon's grip his face was calm, and his voice was calm too, saying, "Mr. Burke . . . Mr. Burke, let me say one thing—"

What did Gordon say? Did he say anything? Did he say: *Say it, you son of a bitch*? Did he say: *Say the last thing you have to say*? He only knew he let the boy stand straight, keeping his grip on his jacket, the boy's hands gripping his wrists, and the square of cloth pressed between the boy's hand and his wrist like some thin bandage he could feel all the way to his heart, and at last the boy said, "Why would I show it to you, Mr. Burke? Why would I do that?" These words and all sound reaching Gordon through a dull roaring like water rushing in his ears.

"Because you want to torment me. Because you want to see if I will kill you."

"No, sir."

"Do you think I won't? Do you think I care what happens to me?"

"No, sir, I don't, but that's not why."

"Why then, God damn you."

"Because . . ." said the boy. "Because it was on the truck. It was caught up in the license plate—"

Gordon renewed his grip and gave the boy a shake. "Boy—what are you telling me?"

"I'm telling you that that deputy shined his flashlight all around that truck and didn't see this piece of cloth, but when I got home I saw it right off. Plain as day."

"Is that supposed to prove something?"

"No, sir. Only . . ."

"Only what."

"Only why didn't he ever say he pulled me over? Why wouldn't he say that?"

Gordon closed and opened his eyes. Black flies swarming all through his vision. A great hard fist pounding on his heart.

"Why didn't *you* say it?" he said. "Why didn't you say the deputy pulled you over?"

"Because I thought they already knew. I thought the sheriff knew. But he never asked me, Mr. Burke. He never asked me about the deputy pulling me over."

The boy staring at him and Gordon blinking—blinking away the black flies until he could see the boy's eyes again. Open and blue and looking into his.

"The deputy," Gordon said. "That's what you're telling me. The deputy put it on your truck."

The boy said nothing.

"He put it on your truck and he never told the sheriff he pulled you over."

"Why wouldn't he tell him, Mr. Burke?"

"Because it never happened. Because you've had ten years to cook up this story."

"No, sir. I've had ten years to wonder how this piece of cloth got on my truck. And all I've ever known is I never touched your daughter, Mr. Burke. Me or my truck."

"But you kept it," Gordon said. "Why did you keep it?"

"I don't know. I don't know . . ." The boy shaking his head. "I thought I might need it."

"The perverts always keep something. Like a kind of . . ." He couldn't think of the word. He was so tired, suddenly. Dead tired. He needed to sit down.

He let the boy go. His hands were cramped and he put them to his skull and ran them backwards, as if to restore order to a head of hair gone wild. He looked toward the woods but did not see them. The whole world a meaningless flat arrangement of shape and color, sickening to see. He turned back to the boy and with effort brought his face into focus. He could see the streaks of yellow in the blue irises.

"Why now?" Gordon said. "Why show this thing now? Do you think anyone will believe you?"

"No, sir. I just didn't want to be the only one anymore. If something happened—" He looked off, toward the house, and looked back. "I just wanted you to hear it, that's all." He put his hand into his jacket pocket, the square of cloth disappeared, and he turned to collect his cap from the bed of the truck.

"And all this while," Gordon said. "Ten years. You never thought of this before—that it was the deputy?"

The boy turned back to him holding the cap. He stood looking into the bowl of it as if finding something there that shouldn't be.

"I was young, Mr. Burke." He looked up and gave a kind of smile, shaking his head. "I just didn't think a man, a cop . . ."

He put the cap on his head and snugged it down.

"Moran," said Gordon.

"Sir?"

"The deputy. Was it Moran?"

The boy held his eyes. "Yes, sir, it was him."

PART IV

41

SHE AWOKE ONCE again in strangeness: the bed not her bed and the room not her room, and neither was it the hospital, or her father's living room. Dim light of day behind the curtains—dawn or dusk, she had no idea. And, oh God, so hot under these blankets, the comforter, whatever else was piled on top of her . . . Audrey shoving at these, kicking and twisting until it all slumped off her and she lay there on her back, getting her breath and feeling the cool air find her.

She was wearing the same flannel shirt of her father's she'd put on when she first got the chills however many days ago, and now she lifted the sleeve to her face and smelled it, but it smelled like nothing and she knew it had not been taken off her and that it must smell terribly, as she herself must.

She sat up, putting her feet to the floor, and sudden moons of color floated across the room. A half glass of water stood on the nightstand and she drank it down, then pushed up from the bed and got to her feet and stood through a second wave of colors and dizziness—then stood listening for any sound in the house that wasn't her own heavy breathing.

No clock in the room, and no sign of her father's phone or his watch. There was a bureau and a vanity and a chair, all in the same unpainted, pinewood style as the nightstand. The bureau top was bare but a middle drawer was pulled partway out, as if recently opened but then incompletely shut in the haste of dressing. She crossed to it and pulled it all the way open. Sweaters. Folded, of muted colors, soft to the touch. Clean-smelling when she bent to smell. In the drawer above she found panties and bras and camisoles. She lifted one bra to see the cup size and put it down again. In the drawer below, a bright bonanza of socks.

On the vanity top sat a wooden box with the lid down, a brush and comb set, and a color portrait in a frame of dull silver, but the image that stopped her was the face in the mirror: waxy, pale face of shadows, of cracked lips and black ropes of hair.

Another girl altogether was pictured in the silver frame—a picture she'd seen before on TV and in the newspapers. It was Holly Burke's high school graduation picture, and she knew that the girl had hated it and would not have placed it here herself. In it she was pretty and honey-skinned, her brushed hair catching the light. Bright-green eyes and a young woman's mouth of glossed lips and white teeth, and nothing in that face to convey a heart with so much in it, so bursting and hungry and bruised and defiant, so alive!

The brush and comb set were not silver as in her dreams but fake tortoise-shell and when she lifted the brush she saw no hairs and when she put it to her nose it smelled of nothing but the synthetic bristles. Brand-new.

Inside the wooden box was a stash of jewelry: silver and gold and colored stones all in a rich jumble. She chose an antique-looking silver ring and slipped it over her knuckle, admired it against the pale skin, slipped it off again and lowered the box lid without a sound.

The floorboards popped and the door hinges creaked and she stepped into the hallway and stood at the head of the stairs looking down, listening. He would've heard the floorboards, the hinges, would've come to the stairs and called up to her, or by some other means let her know of his presence, but he did not and she knew she was alone in the house.

The bathroom looked like a bathroom in a hotel: not a thing in it to indicate a man had used it even once. Pale-blue towels folded and stacked largest to smallest on the counter. A new tube of toothpaste and a toothbrush still in its packaging placed beside an empty glass. A pink razor in its packaging next to ladies' shaving cream. Ladies' deodorant. New bar of soap in the wire rack under the shower head, matching bottles of shampoo and conditioner.

There was a bolt on the door and it popped cleanly into its socket.

She pulled the flannel shirt over her head like a dress and stripped off the heavy socks and stepped out of the panties and stood looking at the creature in the mirror. White as bones. Thin as bones but for the fat purple club at the end of one arm.

She'd have stood under that showerhead forever, just forever, but she didn't want to use up his hot water, and at last she shut off the valves and ran the largest towel over her skin and made sure the bottoms of her feet were dry before she stepped on the bath mat. Then, with the towel wrapped around her, she peered into the hallway and listened again—not a sound, not even a light on downstairs that she could see—and then she scooted back to the bedroom, her dirty clothes clutched to her chest, and shut the door behind her.

42

HE CROSSED INTO Iowa on the 52 and twenty minutes later he found the building on Main Street and there was an open space out front and he took it. It was just 2:15, a cold and gray Wednesday afternoon in Iowa, as it was in Minnesota.

Her fever had broken and she'd opened her eyes long enough to see him sitting there beside the bed, and he'd told her he'd be back in a couple of hours, and she'd nodded and shut her eyes again and was asleep before he'd stood up. He didn't like leaving her alone in the house like that, but the fever had broken and she was going to be all right and he couldn't wait any longer.

He went up the steps and opened the glass door and stepped into a large room. There were four wooden desks and only one of them manned—a young deputy on the phone, looking Gordon over and holding his forefinger in the air.

"Yes, ma'am," the deputy said into the handpiece. "I don't blame you one bit, ma'am."

Gordon stepped up to the desk.

"Yes, ma'am, I'll let him know the second he gets back. You have a good day, ma'am." The deputy hung up the phone and shook his head and looked up at Gordon. "Afternoon, sir. What can I do for you?" The ID on his pocket flap said DEP. KURT SHORT. Gordon read it twice to be sure.

"I need to speak to the sheriff."

"All right. I bet I can help you out. Did you want to report something?" He fetched a form and readied his pen.

"No, I just need to speak to the sheriff. Is he here?"

"'Fraid not. He's out on a call."

"How long."

"Sir?"

"How long will he be out."

The deputy tapped his pen on the form. "Can't say, sir. How about you give me your name and your trouble and I can pass it on to him when he gets back?"

"What makes you think I've got trouble?"

The deputy stopped tapping his pen.

"Sir, either you let me help you out or you let me write something down or you go sit in a chair over there and wait for the sheriff to get back."

"You forgot one."

"One what."

"One option."

"I don't believe so."

"You forgot the one where you call up the sheriff and say Gordon Burke drove down from Minnesota to get Audrey Sutter's things and he's standing right here in front of my desk, Sheriff, what do you want me to do."

Fifteen minutes later he'd loaded the last of it into the back of the van and he was just closing the rear doors when a sheriff's cruiser pulled into the spot beside him and Ed Moran stepped out.

"Hey, Gordon."

"Hey, Sheriff."

"You get everything all right?"

"I don't know. I didn't exactly have a list."

"Well, whatever the Prices didn't take, the rest is hers."

"Then I guess I got it all."

"Sorry I wasn't here to help you. I had to go pick up a sick boy from school and find him a sitter."

"One of yours?"

"My youngest, Eli. Sick as a dog."

"It's going around."

"So I hear. How's she doing?"

"Her fever broke, anyway."

"That's good."

"So I thought I'd run down here and get her stuff."

Moran nodded. Hands on his hips. "Can I ask you something, though?"

"Go ahead."

"How the heck did she end up at your house in the first place?"

Gordon told him about the firewood, the girl burning up with fever, the ice-cold house, and Moran shook his head.

"Like she hasn't been through enough as it is," he said.

Gordon watched the sheriff's face in the shadow of his wide hatbrim. He looked like he might have another question on his mind, but if he did he didn't ask it. Gordon said, "You made any progress on any of that?"

"Not as much as I'd like. County attorney says we're about one eyewitness shy of a case."

"She told me you showed her some pictures—the girl did."

"She tell you what her old man did down here?"

"Told me that too."

Moran shook his head again. He squinted up at the blue winter sky. "Well, I guess I best get back to work here."

"I don't suppose you care to have a cup of coffee, Sheriff."

Moran looked at him.

"On me," Gordon said.

Moran slid back his jacket sleeve to check his watch.

"Yeah, I might could use a cup," he said. "Why don't you go on ahead to the Blue Plate just down the street here—it's that blue sign, you can see it from here—and I'll come along soon as I check in with the boys."

"Boy," said Gordon.

"How's that?"

"There's just one boy in there."

The waitress told him to sit wherever he liked and he took the booth in the far corner with his back to the wall. The lunch hour was over and the place was empty but for one old man at the counter, the old man stirring his spoon round and round in a white china mug. From where Gordon sat he could see the plug of skin-colored plastic fitted into the old man's ear.

The waitress came over and said, "What can I getcha, hon?" and Gordon ordered a coffee.

"That's it?"

His eyes went to the patch of bright pink on her neck—burn scar, or birth-mark maybe—and back to her face. "That's it for now, thanks."

"All right. I'm gonna brew you some fresh—how's that sound?"

"That sounds jim-dandy."

"Ha," she said, "'jim-dandy,' I like that," and went away again.

The tabletop was striped with lighter bands of laminate and after a while he connected the stripes to the window slats to his left, and he put his hands into the light to see it bend around them. He'd not slept and his own mind seemed feverish to him, jammed full of voices and images, some of them real and some of them having come some other way into his head in the long hours since the boy showed up in his driveway, when was that—yesterday. And now here he sat in a diner in Iowa waiting on a man who was sheriff now but who back then was just another half-wit deputy pawing through her dresser drawers, lifting up her mattress, digging his fingers into her jewelry box—

The white china mug that dropped suddenly into his vision made him jump, and the waitress put her hand on his shoulder and said, "Oh gosh, sorry there, hon—maybe I should of brought you decaf!"

"Maybe so."

"You sure you don't want nothin else?"

Moran appeared at her side. "This man giving you trouble, Rhonda?"

"Oh no, Sheriff. I just snuck up on him and scared him."

"Well, how about you scare me up a cup of what he's having, hey?"

She went away again, and Moran got out of his jacket and tossed it on the booth seat opposite Gordon, tossed his hat on top of that and sat down. He set his phone on the table, off to the side, and slid his napkin and silverware over there too. The two men were silent, looking around the diner, until the waitress returned with a second mug and the pot of coffee.

"There you go, Sheriff. How about you, hon, can I top you off?"

"No, thanks."

"Anything to eat, Sheriff?"

"No, dear, that's all," Moran said, and she went away again.

Moran raised his mug and sipped and set it down again. He sat watching Gordon. Then he said, "Well, Gordon. I'm gonna go ahead and guess you've got something on your mind here."

Gordon was looking down into his own mug. The oily surface of the coffee, the wisps of steam in the bands of light. He rocked the mug a bit to see the liquid move.

"I'm trying to pick someplace to begin," he said.

"The beginning generally gets the job done, in my experience."

"The beginning goes a long ways back, Sheriff."

"Then you best get started."

The old man at the counter sat watching them over his shoulder. Gordon stared at him until the old man faced forward again.

"Don't mind old Harold there," Moran said. "He couldn't hear a firecracker in a football helmet."

Gordon placed one hand over the other on the tabletop and looked at the sheriff. "A man told me a story yesterday."

"Who was the man?"

"Danny Young."

The sheriff's eyes narrowed. "I had a feeling you were gonna say that name. I had a little talk with that SOB not two days ago. Told me somebody took a potshot at him. You'd think he might've gotten the hint."

"It wasn't me."

"I didn't say it was. Could have been any number of people. Did he think it was you?"

"I believe it crossed his mind."

"Did you uncross it?"

"Tried to."

Moran lifted his mug. Gordon watched him.

"How was it you came to have a talk with him?" Gordon said.

"How's that?"

"Said you had a little talk with him not two days ago."

Moran drew his thumb and forefinger down the corners of his mouth. "I had some business up there anyhow, with the Sutter case—those two girls—and a man told me he'd seen him in town so I swung by the house for a chat. Was that part of his story?"

"No, that wasn't part of it."

"Well," said Moran. "You've got my attention, Gordon."

"He said you pulled him over that night."

"That night?"

"In the park. Ten years ago. Said you pulled him over as he was coming out of the park."

Moran was silent. He raised a hand to scratch at the side of his nose and lowered the hand again. "That's what you wanted to talk to me about?"

"Yes, sir. Because, the thing is, I don't remember that ever coming up before."

Moran looked off through the window slats to his right. "Well, that was ten years ago, Gordon."

"I'd of remembered that. No way I'd of forgot that."

Moran turned back to him. "Not sure what fish you're after here, Gordon."

"I'm just asking you, Sheriff. Did you pull the boy over that night?"

Moran held his eyes. Did not look away or blink. "I pulled him over, Gordon. He'd been in the park and I gave him a warning and let him go."

"And then you told Sutter about it. After my daughter . . . You told Sutter about pulling the boy over?"

"Of course I told him."

"Then why wasn't it on the record? Why wasn't it in the report?"

"I have no idea. You'd have to ask Sheriff Sutter about that."

Gordon stared at him. Moran staring back. Finally the sheriff looked at his watch. "Was that all you wanted to know, Gordon?"

"No. The boy said something else."

Moran waited. He opened his hands. "What else did he say?"

"Not so much what he said as what he showed me."

"What did he show you?"

"Showed me the pocket from the shirt she was wearing that night. The blouse she was wearing."

The waitress came by and put her fingers on the tabletop. "You boys all right here?"

Moran looked away from Gordon and gave her a smile. "We're good, Rhonda. Thank you." She moved on and he watched her go, or seemed to. Then slowly turned back to Gordon.

"The pocket from her blouse," Moran said. "And what makes you think it was the pocket from her blouse?"

"Well, I had a long night, Sheriff. I had plenty of time to think things through. And one thing I thought was, what would even give him the idea to bring a fake? How would he even know about it?"

"Unless he was the one ripped it off her blouse. I'm sorry to be blunt about it."

"Unless he was the one," said Gordon. "And in that case, why bring it at all? And why now?"

"Those are good questions. Did you get the answers?"

"I got his answers."

"What were they?"

"As to the why, he believes that pocket was put on his truck, on the license plate, by somebody else, and there wasn't nobody else could of done that between the park and when he found it but one man, and that was the man who pulled him over."

"Unless it happened before the park. At the bar, for instance."

"I thought about that too. But nobody said anything happened at the bar. Nobody said anything about a torn blouse when she left there."

Moran raised his coffee and sipped and set it down again. "And why now?"

"How's that?"

"Why did the boy wait till now."

"Well, to hear him say it, he just didn't know what to do when he was a kid. He was confused. Now he's older and he's tired of being blamed, I guess, so here he's got something he's held on to all these years and it's something only a crazy person would show now, so either he's crazy or he's telling the truth, and he's hoping I'll think one thing and not the other."

"To what end?"

"How's that?"

"To what end. What does he expect you to do?"

"God damned if I know. Stop blaming him, for one thing."

Moran sat there. He rubbed at something on the lip of his mug.

"Have you got it with you?" he said. "The pocket?"

"No. He kept it."

"Ah." Moran frowned into his mug. "I wish you'd held on to it, Gordon. That's evidence of a crime. If he panics, or runs, we might never see it again."

"Is he crazy?" Gordon said.

"What?"

"Is he crazy, or is he telling the truth?"

Moran looked at him with sadness in his eyes. Sorrow even. "The fact that you'd even ask is discouraging," he said.

"I don't think I'm asking that much, Sheriff. A man . . ." he began. "A man just wants to know the truth, that's all."

"I understand. But you've already put me on a level playing field with that son of a bitch and that just doesn't sit too great, I have to say."

"I wouldn't say level. I wouldn't say level by a long shot."

Moran stared at him. Then he picked up his phone and lit up its face and stared at that, then set it down again, facedown, on the tabletop.

"Something else just occurred to me here, Gordon."

"What's that."

"It's that for you to even consider his story might be true, you'd have to think some other man—this man who pulled him over—had that pocket on him for one reason only. You realize that?"

"I realize that."

Moran sat searching his eyes. The color had come up in the sheriff's face. A light in his eyes that had not been there before.

"Well, I just don't even know what to say to that, Gordon. I truly don't. You come on down here, into my town. Walk into my office. All the while thinking this."

"I'm sorry to do it, Sheriff. Like I said, I had a long night and I thought about a lot of things. And one thing I thought about . . . something I'd never really thought about before, was those times you brought her home. You remember that?"

"I brought a lot of kids home to their folks, Gordon. Brought them home drunk, high, beat-up. But alive. Always alive."

"I know it. But she never talked about it."

"I don't follow you."

"When you brought her home she wouldn't talk about it."

"Why would she? Would you?"

"Maybe not. Just, thinking back on it, it seemed she was more than embarrassed. Seemed she was more than that."

Moran's hands had been flat on the tabletop and now he lifted one in the air, palm out, as if to halt traffic. "All right, Gordon. Let's just—slow down here a minute." He leaned forward and said in a low voice, "Can you hear yourself, Gordon? Do you know what you're saying?"

Gordon did not look away.

"Because I'm having a hard time believing what I'm hearing." He sat looking into Gordon's eyes. As if he might read there some other story altogether—or else the madness that would explain this one. Finally he shook his head and looked down at his hands on the table.

"I'm trying real hard to stand in your shoes, Gordon, but it's difficult. I've never gone through what you've gone through and I pray to God I never do. I just don't see how a man would ever be the same after something like that." He took a breath and looked off and let the air out slowly. "So I'm sitting here asking myself what's the best thing to do right now, and there's two or three ideas going around. But I think the best thing for me to do is just get on back to work and let you be."

He picked up his phone and gathered his jacket and his hat.

"You never said," Gordon said.

"Never said what."

"If he's crazy or not."

"Well, Gordon, you might ask yourself this: What would you expect me to say?"

He stood from the booth and put his hat on. He got into his sheriff's jacket, then pulled his wallet from the inside breast pocket, removed several bills and dropped them on the tabletop. He replaced the wallet and stood looking down on Gordon from under the hatbrim.

"Crazy has got a way of spreading, Gordon. I just hope you've got sense enough not to be the one goes spreading it." He held Gordon's eyes, then he turned and made his way toward the door. He called, "So long" to the waitress and he clapped the old man on the back and yelled to him, "Seeya, Harold," and then he pushed out through the door into the daylight and was gone.

43

WHEN GORDON BURKE came home the sun was just down and she was sitting on the edge of the porch with her boots on the step below and a mug of hot tea in her hands. She was wearing her father's canvas jacket and a pair of faded Levi's and a billcap she'd found in the downstairs coat closet. Under the jacket she wore a red fleece pullover and under that a white cotton tank top that smelled faintly of perfume. Or so she believed. His headlights swept through the trees, and she watched as he pulled up to the garage or whatever it was across the way and got out and walked to the rear of the van, opened the back doors, collected a large black garbage bag in one hand and several plastic grocery bags in the other and closed the doors again with his shoulder. He paused at the sight of her, then came along the path with the bags and stopped just short of the porchsteps and stood looking at her in the dusk.

"You shouldn't be out here in the cold," he said, and his voice was strange. Like he himself was sick, or had talked himself hoarse. She looked at him more carefully: the unshaved, ashy face, the shadowed eyes.

"Are you all right?" she said.

"Am I all right?"

"You didn't catch it, did you?"

"No, I didn't catch it. I just didn't sleep too good last night."

"I'm sorry."

"It wasn't your fault. Had nothing to do with you."

She sat looking at him. His eyes went to the billcap on her head but he said nothing.

"What day is it?" she said.

"Friday."

"How long have I been here?"

"Two days, two nights."

She nodded. "Thank you. For bringing me here. For taking care of me."

He adjusted the bags in his grips, then set them down on the path. "Wasn't just me," he said. "Doc Van Allen came out and looked you over. You remember that?"

"No. I didn't think they did that anymore."

"Did what?"

"House calls."

"They don't." He looked up at the sky, then at her again. "Anyway your fever broke, so I thought I'd take off for just a little bit." He nudged the large garbage bag with the side of his boot. "Drove on down to post bond on your clothes."

She said nothing, and he said, "That's a joke. There wasn't no bond."

Her eyes began to sting. "You didn't have to do that."

"I had to talk to a man down there anyhow."

An owl hooted from the woods and he looked toward the trees as if he might see it, but there was nothing there to see. The trees. The snow. The cold early stars in the purple sky.

She said, "I hope you don't mind I found some clothes."

"No, I expected you might."

"Took a shower too. Maybe the best one I ever had."

He looked back at the van and said, "I got the luggage in the back of the van there. Your backpack. I don't know if there's much left you can use but I took it all anyhow. I think they put these clothes through some kind of wash but I don't believe they ever heard of detergent down there. Thought I'd run them through again."

"I can do it."

"All right." He looked at her. "You best come inside now."

"All right."

"I can take you on home later if you want. The gas and electric are back on."

She stared at him, her eyes stinging. "Mr. Burke . . ."

"Mr. Burke nothing. I asked the woman there at Water & Gas, 'Ma'am, what do you think is gonna happen to the waterpipes when you turn off the heat?' She just looked at me." He shook his head. "So then I go back to the house to light the furnace and water heater and guess what I see?"

"What?"

"I see that someone has left all the faucets dribbling."

"Someone must've broken in."

"That's what I figured."

She looked into her mug, the pale tea. Dark curve of sediment down there like a letter C against the white.

"What are you drinking there?" he said.

"Tea."

"Tea," he said. "That's gotta be over ten years old. Come on now," he said. "Let's get you inside and get some food in you."

HE MADE SPAGHETTI with meatballs and she ate two plates of it and wiped the plate clean with the last slice of garlic bread and ate that too, and then with her cup of coffee she ate a slice of store-bought cherry pie that had been warming in the oven and when that was gone she pushed the plate away from her and puffed her cheeks and blew.

In the utility room off the kitchen her clothes were tumbling in the dryer. Zippers and jeans rivets ticking irregularly on the drum.

She was looking around the kitchen and he looked too, as if he'd never done so before. Spare and neat and not much in the way of décor to suggest a wife and a daughter—their coming and going, their cooking, their teasing, their arguing. Their standing shoulder to shoulder at the sink. The sight of one or both of them at the window when he'd come home from work and was crossing the cold path toward that light, that warmth. He'd seen that, she knew. Felt that.

He began to fuss with the plates and she said, "Let me do it. You drink your coffee," and she stood and took the plates to the counter.

"There's a good dishwasher there," he said.

"I'm a good dishwasher. Is that OK?"

"Can you manage with that cast?"

"I can manage anything with this thing."

Steam rose from the sink and she scrubbed the silverware first, thinking, Did Holly Burke hold this knife, eat from this fork? Her own reflection was in the window, but beyond that a skewed rectangle of light lay on the snow, her shape in the center of the rectangle like some parallel girl looking back at her. She said, "I had such crazy dreams. When I was sick."

"Fever dreams."

"I saw my father clear as day. He sat there on the bed and called me Deputy."

"Maybe it wasn't a dream."

She turned to him. "You believe that?"

"Doesn't matter what I believe." He looked down at his coffee, and she turned back to the sink. She watched her good hand moving white and slow under the suds.

"When I went into the river that day," she said, "when we went through the ice and we were in the water, I think I must've drowned. I think I must've died."

He said nothing. She heard him return the mug quietly to the tabletop. She turned around again. "I'm sorry—I shouldn't have said that."

He shook his head and made a face that said it was nothing, no harm done.

"What makes you think you drowned?" he said.

"I saw things under there, in the water. I don't know how else I could've seen them otherwise." Before he could ask what she'd seen she said, "My dreams were like that, when I was sick. It was like being in that river all over again."

I felt her heart, she would've liked to tell him. *All its pain but all its love too.*

He sat watching her. The laundry thumping and ticking.

"I remember looking out the window upstairs and seeing two men standing in the snow talking," she said.

"That wasn't no dream," he said. "I come back upstairs and there you are lying on the floor by that window, and the window wide-open."

"Sorry."

He looked into his mug again. She turned back to the sink and began scrubbing the saucepan.

"You hear what those two men said?" he said.

The saucepan slipped out of her grip and splashed in the water. She retrieved it and resumed scrubbing.

"I heard," she said, "but I thought it was just part of the dream."

"What did you hear?"

She worked at the saucepan. Then, without turning around, she told him what she'd heard—about the deputy, about the piece of cloth. Feverish, crazy things.

Gordon was silent. She rinsed the saucepan one-handed and racked it.

"You heard all that?" he said, and she turned to him again.

"That was Danny Young," she said.

"Yes, it was."

"I didn't think he lived here anymore."

"He doesn't. But he's back now. Came out here to tell me he didn't do it. All these years later."

She leaned against the counter and dried her good hand with the dish towel.

"Do you believe him?"

"I don't know." He put his hand to his forehead. "I went down there and talked to that deputy. Sheriff, now."

"What did he say?" she said—and heard herself and said, "I'm sorry. It's none of my business."

"He said what you'd expect him to say," Gordon said. "Had an answer for everything." He looked up again. Watching her standing there. "What?" he said.

"What what?"

"You were gonna say something."

She shook her head, but then she said it: "My dad didn't like him."

"Who?"

"Ed Moran."

"The world's full of people who don't like each other."

"I know. But I think—"

He waited.

"I think he knew something about him," she said.

"Like what?"

She thought about that, but there was nothing specific, no single thing she could put into words. "I don't know," she said. "But I asked him one time why

Moran was leaving the department and he didn't say. He said it was none of my concern."

"Was he wrong?"

She shook her head again. "But it was the way he said it. Like there was something there he didn't want to talk about. Not with me, anyway."

Gordon narrowed his eyes at her. "If you're trying to say he knew about this . . ."

"No, not about this," she said quickly. "Not about Holly. I mean—" she said, but then lost her voice in the rush of her thoughts . . . because if her father had known that Moran might've been involved in Holly's death, if he'd had any suspicion whatsoever, then he never would've let him go down to Iowa like that—he'd have kept him in Minnesota until he had his case. Until he could bust him and hold him. And he certainly would not have allowed him to become an Iowa deputy . . . and so whatever he'd known, or whatever he'd suspected about the deputy, it hadn't been enough to act on, and it hadn't been enough to say something against him to the Iowa sheriff.

Or did he just say nothing at all, as he'd done with her? *None of your concern.*

"I don't know what it was," she said finally. "But it wasn't about Holly. It couldn't have been."

Gordon looked at her. Then he looked into his coffee again. Silent. Far away in his thoughts, in his pain, so that when he spoke again she knew it didn't matter that she was there to hear it.

"I watched that boy grow up. Him and his brother. Their daddy was my business partner. Our kids used to play together when they were little." He tilted his mug, watching. "I saw the other one just a few days ago, over at Wabash's. Or I guess it was longer ago than that."

"The other one?"

"Other brother. Twin brother. Marky. He works there. And after that I go on out to their mother's place, I don't even know why, I haven't said one word to that woman in ten years, and here she is trying to bury a dead dog in the frozen ground." He shook his head. "The world is just too strange for words, that's all."

She watched him. Then she stepped back to the table and sat down again.

"So what are you going to do?" she said.

He didn't look up. "About what?"

"About what he told you—what Danny Young told you."

He looked up then, and she felt the blood rising to her face.

"What am I supposed to do?" he said.

"You could go to the sheriff, Mr. Burke. Sheriff Halsey. Or a lawyer. I know a good one, I could—"

"Lawyer? I don't need no lawyer. And I can just see the sheriff's face. This boy comes to tell me a story about a deputy—a full sheriff now—trying to frame him ten years ago? Hell, he'd lock me up."

"But there's evidence now."

"There's a piece of cloth ten years old, and I don't even have it. He took it with him."

"But the sheriff—"

Gordon pushed back from the table and stood, as if remembering something he'd forgotten to do, but then did nothing, just stood there. Then he went to the sink, and after a moment there was the sound of his mug going into the water, the dull, underwater note of it hitting bottom.

"I'm sorry," she said. "It's none of my business."

He stood staring into the water. "Nothing to be sorry about," he said. "But to tell you the truth, I wish like hell you never opened up that window. We wouldn't even be having this conversation."

She watched him. The back of his neck.

"I don't know, Mr. Burke," she said. "Maybe I was supposed to open that window."

He glanced back at her then without quite looking at her. "Supposed to?"

"Yes. If you think about how it all happened . . . me getting sick, you bringing the firewood, then bringing me here. Danny Young showing up like that. The fact that it was my dad's case . . ."

He turned back to the kitchen window. "You're a strange girl, you know that?" He was silent a long while, and she was too. Then he said to the window, "I went on up there to Rochester, to that hospital, when you were there. He tell you that—your dad?"

"No."

"Well. Can't say I'm surprised, after what I said to him."

"What did you say to him?"

"Said I wished it on him. What happened to you. It was a long time ago, but after he let that boy go, after he let Danny Young walk away, I wished it on him. Just so he'd know what it was like."

She watched him but he would not turn to look at her.

"You don't think . . ." she began. "Mr. Burke—you don't think that had anything to do with what happened to me and Caroline, do you?"

He didn't move. Staring out the window.

"Mr. Burke?"

"I don't know what I think. I just got a funny feeling that if you never went into that river, you and Caroline, Danny Young never would of come to show me that piece of cloth. And don't even say it," he said, turning toward her again. "I know how it sounds."

He held her eyes, then turned away again. "I just wanted you to know I wished for it, that's all. I wanted you to know that about me."

She was silent, imagining that moment: Gordon Burke standing with her father in the hospital and telling him that—that he'd wished harm on her.

"What did he say?" she said finally.

"Who?"

"My dad. When you told him that."

"Said what a decent man would say. Said he was sorry."

"He was, Mr. Burke," she said. "He never got over it. He never stopped thinking about it. I know he didn't. I know that's why he went down there and shot that boy in the hand like that. It wasn't just about me and Caroline. It was about Holly too, and Danny Young, and—"

Gordon had raised his hand, and he kept it raised. As if demonstrating the act itself—how a hand was raised for its own shooting. "That was about you," he said. "Trust me. I know what was in his heart. And I know he let that boy off easy."

"He shot a boy with no evidence, Mr. Burke."

"No evidence doesn't mean no reason."

She shook her head. Her heart was pounding. How did they get here—with her condemning her father's actions and Gordon Burke defending them?

"And what about those pictures?" she said. "The photo line-up? I couldn't ID him myself."

"Doesn't mean it wasn't him."

"And Danny Young?" she said—she blurted.

"What about him."

"I mean—should he have shot him too?"

He stared at her and she did not look away, her heart pounding, and there was no sound but the tumbling of her clothes in the other room, that constant thumping and ticking, until suddenly an alarm sounded, so loud and urgent she jumped. It was the dryer. It blared and stopped and the drum stopped turning and they studied each other in a new silence.

"I think your dad was right about one thing," Gordon said. "It's none of your concern."

She saw him again, her father, sitting on the bed, his cool hand on her forehead, *You have to help him now, sweetheart.* She felt Holly Burke's heart beating in her chest again—or the memory of it, the emptiness that so much feeling left behind.

"And if he was here," Gordon went on, "I think he'd say it was time for you to get back to school where you belong."

"How do you know what he'd say?" she said, and she saw how these words struck him, and she said, "I'm sorry . . . Mr. Burke, I didn't mean that how it sounded, I—"

He raised his hand again and shook his head. Suddenly he looked very tired and very old.

"We keep saying things we're sorry we said," he said. "Which tells me we should just stop talking about it." He looked at her with kindness, or his idea of it in that moment, and Audrey nodded, and smiled, and wiped her eyes. Then she stood from the table and went into the utility room to get her clothes.

44

IT'S NONE OF your concern.

Her father had told her that years ago, and Gordon Burke had said he was right.

But her father had also said, *You have to help him now, sweetheart.*

Help who? Mr. Burke? Danny Young?

All that day—the day after Gordon Burke brought her home—she did not leave the sofa except to make herself soup, except to use the bathroom, and by nine o'clock the next morning she was done lying around on that sofa.

She'd not been back to the building since his retirement but it had not changed, and its smell was still the smell of her father: leather belts and coffee and cigarettes and dusty wooden floors and the smoky wintry smell of his sheriff's jacket when he would let her wear it as she sat reading in the old wooden armchair, waiting for him to finish typing at his computer, finish his phone calls, finish talking to his deputies, to Gloria, his secretary, before at last jingling his keys and putting his hand on top of her head, *Ready to roll, Deputy?*

Ready, Sheriff.

"Oh, goodness—hello, sweetie," Gloria now said, turning from her computer with her smile. Older now. Old. Hair gone to silver, cigarette voice deeper, but the same kind eyes peeping out of the same enormous glasses. At the funeral she'd wept like a widow and hugged Audrey for so long her husband had to pry her loose.

There was no one else around, the deputies out on call, or back in the jail, or behind the closed door that once bore her father's name on the frosted glass and now bore the name of the new sheriff, SHERIFF WAYNE G. HALSEY, in black-and-gold letters.

"How are you getting along, sweetie?" Gloria said, glancing at the purple cast.

"I'm doing all right," Audrey said. "You know."

Gloria looked at the too-big canvas jacket and shook her head. "Not a day goes by I don't think of him." She plucked a tissue from the box and dabbed at her eyes. Audrey thought to put a hand on her shoulder or squeeze her hand, but then Gloria sniffled loudly and tossed the tissue into a wastebasket and looked up smiling again.

"So. What can I do for you?"

"I was hoping I could talk to him for a minute. The sheriff."

"Sheriff Halsey?"

"Yes."

"Are you sure you're all right?"

"Oh, yes. I just wanted to ask him something."

A crease appeared between the older woman's thin, painted eyebrows. "Let me just make sure he's not on his cell phone," she said and picked up the handset and pushed a button, and from behind the office door they heard the beep-beep and they heard him say, "Yes?" and Gloria spoke into the handset, and her voice was in the speaker in his office at the same time, "There's someone here to see you, Sheriff."

"Well, who is it?"

"It's Audrey Sutter."

He said nothing. Then he said, "I'll come out," and Audrey wondered how Gloria could've thought he was on his cell phone with that voice of his.

Halsey himself was larger than her father, even when her father had been healthy. Taller, heavier, louder. As a deputy he'd looked more like the sheriff than her father had. He looked like he'd been raised from birth to be sheriff, although she knew for a fact that he'd been raised by two English professors at the University of Minnesota.

He walked her back to his office and she sat in the old wooden armchair and he sat in her father's old swivel chair behind the desk. Behind him on the wall was the big map of the county, all in yellow but for the river looping through it in a blue cursive.

He watched her looking around the office and said, his voice just a little softened, "I imagine it's not easy for you, coming back here."

"Not easy but not bad either. I always loved it here."

He scratched at the back of his head. His hair was dark and thick and it held the depression from the sweatband of his hat all the way around. Finally he put his hands together on the desk and said, "You're always welcome to pay a visit, of course."

"Thank you, I appreciate that."

"But this isn't a social visit. Is it."

"No, sir."

He checked his watch and said, "Well, I've got ten minutes before I have to be somewhere else, so we'd best get to it."

"Yes, sir." She turned her father's watch on her wrist and then held it still. "I just wanted to ask you about Deputy Moran," she said.

He looked at her. "You mean Sheriff Moran."

"I mean when he was still a deputy here."

The sheriff sat regarding her blankly. Then he stood up and came around the desk and shut the door with a quiet click and walked back and sat down again.

"What did you want to ask?"

"I wanted to ask why he left the department."

"Why did you want to ask that?"

She was not expecting the question and she sat trying to think, her heart beating.

"Since the accident," she said, "my accident, in the river, I've been thinking about Holly Burke. I've been thinking about her a lot."

"I guess I can understand that," he said.

"And I've gotten to know her father a little bit too—Mr. Burke."

"I saw him at your father's service. Was somewhat surprised by that, I have to say."

"Well. He came to bring me firewood—this was after the funeral—and I was sick with the flu and he took me in. He took care of me."

The sheriff moved a pen on his desk from one place to another. She could see him trying to imagine all of that. He looked up again, waiting for her to go on.

"So, I've gotten to know him," she went on, "and he's told me a little about . . . back then. About Holly. And I know how bad my father felt about that case. I know how much it bothered him."

"It bothered all of us."

"Yes, sir. Well, all of this got me thinking back to that time, and how it wasn't long after the Holly Burke case that Deputy Moran quit the department and went down to Iowa"—she looked to the sheriff to confirm the timeline and the sheriff nodded—"and I remember asking my dad why he was leaving, why Deputy Moran was leaving, and my dad saying it wasn't any of my concern."

Halsey said nothing. Waiting to hear something that required his response.

"Which of course it wasn't," she said. "But now, after going in the river, after Caroline, and after—" She stopped, hearing the struggle in her own voice, the distress of it. A kind of choking, childhood feeling. "I'm sorry," she said.

"It's all right," said Halsey. "Do you want some water?"

She shook her head. "I'm fine." And after a moment she was: her heart no longer racing, her lungs working again.

"After everything," she said, "I guess I just wanted to know what it was. What he wouldn't talk to me about."

Halsey picked up his pen and tapped it once on the desk on its ballpoint and then once on the other end, and set it down again.

"Did your dad generally talk to you about his work? About the goings-on of law enforcement?"

"Yes, sir." She'd been his deputy herself, she wanted to remind him, but she couldn't say that.

"And his deputies? He talked about us too?"

"Sometimes," she said. "Not about you, though."

"No, of course not." He picked up the pen again and gave it a click with his thumb. He leaned back in her father's old chair and regarded her from that new distance. "And so you've come here hoping I could tell you something your father wouldn't. About Sheriff Moran. Do I have that right?"

"Yes, sir."

He nodded. "All right." He clicked the pen. "And why would I do that? I mean, even if I knew what he didn't want to talk to you about, why would I talk about it?"

"I don't know," she said. "I guess because that was ten years ago. I guess because what does it matter now?"

"That sounds like my argument. What does it matter now? What good can it possibly do you?"

She held his eyes. "I can't explain it. Maybe after you tell me I can, but otherwise . . ." She sat watching him. The sheriff watching her.

"And what if I have nothing to tell you?"

"I don't know. I'll have to think about that when we get there."

He looked at her a long while, saying nothing. Then he leaned forward again and put his forearms on the desk and sat turning the pen between his fingers, frowning at it. Her father's watch was ticking away on her wrist. Finally the sheriff looked up and said, "I just can't imagine what good it can do anyone to rehash any of it, but if you want to know did Deputy Moran leave because of anything having to do with the Holly Burke case, then I can tell you unequivocally and categorically no. As to whatever it was your dad didn't want to talk to you about, I find his own words entirely . . . adequate. None of your concern. I don't mean to be harsh about it, but I don't know what else to tell you."

He paused, watching her, but she had nothing to say, and after a moment he said, "Ed Moran by all accounts has been a fine sheriff. And I'll say further that I sympathize with the man's frustration in your own case down there. Under the circumstances."

She watched him, and seeing that he'd finished she nodded and thanked him and began to stand.

"Now hold on there a second."

She sat again.

"You said you'd think on things once we got there, and now we've got there."

"Yes, sir. Well. I guess I can't think what good it would do to tell you anything more right now myself. I guess we need to go some other route."

"Some other route?"

"Yes, sir."

He watched her. "Young lady, I sure hope you're not getting mixed up in something here."

She stood and he watched her stand. He didn't get up. Then he got up and came around the desk and reached in front of her for the doorknob.

"Thank you, Sheriff."

"You take care," Halsey said. He watched her pass through the outer office toward the glass doors and he was standing there yet, holding the edge of the door to his own office after she'd gone.

GLORIA STOOD AT the bottom of the steps in her overcoat, and when Audrey came down the steps the older woman smiled and held up a cigarette and said, "Nasty old habit." The cigarette was just-lit, and there was a whiff of butane in the air.

"Not so nasty," Audrey said.

"Oh, did you want one?"

"No, thank you."

"Good for you. Ginny, my daughter, started nagging me to quit when she was nine and has never stopped." She looked at Audrey, standing there in the canvas jacket. "Your dad," she said, "he'd say, 'You need to quit those things, Gloria,' and I'd say, 'I will if you will, Sheriff,' and he'd say, 'That's a deal.' And then we'd both finish our smokes and get back to work." Her eyes shone behind the lenses, and Audrey looked down at the concrete.

When she raised her head again Gloria was still looking at her.

"Well," said Audrey, "it was nice to see you, Gloria." But before she could turn away, the woman reached with her free hand and took hold of Audrey's sleeve. She glanced back up at the glass doors, then leaned in so close that Audrey could smell her cigarette breath.

"I don't want you to think I was eavesdropping, but sweetie I hear every word that man says in there, since day one. Sometimes I have to remind him to lower his voice but he just doesn't seem capable of it."

Audrey didn't know what to say to that.

Gloria said, "Well, I heard enough and I'm sorry I heard and I don't want to stick my nose where it doesn't belong but I'm gonna tell you one thing, so long as you promise me you never heard it from me, all right?"

Audrey nodded. "I promise."

The woman took a fast drag on her cigarette and glanced once more at the glass doors and blew the smoke from the side of her mouth and said, "Katie Goss."

"Katie Goss." Audrey knew that name but didn't know how. Then she did: Katie Goss had been Danny Young's girlfriend, all those years ago.

"Katie Goss," said Gloria. "She's up in Rochester now. She works at the nursing home up there, Green Fields or green something."

Audrey looked at the woman. The eyes behind the big lenses watery but bright.

"All right?" Gloria said.

"All right."

"Good." She dropped her cigarette on the concrete and mashed it under her tennis shoe and left it lying there. "Tell you one more thing," she said.

Audrey waited, looking into those eyes.

"She wasn't the only one," Gloria said.

45

IT WAS CALLED Green Meadows, not Green Fields, and the woman who answered the phone put her on hold and she sat in the sedan with the phone to her ear listening to recorded music. The sun was going down, and from where she was parked she could see a stoplight turning green, yellow, red . . . green, yellow, red. At last the music ended and another woman said, "Hello?"

"Katie Goss?"

"Yes?"

"My name is Audrey Sutter. I'm so sorry to call you at work but—"

"Audrey Sutter?"

"Yes. I couldn't find any other number for you, I'm sorry . . ."

There was a silence that went on. Audrey could hear the other woman breathing. She could hear people talking in the background. From a distance someone yelled as if he'd just been stabbed.

"Hello—?" she said, and Katie Goss said, "Yes. I'm here."

THE APARTMENT BUILDING was not three blocks from the hospital where she'd woken up with men in the room and a purple cast on her arm. The front entrance would not be locked, Katie Goss had said, and it wasn't. A small dog yapping behind a door somewhere. TVs going. Smell of grilled onions in the air. She went up the stairs, her boots thumping dully on thin brown carpeting, and at the top of the stairs the door with the number 4 on it was not quite shut all the way. She rapped on the door, trying not to open it any farther, and a voice called out, "Audrey—?"

"Yes."

"We're back here in the bathroom."

She stepped in and shut the door behind her and waited to see if Katie Goss would poke her head from the lighted doorway down the hallway but she didn't. There was splashing, a child's voice. The living and kitchen area were all one space, separated only by a short length of half wall. A TV played to an empty loveseat and a herd of toy horses on a coffee table, the horses all on their feet and of all different colors and sizes. Food-smeared plates and milk glasses had been left on the little dinner table.

She moved down the hall and as she neared the open door there was the smell of bathwater and steam and baby shampoo. She eased her head around the jamb and it was the child who saw her first—great brown eyes looking up, then looking down again at the bathwater, at the colorful things bobbing before her in the suds. Kneeling beside the tub in her nurse's uniform, purple top and pants, was Katie Goss, her hair gathered up in clips and a few blond tails fallen loose. She saw Audrey and she smiled the tired smile of a mother and said, "Ah, there she is, sweetie, there's Audrey. Can you say hello?"

The little girl didn't look up but continued playing with her toys, her lips moving as she talked to them.

"Shy tonight," said Katie Goss.

"What's her name?"

"Melanie. We call her Mel."

"Hello, Mel. Is that a mermaid?"

The mermaid dove underwater, where Audrey couldn't see her anymore.

Katie Goss lifted a sudsy hand from the child's head. "I'm Katie. I'd shake your hand, but . . ."

"I'm Audrey. Maybe I should come back later?"

"Why?"

"You have your hands full."

"My hands are always full. I'll tell you what you can do, though."

"What?"

"You can go out to the kitchen and find that bottle of wine I set out and open it and pour yourself a glass. Do you drink wine? Otherwise there's juice in the fridge, or water."

"I drink wine. Should I wait for you there?"

"God, no. It's Friday. Bring me back a glass of that wine. And take off your jacket."

In the kitchen she hung the jacket on a chairback and found the bottle of wine. The opener was beside it and she twisted the skewer into the cork as Caroline had taught her and drew down the arms and pulled the cork free with a deep pop. You were supposed to let it sit for a while, breathe, so she carried the dirty plates and the glasses and the silverware from the table and set them on the counter. Ominous music was playing from the TV as a man spoke of a fresh twist in the case; a woman had murdered her husband with a pair of scissors—or had she?

Audrey returned to the bathroom with the two glasses and Katie said, "Oh, you're in a cast—I'm sorry, I wouldn't have asked you to open the wine."

"It's fine. Should I . . .?"

"Yes, just set mine there, please."

The little girl was standing now, with her hands over her face, as Katie filled a plastic Cool Whip container from the spout and emptied it over her head. The girl's wet hair hung in a dark curtain down to her little biceps, islands of suds slipping down her tummy and down her legs and she stood with no embarrassment at all; her nudity was nothing to her.

"How old is she?"

"How old are you, Mel?"

One little hand came out from under the hair with four fingers raised and went under again.

"Four?"

She nodded.

Katie tossed a towel over the girl's head and lifted her out of the tub and set her on her feet and began rubbing at the body under the cloth. As she rubbed she looked at Audrey more carefully, as if it were only now possible to do so.

"I saw you on the news," she said. "You're lucky to be alive."

"What?" said the girl, her small voice muffled and shaken.

"I'm talking to Audrey, baby."

"Oh."

Audrey sipped her wine.

Katie said, "I'm sorry about your friend. Caroline?"

"Yes. Thank you."

"Just so awful."

"Yes."

"I'm sorry about your father too."

"Thank you."

"You've had a rough time of it, haven't you."

"I'm all right."

"How old are you?"

"Nineteen."

"Nineteen. Lord. How's that wine?"

"It's good. Thank you."

"Is Audrey sleeping over?"

"No, baby. Audrey and Mommy are going to talk for a while after you go to bed like a good little citizen."

"I wanna talk too."

"No, you don't. This is grown-up talk."

"So?"

"Come on," she said, lifting the girl again. "Let's get you in those jammies."

Audrey sat on the loveseat and watched the crime show with the volume turned down, and after a while the little girl came thumping out and dropped to her knees in the space between the sofa and the coffee table and began moving the horses around.

"What are their names?"

"This is Lavender and this is Strawberry. This is Peaches, she's Strawberry's sister, and this is Dave."

"Dave?"

"Mm-hmm, and this is the corral and that's the meadow where you're sitting."

"Should I move?"

"No, they already runned in the meadow before."

"Oh, good."

"What did you do to your hand?"

"I broke it."

"Does it hurt?"

"Not anymore."

"Can I touch it?"

"Sure." She held out the cast and watched as the girl stroked it like it was a soft pet.

"I like the color."

"Thank you. I do too."

Katie came out in sweatpants and a University of Minnesota T-shirt. "I slipped into something a little more comfortable, as they say." She went to the kitchen and came back with the wine bottle and set it on the coffee table away from the horses. They sat and watched the crime show while the little girl played with her horses and chattered. At the end of the show you still didn't know if the wife had done it or not; she was in jail awaiting her trial. There was no end and no answer.

"They always end like that," Katie said. "It's one big tease."

Audrey was feeling the wine. She'd almost forgotten why she was there. She thought she could curl up on the loveseat and sleep over after all.

"Will you be all right while I put her to bed?"

"Sure."

"We read for a bit. It could be awhile."

"It's OK. Take your time."

"Say good night to Audrey, baby."

The girl came around the coffee table and lifted her face, her lips, and Audrey leaned forward for the softest kiss. "Good night, Audrey."

"Good night, Mel."

When they were gone she put her head back and closed her eyes and soon she heard Katie's reading voice down the hall, and then it was as if she were in the bedroom herself and the voice were reading to her, and next she knew a hand was on her shoulder gently shaking and Katie was sitting facing her with one foot tucked up under the other leg. The TV had been shut off and music was playing quietly from somewhere.

"I'm sorry . . ." Audrey said.

"Don't be. I almost didn't wake you. I almost threw a blanket over you and went to bed. But then I remembered you wanted to talk to me."

Audrey sat forward and felt the blood go to her head with a deep thump of pain. "Maybe I'll have some of that water now." She pressed the heel of her hand to her forehead.

"I shouldn't have let you drink all that wine. Did you eat anything?"

She couldn't remember. "Yes," she said.

Katie got up and Audrey turned her father's watch on her wrist. It was just nine o'clock. The second hand seemed connected to the pulse in her head.

Katie came back with two aspirins and a large glass of water and sat as before and watched as Audrey took the pills and drank down half the glass.

"Do you feel sick?"

"No, I just feel like . . . like I don't know where I am."

"You're here, with me, in my apartment. You wanted to talk to me."

"Yes. I just don't know where to begin."

"How about why."

"Why?"

"Why me."

Audrey shook her head. "I don't know. I mean—I was just trying to figure something out about something. About someone."

"Who?"

"A man named Ed Moran."

Katie stared at her. Just stared, no expression. Then she picked up the wine bottle and refilled her own glass and set the bottle down again.

"Do you know him?" Audrey said.

"I know he used to be a sheriff's deputy down there."

"He's a sheriff now, down in Iowa."

"Lucky Iowa."

"Why do you say that?"

She shrugged. "Smart-ass reflex. So what about him?"

"He's investigating my case. Mine and Caroline's."

Katie nodded slowly, recalling. "There was a second car, they said. Did they ever find it?"

"No. Or those two boys either." She didn't want to go into what her father had done. Or Moran's photo line-up.

"Two boys?" said Katie.

"From the gas station."

Katie shook her head and Audrey said, "The ones who tried to—who grabbed me?"

Katie stared at her. "I don't remember anything about two boys."

"Young men, actually."

Katie was silent. Then she said, "What did they do?"

"Nothing. Caroline got them with the pepper spray. We were driving away when we went off the road."

"And was it them, those two pieces of shit, who pushed you over the bank?"

"I don't know. We could only see the headlights."

"Jesus," Katie said. Then she said, "All right. So what has this got to do with me?"

"I don't know. This person I know . . . this woman who worked for my father—"

"Your father the sheriff."

"Ex-sheriff, yes. She gave me your name."

"Gloria Walsh."

Audrey opened her mouth, and closed it.

"I went to school with her daughter," Katie said, answering the question Audrey had not asked. "Does she still work for the sheriff?"

"Yes. I went to talk to him, the sheriff, but it was her—Gloria—who gave me your name."

"And why did you go talk to the sheriff, if you don't mind me asking?"

"Because of Danny Young."

"Danny Young—?" Her eyes grew large, and Audrey thought she was about to stand up, but she only shifted in place and tossed her free arm over the back of the loveseat.

"You and he . . ." Audrey said.

"Yes," said Katie. "About a million years ago. He was my brother's best friend. A year older than me. How do you know him?"

"I don't. I only know him through my dad. Through the Holly Burke case."

"Holly Burke. God, there's another name I haven't heard in forever."

"Did you know her?"

"I knew her. We weren't exactly friends."

"You weren't?"

"No. Most of her friends were boys. Or men. She was known as bad news, generally."

Audrey thought of Gordon Burke, his good old face and his big hands and his kindness to her, his gentleness when she was sick.

She said, "I've gotten to know her father a little bit since I've been home. Mr. Burke."

"Oh God, that poor man. I thought he'd moved away."

"No, he's still there. And so a few days ago Danny Young came out to Mr. Burke's house, and—"

"Wait." Katie raised her hand. "Danny Young went to Gordon Burke's house?"

"Yes."

She sipped her wine. "All right. I'm just going to shut up now and listen. Go on."

And Audrey went on, telling her all that she herself had learned in the last two days, and when she was finished Katie sat looking at her.

"You sound like that TV show, Audrey."

"I'm sorry."

"Don't apologize." She took another sip of her wine, and Audrey drank her water.

"So, what are you telling me here? That Deputy Moran had that torn pocket?"

"Yes. I mean, according to Danny Young."

"And he pulled Danny over so he could plant it on his truck, and then he just—let him go . . . but then they never found it?"

"Right. Danny found it first."

"And held on to it for ten years."

"Yes."

"And then all of sudden decided to show it to Gordon Burke."

"Yes."

"Because . . . ?"

"Because he wants Mr. Burke to know the truth."

"Why didn't he do it ten years ago?"

"I don't know. I don't think he understood it back then. I think he was just a scared kid."

Katie set her glass down on the table and turned it around slowly by the stem, watching it. "And that's why you're here. Because you want to believe Danny Young."

"Because I want to . . ." she said, and faltered. The beat in her head thumping on. "Because I want to know the truth."

"And you think I can tell you that?"

"I don't know. I only know that Gloria gave me your name."

Katie stared at her—then put her face in her hands, as her little girl had done in the bathtub to keep the water out of her eyes. "Jesus," she said. "What a convoluted cluster-fuck of goings-on."

"I know, I'm sorry. I didn't know how else to tell it."

"How else could you tell it? It's impossible."

Katie dropped her hands and sat looking across the room, at the wall, or maybe at something beyond the wall.

"Well, Audrey," Katie said, "well . . ." and was silent again.

"Holly Burke . . . Jesus," Katie said. "That girl. We heard all kinds of things about her. Said all kinds of things about her too, little bitches that we were. She was sleeping with this boy and that boy. One DUI after another. Giving married men blowjobs for money." She shook her head. "But did she have dealings with that deputy? Could he have had reason to kill her? Is that what you want to know?"

It was the first time Audrey had heard the idea expressed out loud. It sounded ridiculous.

"Yes," she said. "That's what I want to know."

"Well, I just can't answer that, Audrey. I'm sorry."

Audrey looked at her own hands where they lay in her lap, the twined fingers. White from squeezing. She untwined them and wiped her palms on her jeans.

"Then why would Gloria give me your name?" she said quietly.

Katie was still looking off.

"Katie—?"

Katie turned and looked at her. "Your dad let him go. He had him and he let him go."

"I know. It bothered him the rest of his life."

"And now it bothers you."

"It bothers Mr. Burke. And it bothers Danny Young and his family," she said, thinking of Danny Young's twin brother. Of that poor woman trying to bury her dog. "It bothers the whole town."

"Why doesn't Mr. Burke," Katie began, and stopped. "Why doesn't Danny . . . I mean, why doesn't he go to the sheriff—the new sheriff—with this?"

"I don't know. I guess because he doesn't think anyone would believe him, ten years later."

"You guess? He didn't tell you that?"

"No. I've never spoken to him."

"You've never spoken to him?"

"No. Like I said, I've never actually met him."

Katie stared at her. Then she lifted her glass and drank and put the glass down again. She shook her head. "Danny Young. God. I thought I was in love. I thought we'd get married, someday."

Audrey didn't know what to say, so she said nothing.

"But it wasn't Holly Burke that ended it," Katie said.

"It wasn't?"

"No."

Audrey was quiet. She tried to breathe evenly and quietly.

"What ended it, really, was one stupid decision on one stupid night," Katie said. And then she told Audrey about the night—August 15, which she remembered because it was Ginny Walsh's eighteenth birthday and Ginny always threw a party at her house, and it was always the last party before the new school year. Ginny's mother, Gloria, was there and so was Mr. Walsh, and everyone was allowed to drink *one glass of champagne each*, and the girls were going to sleep over. But then at three in the morning Katie had slipped away; she'd wanted to go see Danny and she thought she could go see him and sneak back in before dawn and no one would know the difference. She'd drunk three glasses of champagne and Ginny Walsh always left the key to her Honda under the seat and all the girls knew this and they would borrow it at lunch hour to drive to McDonald's and Ginny didn't care and Katie didn't think she'd care this night, and she let the Honda roll down the driveway before she turned on the engine and the lights, and she was doing all right, she was doing just fine, until she rolled through a stop sign on Old Indian Road and the colored lights lit up in her rearview and *Shit, oh shit,* she was so screwed. Arrest. DUI. Her parents. College—it all just flashed before her eyes.

Audrey knew before Katie said it: it was Moran. Although Katie didn't know him then. Had never seen him before, or if she had, had never noticed him.

He came up and put his flashlight on her and said, Can you turn that engine off for me, miss? and she did, and then she saw that his headlights were off too; just the colored cop-lights flying around in the night, in silence, lighting up the side of his face blue and red where he stood. Moran looking down at her, flicking his light around the inside of the car, over her knees, the short skirt she'd worn for the party. He said he knew this car and it wasn't hers. She said her friend said it was OK to borrow it.

She did, did she, said Moran.

Yes, sir.

And where were you taking it?

She hesitated. Nowhere special. I just felt like a drive.

Just felt like a drive, so you took off in your friend's car at three in the morning.

Yes, sir.

How much have you had to drink tonight, miss?

Just a little champagne, Officer. At my friend's birthday party. Her parents were there.

Were they.

Yes, sir. They bought the champagne.

He watched her. And how old are you?

Eighteen.

Can you prove it?

Sir?

Can I see your license.

Yes, sir.

She handed it to him.

He put his light on it and handed it back.

He took a breath and put his hands on his hips, the leather belt creaking. They were all alone out there on the county road. No lights anywhere but the colored lights flashing silently.

We got us a situation here, Miss Goss.

I know.

I don't think you do. I got you for failure to stop at a stop sign, driving under the influence, and possession of a stolen vehicle.

It's not stolen, I told you, I—

Miss. Please. I don't like this any more than you do. Young girl with her whole life ahead of her. College. But what am I supposed to do? What kind of officer would I be if I let you kids go driving all over the county like this, endangering the lives of others? What would your parents want me to do?

She'd begun to cry. She hated herself but she couldn't help it—what her father would say, the way he'd look at her—or not look at her—when he came to collect her from the jail . . .

Officer, please, I promise . . .

He sighed. He clicked off the flashlight. He looked up and down the road.

Well, look, honey. There's a solution here. Very simple. It will require just a few minutes of your time, but then you'll be free to go on your way. You think you're up for that?

She was looking up at him, trying to see his whole face under the brim of the hat but only half the face was there, the other half still glowing blue and red.

Either that, he said, or you get in this cruiser with me and we go back to the station and we take it from there, by the book. That how you want to do it?

No, sir.

All right then. We'll do it the easy way. Come on back to the cruiser with me. You said . . .

We're not going anywhere.

And she got out and he walked her to the passenger side of the cruiser and opened the door for her and shut it again once she was in. She watched him walk around the front of the cruiser and then she just stared at the back end of her car—Ginny's car—as he opened the driver's-side door of the cruiser and got in, rocking the car with his weight. He shut the door and the dome light went out. He took off his hat and put it on his knee. He looked up and down the road again but there was no one, no lights, and there never would be on this road at this hour, and if someone did drive by they'd see the cop-lights and keep going—they'd be drunk or part-drunk themselves and they wouldn't even look at those colored lights, they'd just drive on by—and she thought of her father and her mother and she thought of Danny Young and she thought of college and she thought of the whole town and she even thought of Holly Burke or some girl like her who would do such things, for whom such things were normal, and then she was doing it . . . his hand was in her hair and she was doing it and it wasn't real and it was, and it was the only way and no one would ever know and when it was over she'd go back to Ginny's house, back to her sleeping bag and no one would know and she would be the same person she'd been when the night began.

But she wasn't the same, and Danny knew she wasn't, and that was the end, really, that night. And two months later Holly Burke was found floating in the river.

46

THE WINE WAS gone. The water was gone. The music that had been playing earlier had stopped and they could hear the TV from the apartment below, a constant mumbling broken only by bursts of muffled laughter.

Audrey sat drawing her fingers under her eyes, one side and then the other. No tissues in sight. Her mind was racing ahead but she said nothing. She wiped her face dry and waited.

"When I got back to Ginny's house," Katie said, "she was the only one up. She was sitting there on the porchswing in the dark. She'd woken up and had seen from the bathroom window that her car was gone. Worried to death, she said, just about to wake up her parents..."

Katie told her she was sorry, she shouldn't have taken her car, and Ginny made her sit down. She took her hands—Hey, she said, hey... what happened?

Nothing.

Did you see Danny? What did he do?

Nothing. I never got there. I got pulled over.

Oh, shit. Shit. Did they make you blow?

What—?

The Breathalyzer machine.

No.

There was a long silence.

They didn't bust you or you wouldn't be here.

They didn't bust me.

What did they say?

Said go home.

What about the car?

What about it?

Did they ask you about it?

This cop, this guy. He said he knew it. He recognized it.

The two girls looking at each other, their faces close, their eyes locked in the dark.

Was it Moran?

Who?

Deputy Moran. The sheriff's deputy.

I don't know.

What'd he look like?

I don't know. He looked like a cop.

Did he have big eyes, like bugged-out eyes?

Maybe. A little. Yes.

Yeah, shit. That frog-eyed goon stopped me one time for speeding. Wanted me to step out of the car. I said, Step out, my ass, Officer, you haven't even asked for my license. I put it in his face and he took a good long look at it and handed it back. Yeah, I said, that Ginny Walsh. I believe you know my mother?

What'd he say?

Said, Get your ass home.

Did you tell her—your mom?

Tell her what? There was nothing to tell her. And nothing she could do about it anyway, except get herself fired.

You can't tell her about this, Ginny.

Katie, what happened? What did he do?

He let me go.

Katie . . .

Promise me.

Katie, the guy's a piece of shit.

He's a deputy sheriff piece of shit.

So?

Katie said nothing.

That's exactly what he's counting on you thinking, Katie.

So, what—just go in there and tell the sheriff?

Why not? Why would you make something like that up?

No. No way. I'm going to college in the fall. I'm going to college, Ginny. This is not going to be my story. This ass-backwards little town. Everybody knowing, everybody talking? My parents—oh God. Danny?

You didn't do anything wrong, Katie.

Katie hanging her head. Crying again. She'd stopped at a gas station and had bought a big Coke and washed out her mouth and chugged the rest until her throat burned, and still the taste was there.

Can we just go to bed now, Ginny? Can we just go to bed and never talk about this again, ever? Please, Ginny?

AUDREY HAD SEEN tissues on the bathroom counter. She got up and went down the hall and found them and brought them back and they both took the tissues and blew their noses and wiped their eyes and set the damp wads on the coffee table at the feet of the toy horses. Down the hall the little girl slept, dreaming a little girl's dreams.

"Katie," Audrey said. "He would have believed you. My father. He would have."

Katie looked at her red-eyed, and smiled. "Audrey, why are you here?"

"What do you mean?"

"How did you find me?"

"Gloria Walsh."

"Gloria Walsh," said Katie. "Ginny broke her promise. She told her mother, and her mother told your father."

Audrey's heart slipped. She shook her head.

"I'm sorry, Audrey, but she did."

"How do you know?"

"Because he came to see me."

"When?"

"I don't know, a few days later. I was home by myself. I saw that sheriff's car and just about pissed my pants."

"What did he say?"

"He wanted to know did I have anything I wanted to talk to him about, and I said no, not that I was aware of. And then he stood there for a long time just turning his hat in his hands."

Audrey waited. Her heart pounding.

"He said, 'Miss Goss, if you don't tell me I can't take any kind of action.' I said, 'What kind of action?' and he said, 'Legal action,' and that was the end of it. I said, 'I'm sorry, Sheriff, but I just don't know what you're talking about.' And then he got back into his car and drove off."

Audrey sat staring at the toy horses. They all seemed about to turn and run, to stampede.

Katie took a breath and sighed. "He knew, Audrey. I'm sorry, but he did."

"But," said Audrey. She swallowed, with difficulty, some rawness in her throat. "He didn't know enough. If you'd told him more, if you'd come forward, then maybe . . ." She couldn't say it. She could hardly bear to have it in her mind.

"Then maybe what? Maybe Holly Burke might be alive?" Katie looked at her with her red eyes. She shook her head. "No, ma'am. Nobody knows what happened that night, least of all you. A deputy sheriff runs over some girl in the park, throws her body in the river, then tries to pin it on some poor schmuck who just happens to be driving by? I never would've believed it even back then, when I knew what he was. And now, ten years later, Danny Young starts waving around a piece of cloth and telling this story and—what, I'm supposed to corroborate that or something? Just hop up suddenly and start yelling rape? Against a sheriff?"

"But there were others," Audrey said. "Gloria said there were other girls."

"Oh, really? Where are they? Why haven't they come forward? Why aren't they responsible? Why didn't they say something before it happened to me?"

"They're scared too."

"Scared?" She spat a piff of air from her lips. "You think I'm scared? I'm taking care of one hundred old people, including my mother who doesn't even know my name, and I'm raising my four-year-old daughter on my own. I left scared behind a long time ago."

Audrey was silent. Staring at the toy horses on the table. When she looked up again Katie was watching her, but her eyes had gone away somewhere, and in a quieter voice she said, "He came to see me again, your dad. After they found Holly Burke."

Audrey said nothing. Waiting.

"He wanted to know if I'd seen Danny," Katie said. "I hadn't. He wanted to know if Danny had called me. He hadn't. He wanted to look at my cell phone just to be sure, and I said, 'Don't you need a warrant for that?' and he said he hoped he wouldn't need one and I said he would."

Audrey thought about that: ten years ago . . . Even back then he wouldn't have needed the phone itself; he could've just subpoenaed the records, same as a landline.

She said as much to Katie and Katie nodded.

"Yes, I know that now. Back then I just, you know . . ." She began tapping with her forefinger at something in her opposite hand.

Audrey looked up from the empty hand and into her eyes. "You deleted the call history?"

"I did," Katie said, and said no more. As if this said everything. Then finally she added: "Danny never called me, but I called him. I called him that night and he was in the park. Chasing his dog, he said."

Audrey's heart was beating in her temple again. "Why did you delete the call history?"

Katie didn't answer. She sat staring blankly at Audrey.

"Because you believed him," Audrey said. "Or because you didn't."

"It didn't matter what I believed."

"It might have to him. It might have to my father."

Katie shook her head. "After everything that happened . . ." She took a breath and let it out. "I just couldn't do it, Audrey. I just couldn't be a part of it. Then they let him go, and he never tried to call me again, and I never called him. We never spoke again."

Audrey sat looking into Katie's eyes.

"What?" said Katie.

"I just," Audrey began, and stopped.

"You just what."

"I just wish you'd given my father a chance, that's all. About Moran."

Katie reached and tucked Audrey's fallen hair behind her ear, then returned her hand to her lap. "Sweetie, it wasn't about that. If I'd told him, it would've meant telling everyone. I was eighteen years old. I just wanted to live my life. I didn't want to be Holly Burke."

47

"Hey, buddy. Buddy . . ."

The shoulder twitched under the blanket and there was a low groan and Danny shook him once more, "Buddy, come on, wake up," and at last Marky rolled over and opened his eyes and lay blinking up at him in the dark.

"Danny . . . what are you doing?"

"I'm waking you up. It's like waking up a dead man."

"What time is it?"

"Keep your voice down. It's two o'clock."

"Danny tomorrow is Monday."

"It's already Monday."

"Danny . . ."

"Just—hey, Marky, come on. I gotta talk to you for a second." He'd been sitting there awhile in the chair and he could see his brother well by the light from the farmlight where it shone through the curtains. Marky dug his knuckles into his eyes and then got himself up on his elbows. He swallowed thickly and opened his mouth to yawn.

"Here, drink some water. Your breath could strip the paint off a car."

"Your breath could strip the paint off a car Danny."

Marky drank the water and smacked his lips and handed back the glass. He piled his two pillows against the headboard and drew himself up into a sitting position. He wore a dark T-shirt and his biceps were white as milk. Danny poked the near one with his finger. When they were teenagers they'd had barbells in the garage—Marky so weirdly, so effortlessly strong that Danny had begun working out in the gym at school to catch up.

"You been working out, buddy?"

"No Danny just working."

"They got you lifting cars down there, or what?"

"No we got the lifts for that."

"Oh, that's right."

Danny glanced around the room, at the dark shapes of the desk and the dresser, the gleam of the picture frames on the desk, pictures mostly from long ago when they were boys and their father was still alive. Missing was the picture of the two married couples, the Youngs and the Burkes, standing before a storefront with their arms all around each other and grinning, that picture lost somehow in the move from the old house to the farmhouse, or so he'd thought until, home for Christmas two years ago and digging in Marky's dresser for wool socks, he'd found it at the bottom of the drawer.

"You like working at the garage?" he asked Marky.

"Sure I do but not as much as the Plumbing Supply though."

"Why not?"

"Cause you're not there Danny."

"Yeah. Jeff's there, though."

"Jeff's there."

"Jeff's been a good friend, hasn't he."

"Jeff's been a good friend Danny we've been friends with Jeff since we were all little boys."

"I know it. How about Mr. Wabash. You like working for him?"

"Sure I like working for him. He could give you a job too Danny."

"Yeah, I doubt it."

"Why?"

"I don't think he likes me very much."

"He likes you Danny everybody likes you."

"No, they don't, buddy. You know that's why I went away. Why I always have to go away."

Marky looked down at his hands in his lap. "It's because of Holly Burke."

"It's because of Holly Burke."

"That was a long time ago Danny."

"I know it."

"And it wasn't your fault you didn't have nothing to do with Holly Burke going into the river."

"Do you believe that?"

"I know that Danny," Marky said, "we used to play with her when we were little she was our friend."

Danny sat looking into his brother's eyes in the light of the farmlight, Marky looking into his. And then Marky looked at Danny's clothes, his heavy winter shirt and his jeans and his socks, and he said, "You're leaving again aren't you Danny."

"I'm leaving again. I'm all packed up. I just wanted to say good-bye."

"What about Momma?"

"I don't want to wake her up—she'll just start crying and she'll be up all night worrying. You can tell her for me in the morning. All right?"

"All right but she's gonna cry anyway Danny she always cries."

"I know it."

"I wish I could go with you Danny."

"I do too. But you got your job, and you gotta take care of Ma."

"I know it," said Marky.

They were silent. Marky's eyes gleaming in the dark. Danny leaning forward, his forearms on his knees and gripping one hand in the other.

"What?" said Marky.

"What what?"

"You're gonna say something Danny."

Danny smiled. "Yeah, all right. I'm gonna say something. But it's just between you and me, OK?"

"OK."

"I don't want you telling anybody else I told you this."

"I won't tell anybody Danny."

"Especially Ma."

"OK Danny."

"Swear on a monkey's uncle?"

"Swear on a monkey's uncle."

"All right then. I'm going to call you tomorrow, Marky. Or later today, Monday. I'm gonna call you on your cell phone later today and I'll be far away by then."

"Where you going Danny?"

"I don't know but I'll call you when I get there."

"OK Danny."

"But if I don't call you . . . Are you listening?"

"I'm listening."

"But if I don't call you by tomorrow night—by tonight—it means something happened to me, Marky, and—"

"Danny don't say that."

"Keep your voice down, will you? Marky, I gotta say it so you know. I can't tell Ma because she'll just start freaking out. You're the only person I can tell. You're the only one. All right?"

"All right Danny."

"And if I don't call by tonight, if you don't hear from me, then I need you to do something for me."

"All right Danny."

He reached for the envelope on the desk. It was one of his mother's envelopes, light blue and birthday-card-shaped, but it was never a card when you saw it in your mailbox, whenever you'd stayed somewhere long enough to have a mailbox, it was a letter, two or three pages of her neat handwriting on matching stationery. On the envelope she'd write your name formally and with a kind of flourish, *Mr. Daniel P. Young*, and seeing it written that way on that blue envelope always made your heart stumble a little.

"What's this?" Marky said, taking the envelope.

"It's a letter, you knucklehead, and it ain't for you."

"You're the knucklehead who's it for?"

"You can read, can't you?"

"It's dark in here."

Danny picked up the cell phone from the desk and thumbed the button and held its light toward the envelope and Marky's face. Marky held the envelope close to his face and bunched his brow as he read it.

"Sheriff Wayne Halsey."

"Sheriff Wayne Halsey. You know him, right?"

"Sure I know him Danny we service the sheriff department's vehicles every spring they got three Chevy Tahoes and one Chevy TrailBlazer and—"

"All right, all right. That letter's for the sheriff and the sheriff only—and only if I don't call you by tonight. Are we clear?"

"We're clear Danny."

"You put it someplace top secret that only you know about, all right?"

"All right."

"And I don't mean your sock drawer."

Marky dipped his head to give him a look. "Give me a little credit Danny."

"Give you a little credit? Where'd you get that from—Jeff?"

"No I just said it." He sat studying the face of the envelope as if by doing so he could know all that was inside.

"Well, get up outta that bed a minute," Danny said.

"Why?"

"Because I'm not hugging a grown man good-bye while he's lying in his goddam bed, that's why."

"Don't cuss Danny."

"That's not cussing. Come on, now."

MOST OF HIS gear was already in the truck—he'd never taken it out—and so he only had to go down the stairs once with a duffel in each hand, the old steps creaking but if she woke up she did not get out of bed, and when the duffels were packed into the cab he shut the passenger door quietly and stood looking at the farmhouse, lit up by the farmlight, and the light casting shadows on the snow. The clothesline post stood at its tilt and its shadow lay like a second post on the snow, the two of them conjoined and bent where they met in a trick of the eye—like it was all one continuous piece that was not planted at all but stood upright from its own T-shaped base, like sculpture. Like a demonstration of some principle. He saw two boys swinging there, one on each side of the T, dropping to the ground when the post began to give under the turf, *Oh shit oh shit* . . .

We used to play with her when we were little she was our friend.

But Holly Burke had not been their friend, exactly. More like a cousin, forced into closeness with them not by marriage but by business, by that hyphen in the Burke-Young Plumbing & Supply sign. Nice enough when she was little, fun enough, but you had to be careful. *Moody*, your mother said. Like the time you were playing tag in the yard and Marky tagged her on her chest and she shoved him hard and called him a retard and you could've hit her, you could've just about gut-punched her like she was some dumb-ass boy on the playground. By middle school there was no goofing around with Holly Burke and no saying hello in the halls even, and if you ever told anyone you'd once wrestled with her on the living room floor she'd call you a liar and a pervert, and by high school you wouldn't even believe such a thing yourself—suddenly it was hard to believe she'd ever been a little girl at all.

You can say it, Danny. She was a good-looking young woman and you desired her. You wanted Holly Burke.

No, sir . . . No, sir.

He saw that night again—the dark road winding through the dark woods, the bending limbs, the boughs that dipped and swayed. What if you'd left the bar a few minutes earlier? What if you hadn't stopped to let the dog out? You'd been drinking. Hell, you were drunk. Taking those turns. The trees tossing and you are in your truck and you are nineteen and nothing can touch you, and you come around the bend and suddenly . . .

And what if you had? What if you'd come around the bend with the beers in your blood and not seen her in time? What if what they wanted to be true was true? What if your life now was exactly the one you deserved?

He walked around to the driver's side of the truck, the night so still and cold there was only the sound of his boots on the packed snow, the sound of his own breath, but then, under these sounds and far off, he heard a tinny jangling, a faint rattling that was the sound of a dog running somewhere and he turned back toward the yard, toward the fields beyond. But there was no dog, no dark shape moving fast over the white. There was only the snow and the farmlight and the dark, unmoving shadows on the snow.

48

HE WAS SITTING at the table eating his cornflakes when she came down and she already knew, it was in her face, her eyes. The way she moved.

"He couldn't wait till I came down?" she said, crossing to the sink to look out the window.

"He left last night Momma."

"What time last night?"

"Two a.m. Momma."

"How do you know?"

Marky stirred his cornflakes, chewing.

"Marky?"

"He woke me up to say good-bye that's all."

"That's all?"

Marky nodded. Spooned up more cornflakes.

"Did he say where he was going?"

"No Momma."

She stood watching him eat. The sound of the cornflakes so loud in his ears.

"So he woke you up to say good-bye but not me," she said, and he looked up at her tired, sad face.

"He didn't want to wake you up Momma. He told me to tell you good-bye for him."

"What was the big rush?"

"I don't know Momma he just said it was time for him to go again."

She lit the flame and put the kettle on the stove and then stood looking out the window.

"He'll come back Momma. He always comes back."

She wiped at her face and then she turned and crossed the kitchen and ran her hand down the back of his head and said, "I'll go get dressed and then we'll go."

"OK Momma." When he heard her on the stairs he got up and checked the kettle, ran tap water into it, and returned it to the flame.

HE SPENT THE morning in the back, stocking shelves and matching inventory to what was on the computer, and it was a long morning. At lunchtime he sat at the little table in the back office and after a while Jeff came back and took his bag out of the fridge and tossed his burrito into the microwave and punched the buttons, then stood looking at Marky as the machine hummed and blew the spicy meat smell into the room. Marky took a bite of his ham sandwich and washed it down with his bottle of Sprite.

"You're awful damn quiet today."

"Yeah I been working on the inventory Jeff."

"I see that. Very shipshape. Very shipshape." Jeff watching him. Marky sipping at his Sprite. "How about that bag of chips?" Jeff said.

"How about it?"

"You gonna eat it?"

"No."

"You're not gonna eat your chips?"

"No do you want them Jeff?"

"Hell, if you don't want 'em," he said, and he popped open the bag and began eating the chips. The crunching loud chip sound. The microwave humming and blowing. Mr. Wabash banging on something in the garage. Then, holding a chip partway to his mouth, Jeff said, "Shit, I know what this is. This is Danny, isn't it."

"Danny left last night Jeff."

Jeff stood watching him. "I'm sorry about that, Big Man."

"It's OK Jeff he'll come back he always comes back."

The microwave dinged and Jeff pulled the burrito out by the plastic wrapper and dropped it fast on a paper plate and sat down at the little table to eat.

"I gotta go to the drugstore now," Marky said, standing.

"The drugstore?"

"Yeah gotta get something for Momma," he said. His heart beating so hard as he said it. Jeff watching him as he bagged up his sandwich and put it back in the fridge.

"Hey," Jeff said, and Marky stopped. Jeff just staring at him. "You knew he'd have to leave again, right? You knew he couldn't stay."

"Yeah I knew it Jeff. Momma and me we always know it and even Wyatt did too before he died."

"Doesn't make it any easier, though, does it."

"No it doesn't Jeff."

He put on his jacket and he got out of the garage without Mr. Wabash seeing him and he walked six blocks through town, stopping only to look at the sheriff's station—one of the white Tahoes parked out front, the 2014 V-8 with the 5.3-liter engine—and then he walked the six blocks back to the garage and Jeff was just finishing his lunch and Mr. Wabash was standing in the lot talking to a woman beside her red car. Danny had not called.

49

THE GIRL CAME in the afternoon, just after Rachel herself got home from errands and before she'd even gotten out of her coat. There were footsteps on the porch and then the doorbell rang and the dog didn't bark and she remembered, once again, that he was gone.

Danny gone now too. The house so empty and quiet.

The girl stood on the porch in big sunglasses and a big canvas jacket, and even with the sunglasses Rachel knew who she was, and her heart gave a strange hop in her chest. She opened the stormdoor and the girl said, "Hello—Mrs. Young?"

"Yes."

"I'm Audrey Sutter. I'm sorry to just show up like this, I tried to call."

"Yes, I know who you are." The girl removed the sunglasses and Rachel saw the purple cast, and she knew it must've happened in the accident, when she and the other girl had gone into the river. "I'm sorry—" Rachel said, and didn't know how to go on. She should give the girl her sympathies, she knew, for her father, and for the other girl too—but instead she said, as kindly as she could, "Is there something I can do for you?"

"I was actually hoping I might speak to your son?" said the girl, and Rachel's heart stumbled, it fell back in time. It was those words—*speak to your son*—as the girl's father had once spoken them, standing just so on her stoop, at the old house, but it was the eyes too: those same blue eyes looking at her again out of that past, those terrible days. And she looked into these eyes now, trying to find the connection between her son and this girl, the sheriff's daughter, but it was impossible. What had she missed?

"My son . . .?"

"Danny," the girl said. "I couldn't find his number anywhere, so finally I just—"

"I'm sorry," Rachel said, "but what is this about?" and the girl was silent. Unprepared for the question. Did she even know what her father had done to Danny? To Rachel herself, to her family? The girl would've been what—nine, ten years old. But you could not grow up in this town and not know. Especially if you were the sheriff's daughter.

"If I—" the girl began. "I mean if I could talk to him for just a minute, Mrs. Young, then I think he could explain it better." And Rachel, her heart beating, said, "You can't speak to him. He's gone."

"Gone, as in left town?" said the girl, and she looked down the road, as if she might catch sight of his departing truck. In the driveway, behind Rachel's car, was the white sedan she'd seen Tom Sutter driving after he retired as sheriff. After the cancer had gotten too far along.

The girl stood there, in that big canvas jacket that must have been her father's, having no idea what to do next. What to say.

When she turned back to Rachel, looking at her again with those eyes, Rachel held the stormdoor wider, and the girl stepped into the house.

IT TOOK TEN minutes, or maybe thirty, for the girl to tell her everything: what she'd heard Danny tell Gordon Burke about that night ten years ago—what she was even doing at Gordon Burke's in the first place! What Danny said about the deputy pulling him over, that piece of cloth . . . Gordon talking to the deputy, or sheriff now, down in Iowa; what Sheriff Halsey up here had not told the girl and what his secretary had; and finally what Katie Goss had told her three nights ago, Friday night, the girl not saying this last outright, careful not to betray a confidence, but her body and her hands and her eyes saying it anyway—sweet, pretty Katie Goss who smelled like strawberries and was her son's first love, and maybe his only love . . . and Rachel all the while holding the mug like it was her own heart, hot and pounding in her hands.

She knew the girl was finished when she picked up her own mug and sipped from it and set it down again quietly on the tabletop. Then the girl began turning a large metal bracelet on her other wrist, her good wrist—or not a bracelet but a man's wristwatch, and that soft clicking was the only sound. Rachel's own hands, clutching the china mug, looked sinister. Like hands wrapped around a white little neck. If the girl had come Saturday, or Sunday—or had called—Danny might still be here.

"I'm sorry," said the girl. "I shouldn't be the one telling you all this. You don't even know me."

Finally Rachel let go the mug, and her breath came back to her, and after a moment her voice did too—or something like it.

"And where is this cloth now—this pocket?"

"I think Danny must have it with him," the girl said. "Or else he left it here." Here, in this house, all this time. And the old house before that. Ten years! Or did he keep it with him, wherever he went, so she would never find it?

She looked at the phone then and saw the blinking red light on the machine, and she got to her feet and crossed to it and played the message, but it was the girl herself, asking if she might speak to Danny, leaving her number. So she did call—but not until this morning.

". . . really so sorry," this same voice was saying, behind her. "I shouldn't be the one telling you any of this, like this—except that I think I can help him. If I could talk to him, I think I could help him."

"Why did you wait?" Rachel said, as if to herself.

"I'm sorry?"

"All weekend . . ." She pushed two buttons on the phone and raised it to her ear again. After four rings she knew it would be his voicemail but her heart kicked anyway at the sound of his voice, as it always did. *This is Danny . . .*

"I'm sorry," said the girl. "I guess I was trying to figure out what to do. If it was even any of my business."

"He's not picking up," Rachel said, and the girl said, "He's driving. He might not even have his phone on."

"Yes," said Rachel. Holding the phone in her hands, holding it to her chest. She'd been here before, in this moment. It was too familiar.

Then she remembered: the night she'd heard the water running, and Danny had been washing the dog, and he'd driven up to the cabin, and she'd called and called but he hadn't answered.

In custody.

The girl said, "He didn't say anything before he left, about where he was going?"

"No," Rachel said, "not to me."

And some few minutes after that she was alone again—the girl having made her good-byes, her apologies once more, and driving off again in the white sedan, and Rachel going immediately upstairs to his room, to stand in the doorway looking in. As she'd stood that night ten years ago, watching him stuff clothes into his duffel. How frightened he looked, in her memory, how terrified. Why hadn't he talked to her? Why hadn't he told her? She could have helped him!

Everything in the room was in order: the sheets and pillowcases pulled off and placed in a neat pile on the mattress for her to wash and no other sign in the room that anyone had been there. The sheriff and his deputies had gone through his room once before, at the old house, and she didn't think he would leave it here, not in this room, and after a moment she stepped across the hall and went into Marky's room, and five minutes after that she was downstairs again, at the stove again, watching as the kettle came slowly, so slowly, to boil. He'd done his best to hide it but her eye had gone directly to the light-blue envelope, one of hers, among the other letters and valentines in the shoebox in his closet. This envelope never opened. This envelope addressed to Sheriff Wayne Halsey.

The kettle began to whistle and she played the seal of the envelope over the steam, helping it along with a butter knife until the flap popped free, then she took the envelope to the table and sat down with it before her.

Inside were several sheets of her stationery, and when she opened these up the square of cloth slipped out and fell without a sound to the table and her heart stopped beating. Just stopped. A square of white silk so sheer she could see the grain of the tabletop beneath it. Her fingertips trembled on her lips and she didn't have to touch the cloth to know; she'd touched it before, in the store, when the blouse lay draped over her arm, and again when she'd folded it into its box . . . you'd have to wear something under it, a camisole, and did the girl have anything like that?—you couldn't ask her father and you couldn't ask the girl herself . . . Well, let her figure that part out for herself, the blouse was not cheap even with her store discount, and she might not even like it, or she might not like it out of spite, but a birthday was a birthday and the girl could always take it back for something she wanted and you just couldn't worry about that, but wasn't it lovely, wasn't it nice to buy something fine for a young woman when all your life you'd bought clothes for boys . . .

And Holly had worn the blouse that night, the night of the river, and one way or another, by accident or by some other encounter gone wrong—by some kind of violence—the pocket had been torn from the blouse and had not gone into the river with her but had been kept, had been hidden, and had been brought out of hiding all these years later to fall without a sound to her kitchen table.

She wiped her eyes, then wiped her hands on her lap and when her fingertips were dry she picked up the three pages of stationery and read the letter her son had written to the sheriff.

50

AFTER LUNCH JEFF got a Chevy Impala up in the air and began tearing out the exhaust front to back while Marky stood by to hand him the tools he asked for, and Danny didn't call and you gotta stay busy is all, you just gotta keep working and not even thinking about it, not watching the clock and not even thinking about it and then he'll call, he'll call to say he's far away now and everything is OK . . . and at 2:15 Tony the parts man came with the new exhaust parts and Marky was entering those into the computer when his phone vibrated in his pocket, and he fumbled for it and got it out and read the screen and it was his mother, and his heart dropped back into place.

"Marky, can you talk a minute?"

"I'm at work Momma."

"I know, but Marky I need to ask you—did Danny say anything else last night, when he woke you up?"

Marky stood with the phone to his ear, his heart kicking.

"Marky—?"

"He didn't say anything else Momma he just said to say good-bye."

"Marky . . . are you telling me the truth?"

"Yes Momma."

He held the phone to his ear, listening. Finally she said, "I've been trying to call him and he won't pick up," and Marky put his other hand flat on the counter, because everything had just gone a little bit crooked, like after you've been spun around and around.

"You always say turn off your phone when you're driving Momma," he said.

"I know it. Has he called you?"

"No Momma."

Jeff began banging on something under the Impala, banging away until whatever it was fell clattering to the concrete, and she didn't speak again until the noise had ended.

"If he calls you," she said, "will you tell him to call me, please?"

"Yes Momma."

"I'm serious, Marky. I need to talk to him."

"I know Momma I'll tell him."

2:15 AND HE didn't call.

2:45 and he didn't.

At 3:05 Mr. Wabash drove off in the wrecker and at 3:35 a white four-door pulled into the lot, and Marky watched through the windows in the bay doors as a girl got out of the car and walked toward the office, and he said, "Jeff."

"What."

"Customer in the office."

"So go talk to him."

"It's a her Jeff."

"So go talk to her, man, I'm kinda up to my elbows here."

"OK Jeff."

She was standing at the counter and when she saw him she smiled and he knew who she was—he'd seen her picture on the news, hers and her friend's, after they went into the river. She was the old sheriff's daughter and her name was Audrey and his heart began to pound again, and the girl looked at his chest, at his pounding heart and said, "Are you Marky Young?"

It was the name patch she looked at, that was all.

"Yes ma'am that's me."

"My name is Audrey Sutter," she said and put out her hand for shaking, but there was a purple cast on it and he held up his own hand to show her the oil stains and she said, "I don't care about that," and she held the cast out and finally he took it and gave it a shake, and it felt funny in his hand.

"Yes ma'am I saw you on the news you and your friend Caroline," he said, and he watched her face to see had he said it all right or would she make the face of not understanding and start looking around for someone else who could speak to her like a normal person. But she did not make the face.

"Yes," she said. "That was me."

"I was sorry about her," he said, "I was sorry about Caroline."

"Thank you, Marky." She stood looking at him, her eyes so blue and so light, and finally he looked away, toward the parking lot beyond her, toward the white four-door in the sunlight.

"Two thousand five Ford Taurus," he said, and she turned to look, and turned back again.

"Good call," she said.

"What's wrong with it?"

"Nothing. Well, probably all kinds of things. But that's not why I'm here."

"You're here about Danny," he said, and she nodded.

"Your mother called you?" she said.

"Yes ma'am she called me a while ago."

"And told you I talked to her?"

"No ma'am she didn't say anything about you."

The girl looked at him. Her eyes moving around his face like something was flying in front of it. Then she said, "Marky, I was hoping . . ." and stopped, and he waited while she got the words together in her head. "I guess I was hoping you might tell me where your brother went. If you knew where he was heading. I need to talk to him about something and I don't have his number and your mother . . ."

He waited again.

"I don't think your mother wants me to talk to him, not before she does anyway, and that's fine, I understand that. But really, Marky, I just need to let him know that I need to talk to him, and then if he wants to talk to me, if he wants to hear what I have to say, then we can just go from there. I know how vague that all sounds but . . . Am I making any sense?"

"Yes ma'am but I don't know where Danny is he didn't say he just went."

"So you talked to him—before he left?"

"He woke me up but it was just to say good-bye that's all," Marky said, and the girl stood watching him, and he saw suddenly how young she was—young like Katie Goss had been back then. Young like Holly Burke had been before she went into the river. Young like Danny and Jeff and himself and even Wyatt had been, before Holly Burke went into the river and nobody was the same anymore.

"And you don't know where he was going?" the girl, Audrey, said, and Marky shook his head, and she stood watching him again. In that silence he heard the wrecker first, then looked beyond her again to see Mr. Wabash pulling into the lot towing a green Toyota Camry with a smashed front end. The girl looked too, then turned back to Marky.

"OK, well . . ." she said. And Marky said, "But he's going to call me today and tell me and then I can tell him something if you want me to."

"He's going to call you today?"

"Yes just to say he's OK."

"That he's OK?"

"Yes."

There was the beeping of the wrecker backing up, and the girl turned again, and when she turned back she said, "Marky, you remember Sheriff Sutter, who was the sheriff ten years ago?"

"I remember Sheriff Sutter he went and got Danny at the cabin and then he let him go. I saw him on the news too."

"You did?"

"Yes," Marky said. "My poppa died when we were just little boys Danny and me." She looked at him with her blue eyes. "I'm so sorry, Marky."

"He smoked too many cigarettes."

"Yes. Mine did too."

The beeping stopped and Mr. Wabash stepped out of the wrecker in his black jacket and began working the levers, lowering the Camry.

The girl was watching Marky. "Marky," she said.

"Yes?"

"My dad let Danny go because he knew he didn't have anything to do with what happened to Holly Burke."

"Danny didn't have nothing to do with that."

"I know. That's why I need to talk to him. I think I can help him." She waited, like he was supposed to say something, but he didn't know what to say. Finally she picked up a pen from the counter and began to write on one of the Wabash

Auto notepads. "I'm writing my name and phone number," she said. "Your mom already has it, on the machine, but I'm giving it to you too."

Mr. Wabash was walking toward the office.

"All I'm asking is that you give it to Danny when he calls and tell him what I told you, about helping him. You don't have any reason to trust me or believe me, but I hope you'll just give Danny my name and number. Is that OK?"

"That's OK," Marky said, "I'll give it to him when he calls," and he stripped the paper from the pad and folded it once and tucked it into the breast pocket of his shirt just as the glass door swung open and Mr. Wabash walked in.

"Thank you, Marky," the girl said.

"You're welcome."

Mr. Wabash stepped behind the counter. He gave Marky a look and turned to the girl. "Is there something I can help you with, miss?"

"No, thank you. I'm all set."

"Something wrong with your car, there?"

"No, sir. I just came in to talk to Marky."

"Talk to Marky."

"Yes, sir."

"What for?"

"Sorry?"

"What did you need to talk to my employee for?"

"I'm sorry—I think that's between him and me."

Mr. Wabash looked at her. He ran his finger over his mustache like a comb. "Then maybe you shouldn't be talking to him on my time, hey?"

"Sir?"

"I pay my guys to work on cars, not stand around answering your questions. Like this boy could tell you anything anyhow."

She looked at Marky and he saw that she felt bad that she'd come in, saw that she wanted to tell him how sorry she was to get him into trouble, and he wanted to tell her it was OK, but he couldn't say anything as long as Mr. Wabash was standing there.

"I know who you are," Mr. Wabash said. "And I got a pretty good idea this has to do with this boy's brother. Am I right about that?"

"I'll just go now," the girl said, still looking at Marky, giving him a smile, and Marky raised his hand slightly but that was all, and the girl turned and went back out the door, and he and Mr. Wabash watched her get back into the Ford, and they watched as she pulled out of the lot and drove away, and then Mr. Wabash turned to look at Marky.

"Well?" he said. "What the heck did she want with you? Was it about your brother?"

He didn't want to lie but he didn't want to tell Mr. Wabash something that wasn't any of his business either.

"I better go help Jeff Mister Wabash."

Mr. Wabash frowned. He shook his head. "Yeah, you go do that, Marky."

And Marky did that, and now it was 3:45 and Danny hadn't called.

51

She was reaching for the doorbell button when the inside door swept open and he appeared in the window of the stormdoor, his face clear for just a moment before the glass began to fog. Rachel raised her hand to him and he opened the stormdoor and she knew before she got a good look at him that he'd not bathed or put on fresh clothes that day, though it was nearly sundown.

"Gordon," she said, "I'm sorry to bother you."

"No, bother," he said, and stood looking at her, his face pale and bristly. A redness in his eyes. Her heart was beating. It was too much like it had been ten years ago, when he did not even seem to recognize her.

"Do you think I might come inside, for just a minute . . . ?"

"Oh," he said. "Sure," and he opened up the door, and she wiped her boot-soles carefully on the welcome mat and stepped in.

No lights on in the kitchen but light enough from the window to see it all as it had been: the yellow-and-blue-tiled counter, the same coffee maker, the deep sink where she and Meredith had stood rinsing dishes and looking out at the summer dusk; the round oak table where they'd sat drinking coffee or sometimes wine while the men watched football and the kids thumped about upstairs in Holly's room.

"Sit," he said, and as she moved to the table something crunched under her boots, bits of cornflake maybe, or cookie crumbs. The broom stood leaning against the counter, as if he'd begun to sweep but had become distracted, perhaps by her arrival. The garbage had gone sour, and there was the smell of woodsmoke too. From where she sat she saw the coals pulsing in the darkness of the living room, the curtains drawn, the face of the TV black and empty.

He went to the counter and began to set dirty plates into the sink. He poured out the old coffee and she said, "Please, don't bother. Could you just . . . ?" and she looked at the broom again, and then she looked at the space beside the refrigerator where it had always been kept and there was something else there, set back into the recess but not far enough that it could not be easily reached. It was a hunting rifle. She never knew he owned one.

She looked away and found him watching her, the empty coffeepot in his hand.

"Can you just sit down with me for a minute?" she said. "Please?"

IT WAS DARKER in the kitchen when she'd finished. The coals in the living room had gone black and there was no sound in the house other than the sounds she and Gordon made themselves, clearing their throats, shifting in their chairs. The three sheets of stationery lay faceup on the table and beside them lay the white square of cloth. Gordon's hands rested on the edge of the table, one hand folded over the knuckles of the other.

"Well," he said at last. "It wasn't me who shot at him. If that's what you're wondering."

"No," she said. "That never even occurred to me, Gordon."

The refrigerator was in the corner of her eye but she would not look at it; would not look away from his face.

"Where has he gone?" he said.

"I don't know. As far from here as he can get, I suppose. He's not answering his phone."

Gordon nodded. "Don't worry, Rachel," he said, but it sounded to her like something one was expected to say at such times. He was staring at the piece of cloth.

"Do you recognize it?" she said.

"I saw it when he showed it to me. Last week, I guess that was."

"I mean before that. From back then."

Gordon frowned. "The better question is, do you?" he said. "It was you who bought the blouse."

She stared at the cloth. "When I first saw it I was so sure. Now that I see it again . . . I mean, it's a silk pocket." She shook her head. "I couldn't swear to it, Gordon."

"You wouldn't have to. That blouse is still in a bag somewheres in the sheriff's evidence room. Wouldn't take much to match it up."

"There could be DNA on it," she said hopefully.

"Yes," he said. "Could be. Could be Danny's. Could be yours. Could be mine."

"Could be that deputy's."

He stared at the silk cloth. As if to see the DNA himself.

"There's something else," she said. "Something not in the letter. Something Danny didn't even know about."

Gordon was silent, watching her with eyes that had seen too much, knew too much, and that now waited to know a little more, and she stopped herself. Did she have to say it? Did he have to know this too?

"Do you remember a girl named Katie Goss?" she said.

"I remember that name."

"She was his girlfriend at the time. Danny's girlfriend."

Gordon said nothing, and Rachel went ahead in a rush—telling him about Audrey going up to Rochester, telling him what Audrey had not told her, Rachel, not in so many words but which anyone—any woman—would know just by looking at the girl. That Moran had raped Katie Goss.

Gordon looked down at his hands.

She watched him, her heart pounding.

"Gordon . . ."

He looked at his hands—at one fist wrapped in the other, a great tight ball of knuckles.

"Gordon," she said again, but he would not look up. "Gordon, we have to try, don't we?"

He said nothing. Staring at those fists.

"I'll tell you what I think," he said at last, without looking up. "But you won't like it."

"Tell me."

He unclenched his hands and flattened them on the table, one to either side of the piece of cloth. He looked up.

"I think just about anybody who isn't his mother is gonna think there's only one way in hell that boy comes up with this pocket ten years later."

She watched him. "Is that what you think, Gordon?"

He didn't answer. Looking into her eyes. Then he looked away, toward the window, as if he'd heard something, and she looked too, and listened, and for just a moment she heard them: The kids, chasing each other in the snow. Laughing, shouting. Any second now a snowball would thud against the house, trying to get them to come to the window, come to the porch, watch us, notice us!

"Doesn't matter what I think," Gordon said, and she turned back to him.

"Of course it does."

"Not to the law it doesn't."

A panic began to rise in her. She had the urge to swipe up the cloth and hold it in her fist.

"Gordon—" She had to swallow. "Gordon . . . you sound like you don't even want to try."

He shook his head. "It isn't that. I don't want anything more in this world than to know the truth. It's just . . . God damn it, Rachel."

"What?"

"What if the truth isn't what you want it to be?"

She looked at him. Was it possible this was the same man who'd held her as she sobbed against his chest? Who'd built the fire and thawed the ground and dug up the earth so she could bury the dog?

Then she saw her own hand moving slowly toward the square of cloth. Palming it up, replacing it in the folded stationery, fitting the stationery back into the envelope, and the envelope back into her purse.

"I'm going to the sheriff with or without you," she said, her voice trembling.

Gordon nodded. "I know it," he said. "I know it, Rachel. And I'd do the same, I were you."

52

HE DIDN'T CALL. 4:50 and he didn't call.

5:00 and he didn't.

Mr. Wabash was in the front office closing out the register, putting the cash and the checks into a zipper bag for the bank. Jeff had pulled the Impala out and was backing it into a tight spot. Marky stood watching through the glass.

"You OK there, Marky?"

"I'm OK Mister Wabash."

Mr. Wabash looking at him, and Marky looking out the glass, watching for his mother's car to pull in. Finally Mr. Wabash zipped the bag shut and said, "OK then," and turned and went back into the garage.

Marky zipped up his jacket and stepped outside and stood in the cold wind. It was not dark yet because it was almost March and the days were getting longer, but everything still looked like winter. Smelled like winter. Jeff came back from parking the Impala, hurrying to get back inside, but then stopped next to Marky and stuffed his hands in his pockets and stood as if he would wait too.

"She's running late, huh."

"She's running late Jeff."

They watched. Jeff shivered and said, "Well," and at that moment the wagon turned into the lot, and Jeff said, "I'll see ya, Big Man," and Marky said, "OK seeya Jeff," and he got into the car, so warm and smelling like his mother—"Hi Momma"—and he shut the door and pulled the seatbelt across him, but then they just sat there.

"Momma?"

She seemed to be watching Jeff as he stepped back into the office.

"Yes?"

"Are we going?"

She turned to him, but it was another second or two before she really saw him, and he knew she hadn't talked to him—to Danny—just as she knew he hadn't talked to him either, because he would've told her already, he would've called her right away like he promised, but of course she had to ask anyway, and he had to tell her, "No Momma he didn't call," and she looked at him then for a long time, just looking at him, before she faced forward again and took her foot off the brake. And it was the longest drive home. Or not the longest because that was the drive home from the hospital after Poppa died, just the three of you now . . . and there was that drive out to the farmhouse after Danny had gone away the first time and you had to move and it was just you and Momma and Wyatt in the car, and this was like that again only without Wyatt, and the two of you just staying in your own heads and not saying anything, and it's worse than if she just said *Marky I know you're not telling me something, I know Danny told you something*, because that's what she's thinking but won't say it because she doesn't want you lying to her again . . . and you not saying what you know is just as bad as lying, but if you tell her, if you tell her everything then you break your promise to Danny and that's even worse, isn't it? And they were almost home before he looked at her again—he would say something, he didn't know what, just say her name—"Momma . . ."

But she wouldn't turn to look at him—she was looking straight ahead and she was looking at something more than just the road, and when he looked he saw it too: a white SUV parked in the driveway near the farmhouse, and he knew the SUV because it was the sheriff's 2014 Chevy Tahoe.

"Oh God," she said.

"It's OK Momma."

She turned into the drive and pulled up behind the SUV and put the car in park and cut the engine. They could see the sheriff looking at them in his rearview. Then the sheriff stepped out, putting his hat on, and walked toward them, and Rachel opened her own door and got to her feet and stood holding on to the door.

"Evening, folks," the sheriff said, nodding to her and then to Marky, who stood behind her now, somehow, a presence felt more than seen, his breaths blowing by in white clouds. "Mrs. Young?" the sheriff said, and she tried to say yes but all of her attention was on his hand, watching to see if he would raise it to his hatbrim and remove the hat from his head. He didn't do it. But neither did he give her any indication that he'd not driven out here to rip her heart from her chest.

He said, "Hey, Marky," and Marky said, "Hey Sheriff Halsey," and the sheriff began to say how sorry he was to just show up like this but he'd tried to call and—

"Sheriff," she said. "What's happened?"

"Well, ma'am, that's a good question. All I know is I've got an abandoned vehicle about a half-mile mile shy of the Mississippi with plates that are registered to Daniel Paul Young of Amarillo Texas, whom I believe is your son. Your other son."

"What kind of vehicle Sheriff Halsey?" said Marky.

The sheriff looked at him, and Rachel said, "He asked what kind of vehicle."

"A dark-blue Ford F-150, two thousand and one."

"XLT?" said Marky.

"Yes, sir."

"Four-by-four?" said Marky.

"Yes, sir, I believe that's right."

"That's Danny's truck Momma."

She was holding on to the door, but the door too began to sway and she stepped back until she felt her son's chest against her and she found his hand and gripped it and he gripped back.

"What else, Sheriff?" she said.

"Well, I was hoping you might tell me. The keys were in the truck and it started right up, hadn't run out of gas or anything like that. No flat tires." The sheriff glanced down, then looked up again. "Mrs. Young, when did your son get back in town?"

She had to think a moment. "A week ago?" she said, looking at Marky.

"Eight days ago Sheriff it was Sunday night he was here when we came home."

Rachel repeated this, and the sheriff nodded. "And did either of you notice anything about the condition of his truck then?"

"The condition of his truck?"

"Any, ah, holes in it, that you saw?"

"Holes, Sheriff?" Her heart was crashing. "More than one—?"

He looked at her. "You know about that, ma'am?"

"I know somebody took a shot at him in the park."

"Momma—"

"What park was that, ma'am?"

"Henry Sibley."

The sheriff stared at her. His lawman's mind working. "Did he have any idea who shot at him?"

She shook her head. Then she said, "No." Seeing that rifle in Gordon's kitchen, beside the refrigerator.

But he wouldn't do that . . . He wouldn't.

The sheriff was silent. Marky silent too, breathing heavily behind her. Then the sheriff said, "Well, there's just the one hole, and not anywhere near the cab, and there's no other signs of foul play, nothing to indicate any harm has come to him personally. His things are packed up in the cab shipshape and—"

Blood, he meant. He meant there was no blood.

"—it looks for all the world like he just pulled over and either got in some other vehicle or else went afoot across the bridge into Wisconsin. Ordinarily I wouldn't get too worked up about an abandoned vehicle, but your son is no ordinary case, not around here, anyway. And there's that bullet hole. So I came out here hoping he'd called and told you where he's at. But clearly he hasn't."

"I've been calling him all day," she said, "but he hasn't answered."

"Momma I have to show Sheriff Halsey the letter now."

The sheriff looked at him. "Letter—?"

"Danny wrote a letter Sheriff Halsey and told me to give it to you if he didn't call first to say he was OK it's upstairs in my room. I'm sorry Momma he made me promise not to tell you—" And he'd begun to go but Rachel held him in place by the hand.

"It's not in your room, Marky, it's in my purse." Then to the sheriff she said, "Sheriff, do you want to come inside out of the cold?"

53

THE LIGHT WAS blinking again and she hurried to it, and once again it wasn't him, it wasn't Danny; it was the sheriff who'd come in behind her.

She erased the message and slipped the handset into her coat pocket. She put the kettle on the burner and got down the mugs, then she walked out of the kitchen and went upstairs to the bathroom. Took off her coat to sit down, and put it back on again after, checking her face in the mirror, white as a ghost, frightened old woman, slapping her cheeks a little and then coming back down the stairs and by the time she walked back into the kitchen the sheriff had given the last page of the letter to Marky, and Marky was reading it slowly as the sheriff sat staring at the white square of cloth where it lay before him on the table. He'd taken off his hat when he walked in but he still wore his jacket, and Marky wore his too.

"I forgot to light the burner," she said, and the sheriff said, "Don't bother with that," and his voice startled her—loud in the kitchen in a way she hadn't noticed outdoors. As if he'd decided she might be hard of hearing.

She sat down across from him. She took the handset from her coat pocket and set it on the table next to Marky's cell phone. One of the two would ring any second now. One of them would.

They waited for Marky to finish reading the letter. His lips moved when he read and the small noises his lips made were the only sounds. Finally he put the last sheet of stationery down and sat looking at the square of cloth. She could see him shuffling the parts of the story around and around in his head, how he wanted to fit them all together before he'd say anything.

The sheriff ran his hand through his hair slowly, front to back, and returned his hand to the table. He looked at the sheets of stationery and after a while he tapped them with his fingertips and said to her, "You didn't show this to anyone else besides Gordon Burke?"

"No, sir."

"And he handled this piece of cloth?"

"He touched it. Just a little."

"And you've handled it?"

"Yes."

"And so has Danny," said the sheriff.

"And so has the person who put that girl in the river," she said weakly.

"Yes, if that is, in fact, the pocket from her blouse." He shook his head. He blew the air from his lungs as a smoker would. "I had a bad feeling about all this the second that girl stepped into my office."

"What girl?"

"Audrey Sutter. Tom Sutter's daughter. The girl who—"

"I know who she is. She came to talk to me too."

"Me too," said Marky, and they both looked at him.

"What did she say, Marky?"

"She wanted to know did I know where Danny was Momma. She said she wanted to help him."

"That's all?" Rachel said.

"She asked me to give Danny her number when he called."

"She didn't say anything about Katie Goss?"

"No Momma I don't think she knows Katie Goss."

"Katie Goss?" said the sheriff. "What's she got to do with this?"

"That girl," Rachel said, "Audrey Sutter, she went up to Rochester to talk to her."

"And why did she do that?"

"Because someone told her to."

The sheriff looked at her. "Someone told her to."

"Yes."

"And what did Katie Goss have to say?"

Rachel glanced at Marky and turned back to the sheriff. "Something I think you already know about," she said.

He looked at her darkly and for a long time. Then he said, "Tell you what I know about Katie Goss. I know some friend of hers told a story got back to

Sheriff Sutter, back then ten years ago, but when he went out to talk to her, to Miss Goss, she had no idea what he was talking about. I know her story doesn't even qualify as a story, legally speaking, unless she's all of a sudden changed her mind about telling it. Is that what you're telling me?"

"No," said Rachel. "But she might change her mind, if the Holly Burke case were reopened."

"And why would the Holly Burke case be reopened?"

"Because of this!" she all but cried, picking up the sheets of stationery. "Because of that pocket."

"That," said the sheriff, nodding at the letter, "is one humdinger of a story, but that's all it is, at the moment. And as for the pocket, even if it does match the blouse, it's ten years old and has been handled by half the county by now. I don't mean to be harsh about it, Mrs. Young, but those are the facts of the situation here. So far it's your son's story against the sheriff's, with no other witnesses and only this piece of cloth, which your son has kept hidden all this time—an unfortunate move on his part, I'm sorry to say, as even the world's sorriest prosecutor would point out that that is a practice consistent not with innocent men but with guilty ones."

"Danny didn't have nothing to do with Holly Burke going into the river Sheriff Halsey," Marky said, and the sheriff nodded, as though he'd understood.

"You're right, Marky. In the eyes of the law, right now, that is absolutely true: Danny is altogether innocent of Holly Burke's death. But it's also true that he was never formally charged and never stood trial."

Though he looked at Marky as he spoke, watching carefully to see that he was understood, Rachel knew he was speaking to her. He said, "Now along comes this new piece of evidence here, and this new testimony—and possibly even the testimony of some third party like Miss Goss—and suddenly you are placing that boy into the hands of a system that may just find him guilty whether he had anything to do with her death or not. Do you understand? He's free now. He might not be afterwards."

"He's free?" said Rachel. "Sheriff, he hasn't been free a day in his life since you all took him into custody ten years ago. And you knew. You all knew about that—*deputy*, back then, and you protected him."

"Momma . . ."

"Mrs. Young." The sheriff looked at his hands on the table, then looked up again. "I can't even imagine what you've gone through. Or what you're going through right now. But I would ask you to ask yourself one thing."

She waited. She was trying not to tremble.

"Why didn't Danny tell his story ten years ago?" the sheriff said.

"He was just a boy, Sheriff. He was confused. He was terrified."

The sheriff scratched his jaw and cocked his head. "He was nineteen, Mrs. Young. And I wouldn't say he was terrified."

She stared at him. "What does that mean?"

"It means I watched his interview, with Sheriff Sutter, and I wouldn't say he was terrified. I'd say he handled himself pretty well, actually."

She just stared at him. No idea what to say to that—was that supposed to be a compliment?

When he said nothing more she tapped her finger on the table and said, "Maybe that's not the right question, Sheriff."

"Ma'am?"

"Maybe the question isn't why didn't he say anything back then. Maybe the question is why would he say anything now? I mean, why would he do that?"

"Yes, ma'am. That is an awfully good question." He cupped his hands together on the table and sat staring at them. As though he'd captured a small bird and was deciding what to do with it. Rachel and Marky watching him. Finally he uncupped his hands, popped the snap on the breast pocket of his shirt and brought out his notebook and pen.

"All right," he said, clicking the pen. "Let's start with what he was wearing."

She stared at him. "What he was wearing?"

"Yes, ma'am. Last time you saw your son, what was he wearing?"

"Sheriff—" she said. Her mind was tumbling. "Sheriff—what about that deputy? Are you not even going to question him?"

"Sheriff, ma'am," he said.

She looked at him. "What—?"

"That deputy is a sheriff now, ma'am, in another county, in another state, and I can't just go down there and question a sheriff across state lines."

"Why not?"

"Well, for one thing, it might make him itchy before I got a chance to charge him."

"So then charge him."

"I can't charge a man across state lines, ma'am. I'd have to convince a judge to issue a warrant for his arrest down there, and even then, well, it could turn out he'd almost have to arrest himself, and he might not care to."

Rachel took this in. She shook her head.

"But—" she said, and the sheriff waited. "What are you saying—if he was up here you could arrest him?"

"I could if I had probable cause. Only problem is, all I've got so far is this letter and this piece of cloth, both of which have been produced not by your son himself but by you, and one abandoned truck with a bullet hole could've been put there by anybody. So unless your son comes walking through that door in the next five minutes, or calls and tells me where he's at, then I'm going to have to go out there and find him. So." He readied his pen again and looked at them both, mother and son. "Can you tell me what he was wearing, last time you saw him?"

54

AFTER THE SHERIFF was gone, Marky went upstairs to get cleaned up and she sat at the table alone, staring at the two phones. Finally she picked up the handset and dialed Danny once more, and once more got the recording. She set the handset down and stared at it again.

And why didn't you tell the sheriff about that rifle? Why didn't you tell him to go talk to Gordon Burke?

Because just two weeks ago Gordon Burke was sitting right here at this table, and because he'd helped you bury old Wyatt . . . and because he'd watched Danny grow up, and because Gordon Burke had once been like a father to her sons and he wouldn't, he wouldn't. He just wouldn't.

When Marky came back down she had soup ready, and they tried to talk like it was just another night but everything they said sounded strange. The two phones sat on the table looking like they would ring, but not ringing. Outside it was snowing again, big white flakes tumbling in the farmlight, but it wasn't pretty, not anymore. The first time it snowed it made you happy, it made you think of being a kid and sledding and making snowmen, and Christmas, and sometimes after that the snow would turn everything white and pretty again, but now the snow was just snow and the winter went on and the spring would never come.

After dinner they each tried calling again, then she called the sheriff, using the card he'd left, and after she hung up she told Marky a deputy had answered and said there was no news and that he'd let the sheriff know she called.

She turned on the TV and they sat down to watch, but everything they saw seemed loud and stupid and fake. Marky sat through one show, then said he was going upstairs, and she muted the TV.

"Is this bothering you? We don't have to watch."

"No Momma I just feel like going upstairs now."

"All right." If he was going upstairs then he wasn't worried, Rachel knew. Or was that just what he wanted you to think?

"I can leave my phone with you if you want me to Momma," he said.

"No, you keep it with you, sweetheart. Just, you know, let me know—OK?"

"I will Momma."

Upstairs he sat on his bed, then stood again and went across the hall to Danny's room. All his things were there, not as many as in his old room but just enough so you knew it was Danny's room. His schoolbooks on the bookshelf, his old skates and his hockey stick. The Big Dam Mug on his desk where he kept his drawing pens and which always made you think about the dam that time you all drove there—Poppa lifting you up so you could look over and down and your insides all rolling over and what if he dropped you on accident and nothing to keep you from falling and you wouldn't look again, you wouldn't even stand there again for a picture.

And next to the Big Dam Mug was the framed picture of the two of you in the canoe with Poppa behind you, you and Danny in the orange life vests that smelled of the river and fish, both of you smiling and Poppa smiling too and it was Momma in the back of the canoe who took the picture with her old camera. That was the year Poppa went back to the hospital even though he didn't smoke anymore and you stood by the hospital bed and he put his arm around you one at a time and said *no crying, you boys are too big for that. I need you to be men, now, all right? I need you to take care of your mother. Will you do that for me?* And at the funeral you each sat to one side of her and held her hand and you watched the machine lower the casket into the ground and that was when you knew for sure he was gone, he was really gone, and it was just the three of you now and you would never see your Poppa again except in pictures and in your memories and your dreams.

And now Danny too. Danny was missing, and what if Holly Burke never went into the river and Mr. Burke never got sad and angry and you all still worked at the Plumbing Supply, you and Danny and Jeff, and you still lived at the old house and Wyatt was still alive . . . But no, Wyatt would still be dead because time was still there and you would be as old as you are now and Wyatt died because he got too old, and you will die one day too, you and Danny and

Momma too, but Danny would not be leaving all the time, driving all over, he'd be making bridges and dams but he could come home and stay home and he wouldn't be leaving all the time because of people saying he had something to do with Holly Burke going into the river when he didn't, he didn't, some other person did that to her, and the sheriff, the old sheriff who was Audrey's father never found who did it and that was ten years ago . . . and now Danny's letter said Deputy Moran pulled him over that night and that's how the pocket got onto his truck, and what did that mean? Did the deputy just find the pocket or did he tear it off of her shirt himself, and what did that mean . . . ?

When he woke up he was in Danny's room, on Danny's bed, the comforter from his own bed thrown over him and it was almost light out and he'd been dreaming and the dream was so bad he'd been crying in his sleep and he went on crying when he was awake because he knew it was true, what he dreamed, he knew it: the phone would not ring, would never ring, because Danny could not make the call. Because Danny was dead now too.

It was like looking over the dam again, your heart rolling and nothing to hold on to and nothing to stop you and nothing but down and down and down.

But you can't tell her. You can't tell her.

You have to get up and brush your teeth, and wash your face, and get dressed for work. You have to go downstairs and turn off the TV and put your hand on her shoulder and shake her gently, *Momma, Momma wake up*, and wait for her to open her eyes and see you, and see how she remembers, slowly, just looking at you, that Danny is missing. You have to tell her you want to go to work, you want to stay busy, you can't tell her you don't want to sit with her all day waiting and waiting, even though Danny would say you should do that, just for her. And then you have to make the tea while she goes upstairs to dress and have a hot mug waiting for her when she comes back down, and you have to remind her that she needs to put the phone back on the machine because it won't charge otherwise and it won't work away from the machine anyway, and when she drops you off at work you have to kiss her on the cheek good-bye and tell her *everything is going to be OK Momma, everything is going to be OK*, and watch as she pulls out of the lot again and turns toward home so she can be near the phone when it rings, and all the time you are just falling, down and down and nothing to stop you not even the river, not even the rocks.

55

HE DROVE BY Wabash's garage at two in the afternoon and when he drove back fifteen minutes later the van was rumbling like a race car and he could see sparks in his sideview mirror where the tailpipe was scraping the concrete.

Wabash came out to meet him in the parking lot.

"What happened there, Gordon?"

"Ran over something." He shut the door and put his hands in his jacket pockets.

"Sounds like you tore the whole muffler out. What the heck did you hit?"

"I don't know. Something big. Wasn't even there by the time I pulled over."

Wabash moved to the back of the van and got down on one knee for a look under the chassis. "Chunk of ice, maybe?"

"Maybe."

"Must of been a big gosh-darn chunk."

"Think you can get to it today?"

"Well," said Wabash, still looking. "Gonna have to order a new muffler and tailpipe, looks to me, so we might not get her done till tomorrow." He stood again and spanked the snow and grit from his knee. "You want me to work up an estimate?"

"No, just want you to do it."

"All right. You want to take the Crown Vic again?"

"If you don't mind."

"That's what she's there for." They both looked at the black car where it sat in the weak afternoon sunlight.

Wabash looked at Gordon and then looked more closely. "You feeling all right there, Gordon?"

"Feel just fine."

"You don't look so hot."

"That right? Well, you don't look so hot yourself."

"Fair enough. I'll get you the key."

AT A QUARTER past six Moran came out of the building and climbed into his SUV and shut the door. Exhaust chugged from the tailpipe, reverse lights lit up the pavement as he backed out of his space, and then the cruiser followed its headlights down the street. When it was a block away Gordon put the Crown Vic into gear and pulled away from the curb and followed. He'd been sitting there since four thirty.

The cruiser hit a green light and Gordon, keeping his distance, stopped on the yellow. He sat through the red light as the cruiser sat through a red at the intersection up ahead and then they both drove on. Gordon hit a pothole and the Crown Vic's license plates rattled on the floor of the passenger side. Beside him, unfolded on the duffel bag, lay the map of the county.

He followed the SUV through town and out onto the county highway going west into rural woods and farmland. The address was listed as Route 10, and Moran was headed that way, and why else would he be going out there? The man was going home.

Home to what? To wife. To smells of dinner. To kids running up to grab his legs.

Could a man live two lives? Could he be this one man in the light of day— this husband, father, sheriff—and another man at night, a second man? Driving the back roads in his sheriff's cruiser, using his badge and his authority for the purposes of the second man. Ugly purposes. How long could he go on like that? How many nights, how many women. Would he still be doing it when his kids were off to college, when he was a grandfather? Or would the needs of the second man weaken with age, his memory weakening too, until he no longer believed he'd ever been that man, done those things. Could his children and his wife stand at his graveside one day believing they'd known the one, entire man? And die themselves believing that?

It was a six-mile stretch of empty highway, the blacktop plowed but with tracks of packed snow, and Gordon kept his distance until they'd gone three miles by his odometer, then he gunned the Crown Vic to close the gap. He drew near enough to see his own headlights in the silver paint of the SUV's back side and then eased off the gas and followed along at that distance. He saw Moran tilt his head toward the rearview and he could see that he was watching the headlights, and he gave him a few seconds to recognize the shape of the car, the headlights, as he knew he would, as any cop would, before he swung into the other lane and gunned the big engine again and blew by the SUV. He'd already dimmed the dashlights, and anyway the moment of alignment between the two drivers was too brief, and in the next moment the headlights of the SUV were in his rearview and growing small as he sped on, and the sign for the turnoff up ahead was bright in his own lights, and he would take the turnoff, he would take it one way or another and it was up to Moran to decide what would happen after that, follow or not follow, go home or not go home, choose one path and not the other . . . and the turnoff was coming up fast on the right, the turnoff was here, and Gordon braked to take it and only then, banking sharply into it—too sharply, the back end of the Crown Vic swinging wide—only then did the cruiser bloom into color behind him, barlights pulsing red and blue, grille lights pulsing red and blue and the headlights lifting as Moran hit the gas hard.

The Crown Vic held the turn, the rear end swung back, and he sped down the road with his eyes in the rearview, and there it came: the cruiser's headlights and barlights spilled into the turn and slurred left and right and straightened and came on fast. Gordon watching his own headlights on the snow and the tiretracks up ahead, and watching Moran's in the rearview. He had a quarter-mile lead, maybe a little more, and that was what he needed. His lights lit up the yellow sign, BRIDGE MAY BE ICY, and then they shaped out the trestlework of the bridge, and the tiretracks went across and there was no ice that he could see, and when he hit the brakes the tires grabbed and held, until they didn't and the car began to drift, and he eased off the brakes, correcting, braking, straightening her out and bringing her to a halt near the far end of the bridge.

He threw the Crown Vic into park and opened the door and stepped out as the SUV's lights bore down on the bridge. Moran saw him in plenty of time and braked to a stop twenty, thirty yards from the Crown Vic, and no way to go around, and there he sat, behind his headlights, the colored lights pulsing. Not getting out of the SUV, not killing the lights, just sitting there. Like it was just another routine stop and he would sit back there awhile doing whatever it was cops did—check the plates, check in with dispatch, send a text to the wife. When Danny Young looked in his rearview that night, the night of the park, this is what he must have seen: the deputy's headlights, his silent colored lights.

And had she seen them too? Ten, fifteen minutes earlier, that night—those same lights coming up behind her as she walked near the river. The colored lights that said *Stop walking now, just stay where you are. Just do what I say.*

Gordon went through his motions and watched himself going through them, moving through space so slowly and at the same time so surely, so expect-edly, as if watching a memory of himself . . . keeping his hatbrim low and lifting his hand in a friendly wave and then stooping back into the car like he had some trouble to attend to there, such as haywire equipment, such as spilled coffee, and from that vantage he saw Moran step out of the cruiser and put on his sheriff's hat and make his way forward in his own headlights. Not reaching for his sidearm but moving just the same like a man who would not be caught off guard.

What are you doing out here, young lady?

Nothing, Officer. Just walking.

You know the park is closed after dark.

It is?

You know it is. Come on, get in. I'll take you home.

From within the Crown Vic he heard Moran call out, "Davis—? Is that you? It had goddam better be, or else I'd better see hands in the air and I mean right now."

Gordon stood up out of the car with the rifle and leveled it, and Moran stopped midstep and put his hand to his pistol grip and Gordon said, "Don't do that," and Moran held still.

"Get your hand off that pistol, you son of a bitch. Right now."

Moran stood with his hand on the pistol and Gordon stood with the stock to his shoulder and his eye to the sights. He'd known it would be close range and he'd removed the scope before he put the gun in the duffel bag. The end of the barrel was steady, the sights dead-centered on the backlit shape of Moran's neck.

"Gordon?" said Moran. "Is that you?"

"Hand off the gun or I pull this trigger right now, no discussion."

Moran hesitated, then raised both hands chest-high, palms forward.

"Take it easy, Gordon. Christ, I thought you were a goddam off-duty cop. Where'd you get that Crown Vic?" He cocked his head to look past Gordon. "Is that Dave Wabash's?"

Gordon watched him.

Moran shook his head. He might've smiled but the lights were behind him and his face was dark under the hatbrim. "Cop car . . . sheriff's hat. You got a badge now too, Gordon?"

"Shut up."

"Christ," Moran said again. He looked slowly from side to side, then up into the trestles, then back to Gordon. His breaths coloring in the lights. "Put the rifle down, Gordon, before you accidentally shoot me."

"Won't be accidental."

"Well, at least take your finger off the trigger till you're ready. I'd hate for you to shoot before you had a chance to tell me just what the fuck you think you're doing."

Gordon flexed his fingers on the forward stock and reset the butt to his shoulder.

Moran shook his head again. "I blame myself, Gordon. I should've seen this coming at the café. Should've got you some help right then."

Gordon said nothing. The rifle barrel steady. He saw something in the cruiser, and his heart went cold: someone in the passenger seat. A small person. A little girl. But when he looked directly into those headlights the little girl—or that shape of her—vanished.

"Put the rifle down and let's talk it over," Moran said. "I can help you, Gordon. There won't be any charges."

"You got that right."

"Gordon." Moran took a step and Gordon shifted the gun and shot into the near headlight of the SUV and immediately chambered another round and leveled the gun at Moran again. The report replayed in the trestlework and died away. The headlight had been in his eyes and now it wasn't. There was no one in the passenger seat. That daughter was home, she was safe . . .

Moran stood looking at the darkened headlight, his profile lit up now by the Crown Vic's taillights. He looked like a man in red face paint. Or one so angered his face had begun to glow.

"You've just made this situation a whole lot harder to walk away from, Gordon."

"I can see your eyes now. I can put the next bullet in either one of them."

"I expect you could, if you were ready to shoot a sheriff."

"Wouldn't be shooting a sheriff. I'd be shooting a liar and a rapist and a killer."

The red and glowing face did not change.

"I don't think you're thinking clearly, Gordon. If you're so sure about this, why don't you go to Sheriff Halsey and tell him?"

"Because it doesn't matter what anybody says. Nobody knows the truth but you and my daughter."

"And you, Gordon. You're so sure, you're ready to shoot a man in cold blood. And then what?"

"And then what doesn't concern you. You won't be here."

"What if you're wrong, though, Gordon? What if you shoot an innocent man?" He turned his palms in a way that changed him from a man at gunpoint to a man in conversation. A man just asking the obvious and reasonable. But he kept them raised, and Gordon considered putting a bullet through one of them, as Sutter had done for his own daughter. And for Caroline Price. And for Holly too. All of them one daughter finally, and their fathers were all the same man with just one desire in him, one purpose.

"I'm just not sure you've thought this through, Gordon," Moran said, and Gordon shook his head to clear it.

"Keep saying my name, you son of a bitch. It won't make me not pull this trigger."

"Just take it easy, all right? I'm trying to help you here. Can you just lower the gun barrel, at least?"

"How many."

"What?"

"How many women. Young women. Girls. How many."

"I don't understand the question, Gordon."

"Hell you don't."

"Lower the rifle, Gordon."

"Think I don't know about Katie Goss?"

"Katie Goss? Am I supposed to know that name?"

"You ought to since you raped her."

"Raped her?" Moran cocked his head. "Where in the hell are you getting your information, Gordon?"

"Doesn't matter."

"It does matter, as I'd like to know who's spreading lies about me."

"Katie Goss said it herself."

"To you?"

Gordon said nothing.

"No, not to you. Why in the hell would she be talking to you?"

"My daughter—" Gordon said, but the words choked him. He saw the gun barrel waver. The colored lights blurred. "She told you no," he said. "She told you no and you killed her. Say it. Say it, you son of a bitch. Say you ran her down and threw her in the river to drown. Say it before I kill you."

"You aren't going to kill me, Gordon." Moran took a step forward, his hands still raised.

"Take one more step and find out."

"You aren't going to shoot me, Gordon, because you're not sure you're right. You've heard a lot of talk, and you've talked yourself into one version of things, but you don't know for sure, and the moment you kill me you'll never know for sure, because if I'm the one who did it, like you say, then I'm the only one who can tell you the truth. I'm the only man who can put your mind at ease. And I won't do that, Gordon, because it would be a lie, and afterwards you would still not know the truth. Kill me, Gordon, and you will still be in exactly the same place, won't you. You still won't know for sure. You will never know, even when you are in prison for the rest of your life. Or dead yourself. You'll die never knowing for sure if you killed an innocent man, a sheriff, a father of two little children himself, Gordon . . ."

Somehow he'd walked nearly to the barrel. The colored lights filled Gordon's vision, Moran just a shape in the glistening pulsing lights, like a figure underwater.

The rifle became heavy and he understood that Moran's hand was on the barrel, lowering it. He let the barrel drop and when it was aimed at the ground he let Moran take the rifle out of his hands. Moran working the bolt, ejecting the remaining two rounds into the snow and recovering them from the holes they made, then digging up the empty casing the same way and slipping all three into his jacket pocket. He carried the rifle to the cruiser and put it in the back seat as if it were his prisoner, then opened the front door and reached in, and the colored lights that had been pulsing all the while stopped and there was only the one headlight casting light on the two of them and the road and the Crown Vic.

Moran stepped to the front of the cruiser and stood looking at the shot-out headlight. Then he walked back to Gordon and stopped before him, his hands on his sheriff's belt. "Well, Gordon, we've got us a situation here. I put you in cuffs and take you in, you're gonna have to explain why you decided to ambush me, and I can't say I'm too crazy about that idea. On the other hand, you have committed serious crimes here, felonious crimes, and damn well could've blown my head off to boot."

He looked up into the trestles then, or the dark sky beyond them, and it was the kind of thing a man would do just before he pulled his pistol and shot you dead, and Gordon considered what that would be like—to be shot dead where he stood. To fall back in the snow and feel the life drain out of you, to see the world go dark. And the face that came to him then, that hovered over him in his last seconds, was not his own daughter's, but Audrey Sutter's, *Oh, Mr. Burke . . . what were you thinking?*

But Moran did not pull his pistol and shoot him. He looked at Gordon again and said, "Give me that hat."

"What?"

"The hat. Give it here."

Gordon reached up and felt the hatbrim. There was a hat on his head. He took it off and handed it to Moran.

Moran held the hat in one hand, turning it upside down and righting it again.

"That's what I thought," he said. "Not even the real deal." And he turned and flicked the hat Frisbee-style over the rail and they watched it fall out of the light and into the darkness below the bridge. Wherever the hat landed it made no sound. As if it had never landed at all.

"Tell you what, Gordon," Moran said, facing him again. "I think we'd best call this whole thing a wash. I'll take care of this headlight and you go on home and get some sleep. Some serious sleep. I won't tell anyone you pointed a loaded rifle at me, and you'll get some sense into your head again." He stood staring at him. "That work for you?"

Gordon said nothing. He hadn't moved since he'd let go of the rifle. He did not know if he would ever move again. Just stand here until the blood stops flowing, until the heart stops beating. Some old farmer coming along in his pickup and seeing the Crown Vic, seeing you standing here in the middle of the bridge, in the snow, *Blue and just stone-dead on his feet, Officer, never seen nothin like it in all my days . . .*

"Go home, Gordon," said Moran. "We both of us dodged one here, and tomorrow will look a whole lot better."

Moran turned then and walked back to his cruiser. He took off his hat and climbed in, and there was the sound of the shifter dropping into gear, and the single headlight began to withdraw toward the far end of the bridge. When the light was beyond the bridge it swung away, lighting up the trees to the side of the road, and then it swung away again as Moran completed his three-point turn and accelerated back the way he'd come. The two red taillights trailed away into the darkness until they were small as the eyes of an animal, and Gordon watched as they rounded the bend, as they shone briefly on the county road, as they blinked through the trees and were gone.

56

SHE HAD SEEN a light, several lights, small and moving way off in the darkness, way off in the trees, and she'd said, There's someone in the park, Daddy.

What?

There's someone in the park.

She was nine and riding shotgun. They'd been out for pizza and they were driving home and it was November and already dark out and you could see the moving lights from the road that went alongside the park; they looked like jumpy little fairies way deep in the woods. He'd leaned to look past her and after a moment said, That's a sharp eye, Deputy. Why are there flashlights in the park at this hour?

Because it's dark out, Sheriff.

Why are there people in the park at this hour, I meant.

Are we going to check it out?

Well, he said. He watched the road ahead. Then he turned to her again. What do you think, Deputy?

She didn't like going into the park at night. At night the park was not a park; it was a woods so dark and deep it made the hair on your arms stand just to think about it—and that was before they pulled Holly Burke out of the river.

I think we'd best check it out, Sheriff.

All right then, he said, and they pulled into the park and drove toward the far-off lights. There were three of them, they saw as they came closer, but when they rounded the bend toward the river the lights all blinked out and did not come on again.

He pulled over and switched on his spot and swept it over the line of trees that ran between the road and the river, lighting up the trunks one by one like faces, and the beam lighting up the black water in the distance between the trees, and he swept it over the white wooden cross and its faded flower wreath, and lastly he swept it over the trees of the woods on the other side of the road.

They're gone now or else they're just gonna ride this out, he said.

Who?

The people with the flashlights. Who do you think?

She didn't answer—not so sure now that it was people at all. Or flashlights.

He got on the speaker and said, The park is closed after dark. Go home. Then they sat in the silence watching the woods for any movement, but there was none, and Audrey turned back to look at the white cross and the wreath, visible in the glow from the headlights.

That's where it happened, isn't it, she said.

He looked where she was looking. Then he placed his hand on her head and moved it like a hairbrush to the back of her head and then down to her neck, and gently squeezed.

That's where she went into the river, yes.

Did Mr. Burke put the cross there?

I don't know. I don't think so.

Who did then?

I don't know. Someone who knew her. Friends, maybe.

Will it stay there, like a gravestone?

Probably not. The park will probably remove it.

She thought about that. They were silent.

And you're going to find who did it? she said.

Yes, I am. He looked at her. Sweetheart—are you worried about that?

She shook her head. She thought she would cry and she didn't know why, but she didn't cry. She said, No, Sheriff. I know you will.

But he hadn't, and the cross had been removed and there were no more flowers or stuffed animals or notes or anything at all to mark the place where Holly Burke had been hit by a car, they said, and thrown into the river still alive, still breathing, they said. There was the bank of snow, shaped by the snowplow blade, and there were the pine trees—jack pines, she thought—and there was the snow between the pines where someone had walked not long ago, and beyond that there was the wide frozen river, patches of icy black in the snow, and all of it lit weirdly blue by a bright, lopsided moon.

Audrey had not been standing long, three minutes maybe, between two pines, looking at the footprints in the snow, when she saw the light, as she'd seen the lights ten years ago from outside the park, and this light was coming along through the park as her father had come along back then, and she took it to be the headlamp of a motorcycle—but who would be riding a motorcycle in the snow and ice? And it wasn't a motorcycle; it was a car with one of its headlights out, some kid or drinker or both cutting through the park in his beater car to avoid the cops.

She'd pulled the sedan over as far as she could against the bank of snow and there was room to get by if the driver was not too drunk, and she stood between the pines watching the single light snake its way through the woods until it came around the bend and shone briefly in her eyes like her father's spot and she closed her eyes until the light passed on. When she opened them again she saw the SUV, the sheriff's cruiser, pulling up behind the sedan. It was not local. It was the same Iowa sheriff's cruiser she'd seen in her driveway when he came to show her the pictures, and seeing it again here in the park she knew one thing absolutely: he'd followed her. Had waited for her somewhere near the house and followed her here.

But why would he do that?

And how had she not seen it—a one-eyed car tailing her across town?

He parked the cruiser behind the sedan but did not get out and she could see his profile in the lights of his dash. She held her breath so he would not see the clouds. Her heart was pounding.

He sat looking at the sedan in his headlight. Then the headlight blanked out and the engine went silent and the last of the exhaust slipped away and he turned and looked right at her where she stood in the pines.

He stepped out of the cruiser and put his hat on and shut the door behind him and stood looking at her.

She let out her breath.

He put his hands in his jacket pockets and walked across the road, the packed snow grinding under his bootsoles like glass. He reached the banked-up snow and stopped.

"Now what in the heck are you doing out here?" he said.

"I could ask you the same thing," she said.

He cocked his head. "I'm here because you're here and this park is closed after dark, which I know you know full well."

"And you're out of your jurisdiction, Deputy."

"Sheriff, young lady. And don't get smart with me."

She looked to her left and to her right, as if some other car might be coming along. She looked toward the far road that ran alongside the park, but there were only trees and darkness, the weird blue light of the moon, and she wondered how you could see flashlights this deep in the park from the road yet not see the lights of the road from here. Like you had traveled deeper than you thought. Or that the physics of time and distance changed once you entered the woods, as it did in fables and certain ghost stories.

She thought of her father's phone. Saw it sitting on the passenger seat of the sedan, charging. Stupid.

She looked at Moran again. From where he stood on the road it was four, maybe five big steps through the snow to where she stood. Even if she could get by him and get to the car—even if you got in it what would be the point? Who would you call? *A cop is chasing me . . .*

Her nose was running and she drew her good hand under it and returned her hand to the jacket pocket. The keys were there. She arranged them between her knuckles, sharp ends out. She wondered for the first time what had become of Caroline's pepper spray—if the little canister had been carried away or if it had ended up in the hands of her parents down in Georgia.

Behind her was the riverbank and the short drop down to the ice.

"What do you want?" she said.

"What do you mean what do I want?"

"What do you want to let me go?"

He stared at her. He removed one hand from its pocket to tip his hatbrim up on his forehead and returned the hand to the pocket.

"Do I look like I'm keeping you from going anywhere? What in the heck has gotten into everybody around here lately? Did you know your old buddy shot out my headlight earlier tonight? Shot it out with a deer rifle." He turned to look at the front of the cruiser.

"What old buddy," she said, although she knew.

He turned back to her. "Who do you think? Your old buddy Gordon Burke."

"What did you do to him?" Her jaw was trying to chatter but she would not let it.

"What did I do to him? Honey, he was the one holding the rifle. What do you think I did? I talked him down and sent him home. Told him to get some sleep and just give all this nonsense a rest." He watched her. "I'm thinking you need to do the same. I'm thinking you are somewhat out of your depth here."

"I talked to Katie Goss," she said. "I know what you made her do."

"Now, see there—that's exactly what I'm talking about." He shook his head. "I didn't put it together right away, when I had that deer rifle pointed at my head. But afterwards I thought to myself, now who would go talking to Katie Goss all these years later, and who would tell Gordon Burke about it? And then I remembered a phone call I got from a man, day or two ago, telling me about a certain someone coming into his place of business, asking questions about Danny Young." He raised his hand again to tap a finger on his temple. Returned the hand to its pocket.

"And so I decided to drive on up here and just have this out, just straighten this all out before someone gets hurt for real. But then I see you driving off and I think, Now where's she going? And turns out you were going here." He looked around at the pines, the snow, the ice beyond her. "What did you think you'd find, hey? Something your daddy and us never saw?"

He watched her. She said nothing. Did nothing.

"What ever happened to you, anyway?" he said. "You used to be this quiet, shy girl." He gave her a kind of smile. "I think you even liked me, once upon a time."

"I think you're mistaken."

"No, I'm pretty sure you had yourself a little crush, back in the day."

She shuddered. It was all so familiar. She'd been here before, at just this moment. There was a foulness and a bitterness in the air. The stink of a greasy hand.

"You're pathetic," she said, and he stopped smiling.

"I'm pathetic. Is that what you said? Are you forgetting who you're talking to?"

"I know exactly who I'm talking to. I know all about you."

He looked down and shook his head. Then he looked up again. Staring at her with those bug eyes. "I think you'd best come on outta that snow now, before you get yourself into some real trouble. Come on now."

"I won't do it," she said. "I won't do what Katie did. You'll have to kill me."

"Kill you?" He stared at her. "I knew you when you were in pigtails. I watched you grow up. Your dad was my boss. And now you stand there talking to me like that?"

"My dad knew what you were. He knew. He just didn't have the proof."

Moran grinned crookedly and huffed a smoky laugh and looked back toward the road. No lights. No one coming or going. Nothing but the trees and the moon.

And then he stepped up over the bank of snow and he was coming for her. "We're done talking. Let's go."

She backstepped, keeping the distance between them, the river at her back— the bank how many steps away? She would not turn to look. Would not take her eyes off him.

He stopped and stared at her. "Where do you think you're going?" He reached behind him and there was a flash of moonlight on chrome and a rattle like dog tags. "We can do this the easy way or the hard way, honey." He swung the cuffs as if to dazzle her with them, their shininess, as you would a child. If he got them on her that was it, it was all over.

"Is that what you told Holly Burke?" she said, and the cuffs stopped swinging. Moran watching her, dark-eyed under the hatbrim. The breaths pulsing from his nostrils.

"You have no idea how crazy you sound," he said, and stepped forward again, and again she backstepped. The bank was there . . . so close. He took another step and she backstepped, and her boot fell through space and she followed it down—stumbling backwards, arms rowing in the air and both legs going out from under her. She landed on her back and went sliding down the short ramp of the riverbank and she knew what was next and raised her head so that she struck the ice with her shoulders, then watched as her legs, following some instinct of their own, carried on overhead, her boots swinging through the stars and landing toe-first in two heavy chops behind her, ice chips flying, so that when she looked up again she was on her hands and knees on the ice and facing the bank she'd come down backwards.

Moran stepped to the edge of the bank and stood looking down on her.

"Come up off of there," he said.

She shuffled backwards on her hands and knees, then got to her feet. She stood listening, feeling—her heart pounding, remembering the water when she first went in, the shock of it, how the entire body jolted in amazement, in disbelief. At the same time, standing there, she knew she would not fall through again, and it was silly, it was irrational, but she believed that the ice knew her. Or the feel of her, her particular weight and stance. She and the ice had a history, and after all it was the same river here as it was across the state line . . .

Moran took a small, careful step down the bank, his hand held out to her, and she turned then and walked out onto the ice.

"Wouldn't do that if I were you," he said. "That ice ain't as thick as it used to be."

She continued on, putting distance between herself and the bank. When he shut up she could hear the thin dunes of snow compressing under her boots, could hear the blood beating in her ears and nothing more—no cracks, no pops. Ten. Fifteen. Twenty steps before she stopped and looked back. He wasn't following. She'd had her hands out for balance and now she slipped them back into the jacket pockets. She stood facing him. The ice would be thinnest in the middle of the river but she would go there if she had to, and beyond, all the way across and into the nameless woods on the far bank.

"Just gonna stand there all night, is that the idea?" He didn't have to shout; his voice carried easily over the hard, flat surface.

She said nothing. The river made no sound—not the ice, not the water flowing beneath it, although it did flow; she could feel it, like her own blood. So fast and silent in its dark rushing and so cold.

Moran folded the cuffs and returned them to their place on his belt. He watched her. Then he took another sideways step down the bank, took one more and then onto the ice, one boot only, but that was enough—she felt the change before it reached her: a shift, a shooting nerve that ran through the ice and expressed itself, finally, in the smallest pop, just beneath her boots.

She took her hands from her pockets.

The ice sighed, it took a breath—then pitched beneath her. A sharp edge rose like a fin, and her boots slipped down the incline of it and she fell to her chest on the upended slab and slid legs-first into the water, plunging into the dark and the cold up to her ribs, clinging to the upended slab of ice, and there was the moment before the cold soaked through her clothes, and then it simply squeezed the breath from her like great jaws clamping down. She clung to the slab of ice but her own weight pushed it under, dunked it like a smaller body she meant to drown and it slipped under the surface of the ice and she let go and grabbed for the ice itself and she could hear the slab scraping and knocking along the underside of the ice, carried away by the same current that shoved her against the edge and pulled at her legs.

"Shit, I goddam told you," said Moran.

She watched him. Her throat wanted to call out to him—*Help me, please*—but she would not let it. Would not speak to him. Already her jaw was chattering.

"You couldn't just cooperate, could you?"

The water so cold and so strong and Moran just standing there. She turned her face so she wouldn't see him. Before her, downriver, the ice banked around the woods and disappeared. If she went under how far could she go? Was there a place downriver where the ice didn't freeze and she could surface? How far was the dam, where Caroline had been found?

But this wasn't that river.

Yes, it was—Upper Black Root, Lower Black Root, all the same river going the same direction, toward the same dams . . . but how far?

The water so cold you couldn't think, couldn't breathe.

But there's another dam, Deputy—remember? Where we fished when you were a little girl?

Yes, Daddy . . . but how far is that?

Fishermen left holes in the ice—but the holes would freeze over an hour later and would be too small anyway.

There was movement, scraping sounds, and she turned to see Moran on his hands and knees, making his way out toward her. He'd left his hat behind and he looked ridiculous and hideous. Like an animal come from the woods to see if this floundering thing in the ice could be had for dinner.

"Go away," she said, or tried to say. Her breath was gone.

He got down on his stomach and drew himself forward on his elbows. The ice popped and he went no farther. Resting there on his elbows, getting his breath, and the breath gusting white from his open mouth.

She turned from him and tried to raise herself on another part of the ice, but there was nothing to hold on to and the current was strong and she slipped down again and stopped trying and rested. All the blood had gone to her heart but her heart was cold too.

Moran breathing, watching her.

"All you had to do was cooperate," he said. "You'd think I deserved that much, at least. All the years we've known each other."

Against her will she turned to look at him—looked into those bug eyes and saw not hostility but . . . confusion. Or something like it.

He looked down at his hands, then cupped them and blew into them. White shoots of breath escaping at the seams. He looked away, downriver.

"You remember when your daddy would send me to pick you up at school?" he said. And looked at her again. "You remember that?"

Her head was shaking and maybe he thought she was answering him.

"Sure you do. You were just a little girl. He'd get hung up and couldn't make it so he'd send me. Trusted me with that—picking up his daughter from school."

She watched him from her hole of ice and water, her backteeth knocking.

"And you'd ride up front with me, and I'd let you use the PA . . . remember? You'd scare the bejesus outta some kid on the sidewalk and then duck down out of sight."

He smiled at her, almost shyly. Then the smile died away and his brows creased. "But then he stopped doing that. Stopped sending me. I figured you must've said something. Must've told him you didn't want me picking you up anymore." He watched her. As if she might have something to say to that. Some kind of confirmation.

"You never . . ." she said with her rattling jaw.

Moran cocked his head. "Never what?"

"Never told him . . . my dad."

"I never told him what?"

"That you pulled . . . Danny Young over. That night. You never told him . . . you were there too."

She watched him, and whatever had been in his eyes, shyness or whatever it was, vanished. He grinned crookedly and shook his head.

"Daddy's little deputy," he said. "And look where it's gotten you."

She turned away from him again. She could not hold on much longer but she wasn't frightened now. She'd been here before and she knew how it would be. In a moment you'll simply let go and he'll see that you let go, that you made the decision yourself. Not him. You walked onto the ice yourself and you will go under yourself and it will be all right.

But Moran would not wait—he began worming his way forward again on his elbows.

"Don't—" she said, and he reached out and she slipped and thrashed and turned from him and held on, and he came at her again.

"Stop that," he said, but she said nothing more—would not speak to him, would not scream. He reached again and she dodged again, splashing, and held on. He would only come so close, would only risk so much. She kept moving to the left and to the right. Like a child going around a tree to keep from being tagged.

He was breathing hard, grunting with his efforts. He came closer still and reached again and she turned away and with her back to him she felt his hand land on her shoulder and felt the strength of his grip. And though she was not facing him she knew from the pressure of his hand, the orientation of his fingers, where he was, and she turned once more in her hole and flung the cast backwards through the air and it landed hard, solidly, as if striking a rock. The impact shook her to her skull and he made no sound and his hand slipped from her shoulder and did not return.

She turned to face him. He was lying facedown on the ice, his mouth open, one bug eye open and staring at her. Something dark ran down his jaw and she saw it was coming from his ear. His breaths puffed snow crystals along the ice.

Instinctively she grabbed at him. As you would grab at a rope, or the branch of a tree. She took hold of his arm, his shoulder, and suddenly he was awake again, and he was moving—rolling once, slowly, like a body turning over in bed, away from her, and her deadened fingers could not hold on. He lay flat on his back on the ice now, his face to the sky. His bug eyes shut. Cold, thin smoke drifting from his open mouth. No part of him within reach.

She watched him. Watched for the smoke to stop seeping from his mouth.

She looked back toward the road—no lights, no movement; the pines and the shadows of the pines, and the dim shapes of the two cars beyond—and when she looked back he was staring at her. Or seemed to be. He'd turned his head and his eyes were open. Bulbous and glassy and empty.

She looked away again, downriver, at the wide plate of ice and the bend that went around the woods and continued out of view. She'd stopped shaking, she noticed. Her teeth had stopped chattering. No longer cold because she was no longer there—arms dead, chest dead. No feeling whatsoever below the ice, not even the sensation of the current pulling at her legs. Nothing now but the dead weight of sleep, of dreaming, of sinking into water that was no longer cold but warm—bathwater warm, and you could see everything under the water, every bubble and every rippling eel of color where the moonlight came through the ice and lit up the underworld, the shape of your own fingers where they slid along the underside of the ice, and there's the slippery and wavering moon following along with you, gliding along on the other side like a bright eye that wants only to keep you in its sight, wants only to light your way as you go, and the journey will be long but you are not alone—the girls of the river are here as they were before, girls of pale arms and long yellow hair . . . and Caroline is with them too, her hand finding your good hand and gripping, her cheek so smooth against yours, her voice so warm and grass-soft in your ear, *Oh, Audrey, here we go again—what is wrong with us?* and it's a voice to fill your heart, to make you want to laugh and cry—*Oh, Caroline, Caroline! God I've missed you!*

Drifting with Caroline and the others in the warm river under the ice, the moon following overhead, and there is no urgency to breathe, no panic about breathing, just the steady current and the feeling of her hand in yours, her body alongside yours, the two of you bumping downstream under the ice.

It's so beautiful, Caroline, isn't it?

It is, Audrey. But hush now, hush, she says in her Georgia voice, it won't be long.

On and on under the ice, in the strange light, your fingertips slipping along the underside of the ice and the girls coming and going like the curious creatures they are, the moon following, and it's two minutes or it's two hours or it's ten years . . . ten years and ten thousand years all the same thing to the world and only one creature in all its history ever keeping track, ever thinking of such a thing as time—ever desiring it or fearing it or losing it, and that was why you'd come home in the first place, because you were running out of time and that was why he'd gone down there looking for that boy, and there'd been even less time than both of you knew. And time had just ended, just stopped cold with no warning for Caroline and her family, for Holly Burke and her parents too . . .

But that's not how it is, Audrey, that's not how things really are once you're outside of time—or inside of it, as you are when you're in the river, when you're in that current and you are drifting. That's not time, because there is no beginning and no ending and you are just in the current and the current is forever and you are not alone, you are never alone in the current and the current itself is . . . is what?

Is love.

Is love. All right. But you have to be in it, inside the current, to ever know that. And once you're in it you can't tell those who are not, who you've left behind, that it's all right, that it's not what they thought it was. And that's the worst thing: that you can never tell them what it's really like. That it all flows on, under everything, even the ice . . . And that's why you can't stay, Audrey: so you can tell them.

But I want to stay.

No, you don't. You're too strong.

You're the strong one, Caroline . . . You are.

Tell that to the deputy!

Did you see?

I saw everything. You fought so beautifully, Audrey. Don't stop now.

But I'm so tired . . .

Almost there, Audrey.

Caroline—

Hang on, now. Hang on, Audrey. See it? Here it comes . . .

PART V

57

THE SHERIFF SAT in the cruiser for a long while, the engine off, watching the building from a distance. He kept thinking something would come over the radio, or his phone, that would require him to pull away from the curb and get back to town. But no one radioed, no one called.

Almost six thirty now and lights were coming on in the windows. He didn't have to watch hers, as he'd already been up there once and she wasn't home, but he watched anyway.

He would wait fifteen more minutes and then he'd go.

He waited fifteen minutes and said, "All right, five minutes more," and two minutes after that a small red hatchback pulled up before the building and parked. A woman stepped out of the car hitching a tote bag to her shoulder, then stood by as a small child—a girl—hopped down to the curb. The woman opened the hatchback and collected a plastic bag of groceries, then took the girl by the hand and the two of them went up the walkway toward the building.

He waited until he saw light in the second-floor windows and then he got out of the cruiser and walked up to the building and pushed through the unlocked entrance. He climbed the stairs for the second time, and for the second time rapped his knuckles on her door. There was a long moment, a long silence, the sheriff watching the lens of the peephole, before the deadbolt clacked and the door swung open and she stood in the opening, still in her coat.

She was older, a little heavier, but otherwise did not look much different than she'd looked ten years ago when she'd been Danny Young's eighteen-year-old girlfriend. She looked like a tired young mother at the end of a long workday. The little girl stared up at him from behind her mother's legs and the resemblance was strong. Like seeing the same person at two different ages.

"Miss Goss?" he said.

"Yes," said the woman.

"Katie Goss."

"Yes."

"My name is Sheriff Halsey. I don't know if you remember me."

"I remember you. You used to be a deputy."

"Yes, ma'am, I did. I'm sorry to just show up like this. I tried to catch you at work but you'd already left."

She stood with one hand on the door, one on the back of the little girl's head.

He said, "Do you mind if I step in for just a minute? I'd rather not talk to you in the hallway like this."

She didn't answer, and he knew what he was asking of her, and he didn't know what he'd say if she refused him. But she didn't; she opened the door and stepped aside.

He removed his hat and stepped inside and she closed the door behind him. He bent toward the little girl and smiled. "Hello, what's your name?"

The little girl flinched at his voice and said nothing.

"That's Mel," said her mother.

"Hello, Mel. My name is Wayne."

The little girl said nothing. He straightened again, and Katie Goss was watching him. She said, "Sheriff, why do I get the feeling you're about to say the name Audrey Sutter?"

"I don't know, ma'am. I hadn't planned on it."

"But that's why you're here."

"No, ma'am. Why would it be?"

"Because of what she told you."

He watched her. "What do you think she told me?"

"Something she promised me she wouldn't."

Halsey stood there. The little girl looking up at him, then at her mother, then at him again. He said, "She kept that promise as far as I know, ma'am. She came to see me before she came to see you, and it sure wasn't me who sent her your way."

Katie Goss watched him. "Then why are you here, Sheriff?"

THE LITTLE GIRL would not go to her room, but finally she agreed to play with her horses on the coffee table, and Katie Goss found a cartoon channel on the TV, and when that was settled she took off her coat and cleared the little kitchen table and poured two glasses of filtered water and sat down in the chair across from him.

Halsey lifted the glass for a drink and set it down again. The TV was playing and the little girl was out of view behind a pony wall, but just the same he tried to keep his voice down.

"I guess you won't be too surprised to know that I know about your talk with Sheriff Sutter, ten years back."

"You mean about Danny Young?"

"No, ma'am, I don't. I mean before that."

She said nothing. Then she sat back in her chair with both hands around the glass of water and the glass on the table. The cartoon voices looped forth in a continuous babble. She began clicking her fingernails on the glass. Halsey watched her nails for a moment and looked up again.

"And just to be clear," he said. "I'm not asking you to tell me anything you don't want to tell me. I'm not asking you to go into any . . . particulars."

Her nails on the glass sounded like a soft typing. She watched him, saying nothing. Finally she stopped clicking and said, "I'm still trying to figure out why you're here, Sheriff. I mean why now."

"Yes, ma'am. I'm trying to figure that out too." He looked at his own glass of water. "They's a thaw to ever freeze, as my granddad liked to say."

"What's that mean?"

"I think it means the past doesn't stay in the past. That it comes back around, eventually."

"And you think it's come back around?"

"I don't know. I'm not even sure what that would look like." He gave his glass a slow half-turn. "When Holly Burke was killed," he said, "I was just a young deputy about as green as I could be. And I believed then that the sheriff, and the rest of us, that we all did the best we could with what we had, and what we had was not much. Now, as sheriff myself, knowing the things I didn't know then, well. I wonder."

"What do you know now?" she said, and he looked up from his glass. The young woman just sitting there, awaiting his answer.

"The truth is I don't know what I know," he said. "But certain . . . information has come to light, with regards to that case, the Holly Burke case. And I'm sitting here now because I think there might be a connection."

"A connection?"

"Yes, ma'am. Between what happened to her and what happened to you, back then."

She watched him, and he could see in her eyes that he wasn't telling her anything she hadn't already considered—maybe even before Audrey Sutter tracked her down.

"Have you spoken to Danny Young?" she said. "I mean recently?"

"No, ma'am. I wish I could. But he's gone missing."

"Missing?"

"Yes, ma'am. Part of me was hoping maybe you'd heard from him."

"Me?" She gave a small huff. "I haven't heard from him in ten years."

"Yes, ma'am. It wasn't much of a hope."

She watched him, and he held her eyes.

"You don't think he killed Holly Burke?" she said.

"No, ma'am, I don't. I don't think I ever did."

"You must be about the only one then. You and your old boss."

"Did you believe it?"

She didn't answer, but she didn't look away either—and at the same time she did; her eyes were on him because he was in front of them, that was all. Then she looked down.

"I didn't know what I believed anymore, Sheriff."

He waited. Turning the glass in his hands. She did not wipe at her eyes and no tears came. The TV played on in the other room. He resisted the impulse to check his watch.

Katie Goss shook her head. "You've got nothing on him," she said, still looking down. Then she looked up and her eyes were focused again.

"Ma'am?"

"You've got nothing on him for Holly Burke."

He watched her, and he knew who she meant.

"No, ma'am, I don't. Not without Danny Young I don't."

"So you'll take him any way you can get him."

"Yes, ma'am. That's right."

She nodded, watching him. Then she shook her head again. "A little late, though, isn't it, Sheriff? Ten years. Why would anyone wait that long to come forward?"

"For good reasons. Because he'd threatened her. Because she was young. Because she didn't think anyone would believe her. Because she wanted to get on with her life."

"And suddenly she decides she doesn't care about any of those things?" said Katie Goss. "Suddenly she doesn't want to protect that life anymore? And if they wouldn't believe her then, what would make her think they'd believe her now, ten years after the fact—the alleged fact?"

"Because, for one thing," he said, "she'd have the full support of the law enforcement apparatus, including the sheriff's department and the county attorney. And for another thing, she wouldn't be the only one."

Katie Goss was silent. Watching him. The cartoon voices, the sound effects playing on in the other room.

"What's that supposed to mean?" she said.

He opened his hands and clasped them together again. "It means, do I think in ten, fifteen, however many years, you were the only one? That it was just your bad luck and nobody else's?" He shook his head. "No, ma'am. If what happened to you is true, and I believe it is, then you haven't been the only one. And you won't be the only one to come forward, once he is served and arrested. I can pretty much promise you that."

"But you don't know it for a fact—that they'll come forward."

"Not for a fact, no, ma'am."

She drank from her water and set it down again.

"Sheriff, I'm no idiot."

"No, ma'am."

"What I mean is, even if you got my statement, aren't you forgetting something?"

"It's possible."

"Statute of limitations," she said, and he looked at her more carefully, and understood her better. She hadn't forgotten. She hadn't put it all behind her.

"Yes, ma'am," he said. "The statute is nine years."

"Nine years. And there's no DNA, no kit, because I never reported. So why are we even having this conversation?"

"We wouldn't be, except that the man in question moved out of state more than eight years ago. Eight years and seven months, to be exact."

"So?"

"So that stops the clock on the statute of limitations. By the law, less than a year has passed since the night he pulled you over. The clock starts running again when I bring him back to Minnesota in handcuffs."

She sat staring at him. Processing this. She took a breath and let it out.

"It may be less than a year by law, Sheriff, but it's still ten years that I didn't say a word."

Halsey nodded. He looked around the apartment again. The little girl just out of view.

"I'll say one last thing, ma'am, and then I'll be on my way."

She waited.

"If a man commits a certain kind of crime," he said, "if he commits a certain kind of offense that is motivated by his sexual impulses, and he gets away with it, then he doesn't just quit. He doesn't just call it a day and become an upstanding, law-abiding citizen thereafter. That same impulse—"

Katie Goss raised a hand to stop him, then lowered it again. "I'm familiar with the argument, Sheriff. I just wish you'd made it to some other girl a long time ago."

"Yes, ma'am. So do I."

He collected his hat from the empty chair and began to get up.

"Which degree?" she said.

"Ma'am?"

"Which degree would he be charged with?"

He sat down again. "Well, that would depend on a number of things."

"I know what it would depend on. It wasn't just contact, Sheriff," she said, citing the distinction.

And to spare her saying the other word aloud, in her own kitchen—*penetration*—he said, "I understand that, Miss Goss. It would also depend on whether or not he was armed with a deadly weapon."

"He was. But he never pulled it. He never threatened me with it."

Halsey nodded. She'd read the codes carefully. "Then how did you know he was armed?" he said.

"Because he was wearing it on his belt."

"In plain sight."

"Yes."

Halsey opened up his hands again. "If that doesn't constitute fear of bodily harm I don't know what does. So there's three of the conditions for first-degree right there. And that's just the one statute. Any prosecutor worth their salt would also make the case for criminal sexual predatory conduct, which could tack on another twenty-five percent of jail time."

"If he goes to jail."

"If he goes to jail, yes, ma'am."

"Mommy?" They both looked over. The little girl had come around the pony wall and stood holding a plastic Appaloosa by its hind legs.

"Yes, baby?"

"I'm hungry."

"All right, we're gonna eat in just one minute."

"I believe that's my cue," said Halsey, getting to his feet. "Miss Goss, I've said what I came to say. I appreciate you hearing me out."

She rose too and walked him to the door. She opened the door and he stepped out and put his hat on and tipped it to her in farewell and turned to go.

"Sheriff," she said, and he turned back. The little girl had come to stand next to her again, to watch him go. To make sure he went, maybe.

"Yes, ma'am?"

Katie Goss held his eyes. "Aren't you supposed to give me your card? In case I want to get ahold of you?"

Halsey hesitated—and stepped back to her. "Yes, ma'am. I've got one right here."

58

THE WOOD HE'D brought her burned most of the night but in the morning the logs were down to their smoky bones, and she lay under the blankets watching them pulse in the drafts, the tossing thread of smoke, before sitting up finally and pushing the blankets off. She hurt just everywhere. It was hard to swallow and when she did she tasted the river.

Weak light of dawn in the windows. Her wet clothes, her boots, her father's jacket, lay on the floor like a scene from some frantic disrobing, which it was— her hands almost too numb to make the fire, to flick the flintwheel, her body spasming, and she should go upstairs and take a hot shower but she didn't want water on her skin, she wanted the fire and the blankets, and finally the flame took and the kindling crackled and the firewood burned bright and hot as she lay shaking under the blankets—she remembered all of that.

And she remembered Moran, fighting him on the river . . . and going under the ice. Drifting, pulled along in the current, the wobbling moon following overhead. The feel of the underside of the ice. The girls of the river. Caroline . . . But how had she gotten home?

Then she remembered the birds—two ducks, drake and hen, crying and beating their wings in panic and dragging tails of light behind them, pieces of light falling back to earth as the dark shapes climbed the sky.

But before that . . . Before that there'd been a different kind of light—not the light of the moon but a yellow light trembling like a thin cloth, like silk—and the light was stuck, the yellow light wasn't moving and she was going toward it, her fingers tracing the ice, but when she reached the yellow light her fingers fell through it, tearing it, and she followed her fingers, her arms, up into the light and she broke through it and suddenly she was above the ice again, sucking in the air and watching the two ducks rise into the sky.

She was in a kind of pool, in the woods, and the yellow light came from a single streetlamp beyond the water, and there was a straight, smooth edge that lay across the water. Then, over her own sounds, her splashing and gasping, she heard the hissing sound of the water spilling over the straight edge—it was a dam, but not the one she knew, not the one she'd fished at with her father—and she knew by that sound that she must swim or else be carried over the dam herself: over it and down into churning water, into the undertow, and from there under the ice again.

And so she swam. In the wet heavy jacket and the boots like concrete she swam for the bank, splashing and kicking, until her fingers clawed at silt and her knees banged against stones and she was climbing up out of the water and heaving herself ashore like a great fish, retching river water from her guts, from her lungs, so much water! And she lay there inhaling the smell of frozen mud, the smell of the woods and even the animals in the woods . . . *But get up, get up now Audrey or freeze* . . . and she'd gotten slowly to her feet, and it was then the other light came, the bright twin beams that could only be headlights, and she thought, first, her heart failing: *Moran.* Moran had come to see if she'd washed up here.

But it was two headlights, and Moran only had the one.

She raised a hand, but the lights were backing away—they swung away and the car was turning around. It showed her its taillights and off it went down the unplowed road. It was no car she knew and it was leaving her. She tried to call out but her throat was frozen, or raw from retching, and the sound that came out was not even human. What had the driver seen? What kind of drowned, white-faced thing had come up out of the water before him in this remote place, in this yellow gloom? She hung her head to look at herself, and ropes of hair swayed and clicked like beads against her face.

When she looked up again the taillights were still there. The car had stopped. A white fog chugging from its tailpipe. Then: reverse lights. The car backing, returning! Brake lights. A door swinging open and a woman shuffling toward her in winter boots—Oh my God, are you all right? Not a woman but a girl, sixteen maybe, and a boy coming up behind her at his own pace, wary, not yet convinced that this thing before him wasn't what he'd first thought: a dead girl or her ghost, risen from the water.

The other girl turning now to the boy and saying, Should we call 911?

No, Audrey answered, coughing. I'm all right.

Into the car with her then, into the back seat, but not before the boy spread the blanket out to keep her from soaking the fabric. Audrey pulling the blanket up around her shoulders, thick woolen emergency blanket that still held their warmth, their smells in its dusty fibers—deodorant and perfume, and deeper scents she didn't want to know about.

What happened to you? The girl hanging over the front seat. Her bright face, her big eyes. The car jostling and slurring down the road through the trees. Eric, turn up the heat!

Fell in, Audrey said.

Fell in? What were you . . . ? Where's your— Did someone push you in?

No. I'm all right.

You are not all right. You're coming home with us. What's your name?

The hell she is, said the boy, and the girl turned to glare at him. Hannah, he said. Your *dad* . . . ?

What about him?

I suppose we'll just tell him we just happened to be at the spillway?

The spillway! thought Audrey. The famous spillway. She hadn't recognized it. She'd never come here herself except the one time, with Jenny White, their hearts beating with what they might see, then seeing nothing: water; a spillway . . . then the sun going down, nothing to eat or drink, no phones, a new kind of scared as they began the long bike ride home, and the sheriff himself pulling up alongside them, *Audrey, Jenny—thank God. I've got the whole department out looking for you, are you all right—are you girls all right?*

Home, said Audrey, and the girl in the front seat said, What?

We could drop her at the hospital, said the boy. His eyes were in the rearview and it wasn't just fear Audrey saw; it was anger. She had interrupted. She had stopped him from getting something he'd wanted very badly and which he'd very nearly had and now might never have, not with this girl, not with Hannah, with her pretty face, with her nice full lips.

Home, said Audrey. Please . . . just take me home.

AND NEXT SHE knew she was lighting the fire. She was naked and shaking under the blankets and she was home.

Now, sitting on the sofa, the blankets thrown off her, she looked at the purple cast in the dim morning light and felt again the unseen blow—the surprise of a swing thrown so wildly finding its target so cleanly, so cracklingly—then turned on the lamp and looked more closely, but there was no blood that she could see. Of course not. All that time in the river, under the ice.

The hardwood floor was cold on the soles of her feet and the air was cold on her skin but still she sat there, the curtains wide-open for all to see, and let them see, let them knock themselves out seeing, until at last she tugged one blanket free from the others and shawled it around herself.

Her father's things lay on the coffee table once again: the Zippo lighter, the aviators, the watch, the old .38 revolver. She did not remember going to the closet for the gun and yet there it sat, the green ammo box beside it.

She listened for a moment, then picked up the watch and held it to her ear. Nothing. She looked at the face. A bubble of water lay under the crystal, rolling as she tilted the watchface. Like the little toy her granddad gave her where you tried to get all the BBs to sit in their holes. The bubble in her father's watch enlarged the hour markers below like a lens and it rolled through all three hands where they'd stopped, fifteen minutes and forty-two seconds past ten o'clock.

Was he still there? All night on the river. Frozen. Dead.

She picked up the remote and aimed it at the TV and waited to see if the service was still working; the bill had not been paid in over a month and yet somehow the service kept going—and it was going still. But the early news programs were all about the weather, the cold last day of February, the endless winter—no one had found an Iowa sheriff frozen on the river, dead from exposure, or a blow to the head, or a combination of the two. No dead Iowa sheriff, period.

She sat thinking about that. She thought about Sheriff Halsey, and she thought about Tuck Trevor, the lawyer. *Self-defense, Audrey, obviously.*

But where was the proof? Who but her could say he didn't go out there to save her?

Indeed, Miss Sutter . . . a man goes out onto ice he knows is too thin—a man sworn to serve and protect, no less, a sheriff—goes out there risking his own life . . . Why would he do such a thing except *to save you?*

She looked at the cast again, exhibit A, and she thought about the hospital, Dr. Breece. It was too soon; six weeks, he'd said. But the cast was wet, the padding under the plaster was soaked and it would have to come off—wouldn't it? There were tools in her father's garage: handsaws and hacksaws and power saws she'd watched him use and that she herself had used, with him nearby, always nearby. But then she saw the slip, and the wound that would send her to the hospital anyway, driving her bleeding self to the emergency room and—

Her heart dropped into coldness once again.

It was the car. The Ford. She'd left it in the park. They would find it there with the sheriff's cruiser. With the sheriff's body.

She looked at the coffee table again—lighter, sunglasses, gun, watch, but no keys.

Then how did you get in the house?

Her mind flew back to the river: She'd parked the car, gotten out to stand by the pines . . . and Moran had come. He'd shown her the cuffs and she'd gotten ready to claw him with the keys, which she held in her good fist, in the jacket pocket.

Hot now, her heart beating, she stood and went to her father's jacket and picked it up by its damp collar and shook it, and there was the sound she'd hoped for: a dull jingling in the left-hand pocket.

Ready to roll, Deputy?

59

"How you doing, Big Man?"

"All right Jeff how you doing?"

"My head is throbbin like a young robin's ass, you want to know the truth."

"What?"

"Never mind. You want to help me with the brake job on that Charger?"

"OK Jeff just let me punch in first."

In a dream he watched the car go up on the lift and somehow all the lugs came off and the tires were dropped bouncing to the concrete and he stacked them off to the side with the chalk marks on them so they could rotate them later . . . then he was at the computer adjusting inventory for the brake pads and then he was taking the pads out to Jeff who was already turning the first rotor and it was only 8:05 and he didn't know how he would get through the day, forgetting for a few minutes but always remembering and falling again, falling and remembering his dream, his brother so blue and cold and his mouth full of the dirty water that tasted of mud and fish.

At 8:15 he swept out the break room, emptied the trash, cleaned the sink, and then on his way back to the garage he saw something through the bay door windows that stopped him. Mr. Wabash was out there, standing in the lot talking to Sheriff Halsey. And his heart jumped, it just flew, because he was wrong! He thought he knew—all morning he thought he knew but he was wrong! Danny was OK and the sheriff had come to tell him so and Danny was home already, or he was in the SUV and you couldn't see him because of the sunlight on the glass . . . But then in the one or two heartbeats it took to have these thoughts he saw that it wasn't the sheriff's white Chevy Tahoe the two men stood before, it was a silver Ford Escape, and then he saw that it was not Sheriff Halsey at all but it was that deputy—the one from ten years ago, from Danny's letter. Who pulled Danny over that night. Deputy Moran. And he was not down in Iowa but he was up here, in Minnesota.

"Yo, Big Man," Jeff called, but Marky had already pushed through the door into the office, and without pausing he opened the outer door and stepped into the sunlight and there he stopped, standing back from the two men as they stood looking at the cruiser. Their backs were to him but it was quiet in the lot and he heard Mr. Wabash say, "What kind of person takes a potshot at a sheriff's vehicle?"

And heard the deputy say, "You tell me."

Mr. Wabash shaking his head, then looking at the deputy and saying, "You look like you had a pretty rough night all around, Ed."

"How's that?"

"Looks like somebody took a hammer to your ear there, for one thing."

The deputy touched his ear. "That was a goddam drunk. Sucker punched me."

Mr. Wabash shook his head again. "When it rains it pours, I guess."

"Can you do it?"

"Let me call up Tony, see if he has it."

"He does. I stopped and picked it up from him. Just need you to put it in."

Mr. Wabash nodded. "How come you don't do it down there?"

The deputy turned to look at him. "If you don't want to do it, Dave, just say so."

"Not sayin that, Ed. Heck, we can get her done if you don't mind waiting."

The deputy looked past Mr. Wabash and said, "I see your loaner's out."

"Yeah, Gordon Burke's got her."

The deputy nodded. "Well," he said, "how long, you think?"

"Twenty minutes, half hour tops."

"All right. I'll walk on down to Irene's and get a cup."

Mr. Wabash looked toward the garage then and saw Marky standing there. They both saw him.

"What's up, Marky?" said Mr. Wabash.

Keep your eyes on Mr. Wabash don't look at the deputy, don't look at his eyes looking at you.

"I can do it Mister Wabash."

"You can do what."

"I can fix the headlight."

Mr. Wabash kept looking at him. Then he turned to the deputy and said, "That work for you, Ed?"

"What?"

"Letting the boy fix the headlight."

"Can he do it?"

"Course he can do it. Do it in his sleep."

The deputy's ear stuck out big and purple and there was crusty blood on it. He was looking at Marky and he was a bad man, anyone could see it, it was in his eyes, but you have to look at him now, you have to look at him so he knows you can do it, so look at him and don't look away.

"Hell," said the deputy, "I don't care who does it, just so they hop to it."

"He'll hop to it," said Mr. Wabash. "Let me drop you at Irene's. I'm goin out on a call anyways."

Jeff pulled the deputy's Escape into the other bay and Marky lowered the bay door and the two of them stood looking at the shot-out headlight.

"What the hell's he doing up here anyway?" Jeff said. "Ain't his goddam jurisdiction no more."

"I don't know Jeff maybe it's because of that girl."

"What girl?"

"That girl Audrey who went into the river down there."

"Audrey?" said Jeff. "Oh, that girl. The sheriff's daughter. The old sheriff," he said, bending closer to the headlight and touching the broken glass with his fingertips. "Who do you reckon would shoot out that gomer's headlight up here?"

"I don't know Jeff."

Jeff stood straight again and then just stood there, staring at the headlight.

"There's a deer rifle in the back seat," he said. "Not locked up or anything." He looked at Marky. "Pretty goddam careless for a sheriff, wouldn't you say?"

"I better get started on this Jeff."

"All right. You need a hand?"

"No thanks Jeff."

"All right. You holler if you do."

"OK Jeff thanks."

60

HER HEART BEAT, it pumped, urging her to go faster, get moving, but her body did not want to do it—begging her to stop this, get out of these clothes, go back to the sofa, go to your bed, fill a tub with hot water and lie in it until you sleep and when you wake it will all be just a dream, I promise you . . . and all the while her head, or the voices in her head, told her what a bad idea it was—the scene of the crime. The biggest mistake you could make.

But which crime? Whose crime? Self-defense, all right, but how do you prove it? If he's alive he denies it and if he's dead there's no other witness but you. Just get the damn car, Audrey. The car is yours so just go get it and you can think about the rest later . . . and in this manner she got dressed—old clothes, old winter jacket and old winter boots she'd last worn when she was in high school—and she got herself out the door, and slowly down the porchsteps, slowly down the drive and slowly along the sidewalk, all the way to the corner where the cul-de-sac began and there she stopped and shut her eyes, the world so bright even with the sunglasses, and drew the cold air into her lungs.

Not too late to call the cab guy. If you had a phone. Her father's was still on the front seat of the car. Or it wasn't.

The only thing was to keep moving, just take it one block, one street at a time, and already she felt a little better, movement itself working the pain from her body, the morning traffic such as it was rushing by and no one paying any attention to a young woman just walking along normally, just going from here to there, and she'd gone four blocks and was well into her fifth when the cruiser pulled up alongside her.

She kept walking. She would not look over. Her heart banging. She took hold of the .38 in her jacket pocket and kept walking. The SUV crawling along, matching her speed and she would not look, until finally she did. Nothing to see but her own reflection in the passenger window, the aviators on her face, and below that, on the door, the Minnesota sheriff's emblem.

Not Moran, at least. Not that bug-eyed goon, back from the dead.

She let go the gun and took her hand from her pocket as the passenger window slid down. Sheriff Halsey behind the wheel, watching her from behind his own aviators. Watching and saying nothing.

She stopped, and he stopped, and she walked up to the open window. No one honked. Traffic flowing calmly around him.

"Where you headed?" he said.

"Just walking." Her voice sounded strange. Her throat still raw. "To the market."

"You're gonna freeze before you get there. You hurt yourself?"

"No, sir. I'm all right."

He watched her. "Hop in," he said. "I'll give you a lift."

"That's OK."

"Get on in here."

She opened the door and got in. The window rose. She drew the seatbelt and, latching it, felt the shape of the gun in her pocket. Halsey signaled and pulled into traffic and got the cruiser up to speed.

"I was on my way to see you when I saw you," he said.

She sat with her hands in her lap, her fingers laced. Watching the road.

"I imagine you're curious to know why," he said.

"Social visit?"

"Not hardly. I know what you've been up to."

She did not look over at him. The world she saw through the windshield was nothing she recognized. Buildings and cars and snow.

"I haven't been up to anything, Sheriff."

"Yes, you have. You've been up to Rochester."

Now she looked at him. "Rochester—?"

He gave her a look. "She told me herself you were there."

Her mind doubled back—found an entire new branch of thinking and went stumbling down it.

"Katie Goss—?" she said.

"Didn't I ask you to stay out of matters that don't concern you? Matters that are matters of law enforcement?"

She unlaced her fingers to scratch at the skin under the cast—damp and cold under there. "Did she call you?" she said.

"No, she didn't call me. I went up there myself."

"Why?"

"What?"

"Why did you go up there if she didn't call you?"

Halsey looked at her. "What part of mind your own business did you not understand?" He looked away again and she watched him, his face in profile. He drove one-handed, checking his mirrors, studying the other cars. Watchful. His sheriff's hat lay in the space between them.

"Let me ask you something," he said.

"All right."

"When you came to see me, why didn't you tell me about Danny Young going out to talk to Gordon Burke? Why didn't you tell me about that piece of cloth?"

Audrey was silent, filling in the blanks: Katie Goss had told him about Danny Young and Gordon Burke. About the piece of cloth.

What else had she told him?

"Did you hear me?" said the sheriff.

"Yes, sir," she said. "I guess I figured you needed to hear it from Danny himself."

Halsey watched her. He seemed to be thinking on that—seemed about to say something. But then he turned back to the road and drove on in silence.

Audrey watching the drab winter buildings, the black trees drifting by.

"Are you going to arrest him?" she said.

"Arrest who?"

"Moran."

"Sheriff Moran?" He glanced over. "I think you know it doesn't work like that."

It took her a moment. "Because he's out of state."

"Not that we're having this conversation. Again, I would ask you, as a personal favor, let's say, since actual authority doesn't seem to—"

"But Sheriff," she said. "What if he wasn't out of state?"

The sheriff glaring at her now. Squeezing the wheel in his big hand. "Meaning?"

"Meaning," she began, and hesitated, her mind dividing once again along two separate paths . . . because once you say it you can't go back, but if you don't say it now and he's dead then they'll say why did you wait to say it . . . but if he's not dead he'll deny everything and—

"Audrey," said the sheriff, startling her.

"I think he might be here in town, Sheriff. Right now."

"And why would you think that?"

"Because I saw him."

"You saw him."

"Yes, sir."

"You saw him this morning?"

"No, sir, last night."

"You saw Sheriff Moran last night, here in town."

"Yes, sir."

"And where was this?"

"In the park. Henry Sibley Park."

He didn't ask her what she was doing in the park at night. He was putting it together for himself. He looked at her again—looking this time for some sign of trouble, of harm.

"What makes you think Sheriff Moran is still in town this morning when you saw him last night in the park?" he said, and she stared at him. The bright morning sky beyond him. Her heart drumming in her chest and in the bones of her forearm under the cast.

"Sheriff," she said. "I think it might be better if I showed you."

61

THE DEPUTY RETURNED at 8:45 and he walked into the office and he looked through the glass door into the garage and then he walked right in—walking past Jeff under the Dodge and coming up to the second bay and bending to look at Marky where he stood hunched under the chassis of the Ford Escape.

"What in the hell are you doing?"

Marky looked at him. "I'm working on your vehicle Deputy."

"I bring this in for a busted headlight and you put it up on a lift?"

"Yes sir you got a leaky oil pan and I put it up in the air to show you that's all."

"What? Don't understand a word you're saying. Where's Wabash?"

"Leaky oil pan," Marky said again.

"Leaky what?"

Marky pointed, and the deputy, muttering, removed his hat and ducked under the chassis to look and Marky stepped away to give him room. The oil was dripping steadily into a pan on the floor, plink, plink, plink.

"What is that?" said the deputy. "Is that the oil pan? This car isn't old enough to have a bad gasket."

"You threw a bolt Deputy." Marky had come out from under the SUV and was standing beside it.

"I what?"

Marky was looking out the bay door windows.

"Hey—" said the deputy, and Marky turned back to him, there under the SUV. Then he looked out the windows again.

"Son," said the deputy, "I haven't got time for this shit. Where is that other one, your little buddy?"

Marky stood beside the lift and when he turned back to the deputy once again he could see the meanness in him, meaner with every second that you don't answer him, every second you stand here looking at him under the cruiser. And then he saw the moment when the deputy saw that Marky was standing so close to the lift release lever, and he saw more than meanness come into the deputy's eyes, and it was like the deputy was seeing him for the first time, and for a long while it was just the two of them staring at each other. But then someone else went, "Whoa whoa whoa!" and it was Jeff coming out of nowhere and bending for a look at the deputy and saying, "Officer, you can't be under that vehicle like that," and then to Marky, "Marky, what the hell? What's this vehicle doing up on this lift?" and the two of them turning to look at the deputy again, who was stepping out from under the SUV at last, moving calmly. Putting his hat back on his head.

"Marky," said Jeff, "what did you put the sheriff's car up on the lift for?" But Marky was watching the deputy, the deputy watching him.

"Leaky oil pan," the deputy said.

"Leaky oil pan?" said Jeff.

"There's a bolt missing Jeff," Marky said, and Jeff looked at him, then stooped under the chassis for a look. He looked for a while and then he came out again.

"There's a bolt missing, Sheriff," Jeff said. "You must of thrown it."

"Yeah, I got that. Can you replace it?"

"Pretty standard bolt, Sheriff. We should be able to scare one up."

"Well, how about you do that, hey? How about you scare one up and right quick?"

"Absolutely, Sheriff, we're on it. And I'm sorry about this, Sheriff. I take full responsibility. When it's just the two of us here, then I'm in charge and I didn't see what was going on. It ain't his fault, Sheriff. He doesn't know any better."

The deputy looked at Jeff and said, "Relax, Goss. I'm not gonna tell your boss. Just get my goddam vehicle down and get me on my way." He looked from one of them to the other. "Christ. You boys. You boys and your bullshit. We should've locked up the lot of you ten years ago and thrown away the key." He eyed them a moment longer, then he walked past them and pushed back through the glass door into the office.

Jeff ran both his hands through his hair and held on to the back of his neck, his elbows up in the air, saying nothing.

"I'll go find a bolt now Jeff."

Jeff shook his head, and from between the wings of his arms he said, "Yeah, OK, Marky. You do that. And maybe Wabash won't fire both our asses."

62

SHE RODE IN the passenger seat and it was like she was the deputy again, except that the sheriff at the wheel was not her sheriff, and the cab did not smell of his cigarettes. And although she was not this sheriff's prisoner, not under arrest, the feeling was closer to that than anything else. A bright and sunny day and the blackbirds were hopping in the bare branches and a man in black leggings and big winter gloves was jogging through the park and he was not under arrest and his life would not be spent in jail, and this is how it would feel if you were the criminal and you were caught and the sheriff was taking you in and it was all over—your freedom, your life. Suddenly and forever done.

Moran's cruiser was not there, and neither was the Ford—no sign of either car, but the sheriff knew the place and he pulled over short of where the cars had been and put his cruiser in park. He cut the engine and sat looking out toward the wide, frozen river, and you could see it from here in the gap between the pines: the small dark hole in the ice where she'd fallen through.

"You stay put," he said and got out, hatless, and shut the door behind him. She watched him walk up the road with his eyes on the pavement. He looked at the place where Moran's cruiser had sat, then he got down into a squat, then stood again and crossed the road toward the river. He stepped through the pines wide of where she and Moran had walked and he stopped at the bank and stood looking out at the ice. He looked again at the snow at his feet, then squatted again and looked more closely. After a while he stood and came back across the road.

The cruiser rocked with his weight and the door whumped shut and there was the smell of the pines and the snow on him. He looked at her and said, "Are you sure you're OK? There's blood in the snow."

"It's his," she said, and raised the cast to remind him.

He looked at the cast. Then he turned and looked at the river again. Drumming the wheel with his fingertips.

"It's gotta be a quarter mile from here to that spillway," he said.

He turned to look at her, and she held his eyes. Either he believed her or he didn't. She saw the ducks again, rising into the sky. She'd frightened them by coming up alive, and if she hadn't been alive, if she hadn't been able to swim, she'd have gone over the spillway maybe and continued on, under the ice again, all the way to the concrete bridge where Holly Burke had come to rest, and from there all the way down to Iowa and the other bridge where Caroline had gone under . . . all way to the Mississippi, all the way to the ocean.

"—and you didn't get their last names?" the sheriff was saying. "Either one of them?"

It took her a moment. "No, sir, it never occurred to me. Hannah and Eric, that's all I know."

"And none of you thought to call 911."

"I asked them not to. I asked them to take me home. They were just kids."

"And why'd you do that? Why'd you ask them not to call 911?"

"Because a cop just tried to kill me."

Halsey stared at her.

"And because I thought I'd killed him," she said.

"You thought you'd killed him."

"Yes, sir. He didn't look too great, last time I saw him."

The sheriff turned to look at the ice again. As if watching the scene play out before him. "Why wouldn't he just let you drown, or freeze to death on your own? Why would he go on out there?" He turned back to her.

"I guess he wanted to make sure."

"You guess. Based on what?"

She was out on the ice again, in that hole—Moran crawling on his belly, reaching for her, grabbing at her, grunting, trying to dislodge her from the ice.

"He wasn't trying to help me, Sheriff."

He sat watching her. Her eyes. Then he turned back to the river once again. Drumming the wheel again.

"Where do you think my car went?" she said.

"Oh, I expect it got towed," he said. "There's a mess of tracks out here."

She watched him, the back of his head. The furrow of his sweatband in the thick hair. Then he stopped drumming the wheel and took his phone from the breast pocket of his jacket, worked it with his thumb and put it to his ear.

"Gloria, it's me. Two—no, three things. Want you to have Deputy Moser stop whatever he's doing and come out to Henry Sibley Park and find me. I'm about halfway in here, by the river. Then I want you to check with impound and see if they've got a white Ford Taurus, two thousand—" He glanced at Audrey and she said, "Five," and he repeated it. "But first I want you to connect me to the Pawnee County Sheriff's Department. Yes, in Iowa. Yes, I can hold."

He turned to Audrey. "If he's there, I have no idea what I'm supposed to say to the man." He looked away again and said, "Thanks, Gloria." And waited. Another few seconds passed before he said, "Good morning, Deputy Short," and identified himself, and asked if the sheriff was in. He listened and said, "Not all morning? All right. Well, yes, I'd call it urgent. Why don't you have him call me as soon as he can." He confirmed the number and hung up and sat holding the phone.

"I have his card," Audrey said.

"His what?"

"His card. At home. With his numbers."

Halsey nodded. "We'll just wait here a minute for the deputy." He looked toward the river again. His fingers were quiet on the wheel.

"Can I ask you something, Sheriff?"

"You can."

"Why didn't you tell me about it? When I came to see you before."

He turned to her. "Tell you about what?"

"About Moran and Katie Goss."

He stared at her. "What could I tell you?"

"You could've told me my dad went up to see her. To ask her about it."

"I could've. But you wouldn't have known any more than your dad knew. Or I knew."

"So you knew about it—back then. About him going to see Katie Goss."

"I knew about it. We all knew. Moran knew."

"Moran knew?"

"Your dad asked him about that girl to his face. Confronted him with it."

Audrey's heart was rolling in her chest, rolling and pounding. "Were you there?"

"No, I was not. He did it in private. Then he told me about it later, also in private."

"What did he say?"

"To me?"

"Yes."

Halsey looked away, up the road. He shook his head, and she didn't think he would tell her. But then he did. "He said he didn't want to tell me what he was about to tell me, but he didn't know what else to do. Said he needed my opinion on the matter. Then he told me what he'd asked Moran: Did he talk that girl into . . . whatever he called it so as to make it seem less than it was. So as to get an admission."

Audrey waited. Watching him.

"That didn't work, obviously," Halsey said. "Moran said it was just a couple of high school girls telling stories to excite themselves. Said he'd swear to that in a court of law."

The sheriff turned to her again.

"His word against hers," she said.

"Yes, ma'am."

They sat watching each other, a long silence.

"And what did you say?" Audrey said finally.

"Told him what he already knew. Here was a girl, a young woman, who didn't report it when it happened, allegedly, and who did not care to report it now. And here was his own deputy who flat-out denied it. Wasn't much of a choice to make."

"So he let him go."

"That's not how I would put it. Your dad made it, let's say, difficult for Moran to stick around. And the man wasn't so stupid or stubborn not to take the hint."

She saw Moran again on the ice, on his elbows, the wounded-dog look in his eyes, a creature holding on to old pains, old betrayals.

"Why didn't he—" she began. "Why didn't my dad . . ."

Halsey waited. "Why didn't he what?"

"Why didn't he say something to the sheriff down in Iowa?"

"Same reason I didn't," said Halsey, and as he said it, the way he said it, the look in his eyes, she understood.

"Because he was a deputy," she said. "Because he was one of you."

Halsey said nothing. He seemed to study the back of his hand where it gripped the wheel, turning the rubbery padding in his fist. Audrey watching him, and with such intensity that his profile began to change, reshaping itself bone by bone—brow, nose, chin—and it was her father's face pushing through, taking over Halsey's face. She could smell him now too, the smoke of his last cigarette, the fuel of his Zippo lighter. But the voice, when he spoke again, was not his, and it all vanished.

"A story," said Sheriff Halsey. "No witness, no corroboration whatsoever. Do you ruin a man's life based on that? A man who's had your back and whose back you've had? What if the tables were turned? What if it was you the story was about?" He turned to her. "What if it was your dad?"

Audrey looked away from his eyes. She looked at her fingers, twined and twisting in her lap.

"But Sheriff," she said, and faltered again.

"Go on," he said.

"Didn't you have a feeling, though? In your gut? Didn't you know?"

His eyes were on her but she could not look up again. So quiet in that cab she could hear her fingers twisting together. Could hear his breaths, her breaths. Her heartbeat. The wind in the boughs of the pines. The shifting, crackling ice; the water scouring away at its underside. And she heard the sound of car tires on the packed snow—another cruiser pulling up behind them—and when she turned to look she saw a young-looking deputy stepping out of the cruiser and coming toward them. Halsey stepping out to meet him, throwing his door shut behind him. Audrey watching the two men through the driver's-side window as Halsey pointed and the deputy nodded. *Secure it*, Halsey's gestures said, *set up barriers, don't walk in the snow.* The place was once again a crime scene.

TEN MINUTES LATER, as they were coming into town, the radio crackled and a woman's voice said, "Sheriff, I got an Iowa sheriff's department vehicle at Wabash Auto on Main Street."

The sheriff picked up the handpiece and said, "Is anyone with it?"

"No, sir, not exactly. It's up on a lift in the garage."

"Up on a lift?"

"Yes, sir. Otherwise I wouldn't have even seen it in the windows."

"You didn't pull in there, did you?"

"No, sir."

"Then how do you know it's an Iowa sheriff's department vehicle?"

"Well, sir, it isn't one of ours, and I saw an Iowa sheriff standing in the office."

"Sheriff Moran?"

"Yes, sir."

"Did he see you?"

"He might of, as I was going by."

"Where are you now?"

"Across the street at the 7-Eleven."

"And he's still there."

"Well, his cruiser's still up on the lift."

"All right, you stay put. I'm not five minutes away."

"Yes, sir, Sheriff."

"And Deputy Lowell."

"Yes, Sheriff."

"If that cruiser comes down and he drives off before I get there, I want you to follow and nothing more—no lights, no nothing. Do you copy?"

"Yes, sir, Sheriff, copy that."

63

JEFF TIGHTENED THE new bolt—he tightened all the bolts—and he wiped down the pan and stood watching for drips, then he came out from under the chassis and lowered the cruiser on the old lift, watching it all the way, until it was on its wheels again. He opened the driver's door to pop the hood and then he went to the front and raised the hood, and the whole time he didn't say a word to Marky or even look at him where he stood off to the side. Then they both heard Mr. Wabash returning with the wrecker and they watched through the glass as he came into the office and began talking with the deputy.

"Marky. *Marky*," said Jeff.

"What Jeff."

"I said bring me a quart of the 5W-30."

"It's synthetic Jeff."

Jeff looked at the engine. "Are you sure?"

"I'm sure Jeff." You could feel it in your fingers and you could see the colors of it and you could smell the difference too.

"All right," Jeff said, "just bring the quart and top this off, all right?"

Marky turned to get the quart and when he turned back, Jeff was walking toward the office and Marky was falling again—not because of what Jeff would say to Mr. Wabash but because Danny was gone. He was gone and nothing mattered now and nothing ever would. But Jeff stopped short and moved to the side of the glass door and stood looking at the red mechanic's rag in his hands.

Marky poured a quarter of the quart into the funnel and waited for the oil to settle.

Jeff returned to the SUV, wiping his hands. "They're just shootin the shit in there. We aren't in any trouble. By some fucking miracle. What were you thinking, Marky? Why didn't you ask me first?"

Marky pulled the dipstick and wiped it clean and fed it back into the spout and pulled it out again and the level was good. He didn't know what to say without saying everything and he couldn't say everything, not to Jeff, so he said nothing. He replaced the oil-fill cap and twisted it tight, then he brought down the hood and wiped his fingerprints from the silver paint.

Jeff shook his head. "Well, open up the bay door and I'll back her out."

He backed the car out and parked it so it faced the street, ready to go, then he wiped down the steering wheel with a fresh rag, pulled the paper mat from the floor and walked back to Marky, mashing the paper into a ball, and the two of them were still standing there when the deputy stepped out of the office and walked toward his cruiser, not looking at them, not even looking their way but going straight to the cruiser and opening the door and climbing in and shutting the door. And they were still standing there watching when a second SUV pulled into the lot and it was the sheriff's cruiser—Sheriff Halsey's white Chevy Tahoe—the sheriff pulling in nose-to-nose with the Escape and putting his cruiser in park. And there was someone else in the cab and after a second Marky recognized her, it was the girl who'd come to see him and wanted to talk to him about Danny and who'd gone into the river down in Iowa and her name was Audrey.

"Hang tight, Big Man," Jeff said. He had him by the arm, to keep him from taking another step toward the SUVs. He pulled him back one step. "Just hang tight."

Sheriff Halsey sat with one hand on the wheel, staring straight ahead, and the deputy sat like a mirror image in his cruiser, staring back. At last Halsey killed his engine and the deputy, taking his time about it, killed his.

HALSEY AND THE girl did not speak, did not look at each other. They sat watching Moran, who sat back in his seat with his hands out of view and with the look of a man who could not guess what might happen next but would sit there patiently, contentedly even, until it did. Finally without looking at her, Halsey said, "You shouldn't be here. I should've dropped you at the station."

"You might've missed him if you did."

"I know it." He tapped the wheel. "I want you to do me a favor, though—all right?"

"All right."

"If this goes bad, if you see any sign of a gun from anyone, I want you to get your head down out of view. All right?"

"All right."

"For now you just sit here and don't do a thing. Just sit here. All right?"

"All right, Sheriff."

He got out then and put his hat on and walked toward the other cruiser. The two mechanics, Marky Young and Jeff Goss, were standing in the open bay door and he didn't like that one bit. He didn't expect Wabash to stay inside either and he didn't; he stepped out from the office and stood watching from there in his black cop's jacket.

Halsey came up to Moran's door with his hands at his sides and he saw his own reflection in the glass, his face layered weirdly over Moran's before the glass slid down and it was just Moran's face, watching him with that look of curiosity, amusement almost.

"Sheriff," said Halsey.

"Sheriff," said Moran. He looked away and nodded toward the Tahoe and said, "I didn't know better, Wayne, I'd say you've executed some kind of a preemptive maneuver here." His hands were in his lap, his fingers laced, his thumbs slowly circling, not touching, round and round, like opposed magnets.

"What are you doing here, Ed?"

"I came to have a headlight fixed."

"Drove all the way up here for that, did you?"

"No, Wayne. Drove up here because I've got an active investigation involving that girl I see sitting in your cruiser there. Some good citizen or other shot out my headlight for me and I thought I'd have Dave fix it while I was here. Nothing more to it than that."

"Some good citizen or other," said Halsey. "You don't know who?"

"I know who. He owns that rifle in the back seat you're eyeballing."

"You got his rifle but not him?"

"That's right. I figure this man has been through enough. I let him go. You want to arrest him you go ahead. I'll give you his rifle. You can look it up and track him down for yourself."

Halsey watched him. "How about we take one thing at a time here."

Moran looked away then, seeing something, and said, "And now here come your deputies."

The two cruisers had pulled in, parking where they could, Bobby and Vickie getting out of the cruisers and approaching. They did not come too close but positioned themselves behind and to either side of Halsey, no weapons drawn or even hands on their weapons but just standing by, following his lead, and he knew all this without seeing any of it directly.

"What's going on here, Wayne?" Moran said.

"Right now it's just a conversation, Ed."

"We could've had a conversation over the phone. But then I'd be down in Iowa and you couldn't exactly run the show down there, could you." He looked around the lot. He looked at the Tahoe again. "And it's a dandy show, Wayne, no doubt about it, but I have to ask—just what the fuck makes you think you can detain me for one second longer than I want to be detained?"

"Like I said, right now it's just a conversation. I thought you might like to have your say before it went any further. Just you and me."

"And if I don't want to have a conversation?"

"Then I'm going to put you in cuffs and take you to the station and book you."

"On what charge?"

"Assault, to begin with, and we'll go from there, depending on the full testimony of the involved parties."

"Parties," said Moran. "What parties?"

"What happened to your ear there, Ed?"

"Sucker punched by a drunk."

"A drunk."

"You heard me."

"It wasn't a girl in a cast?"

Moran turned to look at the Tahoe again and turned back. "If some little girl hit me with her cast don't you think your assault charge would be going the other way?"

"Not if she was fighting you off. Not if she was fighting you off while you were trying to drown her in the river. Which of course would be another kind of charge altogether."

"Is that what she told you?"

"That's her story."

"And you believe her."

"Let's say I've got reason to believe she has no reason to make up a story like that."

"I'll give you a reason."

"All right."

"The reason is she's got it in her little head that I had something to do with a case ten years old, a case her daddy couldn't solve and so now she's trying to solve it by believing some crazy story she hears. But because that story is crazy and she knows it, she figures she can make up a new one and get me arrested on that charge."

"Yeah," said Halsey. "I considered that version of things myself. But I don't think she's that crazy, Ed. And I don't think—" He stopped himself, remembering Jeff Goss at the last second. "I don't think the other one is crazy either."

"Other what?"

"The other girl who says you used the authority of your office to do something I won't even say right now."

Moran stared at him. "What girl said that?"

"Never mind her name. What matters is I've got two accounts from two different people, I've got a hole in the ice on the river, I've got bootprints coming and going, I've got blood in the snow and I've got that split-open ear on the side of your head. I guess you could say I'm beginning to see the makings of a case here, Ed. And that doesn't even include Danny Young."

Moran's expression did not change. "Danny Young."

"Danny Young who's gone missing but who wrote me a letter."

Moran said nothing. Staring at him. Then he threw up his hands and Halsey put his hand on his pistol grip, and his deputies drew their sidearms and held them two-handed and aimed at the ground. Moran looked at the roof of the cab and said, "The whole world has gone shitbird crazy on me, I swear to God."

"Ed," said Halsey.

"What."

"Do you want to tell me about last night? About the river?"

Moran shook his head. "Sure, Wayne, I'll tell you about last night. I'll tell you I had to go out on that ice to try to save that dumb-ass girl from drowning, risking my own goddam neck, and she clocks me with her goddam cast. I should've just let her drown, you want to know the truth. And now this."

"Why did you lie to me just now? About your ear?"

"I guess we'll have to chalk that one up to pride, Wayne. Didn't want you to think some little girl coldcocked me."

"What were you doing in the park in the first place, Ed? What were you even doing up here?"

"I told you, I've got an active investigation. I was actually looking for that girl so I could give her an update."

"You might've just called her."

"I might've, but I didn't, and last I checked there's no law against a law officer going to see his witness in person."

"Why'd she go out on the ice?"

"You'll have to ask her."

"I already did. She said to get away from you."

"She had no reason to get away from me."

"She thought she did."

"Nothing I can do about that, Wayne."

Halsey looked at him. Then he looked toward his Tahoe—the girl sitting there watching. The two mechanics in the garage bay watching. Wabash watching. The deputies with their weapons.

He turned back to Moran. "Why didn't you report it, Ed?" he said, and he saw the question land in the other man's eyes, the flinch that played out in some way Halsey couldn't even say, and he knew at once what Moran thought he was asking: *Ten years ago, Ed—if you pulled Danny Young over that night in that park, why didn't you report it?*

And why didn't you ever say so, once he became a person of interest?

And if the boy had brought it up himself, that day we watched the sheriff interviewing him—what would you have said then?

But that wasn't what Halsey was asking; this wasn't the time for those questions.

"Report what?" Moran said finally, and Halsey said, "Why didn't you report a girl falling through the ice, Ed? Or a girl drowning, for all you knew?" And then he watched as this question landed too, the few seconds Moran took to process it, before looking away and shaking his head again.

"I don't know, Wayne. I don't remember a whole lot after that cast on the side of my head. Except waking up on the ice half-froze to death—I remember that."

Halsey watched him. Then he said, "You want to come down to the station with me, Ed?"

Moran took a breath and let it out. "No, Wayne, I do not. What I want is for you to move your vehicle so I can be on my way already."

Halsey said nothing. He nodded, then he said, "In that case, Ed, I'm going to have to ask you to step out of this vehicle now, with your hands in the air."

Moran didn't move. "Don't be an idiot, Wayne. You got no probable cause."

"I believe I do." He drew his gun and held it one-handed at his side. Then with his free hand he lifted the latch and swung the door open. "Now show me your hands and get up out of the car for me, Ed."

Moran sat watching him. He looked again toward the Tahoe, the girl. He looked at the deputies. Then he put his hands in the air and stepped out of his cruiser.

"This won't stick, Wayne," he said, turning, lacing his hands behind his head.

"Spread your feet for me, Ed," Halsey said. Moran did so, and Halsey took the laced fingers in his grip and holstered his gun and relieved Moran of his. He reached back with the .45 and one of his deputies stepped forward to take it from him. He drew Moran's right wrist down and snapped on the cuff, then brought the left down and did the same, and when Moran was cuffed he turned him around and unbuckled his utility belt and handed that off to a deputy too.

"You won't be able to hold me," Moran said.

"We'll see," Halsey said. He asked Deputy Moser to get the rifle from the back seat and mind his fingerprints and the deputy did so, carrying the rifle by the barrel to his own cruiser and laying it with care on the back seat.

Moran looked once more at the Tahoe, and Halsey looked too. The girl sat there as before. She had not put her head down but instead had watched it all. Halsey held Moran just above the elbow and he made him stand there so he could see the girl. So the girl could see him. But the girl's eyes were not on Moran, they were on him.

"Do you know what you're doing here, Wayne?"

"I'm busting you, Ed."

"You are killing me, Wayne. Some little girl tells you a story and you arrest me like this, in public, for the whole world to see? Small town like this. You're killing me, Wayne. Just killing me."

He led Moran by the elbow toward Deputy Lowell's cruiser. "Edward Moran," Halsey said, "you might think about shutting that mouth of yours and waiting for your lawyer."

Throughout it all Moran had not looked once at the two young men standing in the bay of the garage, the mechanics, but he looked at them now—he looked at the two of them, and then he looked at Marky Young alone, and Marky Young did not look away. He kept his eyes on Moran's, and even after the lady deputy took Moran from Sheriff Halsey and made him get into the back of her cruiser, placing her hand on the top of his head, on his hair, and even after the cruiser door was shut Moran continued to stare at Marky through the glass, and Marky did not look away. And after they were all gone—Moran and Sheriff Halsey and his deputies and the girl Audrey Sutter—Marky and Jeff went out into the cold and helped Mr. Wabash hook up Moran's cruiser to the wrecker and they were standing in the cold yet when Mr. Wabash drove out of the lot, hauling the Escape behind him on his way to the sheriff's impound lot.

64

THE NURSE WHO called her name and took her into the examination room was a young woman with dark eyes and an accent that made you think of islands, of great flowered plants and a turquoise sea. She'd never seen the beautiful nurse before and she wondered if she'd ever seen such a face her whole life before going south to school. As if such a face could not survive up here in so much whiteness, the way a parrot, or any other colorful thing, could not.

The nurse took her temperature and blood pressure and wrote these things down and then said, "Come with me, baby," and left her in the care of the radiologist, himself a young man whom she'd never seen before either, and she realized then that she didn't recognize any of the staff on this floor, and that none recognized her, or gave any indication that they did—as if all of that, her long stay and her long walk on the last day to see her father behind the curtain, had happened in some other hospital, or some dream of a hospital. Which it hadn't, of course, and when she saw Dr. Breece again for the first time since that day, the doctor floating into the examination room with the beautiful nurse behind him, she had to swallow down her heart, but after that she was all right.

"How are you, Audrey?" He'd let his hair grow out just a little. He smelled as before of hand sanitizer and mint.

"I'm fine, thank you. How are you?"

"Never better." He looked at her, and she held his eyes. "Any trouble with the cast?" he said.

"Other than getting it wet, no."

He didn't ask how it happened, getting it wet, but instead simply took the cast in his hands as if taking it from her, as if relieving her of its care. Turning it this way and that and her heart skipping, not because she thought he knew how it had been used and was looking for signs of that day on the river—that violence, those details had not been in the news, and certainly not her name; Sheriff Halsey had kept his promise about that—but because she thought he knew she'd intentionally not covered the cast when she'd taken her shower the night before.

The doctor slipped two fingers between the padding and her forearm and slipped them out again and rubbed them with his thumb. He returned the cast to her and sat down to study the x-ray image on his computer screen, then checked her chart again, his lips pursed.

"Five weeks is cutting it close," he said. "But it was a clean break and the x-ray looks good. You're a good healer."

"Thanks," she said. The feeling of his fingers where he'd slipped them in under the cast remained in a distracting way.

He watched her. Then he said, "Well, you drove all the way up here. Shall we cut that sucker off?"

He uncapped a Sharpie and drew a line from one end of the cast to the other on both sides, top and underside, and the beautiful nurse handed him the cutter—it looked like one of the power tools from her father's garage, the ones she'd thought about using herself—and the doctor explained how the blade did not spin but oscillated and therefore could not cut her skin, and then he thumbed it on and the little machine filled the room with its furious noise. He dipped the blade into the line he'd drawn and the vibrations traveled through her bones up to her teeth. He followed the line precisely end to end before turning the cast, and when both lines were cut the nurse handed him a large instrument like a pair of pliers and he inserted the instrument into the underside seam he'd made and moved along the seam, parting it until the cast cracked open like a clamshell and he slipped the entire thing from her arm. The nurse handed him scissors and he ran them under the damp padding, snipping, until that fell away too and her arm lay naked and pink and strange. As if it were not the one she remembered but had grown inside the cast into some other kind of arm.

A rank, humid odor rose from it and she knew that the doctor and the beautiful nurse must smell it. The nurse, washing the arm with a warm cloth, said,

"How's that feel?" and Audrey looked into her dark eyes and smiled and nodded but could not answer.

The doctor took the arm in his hands again and felt along the bone with his fingers and thumbs.

"Does it still work?" he said, and she made a fist and opened it and rolled her wrist around until it popped deeply.

"Works jim-dandy. Thank you."

"You'll have to take it easy with that arm for another six weeks. No push-ups. No heavy lifting. No karate chops."

She looked at him.

"Joking," he said. He picked up the split purple shell and showed it to her. "Memento?"

She wanted with all her heart to never see it again, to watch him drop it into the trash, but she'd promised the county attorney she'd keep it; they would put it back together again for the trial, with duct tape maybe, so she could show the judge and jury.

And if you were not facing him at that moment, Miss Sutter, then how did you strike him?

Like so.

"Do you have a bag I can put it in?" she asked the doctor, and he handed the two pieces to the beautiful nurse.

And why did you strike the deputy, Miss Sutter?

Because he was trying to drown me.

Was he?

Yes.

And how did you know that, Miss Sutter? Miss Sutter . . . ?

The beautiful nurse was looking at her, holding the purple cast.

"Sorry?" said Audrey.

The nurse laughed and said in that voice of islands and waves, "I asked did you want that gift-wrapped too, baby?"

65

THE WEATHER HAD turned and the snow was dropping from the pines in heavy clumps, and when the sun hit the boughs you could smell the pine like you'd been sawing into it. By the middle of March the house was sold, and a week later it was empty and clean, and on that Saturday afternoon Gordon backed his van into the driveway and they loaded up the few remaining things she wanted to keep for herself—her own things and some of her father's, such as his sheriff's jacket and hat, his old rod and fly reel that had been his grandfather's, the supposedly antique bass bookends she'd given him, and also certain precious things of her mother's he'd kept for her—they loaded it all into the van and the car and then she stood on the porch for the last time, looking out over the cul-de-sac as her father had done so many mornings, smoking his first cigarette of the day. Finally she got into the sedan and backed out of the drive and waved good-bye to Mr. Larkin, who stood in his driveway watching them go and who was standing there still when they turned the corner and passed out of sight.

MELTWATER RAN ACROSS the roads in streams and hissed under the tires and you could put the window down and smell the earth and you knew the winter wasn't forever after all and the land would be green again, the river would flow again, and from the bridges you could see the slabs of ice jutting into the air, and if you pulled over and stood on the bank you could see the slabs moving and grinding against each other like icebergs, like ships, all in a tight puzzle-work of pieces and all of it moving together foot by foot downriver, cracking and popping and grinding as the river below swelled with the thaw and pushed and surged and would not be stopped.

He pulled into the lot and cut the engine and they both got out and stood in the sun, breathing the air.

"Ready?" she said, and he nodded.

"Ready."

The graves were in the old part of the cemetery with all the old graves, including the graves of her grandparents on her mother's side. Her father was from Illinois and had met her mother there, in college, and they'd come back here together so she could be close to her family. By the time Audrey was seven he was county sheriff and her mother, a high school counselor, was dying.

The snow over the plot had melted away into the dirt, and in a few weeks the caretakers would lay down the sod; that was part of the deal and she didn't have to worry about that.

She took off the aviators and put them away, then stood reading her parents' names on the stone, their dates. The inscription:

> *More than all the rain that ever fell*
> *Or ever will*
> *More than all the sun that ever shined*
> *Or ever will*

Does that about cover it? he'd asked, holding her hand. The old engraver man standing by.

Yes, Daddy. It's perfect.

Do you know how much she loved you?

Yes, Daddy.

Well, if you ever forget, there it is, right there.

I won't forget, Daddy.

She told them the house had sold and the bills were paid and she was going back to school in the fall. She told them not to worry about her, and she told them she loved them and that she knew they were with her, that they looked out for her, and lastly she told them that she was not afraid of it now. Any of it.

Then she turned and walked back to where he stood, his hands in his pockets, looking up into the big open sky, and she stopped before him and looked up too. Blue, cloudless sky as far as you could see. A single large bird—hawk, or eagle, maybe—riding the blue, way off in the distance.

Holly Burke, or her body, had been buried in the new part of the cemetery, on the far side of the oak trees. A modest stone of white marble, rough around its edges but glass-smooth on the face.

"Come up here with me," he said, and she did so, and they stood before the stone in silence.

Holly Catherine Burke
Beloved Daughter

A wind came to push at them head-on, and when he spoke the wind tried to carry his words off but she heard them clearly: "I know how people talked," he said. "But she was a good girl. She was a good person and she was not afraid of anything."

She waited for him to say more but he didn't. He lifted his face to the sun and shut his eyes. Her own eyes stung in the wind, and when she blinked, tears ran in cool tracks to her temples. There was so much she wanted to tell him it choked her heart. Finally, into that wind she said, "I told you that I thought I—that I thought I died, when Caroline and I went into the river. Remember?"

He nodded, face to the sun, eyes shut. "I remember."

"I mean, I know I didn't. Obviously. But if I had, it would've been all right. I wasn't scared and I wasn't sad to lose my life and I didn't feel alone. I wasn't alone. That's what I want to tell her mother. Her father. That's why I have to go down there, Mr. Burke. So I can tell them it's all right. That Caroline wasn't afraid and she wasn't alone and that she's all right, now. I can tell them that, can't I?"

He turned to her and opened his eyes. Watching her face. Her eyes.

"Yes. You can tell them that."

"And they'll believe me?"

He looked at the gravestone again. "I don't know, Audrey. I don't know if they will or not."

They stood there, the wind gusting at their clothes, and on this wind came the sound of the birds first, then the birds themselves—a pair of loons, directly overhead, their bellies flashing white against the blue, their calls like a wild hysteria for home, for all the feeding and nesting and mating of the lakes to the north.

"I know your mind is made up," Gordon said when the birds, and their cries, had passed on, "but that's an awful long drive to do alone."

"I'll be all right, Mr. Burke."

"I don't want you driving through that town down there again. I don't want you going anywhere near it."

"I won't."

"I'm serious here."

"I know. I promise."

They were silent again. Her heart was beating. He seemed ready to go, and if they went now, if they got in the van and drove back to his house, she would never say it, so before he could move she said it.

"There's something else I want to tell you. But I don't want you to think I'm crazy."

He looked at her again. "You're talking to a man who near about shot a sheriff—you know that, right?"

"Yes, sir," she said, and smiled, and he turned once more to the gravestone.

"I can't tell you how I know it," she said. "I mean, I can tell you how I think I know, but that wouldn't make it true."

"I'm listening."

"She had a good heart, Mr. Burke. Holly did. She had a strong heart, and that night—that night by the river, she *fought*. She fought really hard, Mr. Burke."

She watched his profile. His jaw trembled, then hardened against the trembling. He stared into the wind and didn't blink.

"How do you know?" he said. And turned to look at her.

"I've always known," she said. "Since the night Caroline and I went into the river. I just never—" And the breath went out of her, or went back into her lungs, as if blown back into her by the wind.

"Never what?" he said.

She turned her face from the wind.

"I never saw him," she said. "I never saw who she fought."

Gordon watching her. Saying nothing. Then he said, "Why couldn't you see?" and she turned to face him again.

"Because it was only girls, Mr. Burke. In the river. It's always been only girls."

They got out of the wind. They returned to the van and climbed in and shut the doors and then sat there listening. An eerie moaning, the van creaking like a boat. Gordon holding the keys in his hand, and his hand resting in his lap. Staring out at the bending trees, the old leaves shuddering on their stems. She said nothing, she waited, and at last he began.

"I have this dream, sometimes," he said. "Or I guess it's a nightmare, but anyway it's always the same. I'm in a car, but I'm in the back seat, and in the front seat there's a man driving and there's a girl, a young woman, and I can't see their faces but I know the young woman by her hair, and because I just know her—in the dream I know it's her, and I can see that the man is talking to her. I can see his breath. And I can see him turn and say something to her, and I try to see his face but I can't, it's like there's a blind spot there, like cloudy glass, or ice maybe, between the front seat and the back."

He reached up with his open hand and swiped vaguely at the air in front of him, as if at a fogged glass. Audrey watching his hand, the fogged glass.

"And I can't hear the man either, but I can see he's getting worked up. He's getting angry because she won't answer him, she won't talk to him, and I can see that she knows she has this one thing over him—she knows that the worst thing she can do to him, the thing that hurts him most, is to just ignore him. And I can feel how that feels to the man, I can feel how angry he is, and I tell her stop it, just talk to him, just talk to him until he calms down again. But she can't hear me because of that glass, or ice, and my heart is pounding, it's just pounding because I can feel how angry he's getting, the man. And this goes on for a while. I can see the trees going past, and I can see the moon shining on the river, and I know what's coming but I can't stop it. It's like I'm strapped down, or handcuffed, and before long the man reaches out to touch her and she just, kind of, jerks away from him, just flinches from his touch, and that's it. That's what does it."

Audrey sitting so still, hardly breathing. The wind pushing at the van.

"And I sit there and I watch him grab her by the hair and there's nothing I can do, just not a goddam thing, I have to sit there and watch this. And she fights. She fights him. He grabs at her and she swings at him and she even bites his hand, and I see him scream and jerk his hand away and that's when the door opens and out she goes. Just right out the door, and he stops the car. He stops and sits there, watching as she gets up, as she walks ahead of him in the headlights. And I watch him watching her and I know exactly what he feels. It's like I'm in the back seat but I'm in the front seat too. It's like I'm inside this man's heart and looking through his eyes and I know how he feels about her, I can feel what this man feels, for my own daughter. I know his rage, but I know that behind the rage is his . . . pride—that *she* would refuse *him*. That this little . . . that she would find *him* disgusting. And it's just . . . it's just . . ."

Audrey didn't look at him, and knew he wouldn't look at her. With his free hand he gripped the padded wheel and she heard the quiet crushing of it in his fist.

"And that's when I know," he said. "That's when I know what comes next, and I tell myself wake up now, wake up, you son of a bitch, and I know it's a dream but I can't wake up, and I have to sit there, I have to sit there as the man takes his foot off the brake and the car begins to move again, toward her. And she doesn't look back—she won't give him the satisfaction—she knows he won't do it, he won't run her down, but I know it. I've known it all along because it's always the same. And he's getting closer to her and she won't look back, but then at the last second she looks back and her face is lit up in the lights, and her eyes are full of the light and I know it, I know what he'll do because I'm inside his heart and I can't stop him, I can't reason with him, I can't change the rage in his heart. All I can do is sit there and watch as he runs her down."

He let go of the wheel and rested his hand in his lap again, next to the hand that held the keys. Audrey was silent. Her heart pounding.

"Anyway what I meant to say was, all these years I could never see the man's face. But now I do. Just before I wake up. The car has stopped again and he's looking all around, like did anyone see . . . ? And finally he looks back. He looks through that glass, that ice, and I see him. I see those eyes of his. I see those froggy eyes looking right at me."

He was silent. Breathing. Staring ahead at the signs of wind, the dipping and lifting branches.

"Then what?" Audrey said.

"Then nothing," Gordon said. "Then I wake up."

66

THERE WAS JUST the one cruiser parked in front of the building, the sheriff's, and she parked next to it and went up the steps toward the glass doors as she'd done so many times before, a little girl following her father; later, a teenager going to see him there, just to sit in the old wooden armchair and do her homework as he worked, just to be near him. The same woman behind the desk today as then, and the glass door had not swung shut behind her before this woman was up from the desk and coming for her—taking her in her arms and murmuring, "Oh, sweetie...Oh, honey..." Smell of powder, cigarettes, hairspray, before Gloria released her from the hug if not from her hold, strong little hands gripping Audrey's forearms. Wet eyes searching Audrey's and Audrey looking into these eyes behind the great lenses, both women silent until, suddenly, painted eyebrows rose and Gloria let go of Audrey's right arm as if it she'd just noticed it was on fire—"Oh, you got your cast off! I'm sorry, did I hurt it?"

"No, it's fine," Audrey said, lifting the forearm and giving it a squeeze herself with her other hand. "Good as new."

"It may *feel* fine," Gloria said, sternly, "but my Ginny broke her arm when she was ten and the doctor said you have to be careful when the cast comes off. You have to be very, very careful."

"I know. I will." She looked over the woman's gray head toward the gray metallic door in the back wall—nothing to indicate what it led to unless you noticed how different it was from all the other doors, all of which were wood and frosted glass and wobbly brass knobs. The gray metallic door was always shut, its latch handle always locked, and for a window there was only the small square of glass with wire mesh in it, too high for a little girl to look into unless she dragged a chair over there to stand on.

The sheriff's door was shut too.

"Is he in there?" she said, and Gloria's eyes lit up behind the big lenses.

"You bet your sweet fanny he is."

"I mean the sheriff," said Audrey. "I mean Sheriff Halsey."

"Oh," said Gloria, putting her fingertips to her lips. "He's in there. He's expecting you. Let me just buzz him." But before she could do so the sheriff's door swung open and there he stood.

"Sheriff, this young lady is here to see you."

"I see that, Gloria. Thank you. Come on in here, young lady."

She did, and Halsey shut the door behind her, then sat down at the old desk, in the old swivel chair with the big map of the county behind him, and Audrey sat down in the wooden armchair facing him.

The sheriff watched her. Taking her in as if he'd not seen her in a long time. Then he opened a drawer to his right and pulled something out and placed it on the blotter and slid it across to her and sat back again. After a moment she reached for it and collected it and held it under her hand on her lap. It was her father's little black notebook.

"Thank you," she said.

"I see you got your cast off."

"Yes, sir."

He picked up his pen and tapped it once on each end and set it down again. "Do you want to see him?" he said, nodding toward the wall to his right.

She thought about that, about going back there again. She'd only been that one time when she was ten, maybe eleven—her father unlocking the metallic door and walking her down the narrow aisle between the empty cells. Stainless steel toilet bowls sitting out in the open. Little stainless steel sinks jammed into the corners. No mirrors. Bunks of bolted steel and thin, scuzzy-looking mattresses. Concrete everything—floor, walls, ceiling.

That's it, he said. *That's all there is.*

Thick stink of dog kennel back there, if dogs smelled also of barf and cigarettes and feet and underarms.

Any questions?

Who feeds them?

Who feeds them? The county feeds them. Three times a day.

I mean who brings it to them.

I do. Or one of the deputies.

She tried to see that, her father bringing food to some filthy, stinking man in a cage. Did they speak? *Hey, Sheriff. Hey, prisoner.*

He'd stood behind her, silent, as she took the bars in her fists. Cold. Scaly, like the bars on an old jungle gym. After she let go and stepped back again he said, *Ready, Deputy?*

Ready, Sheriff.

OK, let's wash those hands and hit that pizza.

To Halsey she now said, "No, sir. I don't need to see that," and the sheriff nodded.

"I expect you'll see plenty of him at the trial."

"I expect so."

He sat studying her. "It won't be any picnic," he said. "His lawyer won't take it easy on you. Just the opposite. But I guess Ms. Kelley has already told you that."

"Yes, she has." Like Mr. Trevor, the county attorney wanted Audrey to call her by her first name—*Deirdre*—but Audrey couldn't do it. She didn't want to be the woman's pal; she wanted to be her witness.

"And I guess you know you won't be alone either," said Halsey.

She looked at him.

"The other women," he said. "Three of them now, not even counting Katie Goss."

Audrey nodded. She looked beyond him, to the big county map. So many roads. So many young women driving them.

She looked at the black notebook in her lap. How far back did it go? Would she find Holly Burke's name there? Katie Goss's? Danny Young's?

She looked up and Halsey was watching her.

"I guess you'd tell me if you'd found him yet," she said.

It took him a moment. "I'd tell you," he said.

She was silent. Then she said, "Do you think he's still alive?" and the sheriff frowned, and nodded.

"Yes, I do."

Audrey nodded too, although she knew he had to say it—had to think it, even. That it was his job to think it until he had proof otherwise.

She looked down again at the notebook. "Sheriff," she said. Turning the notebook in her hands, rubbing her thumbs over the worn, leathery surface. "Sheriff—do you regret it?"

"Regret what?"

"Letting him go down to Iowa like that. Moran. Back then."

She looked up and he held her eyes. Finally he picked up his pen again and stood it on its tip, as if about to write something on the desk blotter. It was a plain blue Bic, the kind she'd used for school all her life. The kind she'd once loaned to Caroline Price.

"Do I regret it?" said Halsey. "As a man, as a human being, yes, I regret it. But would I have done anything differently?" He frowned again. He shook his head. "We got him out of our county. Out of our state. We knew it was the best deal we were gonna get."

He set down the pen and put his hands together.

"And down there in Iowa?" he said. "It's like I told you before: the man did his job. If he was doing any of that other business, pulling girls over . . . well, we never heard one peep about it up here."

Audrey nodded again. She wiped her cheeks with her fingertips. "OK," she said. And sat there. Halsey watching her.

"Your dad never knew the whole story, Audrey. Remember that. He never knew about Moran and Holly Burke, or any other girls. All he knew was one story he couldn't prove, and so he did what he thought was the best he could do, given what he didn't know. And still it dogged him. I know it did." He looked down again and shook his head. "I remember the day we heard he was running for sheriff down there—Moran. I remember the day we heard he'd been elected. Your dad and me, everyone here . . . none of us said a word. It was like . . . Hell, I don't know what it was like. We just got on with it. We got back to work."

She looked up again and she saw something more of his eyes, or in them, than she'd seen before. Like stepping through that gray metallic door for the first time.

"I can't even imagine what it was like for your dad," he said, "seeing Moran—Sheriff Moran—standing in your hospital room like that, asking you questions."

She held his eyes. He'd joined the department after Moran and the other deputies, Halsey had, her father's youngest, greenest deputy, and he'd never known how to talk to her, how to even be around her. This big young man with no idea about children, about little girls. His technique was to pretend he didn't see you.

In the silence she heard her father's watch ticking on her wrist—felt it— before she remembered she wasn't even wearing it; it was at the jeweler's—an old man with shaky hands who said it probably wasn't worth the cost of fixing it. It was, she told him.

"Do you think," she now said, and hesitated. "Do you think he would've gone down there like that, to Iowa, and shot that boy in the hand if it had been anyone other than Moran in that hospital room?"

The sheriff looked at her for a long while.

"I'd have to call that a damned interesting question, Audrey. I'd have to call that altogether worth considering." He gave her a smile then, and pushed up from the chair, and Audrey stood too.

"You let me know your whereabouts," he said, coming around the desk, "you go back down south or wherever. I want to know you're OK out there. All right?"

"All right. Thank you, Sheriff."

"Don't thank me." He opened the door. "Go on, now. I'll see you when you get back here."

"You will?"

"Of course I will—in court. Every day. You just look at me if you need to, and I'll be there. All right?"

She nodded. She was about to thank him again but caught herself. She wanted to put her arms around him, just once, just quickly, but she knew it would embarrass him, alarm him even, this man with no children, no daughter of his own, and finally she just turned and walked away.

67

SHE WAS WEARING the aviators when she drove into town and she saw the town as he'd seen it himself through those lenses: the wide lanes of Main Street with the cars and trucks all parked at angles to the curb, the glass-and-brick storefronts, the Iowa sun flashing in the windows. But there was no snow in the streets now, and the smell that blew into the car's open window was the smell of the earth and the trees and the sky, and even of the sun itself.

Her father had not written the name down in the little black notebook, or if he had he'd ripped it out and destroyed it. She might've asked Halsey and she might've asked the lawyer, Trevor, but both would've asked why she wanted to know. And what would she say?

The last three entries in the notebook, in that large but nearly unreadable scrawl of his, were the names and addresses of the garages, and she went to the nearest of these first, Yoder Auto Repair, and there she was met by Yoder himself, who stood wiping his hands with a red rag as she explained who she was and why she'd come. Strong smell of oil and gasoline in the garage. A radio voice talking and talking from a shelf at the back until Yoder stepped over to it and shut it off. He came back and looked at the large canvas jacket she wore, then he looked her in the eye and said, "I'm sorry for your loss, miss."

"Thank you."

"I only met him the one time when he came in here himself, but from what I hear he was a good man. And a good sheriff. Despite what he came down here and did. And even that . . . well." He frowned. "I got a daughter myself about your age. She's off to college down in Kansas and—" His voice caught, and he looked down at his hands. She saw a vein jump with blood in the side of his neck. He looked up again and said, "Way I see it, he let that boy off easy."

"Yes, sir," Audrey said. "If it was the right boy."

Yoder frowned again. "I reckon your dad was pretty good at finding the right boy."

Audrey said nothing. Did they even know about Holly Burke down here? Would that name, or the name Danny Young, mean anything at all? How quickly did you forget about people when they weren't your people? When it wasn't your town. Wasn't your river . . . even though, really, it was the same river.

Yoder began wiping his hands again with the red rag. "Well, it never was in the papers," he said, "but it might as well of been. You could of asked anybody and they'd of told you: the boy's name is Ryan Radner. Do you know Anderson Auto, down on Frontage Road?"

"Yes, sir. I've got it on my phone."

"I figured you would. But he won't be there."

"He won't?"

"No, he won't."

"How do you know?"

Yoder tucked the rag into his hip pocket. "I've been in this business since I was sixteen and in all that time I've only known one mechanic who didn't have two of these." He showed her his open hands. "That was old Boots Franklin who worked for my old man. Best damn auto mechanic I ever knew but then he'd been born with just the one good hand. Now maybe getting shot in the hand isn't much of a reason to fire a good mechanic. But then again maybe it is. In any case that boy got fired."

"Ryan Radner," she said.

"Yes, ma'am, but don't ask me where he lives. I don't know and I wouldn't tell you if I did. I'd more likely tell the sheriff—the new sheriff. Ask him to come and have a word with you."

"Thank you, Mr. Yoder."

"All right. Well." He frowned. He nodded. "You take care, young lady."

"Yes, sir," she said, "I will."

THERE WAS ONLY one Ryan Radner in that town and he lived in a mobile home park a mile south of the last stoplight, and if that was his truck parked beside the trailer then he drove an old two-tone pickup truck, green and a lighter green, of a year she couldn't even guess and nothing about it to distinguish it from any other two-tone truck she'd ever seen or ever would see. She saw her father opening it up, shining his light, searching for something he'd never seen but knew must be there, it *must* be . . .

She sat in the sedan watching the trailer, the curtained windows. It was late in the day but the sun was not yet down, the days getting longer as they got warmer, and there were kids' toys and bikes strewn in the patches of dead grass between the trailers, but no kids. As if they'd all abandoned play and run inside at her arrival. Nothing moved anywhere but a single cat, a large orange tabby crossing the pitted and muddy road on delicate paws, and she watched as the cat made its way toward the Radner trailer, as it found a crack in the plywood that ran around the base of the trailer and stepped warily into the crack—head, body . . . and when the last of the tail twitched from view she reached into the glovebox and took out the .38 and slipped it into the hip pocket of the canvas jacket. She'd washed the jacket but it was still stained from the mud of the spillway and it still gave off a whiff of the river.

She got out of the car and shut the door behind her. Dogs began barking from other trailers up and down the road but no one came to the door or to the windows of the Radner trailer. From inside she heard the voices of a TV show, the applause of an audience.

She thought her heart should be pounding but it wasn't, and she thought about Caroline with her arm raised so straight and steady, her voice steady too, *Say that to my face, you slackjawed muppetfucker*, and a wave of love went through her.

The three iron steps and the railing were all of a piece and they wobbled independently of the trailer as she climbed them, and there was no bell that she could see and when she rapped on the aluminum stormdoor the dogs in the other trailers barked the more crazily and were joined by other dogs and none of them visible anywhere. She rapped a second time and the TV was abruptly silenced and she thought she could see the trailer itself shuddering as footsteps neared the door. There was a window in the inside door and a curtain was drawn aside and a man's bearded face appeared, looking out, not liking what he saw, and the curtain fell again and the inside door swung open.

He stood in a red sweatshirt and blue jeans, his dark hair lifted and tossed and held in place by its own oils. "Can I help you?" he said through the storm-door, the plexiglass, and it was as if there were no door at all between them. Lidded dark eyes staring out from a puffy face. The face of a man who has been sleeping and watching TV and not much else. In the bristles of his beard lay a pair of girlish lips, pink and wet. She thought she should recognize the eyes, those lips, but she didn't. And if there were still signs of the scratches on his face these had been overgrown by the climbing, untended beard.

"Are you Ryan Radner?"

"Who's askin?"

"Audrey Sutter." She removed the sunglasses but she didn't have to, he knew the name. He raised his hand to scratch at the right side of his face, at the beard. He moved his whole hand to scratch, as you would a wooden hand, and before he lowered it again she saw the wound, the bright-red puckering in the back of his hand where the bullet must have exited. He looked beyond her to the white sedan and then looked at her again through the plexiglass.

"I know that car. What are you, Daddy's little deputy?"

She didn't answer. Searching this face as she'd searched the faces Moran had brought her, trying now to match this one up with one of those, which was all backwards she knew, but what did it matter if there was a match?

Because it did. Because it only worked the other way.

"*Hello—?*" said the face, larger suddenly in the plexiglass, the wet pink lips holding the O shape perversely.

"I came to see you face-to-face," she said. "To see if I remembered you."

"From what?"

"The gas station. The ladies' room."

He smirked. He shook his head. "Just as crazy as your old man. You got a gun too? Excuse me a second while I make a quick phone call." He patted his jeans pockets and looked around but he did not turn away from the door. As if he would not turn his back on her. He looked at her again. Thinking things over. He said, "I know you already know the case was dropped. Your daddy shot the wrong man, Little Deputy."

She looked past him, into the cramped darkness that was his home, and she remembered opening a metal door and flicking a filthy switch, stepping out of the bright stink of the ladies' room into darkness, into that blindness after a light is turned off, and she remembered a hand reaching out of the darkness to touch her, to stop her with its fingers, a voice—*Where you goin, little girl?*—and she remembered trying to duck under the hand, and the hand grabbing at her head, and there was the electric crackling and sparking of her hair suddenly . . . And she had not remembered that until this moment, standing here. She'd thought she'd lost it in the river, along with everything else. But he'd taken it from her there, at the ladies' room.

Radner turned to look too, to see what she was staring at, and turned back. "What are you looking for?"

"Something you took from me."

"For instance?"

"My cap. My black knit cap. I'd like it back."

Dark eyebrows rose into a rumpling forehead. "You really are crazy, aren't you." She waited.

He shook his head again. "A," he said, "what would I want with your stupid cap? And B, even if I took it, do you think I'd be dumb enough to keep it?"

She said nothing, watching him. Trying once more to match this face to her memory of hands—of fingers so hard and strong as they snatched the cap from her head. As they jerked the backscratcher from her grip. As they pinned her arm against the wall. As they covered her mouth with a stink and taste that made her want to gag even now.

Radner grinned and opened the stormdoor. "Well, come on in and look for it then," he said, and she stood looking in at the shabby, dark furnishings. A boxy old TV throwing its light on a patch of stained brown carpeting. The smell coming out of there was just awful, and she turned her face from it. There sat the two-tone truck, and it had the look of him too—dirty, run-down, mean. Like it was just waiting for the chance to do harm.

"Your daddy already searched the truck," he said. "Him and the real sheriff. But you go ahead. Check it out. It ain't locked."

And that voice—she should know that voice, at least. *See there, Bud? We're all gonna be friends here.*

But she didn't. She didn't. And the more she looked at him, and the more he talked, the less certain she became. Or the less clear her memories became, and she felt once again, as she had when Moran showed her the pictures, that she was in danger of losing her memories altogether—not just of that moment, of his hands on her, but all the moments after too: Caroline with her pepper spray, her fierceness. The pounding of their hearts as they ran for the car. The moment on the riverbank, that pause before the other car came, Caroline's laugh. The strength of her hand as you dropped toward the ice. Your spinning hearts. The look on her face when you heard that first crack, that deep pop in the floor of the world. The light under the water and Caroline in the light, swimming so hard to come back, swimming so beautifully . . . And the other girls too, Holly Burke and the others, with their hair like seagrass in the current. All this was real. All this had happened and she must protect it at the cost of everything else—at the cost of certainty, even, so Caroline's parents would see it, so they would know it when they looked in her eyes.

The dogs had not stopped barking and now they seemed inside her head, of her head's own making, and each bark lingered and replayed over those that followed in a ringing continuum, on and on. "I'm sorry to bother you," she said, or tried to say, and began to backstep down the wobbling steps.

"It's no bother, honey," he said. He'd seen the change in her, her failure to recognize, to know, and now he stepped out onto the highest step just as she stepped from the lowest. "I wasn't kidding about coming in. I got some beers in the fridge. How about that? We can just bury the ol' hatchet, as they say. I figure it's the least you can do after your old man shot me and got me fired and pretty much ruined my life. What do you say?"

She kept backstepping, toward the car. The gun riding solid and heavy in the pocket at her thigh. Radner looking down on her from the top step. He took a step down and let the stormdoor slap shut behind him.

"I gotta say I like how you come out here by yourself," he said. "I like your pluck. No partner. No backup. Even though I am not the man you think I am, still—very impressive."

She had reached the car and she turned and put her hand on the latch. He stepped to the bottom step and stopped there. Standing in his sockfeet with his hands in his jean pockets, watching her. Then he said in a voice she almost didn't hear over the dogs, "What made you think I wouldn't just grab you and take you into this house, hey? If I was that man—what made you think I wouldn't do that?"

"Because you'd figure I didn't come out here without my father's gun."

He looked at the sky and laughed. And looked at her again. "You think I'm afraid of a little girl and her daddy's gun?"

She opened the door and stood behind it, watching him.

"Want to know what I think?" he said. He took the last step down and she slipped her left hand into the pocket and took the gun into her grip. She knew that behind the curtains and behind the barking dogs someone was watching, and she knew he knew it too.

He stopped and stood as before with his hands in his pockets. Watching her. "I think you wanted me to grab you and throw you in that house," he said. "I think that's what you come out here for, even if you didn't know it yourself. What do you think about that, Little Deputy?"

"I don't think about it," she said. "And I never will." Then she got into the car and started the engine and put the car into gear and drove away.

68

SHE KNEW HE was coming, he'd called her first, but even so the sight of the truck pulling into the drive made her heart rise, made it fly—until she saw the officer, the sheriff's deputy, get out of the truck, just him, and her heart fell once again, and fell too far for such a brief rise of hope.

The sheriff pulled in behind the truck and got out of his cruiser and it was like that day ten years ago when Tom Sutter and the other deputy, Moran, had come to talk to her about Danny. A different truck then. Different case. Or the same case, really, just a new branch of it now, set in motion somehow by those two girls going into the river. The same river too, and Moran the bridge that connected Holly Burke's death to Danny's disappearance.

This time the sheriff's deputy stayed behind, leaning on the cruiser and checking his phone as Sheriff Halsey came up the drive alone.

Rachel slipped into her shoes and went out to meet him in her sweater. The snow was melting and there was the smell of the earth again, of farmland and wet trees, and there were the high, giddy cries of loons in flight, and all of it terrible. Because when a son had gone missing in the hardness of winter you did not want to see the vanishing snow, or the bright shoots of the tulips, or the tender new grass, or the river flowing again from bridge to bridge without its thick shell of ice.

She came down the porchsteps and the sheriff came forward and tipped his hat and said Morning, Mrs. Young, and she said Good morning, Sheriff.

He glanced back at the truck. "Is that all right there?"

"That's fine. We can move it if we need to."

"Here's the keys. Everything else is inside the cab just like we found it."

She took the keys and held them in her fist. "Thank you, Sheriff. It'll just sit here, like you said."

"I appreciate that," he said. "The deputy and I can unload it if you want."

"No, that's all right."

"It's no bother."

"I'll have Marky do it after work."

He nodded. He looked up at the house and perhaps the sky beyond it. She thought he would say something about the weather, the beautiful day, but he didn't.

She stood waiting. Holding the keys in her fist.

The sheriff cleared his throat. "We haven't forgotten about him," he said, and clarified: "Your son. His picture is out in four states, and between that and the posters, well. He's a top priority, Mrs. Young. We'll follow any lead that comes in."

She looked him in the eye. "And Moran?"

"Sitting in that jail, ma'am, and not going anywhere. I've had three more girls—women—come forward with their stories. All pretty much the same as Katie Goss's."

"I read about that," she said.

"And the judge read Danny's letter, too," he said. "Whether or not it influenced his decision to deny bail, I can't say, but the result is the same, which is Moran sitting in that jail until trial."

"But that doesn't get you any closer to finding my son, does it?"

"No, ma'am, it doesn't. I've got nothing to connect Moran to your son's disappearance except that letter, and that doesn't help us find him."

"And that bullet hole?"

The sheriff glanced at the truck. "Well, like I said on the phone, we couldn't find a match with Moran, so we're continuing to run down local registrations, but that's a lot of rifles and a lot of"—he hesitated—"innocent citizens."

He'd been about to say dead ends, she knew.

"And it wasn't Gordon Burke's," she said.

"No, ma'am. Not even the right caliber. Far as I know, the only vehicle that rifle ever shot was Moran's."

She nodded. She didn't know what else there was to say. To ask. She would have to sit and wait. Get through each day. Each hour. As she'd been doing since the day he didn't call.

The sheriff glanced back at his deputy, and the deputy put away his phone and opened the door of the cruiser.

But the sheriff didn't go. He stood looking down at the gravel, or his boots.

"There's just one more thing," he said, and looked up again.

Rachel waited.

"I thought maybe you could shed a little light on something for me," he said.

"All right."

"I asked your son about it—I asked Marky—but he didn't seem to understand what I was asking."

"What did you ask?"

"I asked him why he put Moran's cruiser up on the lift like he did. Did you know about that?"

"No, I didn't."

"Well, he did. He was supposed to just fix the light, but then he got it up on the lift and found a leak in the pan."

"So?"

"Oh, it's nothing he did wrong." The sheriff scratched at his forehead, lifting the hatbrim, dropping it again. "It's just the thing is, if he hadn't've done that, Moran would've been on his way to Iowa, and he might not be sitting on his ass in my jail right now."

Rachel watched him. The sheriff watching her.

"I'm not sure I understand the question, Sheriff," she said, and he waved his hand and said, "Well. I'm not sure I do either. I just thought maybe he'd said something to you about it, that's all."

Rachel shook her head. "I'm sorry, Sheriff."

"All right then," he said, and glanced toward his deputy. "We'd best be on our way. You have my number."

"I have your number."

He tipped his hat again like some old cowboy and turned and went back down the drive toward the cruiser, his boots crunching in the gravel.

When they were gone she went to the passenger side of the truck and opened the door—not glancing toward the rear tire, not seeing what was there in the otherwise-clean blue fender—and she stood looking in at the duffels, the cardboard box, the kits of tools all packed away, but not packed as he'd have done it himself. They'd searched through everything, of course, as they'd once searched his room, and this time they'd put it all back together again as best they could but it was not as he'd done it himself; it was not his work she was looking at but only his things, and before she could think too much about that she shut the door again and went back into the house to make the tea she'd been about to make when she'd seen her son's truck pull into the drive, and a few minutes later she carried the mug up the creaking stairs and there was no dog to follow her or to carry in her arms, or to follow her into his room, wagging his old tail expectantly, as if this time he would be there, surely this time . . .

The bed gave a squeak when she sat on it. Same little bed the four of them had sat on one night playing cards—the five of them: she and the boys and Katie Goss and Wyatt. Danny and Katie laughing and teasing and so young.

She sat looking around the room: his desk, the bookshelves. His hockey stick and skates in the corner. The bare plaster walls. The window. After a while she got up and set her mug on the desk and went to the window and lifted—and lifted harder until the frame abruptly raised and the sash weights knocked and rang in the wall like dull bells. She'd never gotten the storm windows up in this room and it must've been so cold at night, the few winter nights he'd slept here.

She stood leaning on the sill and breathing in the spring and looking down on the backyard, yellow and green with the thaw. The old clothesline post and the brown patch of earth there. Her boys running around the yard and swinging from the clothesline until it had gone crooked and Grammy Olsen asking, *What the heck happened to my clothesline post?* and Rachel shrugging and saying, *I don't know, Grammy, maybe it was the wind.*

She heard something—kids, coming home from school. Their high voices as they spilled from the bus into their yards. And within those cries she heard her own sons' voices, and Holly's too, and she saw the girl once more in her purple Easter dress, running through Gordon's woods, a bright spot of color searching for smaller spots of color, the poorly hidden eggs. Her squeals, her happiness!

But there were no children out this way—or none close enough to hear, unless it was the McVeigh kids, who lived in the house on the other side of the rented field, and unless the wind was just right. Which maybe it was.

She wiped her face with her fingertips and turned back to collect her tea from the desk, and it was then she saw it—the piece of metal on the desktop, next to his Big Dam Mug. It was a bolt. Placed upright on its hexagonal head. Heavy. Not old. Well cleaned but smelling of oil. She stood looking at it a while, her heart knocking dully in her chest, then returned it carefully to the desktop, exactly as she'd found it, so that it would be there when he came home.

69

SHE FOLLOWED THE county road out of town and it was the same road they'd been on that night and this time the station appeared on her right instead of her left and when she saw it in the early dusk, the bright square of window, the pumps standing in the garish light of the tin shelter, her heart broke freshly and she had to swallow down a sob, *Oh, Caroline!*

It wasn't the woman with the soft pink face in the window when she pulled in, but a skinny man who stood bent at the waist and leaning on his elbows, his head hung down below his shoulders like a man in sorrow, and he did not look up. She parked to the side, away from the pumps and next to the only other vehicle in the lot, a white and dented pickup with blisters of rust around the wheelwells. She cut the engine and sat there with the windows down, and she could smell the river, the icy yellow water, the taste of it even. As if it had been this car and not the RAV4 that had gone under the ice and filled with the river and had been fished out again and drained and put back on its wheels again, *There you go, miss, good as new, and—*

Audrey?

Yes?

What are you doing?

Nothing.

Are you going buggy on me?

No.

Then get your ass in gear, girl. We haven't got all night.

The skinny man had not moved and as she passed by the window she watched to see would he move at all, and just before she stepped out of view he flipped the page of a magazine and the bill of his cap followed the page and he was still again.

She stepped into the shadows where the shelter lights did not reach and she stood on the concrete as she'd stood that night, and she could smell the ladies' room through the door to her back but she could not smell the boy. Could not smell the gas on his clothes or the beer and cigarettes on his breath or the grease on his hand when he put it over her mouth. Could not even smell the pepper spray. Beyond the concrete was a coarse terrain, barren but for yellow weeds and a solitary pine tree, and she took a few steps into that meaningless land, but it was hopeless; he could've thrown it any direction and he would've thrown it far, and would there be anything under its little wooden fingernails anyway, or would it be useless, like her memory?

He's gone, isn't he.

They're both gone.

It figures.

Why?

Because there wasn't anything to them in the first place. Faceless, useless boys. They run all over the world like rats.

I'm sorry.

Why are you sorry?

Because it isn't fair.

Caroline laughed. *Fair? Oh, Audrey!*

She was out of the wind where she stood, but overhead the pine tree swayed and whispered, and she looked at it more closely and identified it as a white pine. She climbed it with her eyes—thirty, maybe forty feet tall—and remembered a young girl walking in the woods, looking for a tree just her height. A father going out to measure the tree year after year.

Audrey.

What?

Time to go.

She drove down the hill toward the trestle bridge and there was no ice or snow now, and the shoulder where they'd gone off the road into the ditch was a wet soft gravel and she pulled onto it and came to a stop short of the bridge and short of the edge of the riverbank where they'd gone over. She cut the engine again and got out and walked to the edge and stood looking down. There'd been the sound of her boots in the gravel and now that she'd stopped she heard the deep silence of the valley. If you could hear a silence. She stood listening and after a while she heard, or became aware she was hearing, a dry rattling and it was the sound of two old leaves in the treetops, brown and curled and hanging on and batting at each other in the wind.

Caroline's family had lived in Georgia for generations. One of her way-back grandfathers had fought in the Civil War. Her father was a professor of mathematics at Georgia State, and when Caroline did her impression of him she stuck her chin in the air and made her shoulders big and spoke from her Georgia chest and you could just see him, you could see the man himself: *A moving vehicle is no place for luck, daughter. May this vehicle be safeguarded by intelligence, by great care and caution, and not the amputated paw of a rodent.*

Her papaw called her Sweetpea and was a mechanical genius who kept the same old pickup running for all of Caroline's life. Her mother was a middle school teacher. Her older brother, James, was going to be a lawyer.

And if you had never asked her for bus fare she would not have driven you.

And if you had never been put in that dorm room together . . . and if she had not asked to borrow a pen from you . . .

Hush now, Audrey, hush.

Colder down here by the bridge and darker but the river was visible in the dusk like a great snake slipping along with no sound, dark and glistening. She was standing at the place above the bank where the car had gone over and where it must have come back up, but there was no sign of those events either, only the grassy fall of the bank, the old yellow reeds twitching in the wind. As if the car had never gone over but instead had kept its hold on the shoulder, the two girls inside it so much luckier than they knew—their hearts racing, the world still spinning as they watched the headlights in the mirrors: the two lights coming slowly down the hill like two little suns descending, the lights growing large in the rear window of the RAV4 as the car or truck or whatever it was pulled up behind them and the driver braked carefully, skillfully in the snow, and stopped—absolutely stopped, in this version, in this dream, well short of the rear bumper. A silence then. A waiting. The girls looking into each other's eyes in the bright light, their hearts beating, until at last a dome light came on in the cab of the truck—it was a truck, they could now see—and there was a brief snapshot of a man in a billcap, just one man, before this man stepped from the cab and shut the door and the dome light went out again . . . and he was coming toward them, cautiously, a jacketed man in his billcap, the dark shape of him in the headlights, faceless as a shadow, his boots so loud on the icy pavement and then in the deep snow, laboring his way alongside the car toward the driver's-side window, gaining it finally and stooping to look inside, and to give them a look: a face lit now by his own headlights and by the escaping green light of the RAV4's dashlights, the worried face of an old man, taking them in through large wire-frame lenses—one girl, then the other—before saying through the window and fogging the glass with his breath, *You girls all right?*

Caroline powering down the glass then, revealing him clearly in the frame of the window—bony, leathery old face with a gray stubble and a rim of creamy dentures showing and deep, watery blue eyes behind the lenses—*We're fine, sir, thank you so much*, Caroline saying, and the old man cocking a large ear at her so that they both see the pink bit of plastic fitted into the inner whorl and Caroline saying again louder, and with such happiness in her voice, *Thank you, sir, thank you so much for stopping!*

It would take a while, the old man being old and the girls not knowing how to help, but he would have a tow rope in the back of his truck, and the good old truck would have four-wheel drive, as does the RAV4, and soon enough they'd be back on the road and he would tell them in his gruff old way—a father himself, you could hear in his voice, a grandfather, maybe great-grandfather—to drive more slowly in this weather, that the bridge would be icy too, and when they'd try to pay him he would not even look at the money but would wave them off and climb back into his truck, and he would follow them across the bridge and for a few miles beyond, until at last they'd see his turn signal, see the headlights swerving off into some dark Iowa woods . . . and only miles later, both of them thinking what might have been had he not come along—not allowing themselves to think what might have been had he been those boys—would they realize they'd never asked his name, nor he theirs. In his memory they would be the two girls he pulled out of the snow by the bridge that time, and in theirs he would be the old man, the kind old feller, who pulled them out of the snow that one winter they drove to Minnesota—who did not bump them, sending them down the riverbank, but instead had saved them—and that's how it would be until the end of all their lives.

ACKNOWLEDGMENTS

It's one thing to write a story—to bang out a kind of beginning, middle and ending—it's quite another to bring a finished, cohesive, ready-to-read novel to readers, and for that I have two superb professional families to thank: At Writers House I thank **Amy Berkower**, agent, guardian angel and voice of clarity every step of the way, and **Genevieve Gagne-Hawes**—too essential to call an early editor, more like my secret weapon. My everlasting thanks also to **Maja Nikolic** and **Kathryn Stuart**, and all the outstanding staff on every floor of that house.

At Algonquin Books and Workman Publishing Co.—simply the greatest publisher any author could hope for—I thank **Elisabeth Scharlatt, Elizabeth Johnson, Betsy Gleick, Brunson Hoole, Michael McKenzie, Anne Winslow, Pete Garceau, Craig Popelars, Lauren Moseley, Debra Linn, Frazer Dobson** and everyone else who has worked so hard on behalf of my books and made such a difference in the course of my life—none more so than **Chuck Adams**, my editor through two novels now and, if my luck holds out, my editor for the next two, and the next two after that.

My thanks to **Robert L. Giron and Gival Press**, who once upon a time honored a short story called "Water" and gave its author a friendly shove into deeper waters. Also, the **University of Memphis**, my superb colleagues in the English department there, and all my students everywhere, who have given me so much more than I've given them.

Closer to home: **Tyler Johnston**, whose influence extended far beyond legal expertise and into essential matters of storytelling; and **Chris Kelley**, who put his keen eye to earliest details and design, and all for the better. For all manner of friendship and inspiration and belief and support, I thank **Mark Wisniewski, PD Mallamo, Randy Larson, Don Foster, Erin Quigley, Mark Carroll and Carmela Rappazzo**. And of course **Carolyn Blais**, whose natural gifts of love and laughter made this book, and its author, better.

Finally, to the person holding this book, whoever you are: Thank you for being a reader of books and for reading this one in particular. You make it all matter.

THE CURRENT

Blue Ink
An Essay by Tim Johnston

Questions for Discussion

BLUE INK
An Essay by Tim Johnston

AFTER THE DIVORCE, it was settled that my little sister would live mostly with my mother, while my two older brothers and I would live mostly with our father. A lawyer himself, our father, tasked all at once with the rearing of three unruly boys, naturally fell back on what he knew, and as a result my brothers and I were exposed at an early age to the principles, and often the consequences, of due process. To what extent this parenting style shaped the adults we became is inconclusive: one son would grow up to become a lawyer as well, while another, taking an alternate path, would often need his brother's services. No judgment here. Just the facts.

The youngest son would follow a third path altogether, becoming a writer of stories and novels. And while it's true that the writer this boy became would be motivated by many of the themes and ideas of his upbringing—themes of guilt and innocence, for instance; ideas of perception and reasonable doubt, which are the qualifiers that make absolute fact, or objective truth, seem entirely impossible the moment the wheels of justice are set in motion—there was little evidence at the time that the boy was taking these concepts to heart. Or even that he recognized them when they were playing out before his very eyes.

Take, for example, the incident of the pulled fire alarm.

I was in middle school, and my friend Randy B and I were skipping second period, wandering the empty halls, when he dared me to pull the fire alarm. That is: he dared me to *pretend* to pull it. To put my hand on the little red handle *as though* I were going to pull it.

Not much of a dare, as dares go, except that we were standing just around the corner from the principal's office, and that made it juicy. That made it irresistible.

The little red handle seemed to hum when I gripped it, like something alive. It wanted me to test it, to see how fixed it was, how resistant to pulling. And so I leaned back a bit, and I turned to give Randy a look, a smirk of victory—and was suddenly sitting on the floor. The alarm was blaring like the end of the world, and Randy, pausing just long enough to lock his eyes on mine, turned and flung himself toward the exit.

In those first stunned, surreal seconds, my feet and my heart and my brain were all in agreement: *Get up and run, you idiot—and do not stop.* But if I was a boy of considerable foot speed in those days—as any smart-mouthed little troublemaker had better be—I was also the son of a lawyer, a man who'd taught his children the meaning of right and wrong, the importance of lawful behavior, and the total irrelevance of all such things once you get busted. And it was that kid who knew that *running*, when the school fire alarm has been pulled, is exactly the worst—the most *incriminating*—thing you could do.

And so I walked. With that alarm clanging away in my heart I walked through the exit, made my way around the end of the building, and walked up to the students filing out and blended myself into their ranks. Randy had the same idea, I saw, but we did not speak and did not make eye contact. The important thing now was to stay cool. To wait for the all-clear, and to file back into the building with the rest of the students and go on with the day as if it were any other one.

And this I did, and with such faithfulness to character that, come fourth-period art class, fire alarm all but silenced in my heart, I got my hands on one of Miss P's ink pads and set about staining my fingers a rich navy blue. Why? Because that was the kind of kid I was, and because this was just any other day.

Five minutes into fifth period, I was in the halls again—not skipping class this time, but on my way to see Vice Principal H, at his request.

I knew Mr. H well, and believed he harbored a kind of head-shaking fondness for me, thinking I was not a bad kid, not really, but only pretending to be one to get attention. He expected me to grow out of such nonsense, I understood, and, if not make something of myself, at least do the world no real harm.

On this day he waved me into his office and closed the door and told me to take a seat. He leaned on his desk awhile in silence, then sat down in the chair beside me.

"Let me see your hands," he said.

I showed him, and we stared at my blue-stained fingers.

He asked how I got blue ink on my fingers, and I told him the truth: fourth-period art class, the borrowed ink pad. Idiotic, immature, to be sure, but hardly worth a visit to his office. But then he told me what happens when a middle school fire alarm gets pulled—it shoots blue ink onto the puller's hand—and a series of realizations began to dawn on me:

a) This visit had nothing to do with Miss P's ink pad,

b) If the alarm had indeed spat ink at me, it missed—perhaps because I'd fallen to the floor,

And c) What were the freaking odds that I would *stain my own fingers* on the day when a booby-trapped alarm had failed to stain them?

I knew I was guilty of pulling the alarm, and I knew Mr. H knew I was guilty of pulling the alarm, but all that mattered to me, the lawyer's son, in that moment, was that the blue ink was not from the fire alarm. It was not *proof* of my guilt.

I wanted to get Miss P up here, I wanted to get those kids who'd witnessed my handiwork with the ink pad, but Mr. H had moved on—explaining that when the fire alarm gets pulled, the fire department is alerted and must respond, and that costs the school district a lot of money—*a lot of money*, he emphasized. A report of vandalism must be filed, and cops must be called in. Detectives . . . would I rather talk to a detective?

I did not want to talk to a detective. I wanted to talk to my lawyer.

And at that thought, the prospect of explaining all this to my father, Mr. H got his confession—a tearful, shameful one in which I swore it was an *accident*, I never *intended* to pull the alarm, I was just *messing around*. (I did not mention Randy B; I may have been a vandal but I was no rat.)

In the end my father was called, he and Mr. H talked, and I was sent home. Two days later I got the verdict: I was to see a child psychologist. A shrink. "It's the best deal you're gonna get," my father told me, and I burned with shame and anger. That I was in fact guilty did not concern me. What mattered was that the evidence that had nailed me was entirely, randomly, *freakishly* circumstantial.

In my new novel, *The Current*, a lawyer tells a young woman, "Justice is blind, but she also can't see worth a shit." Not to equate my little tale of school vandalism with what happens to this young woman, or any other injustices of real consequence in the real world, like wrongful conviction, like victims who are not believed, like the guilty walking free, but I can see the connection between that boy with blue ink on his fingers and the writer I've become. And as I wrote *The Current*, it was not so much the wheels of justice that drove the story, although those machinations do fascinate me; it was what happens the moment someone, somewhere, *breaks the law*. Or is accused of it. At that moment, due process is only one component—and possibly the least consequential—of the great wave of human behavior set in motion, the irresistible undertow of cause and effect as lives are pushed along toward actions and reckonings they never would've foreseen.

I pulled that fire alarm. I did it. But all these years later I feel the pang of being accused of it—and confessing to it—for the wrong reasons. I wonder how I ended up in Mr. H's office that day, really. Had word gone out to teachers to look for a kid with blue ink on his hands? Do school fire alarms even shoot blue ink when pulled, or had Mr. H, seeing the ink on my fingers, improvised that little detail on the fly? If so, my hat is off to the man.

Or did Randy B, whose name I never mentioned to Mr. H, rat me out?

Innocence and circumstance play out in many ways, sometimes benignly, sometimes with dire results.

In real life, two boys wander an empty school hallway. There are consequences.

In *The Current*, a young woman walks a dark road at night, by a river. Lives are changed forever. Ten years later, two young women stop for gas in the middle of the night, in the middle of nowhere. There's time and place, and there's deciding to do one thing and not another—that moment of choice—and then there's everything after.

QUESTIONS FOR DISCUSSION

1. How would you describe Audrey and Caroline's friendship when the two young women set off for Minnesota? Do you feel more drawn to one of the girls, and if so, why? By the time they are plunging toward the Black Root River, has their relationship changed? Have your feelings about them changed?

2. After a tense opening chapter set in the present, the novel transitions to explore the past, dealing with the murder of Holly Burke in the same Black Root River, and with her relationship at the time with Danny Young. Other than the involvement of Audrey's father, the ex-sheriff, what connections did you make between the two crimes? Why did what happened to Audrey and Caroline have such an impact on the Burke and Young families? From the outset, did you suspect any characters of having been involved somehow in both crimes, and if so, why?

3. What compels Tom Sutter, who as a sheriff always operated strictly "by the book," to go to Iowa to look for the men who assaulted his daughter? Doesn't he realize that his actions might compromise the case? Why does he shoot Radner in the hand? Do you feel his actions were justified?

4. Throughout the book, Audrey seems to experience the sense of encountering Caroline and other girls in the river under the water; at one point she even seems to speak with Caroline under the ice. What do you feel these visions mean to Audrey? What do they mean to you, and to your reading of this novel?

5. In what ways does the title of this novel connect to the story, beyond the current of the river?

6. Why do you think Audrey seeks out Gordon Burke that day in the woods outside his house? Why does Gordon Burke—no friend of Audrey's father—bring her firewood? By the end of the novel, what have Audrey and Gordon come to mean to each other?

7. Both Danny Young and his ex-girlfriend, Katie Goss, have been keeping individual secrets for ten years. Why do you think Katie didn't report what happened to her all those years ago? What has changed to cause her to consider coming forward now? And why do you think Danny hid the piece of fabric for ten years? Why is he bringing it out now? What has changed for him?

8. For a book with so many crimes, there seems to be little absolute certainty as to guilt. In the absence of definitive proof, how is guilt communicated to the reader? At the same time, how are doubts raised about that guilt? By the end of the novel, do you believe Radner was one of the boys who assaulted Audrey and Caroline? How sure are you that Ed Moran killed Holly Burke and then tried to frame Danny Young for the murder? If you were on the jury that heard these cases, and you had no more evidence than what the author provides with which to convict, how would you decide?

9. Another ambiguous moment in the novel comes when Moran goes out on the ice after Audrey falls into the river. Do you think he intends to make sure she dies, or is he trying to help her—and how did you come to this conclusion? What is the effect on the reader of not having absolute certainty as to guilt?

10. Though completed more than a year before the rise of #MeToo, many of the themes in the novel speak to the causes behind that movement. What actions and events in *The Current* speak most clearly to the discussion begun by #MeToo? Do you feel the novel contains an accurate representation of the attitudes that

brought about the changes so evident in how we discuss male/female relationships today, and in how we view the integrity of law enforcement?

11. Why do you think the author chose to leave Danny's fate unresolved? What do you think happened to Danny, and why do you think so?

12. If you were to encounter any of these characters in another ten years, do you think you would find them greatly changed, or would they still be held in the grip of their pasts? If you think they would have changed, why and in what ways? If you don't think they would have changed, how did you reach that conclusion?

CHRISTINE BEANE

TIM JOHNSTON'S previous novel, *Descent*, was a *New York Times* bestseller. He is also the author of the story collection *Irish Girl*, which won the Katherine Anne Porter Prize in Short Fiction, and the young adult novel *Never So Green*. Johnston lives in Iowa City. Visit him online at www.timjohnston.net.